Sara
Paretsky
CRITICAL MASS

Sara Paretsky

CRITICAL MASS

HODDER &
STOUGHTON

First published in the United States of America in 2013 by The Penguin Group
First published in Great Britain in 2013 by Hodder & Stoughton
An Hachette UK company

1

Copyright © Sara Paretsky 2013

The right of Sara Paretsky to be identified as the Author of the Work has been asserted
by her in accordance with the Copyright, Designs and Patents Act 1988.

A CIP catalogue record for this title is available from the British Library

Hardback ISBN 978 1 444 75867 2
Trade Paperback ISBN 978 1 444 75868 9
Ebook ISBN 978 1 444 75869 6

Printed and bound in Great Britain by Clays Ltd, St Ives plc

Hodder & Stoughton policy is to use papers that are natural, renewable and recyclable products
and made from wood grown in sustainable forests. The logging and manufacturing processes
are expected to conform to the environmental regulations of the country of origin.

Hodder & Stoughton Ltd
338 Euston Road
London NW1 3BH

www.hodder.co.uk

For Courtenay,
who taught me to
seek the beauty
of Nature's secrets

THANKS

Many people helped me create this novel. My biggest debt goes to my personal physics adviser, S. C. Wright, from the University of Chicago's Enrico Fermi Institute and Department of Physics. He directed my reading and answered the questions of a physics novice with great kindness and thoroughness.

Dr. Johann Marton, director of the Stefan-Meyer-Institut in Vienna, was generous with both his time and his insights in stepping me through the history of physics in Vienna in the twentieth century.

Thanks to Dr. Marton, I received advice from Dr. Stefan Sienell, MAS, director of the Archives of the Austrian Academy of Sciences, as well as from Dr. Thomas Maisel, director of the Archives for the University of Vienna.

Michael Geoffrey, Chicago patent lawyer, was a most helpful resource for the part of the novel that deals with patent law, with whether patents held by foreign nationals were recognized in U.S. courts, and other critical plot issues.

Leah Richardson, librarian at the University of Chicago Library's Special Collections, advised me on library policy for digging up names of people consulting library materials.

Margaret Elliot of Scotland discussed the education high school girls received in chemistry and physics in the 1930s.

Vicki Hill assisted with the German used by Kitty Binder and Lotty Herschel in this novel.

Jonathan Paretsky, who has reviewed trial records for drug cases, helped describe the drug-manufacturing subculture, especially meth production. He also researched federal warrantless searches and the action of chapter 26 for me.

I'm indebted to the late Stan Ovshinsky for the motto "In God We trust, all others show data."

Karen Pendleton was my inspiration for the offerings at Wenger's Prairie Market.

The technical description of the Innsbruck reactor is copied loosely from Giacomo Grasso et al., "Neutronics Study of the 1945 Haigerlich B-VIII Nuclear Reactor," *Physics in Perspective*, September 2009.

All mistakes in this novel are completely the creation of the author, as are all the fictional events. Although some historic figures are mentioned in passing, such as Enrico Fermi and Edward Teller, the main players on my stage are complete fabrications whose strutting and fretting are due to me alone.

CONTENTS

VIENNA, 1913
And There Was Light

O H." The syllable is a soft cry of ecstasy. She has never seen colors like those on the floor, red running into orange, yellow, green. The purple is so rich, like grape juice, she wants to jump into it. When she runs over to look, the colors disappear. Her mouth rounds with bafflement: she thought Frau Herschel had painted the rainbow on the floor. Then she sees it reappear on her arm. Against the starched white of her sailor shirt, she can see the purple, which the wooden floor had swallowed. She strokes it and watches the color ripple on her hand.

"Martina!" her mother whispers harshly. "Your manners."

She turns reluctantly and bobs a curtsy to Frau Herschel. Her black boots hold her ankles so stiffly that she can't move well and she almost falls. Her mother frowns, desperate for her awkward child to make a good impression on her employer.

Birgit, the *Kindermädchen*, doesn't bother to hide a smirk. Little Sophie Herschel doesn't laugh, just pirouettes in her white slippers and sinks into a deep curtsy in front of Martina's mother.

"I believe the child hasn't even noticed the rocking horse," Frau Herschel says, laughter barely covering her annoyance. "But Sophie will help her. You may leave her here in the nursery, Frau Saginor. You can go down to the sewing room to begin the white work. Birgit will feed Martina when she brings Sophie her lunch."

The six-year-olds are left to stare at each other. Sophie's hair is the color of flax and is arranged in sausage curls tied away from her face with a rose ribbon. Martina's black hair is plaited, pulled so hard from her face that you can see white half-moons of skin behind her ears. Sophie is in a dress beautifully embroidered and smocked by Martina's mother, but Martina herself wears a sailor top and dark skirt. Even if there were money at home for the fine thread and fabric in Sophie's dresses—which there isn't—it wouldn't do for Frau Saginor's daughter to be seen in such delicate clothes.

Later, the little girls will spend so much time together that they won't remember this first meeting, not the meanness of Sophie, flaunting one expensive toy after another, nor of the nursery maid Birgit, giving Martina a piece of bread with goose fat for lunch while Sophie has thick soup and an orange, nor of Martina upstaging Sophie with Signor Caperelli, the Italian who was teaching music to many of Vienna's bourgeois children.

"And this one? She play also?" Signor Caperelli asks Birgit, after yawning over Sophie's haphazard performance for half an hour.

"She is just the sewing woman's child, brought in to amuse Fräulein Sophie," Birgit sniffs.

"But at home I play on my auntie's flute," Martina says. She is made bold by the foreign man's obvious disappointment with Sophie and sees a chance to pay the other girl back for her snubs.

Signor Caperelli produces a child-sized flute from the carpetbag that holds his music. Martina blows on it to warm it, as her auntie has taught her. She shuts her eyes and sees the rainbow spilling onto the nursery floor. Each color has a note and she plays the rainbow, or tries to. She wants to cry, because she hasn't made the sounds come out to match the colors. She hands the flute back, scarlet with shame.

Signor Caperelli laughs. "Your auntie, she love the noise of Herr Schoenberg? To my ear, he is not making music!"

When Martina doesn't answer, still staring at the floor, Caperelli rummages in his bag again and extracts a sheet of simple music. "You can read the notes, yes? Give this to your auntie. At your little age, already you are in love with sound, but now you learn to make a song, not the howling of cats on the Prater like Herr Schoenberg make, *si*?"

In later years, Martina remembers none of that, although the flute will always calm her. She remembers only the rainbow on the floor, and the discovery that the cut glass in the nursery windows created it.

1

HELL'S KITCHEN

THE SUN SCORCHED my back through my thin shirt. It was September, but out on the prairie, the heat still held a midsummer ferocity.

I tried the gate in the cyclone fence, but it was heavily padlocked; when I pushed hard to see if it would open enough for me to slide through, the metal burned my fingers. A camera and a microphone were mounted on top of the gatepost, but both had been shot out.

I backed away and looked around the empty landscape. Mine had been the only car on the gravel county road as I bumped my way from the turnoff in Palfry. Except for the crows circling and diving into the brown cornstalks across the road, I was completely alone. I felt tiny and vulnerable under the blue bowl of the sky. It closed over the earth in all directions, seeming to shut out air, to let in nothing but light and heat.

Despite dark glasses and a visored cap, my eyes throbbed from the glare. As I walked around the house, looking for a break in the fence, purple smoke rings danced in front of me.

The house was old and falling down. Glass had broken out, or been shot out, of most of the windows. Someone had nailed slabs of plywood over them, but hadn't put much effort into the job: in several places the wood swung free, secured by only a couple of nails. Behind the plywood, someone had stuffed pieces of cardboard or tatty cloth around the broken panes.

The steel fence had revolving spikes on top to discourage trespassers like me. Signs warned of guard dogs, but I didn't hear any barking or snuffling as I walked the perimeter.

In front, the house was close to the fence and to the road, but in the back the fence enclosed a large stretch of land. An old shed had collapsed in one corner. A giant pit, filled with refuse and stinking of chemicals, had been dug near the shed. Jugs, spray cans of solvent, and all the other fixings of a meth operation fought with coffee grounds and chicken bones for top stench.

It was behind the shed that I found the opening I needed. Someone had been there before me with heavy steel cutters, taking out a piece of fence wide enough for a car to drive through. The cuts were recent, the steel along the pointed ends shiny, unlike the dull gray of the rest of the metal. As I passed between the cuts, the skin on my neck prickled with something more than heat. I wished I'd brought my gun with me, but I hadn't known I was coming to a drug house when I left Chicago.

Whoever cut the fence had dealt with the back door in a similarly economic way, kicking it in so that it hung on one hinge. The smell that rolled out the open door—metallic, like iron, mixed with rotting meat—was all too easy to recognize. I pulled my shirt up over my nose and looked cautiously inside. A dog lay just beyond the doorway, his chest blown open. Some large-caliber something had taken him down as he tried to protect the losers he lived with.

"Poor old Rottweiler, your mama never meant you to guard a drug house, did she?" I whispered. "Not your fault, boy, wrong place, wrong time, wrong people."

Flies were busy in his wounds; the ends of his ribs were already exposed, patches of white beneath the black of dried blood and muscle. Insects had eaten out his eyes. I felt my lunch start to rise up and made it down the steps in time to throw up in the pit by the shed.

I went back to my car on wobbly legs and collapsed on the front seat. I drank some water from the bottle I'd brought with me. It was as hot as the air and tasted rubbery, but it settled my stomach a bit. I sat for some minutes watching a farmer move up and down a remote field, dust billowing around him. He was too far away for me to hear. The only sound came from the wind in the corn, and the crows circling above it.

When my legs and stomach calmed down, I took the big beach towel I use for my dogs from the backseat. In the trunk I found an old T-shirt that I slit open so I could tie it over my nose and mouth. Armed with this makeshift mask, I returned to the house. I waved the towel hard enough to dislodge most of the flies, then covered the dog.

When I stepped over his body, it was into a kitchen from hell. A scarred wooden hutch, once painted white, was filled with spray cans of starter fluid, drain cleaner, jars part-full of ugly-looking liquids, eye droppers, Vicks inhalers, and gallon jugs labeled "muriatic acid." A makeshift lab hood with an exhaust vent had been constructed over the hutch. Half buried in the filth were a number of industrial face masks.

Whoever had kicked in the door had also pulled linoleum from the floor and pried up some of the rotting boards underneath. I squatted and pointed my flashlight through an opening between the exposed joists. Water heater, furnace, stood on the dirt floor below me, but no bodies as far as I could tell. Cool air rose from the basement, along with a smell of leaf mold that seemed wholesome in contrast to the chemicals around me.

I straightened and played my light around the room. It was hard to tell how much of the shambles had been caused by the dog killers and how much by the natives.

I stepped over jugs that had been knocked to the floor, skirted a couple of plug-in heaters, and moved into the rooms beyond.

It was an old farmhouse, with a front room that had once been a formal parlor, judging by the remnants of decorative tiles around the empty fireplace. These had been pried out of the mantel and shattered. Someone had held target practice against an old rolltop desk. An angry hand had smashed the drawers and scattered papers around the floor.

I stooped to look at them. Most were past-due notices from the county for taxes and for garbage pickup. The Palfry Public Library wanted a copy of *Gone With the Wind* that Agnes Schlafly had checked out in 1979.

Scraps of photos were all that remained of a savagely mangled album. When I dropped it back on the scrap heap, it dislodged one intact picture. It was an old photo, bleached and scarred from its time in the meth house, which showed a dozen or so people gathered around a large metal egg balanced on a giant tripod. It looked like a cartoon version of a pod landing from outer space, but the group around it stared at the camera with solemn pride. Three women, in the longer skirts and thick-heeled shoes of the 1930s, sat in the middle; five men stood behind them, all in jackets and ties.

I frowned over it, wondering what the metal egg could possibly be. Pipes ran through it; perhaps it was the prototype of a machine to ferry milk from cow to refrigerated storage. Just because it was an oddity, I stuck it into my bag.

The adjacent room contained a couple of card tables and some chairs with broken backs. Empty pizza cartons, chicken bones, and a bowl of cereal that was growing mold: I could see it as a Bosch still life.

A staircase led to a second floor; tucked underneath it was a stopped-up toilet. A better detective than I might have looked inside, but the smell told me more than I wanted to know.

Three bedrooms were built under the eaves at the top of the stairs. Two of them held only mattresses and plastic baskets. These had been upended, spilling dirty clothes over the floor. The mattresses had been slit, so that hunks of batting covered the clothes.

There'd been an actual bed and a dresser in the third bedroom, but these, too, had been ripped apart. An eight-by-ten of a young woman holding a baby had been torn from the frame, which itself had been broken in half and tossed onto the shredded bedclothes.

I picked up the photo, cautiously, by the edges. The print was so faded that I couldn't make out the woman's face, but she had a halo of dark curls. I slipped the picture into my shoulder bag along with the one of the milk pod.

A large poster of Judy Garland, with the caption *Somewhere Over the Rainbow*, hung by one corner over the bedstead, the tape ripped away from the other edges. I wondered if that was the drug user's joke: "way up high." It was hard to imagine a meth addict as a purveyor of irony, but it's easy to be judgmental about people you've never met.

The few clothes in the closet—a gold evening gown, a velvet jacket that had once been maroon, and a pair of designer jeans—had also been slit.

"You got somebody pretty pissed off, didn't you," I murmured to whoever wore those clothes. My voice sounded odd in the dismembered room.

If there'd been anything to find in this ruined house, the dog's killers already had it. In my days with the public defender's office, I used to see this kind of destruction with depressing frequency.

Most likely the invaders had been hunting for more drugs. Or they felt the drug dealers had done them out of something. The addicts I'd known would have traded their mother's wedding ring for a single hit and then come back to shoot up the place so they could retrieve their jewelry. I'd represented one woman who killed her own son when he couldn't get back the ring he'd traded for a rock of crack.

I climbed down the steep stairs and found the door that led to the basement. I walked partway down the stairs, but a spider the size of my hand scuttling from my flashlight kept me from descending all the way. I shone my flash around but didn't see signs of blood or battle.

I left through the front door so that I wouldn't have to wade through the kitchen again. The door had a series of dead bolts, as unnecessary an investment as the security camera over the padlocked gate. Whoever had been here before me had shot them out.

Before retreating through the gap in the fence, I found a board in the high weeds and used it to poke through the open pit. It held so many empty bottles that I didn't want to climb down in it, but as far as I could tell, no one was hidden among them.

I took a few pictures with my camera phone and headed for the exit. I was just skirting the fence, heading to the road, when I heard a faint whimpering from the collapsed shed. I pushed my way through weeds and rubble and pulled apart the siding. Another Rottweiler lay there. When it saw me, it feebly thumped its stub of a tail.

I bent slowly. It made no effort to attack me as I cautiously felt its body. A female, painfully thin, but uninjured as far as I could tell. She'd gotten tangled in a mass of old ropes and fence wires. She'd fled into the shed when her partner was murdered, I was guessing, then panicked and worked herself deep into the makeshift net. I slowly pried the wires away from her chest and legs.

When I moved away and squatted, hand held out, she got to her feet to follow me, but collapsed again after a few steps. I went back to my car for my water bottle and a rope. I poured a little water over her head, cupped my hand so she could drink, tied the rope around her neck. Once she was rehydrated, she let me lead her slowly along the fence to the road. Out in the daylight, I could see the cuts from where the wires had dug into her, but also welts in her dirty black fur. Some vermin had beaten her, and more than once.

When we reached my car, she wouldn't get in. I tried to lift her, but she growled at me, bracing her weak legs in the weeds along the verge, straining against the rope to get out into the road. I dropped the rope and watched as she staggered across the gravel. At the cornfield, she sniffed among the stalks until she found what she was looking for. She headed into the corn, but was so weak that she kept falling over.

"How about if you stay here and let me find what you're looking for?" I said to her.

She looked at me skeptically, not believing a city woman could find her way through a field, but unable to go any farther herself. I couldn't tie her to the corn—she'd pull that over. I finally ordered her to stay. Whether she'd been trained or just was too weak to go on, she collapsed where she was and watched as I headed into the field.

The stalks were higher than my head, but they were brown and dry and didn't provide any shield from the sun. All around me insects zinged and stung. Prairie dogs and a snake slipped away at my approach.

The plants were set about a yard apart, the rows appearing the same no matter which direction I looked. It would have been easy to get lost, except I was following a trail of broken stalks toward the spot where the crows continued to circle.

The body was splayed across the corn like a snow angel. Crows were thick around the shoulders and hands and they turned on me with ferocious cries.

2

DOG-TIRED

YOUR FRIEND WASN'T THERE, but I did find one of her fellow communards. Or drug dealers, as we call them on the South Side." I was in Lotty Herschel's living room, leaning back in her Barcelona chair, watching the colors change in the glass of brandy she'd given me.

"Oh, Vic, no." Lotty's face crumpled in distress. "I hoped—I thought—I wanted to believe she was making a change in her life."

It was past nine and Lotty was almost as tired as I was, but neither of us had wanted to wait until morning to talk.

I'd driven the crows away from the dead body by flinging my flashlight and a screwdriver at them. They took off in a great black circle, just long enough for me to look at the body and see that it had been a man, not a woman. After that I backed away as fast as I could through the dead corn. I didn't call the sheriff until I reached the edge of the road.

The dog wouldn't leave her vigil at the entrance to the field, despite my pleas and commands. While we waited for the law, I poured more water over her head and into her mouth. She tried to lick my arm, but fell asleep instead, lifting her head with a jerk when two squad cars pulled up. Two of the deputies, a young man and an older woman, followed the bent stalks of corn to the body. The third phoned headquarters for instructions: I was to go into town and explain myself to the sheriff.

"Oh no, get the crows off of him." It was one of the deputies in the field. We heard them flailing among the stalks, trying to beat the crows away, but they finally fired some rounds. The crows rose again.

I asked the deputy to help me lift the dog into my car. "Even though the dead guy in the field might have given her some of these wounds, she won't leave while he's out there," I said.

When the deputy came over, the dog curled her lip at him and growled.

The deputy backed away. "You should just shoot her, weak as she is and mean as she is."

I was a hundred miles from home, the law here was a law unto itself – and could make my life miserable. I needed to not lose my temper. "You could be right. In the meantime, she's innocent until proven guilty. If you'll take her back legs, I'll get her around the neck so she can't bite you."

The dog struggled, but feebly. By the time we had her shifted into the back of my Mustang, the two other deputies lurched out of the field at a shambling run. They had both turned a greeny-gray beneath their sunburns.

"We gotta get a meat wagon out here while there's still some of the body left for the ME," the woman said, her voice thick. "Glenn, you call it in. I'm going—" She turned away from us and was sick in the ditch by the road. Her partner made it as far as their squad car before he threw up.

My deputy called back to headquarters. "Davilats here. Got us an 0110 . . . Don't know who; I drew the long straw and didn't have to see the body, but Jenny says the crows been doing a good job having dinner off of it."

The voice at the other end told Jenny to guard the entrance to the field; I was to follow Officer Davilats back to the county seat. To my surprise and great gratitude, Sheriff Kossel didn't keep me long. He had me stay while Davilats drove him to the cornfield. Once Kossel returned from viewing the body he demanded my credentials.

"Warshawski? You related to the auto-parts people?" he asked.

"No," I said for perhaps the fifty thousandth time in my career. "They spell it with a 'y.' I'm related to I. V. Warshawski, the Yiddish writer." I don't know why I added that, since it wasn't true.

Kossel grunted and asked what I was doing down here. I gave him some names in the Chicago PD who could vouch for me.

"I was sent down here to look for a woman named Judy Binder," I explained when the sheriff had gotten Chicago's opinion of me ("Honest but a pain in the ass," I heard one of my references rumble). "I didn't know she lived in a drug house, but I went through the place and didn't see any trace of her. Was the dead guy the only person living there?"

Kossel grunted. "It's a shifting population and we don't know all their names. Every time we bust them it's been a different crew. House stood empty after the old couple who farmed that land died, then one of the grandsons showed up, started holding open house with his buddies and their girlfriends. We closed down the operation three times, but you know, it's not hard to buy the components and start up again. The gal, Judy you say? We've never picked her up. They don't have a phone, landline, I mean. If she was calling for help she did it from a cell, or a pay phone. Looks to me like the thieves had a falling-out and she got away with her skin in the nick of time."

"The house was really torn apart," I said.

"Could be they did it themselves while they were high. Nearest neighbors are a quarter section off to the south, and they hear gunshots out of there every so now and then. One time, those morons forgot to vent their ether and blew out some windows. Heard the explosion all the way over to Palfry, but when we went out to look they wouldn't let us in. Between the drugs and the guns and the dogs, everyone in the county kept a distance. We only arrested them when they started selling their shit out by the high school. Why'd you say you were looking for this gal Judy?"

It was the third time he'd asked: a test, to see if putting the question abruptly, out of sequence, got him a different answer.

"She left a message on an answering machine saying someone wanted to kill her. I got a call asking me to find her; the address down here was the only one I could turn up."

This was exactly what I'd said the first two times, but I repeated it patiently: strangers who turn up at meth houses have to answer questions, no matter how many Chicago police officers vouch for them.

"This answering machine belong to anyone?"

"I'll find that out and get back to you," I promised.

"You've traveled a long way for someone you don't know to find someone you say you never saw in your life." Kossel studied me closely; I tried to make my face look open, trustworthy, naive. "But I've got your name and address and they match what the Internet is saying, so you drive on back to the big city. I'll call you if I need you. You see crows circling around any more cornfields, just keep driving, hear?"

I took that as a dismissal and got to my feet. "You can bet your pension on that, Sheriff."

Tension and dehydration had left me light-headed. I refilled my water jug at the station's drinking fountain, poured water over my head in their women's washroom, and took myself and my orphan dog back to Chicago.

Palfry Township was a hundred miles south of the city. What with rescuing the dog, finding the body, talking to the sheriff, I hit the Dan Ryan Expressway at the height of the evening rush, but I didn't care. It felt good to be surrounded by thousands of cars and millions of people. Even the polluted air felt clean after the terrible stench of the country.

I drove straight to the emergency veterinary clinic on the North Side. The Rottweiler had lain so quietly throughout the drive that I was afraid she might have died on me, but when I lifted her out of the car at the clinic, I could feel her heart thumping erratically. She was so weak when I set her on the sidewalk that I had to carry her inside, but when I set her on the counter, she stuck out a dry tongue and licked me once.

I told the intake staff how I'd found her, said I had no idea of her age or temperament or whether she'd been spayed but yes, I would pay bills within reason. After half an hour or so, a young woman in scrubs came into the examining room to talk to me.

"Right now her main problem, at least on the surface, is starvation, but she's been beaten badly and there may be internal injuries," the vet said. "Also, a dog in a drug house was probably trained to attack, so once she's regained her strength she may prove too violent to keep. We'll do a thorough workup when she's had enough IV fluids and food to handle the exam. If she is salvageable, she'll have to be spayed."

"Yes, of course."

The vet added, "You may have found her downstate, but we get them all the time in here, dogs beaten to a pulp for not fighting hard enough, or for losing, or just beaten for the hell of it. We'll do our best for your girl here. I just want you to know that not every rescued dog can be saved."

I bent to kiss the dog's muzzle, but as I turned to leave, the vet added that I should shower and shampoo my hair and wash all my clothes without putting them into a hamper first because of the number of ticks and fleas on my charge.

No one who knows me has ever accused me of being germ-phobic, but ticks and fleas turn even a sloppy housekeeper into a compulsive Lady Macbeth. I stopped at a car wash, where I threw out all the towels and T-shirts in the car while they cleaned the interior. At home, I ran my clothes through the laundry with bleach and scrubbed myself until my sunburned arms begged for mercy.

Lotty had called several times while I was driving home. I called from the car wash to say I'd stop by as soon as I could. She was waiting for me when I got off the elevator. Even though her face was set in hard

worry lines, she insisted that I eat a bowl of lentil soup to restore my
strength before I did any talking.

As soon as I'd put the soup bowl down, Lotty said, "Rhonda Coltrain told me why she called you in, but of course we didn't talk until
after I finished my surgery roster."

Rhonda Coltrain is Lotty's clinic manager. When she arrived at
seven-thirty to prepare the clinic for the day, she heard a frantic message
from someone who only identified herself as "Judy" on the machine.
That was how my day started: Ms. Coltrain woke me, begging me to
come to the clinic. Lotty was in the middle of an intricate repair to a
prolapsed uterus that couldn't be interrupted.

In Lotty's storefront clinic on Damen Avenue, I replayed the terrified outburst several times until I could make out the gabbled speech.
"Dr. Lotty, it's me, it's Judy, they're after me, they want to kill me, you
have to help me! Oh, where are you, where are you?"

I didn't know any Judys who might be calling Lotty in the predawn,
but Ms. Coltrain did. She's usually completely discreet, but when she
realized who was calling, she snapped, "I'm not surprised. She only calls
Dr. Herschel when she's been beaten up, or has an STD. And why the
doctor keeps trying to help her, I don't know, except they seem to have
some kind of history together. I don't like to ask it of you, but you'd
better try to find her."

She found the downstate address in Lotty's private files. None of
my databases could produce a phone number or even a photograph. In
the end, not sure what else to do, I'd made the trek downstate.

After I described the unspeakable mess in Judy's so-called commune to Lotty, I said, "The sheriff down in Palfry wants your name,
and he wants to know what your involvement is with this Judy Binder.
I protected your privacy today, but I can't forever. It would help if I
knew who she was and why you care so much."

"I didn't ask you to drive down to Palfry. If I'd been in the clinic, I
would never have bothered you."

"Lotty, don't try that on me. If you'd been in the clinic, you know darned well that your first call would have been to me, to ask me to trace the call, which, by the way, I lack the legal authority to do—you can sic Ms. Coltrain on the phone company in the morning, if you want to find out where Judy was calling from. And then you would have said, *Victoria, I know it's an imposition, but could you possibly check up on her?*"

Lotty grimaced. "Oh, perhaps. Just the way you come in every time someone puts a bullet through you and say, *I know it's an imposition but I don't have enough insurance to pay for this.*"

I sat up in the Barcelona chair and stared at her. "You want to start a fight to keep me from asking about Judy Binder. I'm too tired for that. I'm not leaving until you tell me who she is. Rhonda Coltrain says you feel responsible for her. Here I've been knowing you thirty years and never once heard you mention her name."

"I know a lot of people you've never heard of," Lotty said, then gave her twisted smile, a recognition that she was being petulant. She put down her coffee cup and walked over to the long glass wall that overlooked Lake Michigan. She stared at the dark water for a long time before she spoke again.

"Her mother and I grew up together in Vienna, that's the problem." She didn't turn around; I had to strain to hear her. "That's the story, I mean. Käthe, her mother's name was in those days, Käthe Saginor. So when Käthe's daughter Judy began needing extra attention, running away from home when she was only fifteen, getting involved with one abusive boy after another, then needing her first abortion when she was sixteen—she came to me for a second when she was twenty-two—I felt—I can't even tell you what I felt.

"I didn't see that much of Judy as a child, so why should I feel responsible, or even affectionate? But I did feel some of both, along with a dash of schadenfreude over Käthe's failure at motherhood. I only know that against all my own beliefs or my normal course of action, I kept trying to rescue Judy."

She turned to look at me. "In an Uptown practice, I see many people caught in the thralls of addiction to one thing or another. I know if they are going to be saved they have to want salvation, which, to be honest, I never saw any sign of in Judy. I don't know why I thought my own willpower could imbue her with the desire."

"She was the daughter of a friend from your childhood," I said, thinking I understood. "That can—"

"I don't like her mother." Lotty cut me off sharply. "Käthe Saginor was always a whiny, nervous girl. I hated that my grandmother thought I should play with her. I was never very nice to her on the days Käthe's grandmother—Kitty, I mean, she changed her name in England—Kitty's grandmother brought her over to our flat on the Renngasse. After the Anschluss, when we had to leave the flat, it was worse because we were stuck next door to each other in those cramped slums in the Leopoldstadt. Käthe used to tell her grandmother—oh, never mind that!"

Lotty flung up a hand, as if brushing a cobweb out of her hair. "Why am I dwelling on those petty old slights and wounds? Still, when my *Opa* put Käthe on the train to London with Hugo and me that spring before the war started, I was scared Käthe would jinx the trip. I worried that she would cry and complain so much that the German guards would throw us off the train, or even that the English would be so cross with her that they'd ship Hugo and me back to Vienna with her. It was a relief when we reached London and she was sent on to Birmingham.

"In the turmoil of the war years, I forgot about her. Then, without warning, she appeared in Chicago, around the time I was doing my obstetrics fellowship at Northwestern. She'd become Kitty—I don't know why I can't remember that. After all, I anglicized the spelling of my own name."

"Did she come to Chicago to find you?" I asked.

"No—she had her own complicated story, which I got tired of hearing. She was married by then, she'd gone back to Austria after the war to interpret for the British Army and married an American GI. They came to Chicago because Kä—Kitty thought her own mother was here, that was her story. I couldn't *bear* hearing about all the people who'd mistreated her, or lied to her, how she found her mother, she hadn't found her mother, her mother left Chicago without seeing her, her mother was dead. We all had our dead to mourn, our lives to build, no one was holding my hand and I didn't want to hold hers!"

I sat still: if I'd gone to her at that moment she would have pushed me away like another cobweb.

Finally she walked back to her chair. "I liked Len—Leonard Binder, that was Kitty's husband. Judy was their only child. Len died about eighteen months ago and that was the last time I saw Judy, at his funeral. She told me she'd joined a commune downstate, that she was turning her life around, and I wanted to believe her even though I was pretty sure she was high at the time."

At that I did go over to her, knelt next to her chair, put my arms around her. Lotty's breath slowly returned to normal. She sat up abruptly and said, "Didn't you say the sheriff down there had never seen Judy? What if she wasn't part of that drug house at all?"

I walked over to the couch where I'd left my handbag and pulled out the two photos I'd found in the wreckage in Palfry. I handed Lotty the one of the mother with a baby.

Lotty looked at it briefly. "Oh, yes. Judy with the one baby she carried to term. Poor thing, she gave him to Len and Käthe when he was a year or so old."

I looked at the bleached-out picture again. It was hard to make out Judy Binder's expression, but she seemed puzzled, like a dreamer who doesn't understand where she's woken up. She'd given the baby to her parents, but she'd kept the picture; that must mean something.

I showed Lotty the picture of the metal pod on stilts that had been on the floor of the meth house. "Do you know what this is?"

"It looks like a child's design for a spaceship. But the people—" She frowned over the photo. "I feel as though I should recognize them, but—I don't know, I think it's the clothes. They make me think of my childhood."

I took back the pictures and put them in a folder in my bag. The mantel clock chimed eleven, startling both Lotty and me. It had been a long day; I was more than ready for bed. As she walked me to the elevator, Lotty thanked me formally for all the trouble I'd taken.

When the car arrived, she held my arm and said with her self-mocking smile, "Victoria, I know it's an imposition, but will you go see Käthe—Kitty, I mean—and see if she knows anything?"

3

FAMILY PORTRAITS

K ITTY BINDER LIVED IN SKOKIE on Chicago's northwest border in a tan brick house. Most of her neighbors had small front gardens, with marigolds and rosebushes set around squares of perfect grass. At the Binder place, a few patches of unmown grass warred with dandelions in the dry ground. The trim around the windows was peeling; squirrels had bitten holes underneath the eaves. Depression, age, lack of money, or all of the above. I sucked in a breath to buoy myself and rang the bell.

Two fingers cautiously parted the blinds in the front window. After a moment, I heard the lock's tumblers clunk as the dead bolts were undone; the front door opened the length of a stout chain. Through the crack I could just make out a shadowy face.

"Ms. Binder? I'm V. I. Warshawski. We spoke earlier this morning."

It had been a difficult phone call. At first, Kitty Binder said she wasn't interested in her daughter, she had no idea where Judy was, and furthermore, why had I let Charlotte Herschel involve herself in affairs that were no business of hers?

When I described Judy's terrified message on Lotty's answering machine, Ms. Binder became even fiercer. She wished she had a nickel for every threatening phone call Judy had made over the years. Judy played on Lotty's sympathies like Isaac Stern with a Stradivarius. Judy knew

that she, Kitty, wouldn't stand for such nonsense, so Judy turned to Lotty instead.

"Not that Charlotte is gullible. She sees plenty of drug addicts in that clinic of hers. She knows exactly what's going on. She just wants to make me look bad in my daughter's eyes by acting as if she were a saint."

I flinched at my end of the phone. Lotty and Kitty definitely were not best friends forever. I didn't want to have to listen to decades of grievances from either of them, so I cut Kitty off abruptly.

"I went down to Palfry yesterday, to the house where your daughter has been living. I didn't find Judy, but the house had been torn apart and I'm sorry to say that I came on the murdered body of a man who'd been living there. I think this time your daughter may have—"

"A murdered man?" Kitty interrupted me in turn, her voice rising in fear. "Who was it?"

"I don't know; I couldn't find any ID on him." I didn't want to say I hadn't looked for any ID with the crows descending on me, claws and caws ordering me away from their feast.

"Come at noon." And she'd hung up.

Here it was, noon, which I'd managed only by rearranging a couple of client visits. Instead of letting me in, Ms. Binder demanded proof that I was V. I. Warshawski. I didn't argue with her, just showed her my various licenses to drive cars, shoot firearms, investigate crimes.

She finally undid the chain bolt. As soon as I was inside, she did up all the bolts again. The house smelled of unopened windows, overlaid with the scent of the face powder Kitty Binder was wearing. The only light in the entryway came through a dirt-crusted transom above the front door. I had trouble making out Ms. Binder, but I could tell she was short, with close-cropped white hair. Despite the hot day, she had on a thick cardigan.

Instead of inviting me all the way in, she startled me by demanding to know if anyone had followed me to the house.

"Not that I know of. Who were you expecting?"

"If you're really a detective you would have kept an eye out for tails."

"If you were really Kitty Binder, you'd want to know about your daughter. You wouldn't be lecturing me on the fine points of detection."

"Of course I'm Kitty Binder!" It was hard to make out her expression, but her voice was indignant. "You're violating my privacy, coming into my home, asking impertinent questions. I have a right to expect you to be professional."

Everyone in America is watching way too many crime shows these days. Juries expect expensive forensic work on routine crimes; clients expect you to treat their affairs as if they worked for the CIA. Not that Kitty Binder was a client yet.

"Is it the DEA you're worried about?" I asked. "If they're looking for your daughter they'll already have a wiretap in place, so they don't need to follow someone like me around."

I thought Ms. Binder's eyes grew round with alarm. "Are you saying that my phone is being tapped?"

"No, ma'am." I was beginning to feel that I'd gotten lost in a conversational thicket the size of yesterday's cornfield. "I'm just saying that we should talk about the murdered man I found yesterday. Who do you think he was?"

"You're the one who found him," she said. "You tell me."

"He either was living in the house with your daughter, or he was one of the invaders. But you know or think you know who it was, because it was only after I mentioned him that you agreed to talk to me."

"Charlotte sent you here to spy on me, didn't she?" Her voice quavered, as if she were trying to whip up anger as a cover to whatever she was afraid of facing.

"Ma'am, could we sit down? If someone's been bothering you, following you, or threatening you, I can help."

"If you're a friend of Charlotte Herschel's, you'll go back to her and tell her what I said so the two of you can have a laugh at my expense."

"No, ma'am, I can promise that if you tell me something in confidence, I will keep it confidential."

Lotty's last words to me came into my mind: the baby Judy had carried to term, she'd given him to Len and Kitty. Could he possibly be the man I'd found in the field? I wondered how old the grandson was by now.

Kitty was biting her lip, unable to make up her mind whether to talk to me or not. I moved past her into the house and stopped at the door to a living room. The blinds were drawn so tightly that I could only make out ghostly shapes of chairs and a couch, the gleam of a TV screen. I could smell the dust.

"Where are you most comfortable, Ms. Binder? In here? Or should we go to the kitchen?"

Ms. Binder pushed past me into the living room. A pity: she might have unbent more in the kitchen. She turned on a table lamp and gestured toward an armchair whose arms and back were covered with lace doilies. Lace dripped over most of the other furniture, including a side table that held a series of photos, some formal, in frames, but most old snapshots. The room was tidy, if crowded, but a layer of dust had settled over the table and television.

"Did you make these yourself?" I fingered the lace covering the arms of my chair.

"Oh, yes. I wasn't a pampered house pet like Charlotte Herschel. We worked in our home. My grandmother made sure I could knit and make lace before I turned five. It's not a skill you forget, not when you're taught it that young. Even my own mother—"

Kitty bit the sentence off, as if it were a thread she was snapping in her teeth. I waited, hoping she might add something.

"When did you last see your daughter?" I finally asked.

Kitty's lips tightened. "She came to her father's funeral. She showed up in black, wearing a big hat, and crying as if she'd been nursing Len day and night. Of course, he was always soft with her, so soft you'd have thought she might come around more when she learned he was sick. Or maybe she did, she probably went to see him at the shop more times than he let on to me. He knew I didn't like him giving her money. I don't imagine a drop will fall from her eyes when I'm gone."

And if she's dead, will a drop fall from your eyes? I wondered.

"Can I talk to your grandson? Maybe he—"

"You leave Martin alone," she said, her tone menacing.

"How old is he?" I asked, as if she hadn't spoken.

"Old enough to know his mother is poison through and through."

I got up and went to look at the framed photos. A young Kitty wearing a New Look suit, carrying a bouquet, stared sternly at the camera. The man next to her, in a U.S. Army uniform with his combat ribbons on his chest, black hair slicked away from his forehead, beamed with pride. They'd met in post-war Germany, Lotty had said. From the man's uniform, I assumed they'd married there. It was a time when many women wore their best suits to their weddings, not a bridal gown. My own mother was married in an outfit not much different, but my dad had filled her arms with roses.

In another photo, the same man, considerably older, but still wearing a proud smile, was standing at a bima with a thin, serious boy. The grandson's bar mitzvah. The two also appeared behind a complicated collection of glass tubes and coiled wires, with a "First Place" ribbon attached to the table. Same proud smile on Grandpa, same serious look from the youth. The only other photo was a faded snapshot, three teenage girls and a plump couple. They all wore old-fashioned swimsuits and were grinning at the camera. Kitty was in the middle; she, too, was smiling.

"Are those your sisters?" I ventured, nodding at the snapshot.

Her face tightened further, but she nodded fractionally.

"Is it possible your daughter went to one of—"

"Oh!" Her cry was almost a scream of pain. "How can you? How can you be so cruel?"

My stomach twisted. I should have known, Jewish refugee from Vienna: her family, like Lotty's, had likely been murdered.

"Forgive me." I rolled a lace-covered hassock up next to her chair so that my head was lower than hers. "I didn't know, I wasn't thinking. Please talk to me about your daughter and your grandson. It's he you're worried about, isn't it? If you can describe him to me, I may be able to tell you if he's the person whose body I found yesterday."

"That's him you were looking at just now." Her fingers twisted so tightly in her lap that the joints turned white.

"How old is he now?"

"He turned twenty in May."

"The man I found yesterday was probably ten or fifteen years older than that," I said, "although his body was so damaged I can't be a hundred percent sure. When did you last see Martin?"

She scowled but didn't answer. She was embarrassed: perhaps Martin had followed his mother in fleeing this musty house with its drawn blinds, its tightly sealed windows.

"Does he work? Go to school?" I asked.

"He takes a few night classes down at Circle, but he works for a living, like my family always has."

"Ms. Binder, what is the problem? Is he doing work that you think will get him in trouble?"

"Of course not," she bristled. "He's nothing like his mother, which just proves all that environment influence they throw at you is nonsense. If he could grow up here and be a decent, hardworking boy, then his mother could have, too, if she hadn't had such a weak nature."

"Then what are you worried about?" I asked.

She twisted her fingers into such tight knots that I couldn't see how she stood the pain. "He took off ten days ago," she whispered. "No one knows where he is."

4

MARTIN'S CAVE

I GOT THE STORY out of Kitty in tiny pieces, as if I were prying gold from a rockface. Martin worked at a company in Northbrook as some kind of computer technician. He took a few night classes at the University of Illinois's Chicago Circle campus, but he made good money at the place he worked: Kitty didn't think he needed a college degree.

Martin hadn't talked much about the job, but he seemed to like it, he often worked late even though he wasn't paid overtime. "I keep telling him, they're just taking advantage, but he says he learns so much he's coming out ahead. Used to say, anyway."

Then about six weeks ago, something upset him. He had always spent a lot of time alone in his room, but now he was either spending all his time there or disappearing for long hours after work. He stopped working overtime; he started treating the job like a job; Kitty thought this was as it should be, or she would have thought so, if he hadn't become so moody.

"Did he say what was troubling him?"

"He's not very talkative. Neither am I." Kitty gave a bleak smile. "I guess we both relied on Len to talk to us and neither of us ever learned how. Anyway, this went on, him brooding, me having to remind him to eat, and then, about ten days ago, he went off in the morning, like he always does. Only he came home after a few hours. He stayed in his room for a bit, then around three he left again."

That was the last his grandmother had seen or heard of him.

"Where did he go?"

"He didn't tell me. He said he'd found something didn't add up, then he took off. I started cleaning—"

She broke off as I involuntarily looked around the dust-covered sitting room.

"Yes, my grandmother would have slapped me for letting a room look like this, but since Martin disappeared I think, what's the point? Why keep cleaning when people keep leaving?"

"Your grandmother would slap me every day if she saw the way my apartment looked," I assured her. "'Something didn't add up.' Could he have been going to the bank?"

She shook her head, her face pinched in misery. "I don't know. He just said there was something he had to look into. Or look at? I'm not sure; I didn't pay much attention. I didn't think it was anything special until he didn't come home."

"When did you start getting worried?" I asked.

"That night. Well, the next day. I thought, who knows, maybe he found a girl to spend the night with. Then, when he didn't come home, I thought maybe he'd gone camping. He would, sometimes, just pack up a light tent and go down to Starved Rock or up to Wisconsin for a few days. He hadn't taken a vacation since he started the job two years ago—he started right out of high school."

"Would he go off camping without telling you?"

"He might. Since Len died, Martin doesn't like to tell me what his plans are. But then when he still hadn't come back, I thought he'd moved into an apartment. We used to argue about that: he could save so much money living at home, and he has his own nice little apartment down in the basement. I thought he'd moved out but didn't have the courage to stand up and tell me to my face. Only—he isn't answering his phone or e-mails or anything."

"It should be pretty easy to check with his employer," I said.

She started twisting the thick cables of her sweater around her fingers; her voice sank back to a whisper. "Last week his boss called: Martin hasn't been to work since the day before he left here. He's not answering their e-mails or phone calls, either."

"That sounds really bad," I said baldly. "What do the police say?"

"I haven't told them. What would be the point?"

I tried not to shout at her. "The point would be that they could be looking for your grandson. He's been gone ten days now. No phone calls, right? No postcards or e-mails? No? Then we need to get the police looking for him."

"No!" she cried. "Just leave him alone. And don't go calling the police, the police are worse than—never mind—but if you go to the police about my business, I'll—I'll sue you!"

I looked at her in bewilderment. It was hard to believe an elderly white woman might be the victim of police harassment. Maybe it was a residue of Austria under Nazi control, when police declared open season on Jews, but her ferocity made me think she was guarding against a more immediate danger.

"Ms. Binder, who are you afraid of? Has one of your daughter's associates threatened you?"

"No! I don't want the police involved. What if they—" She cut herself off mid-sentence.

"What if they what?" I demanded sharply.

"People like you think the police are there to help, but I know different, that's all. We solve our own problems in my family. I don't need police, I don't need Charlotte Herschel's condescension, and I don't need you!"

I couldn't budge her from that stance, even though I didn't mince words about the danger her grandson might be in.

"How did he leave? Car?" I finally asked, thinking that with the plate number I might get state police to help look for him.

"Len bought him a used Subaru, when I—when we said—when Martin agreed that college would be a waste of time and money, but he didn't take it; it's still out front."

She couldn't imagine how he'd gone; she thought she would have heard a taxi. He might have just walked to the bus stop.

"What did he take with him?" I asked.

"I don't know. I told you, I wasn't really paying any attention."

"Have you looked in his room to see what might be missing?"

She stared at me blankly, as if I'd suggested she sacrifice a sheep to predict the future. When she didn't respond, I said, in the bright tone you reserve to mask your anger, "Why don't we go to his room now, and you can tell me whether he took camping gear or a laptop, or what."

After fiddling with her hands and her sweater for another moment, Kitty got to her feet and stumped off toward the back of the house. I followed her through a dining room crammed with sideboards and more lace into the kitchen. This was where she lived; it held a television, bookshelves, and stacks of unopened mail.

She opened a door to a set of open-backed stairs and led me down them, past the mechanicals, to a wall made of dark-stained wood with a door set in the middle.

"I did most of this work," Kitty said. "My dad was a builder and you knew when something broke he could fix it. He taught all us girls the same. When I married Len—we met in Vienna; he was working in the army motor pool—I thought he might be like my dad, but Len wasn't a builder. He was good with machines, but he couldn't do carpentry. I ended up doing all those kinds of things." The words might have been part of an ongoing plaint, but it was clear from the way she looked at her knobby fingers that she was proud of her skills.

She pushed open the door to her grandson's room. A deep voice intoned, "Beware, mortal, you are entering Sovngarde, where Alduin has set a snare for your soul."

I jumped back and flung a protective arm around Kitty, but she wasn't disturbed. She even produced a faint smirk at seeing me knocked off balance.

"I'm so used to Martin's gadgets, I don't notice them. Martin is a clever boy with engineering projects, so if anyone besides him opens the door, they hear a warning. The message changes; he's got five or six programmed in."

Peering closely, I saw a small speaker and two tiny camera eyes mounted into the door frame. Martin must be a clever boy indeed to disguise their mounting so carefully.

When I walked into the room, I thought if Kitty had built this space, she was pretty clever herself. Soffits were set into the low ceiling, with three sets of recessed lights. One illuminated the built-in workstation, which held two computer monitors, a second an alcove where Japanese-style screens were open to show a carefully made bed. The third set of lights covered a separate little living area where Martin and his friends met—if he had any friends, poor guy.

The floor was tiled in a soft-colored stone. I opened a door and saw a bathroom, tiled in the same pale stone. An old tube of toothpaste and a dried-out bar of soap sat on the sink, but a trailing vine, its leaves still thick and green, covered part of the wall next to the shower.

I wondered if Kitty came in to water it, then saw that a little hose hung over it, attached to an electronic timer. "Was this your invention or Martin's?" I asked.

She gave a half-smile. "That was one of the tricks we learned from my dad. Martin made the electronics for it, though. The last thing we ever did together."

Back in the bedroom, I poked my head into a walk-in closet, where a lone sports jacket hung. Most of the closet was a storeroom for Martin's overflow of electronics, old computers that he was hanging on to, a bassoon, some stereo speakers. His whole little apartment was severely bare, as great a contrast as possible to the musty rooms above with their collection of junk.

Two rockets about a yard long, made with a painstaking attention to detail, stood on a shelf above the computers. In between them was a framed snapshot of Martin as a young teen, holding up a plaque that read "First Prize." His grandfather stood next to him, beaming with pride.

The rockets and photo, with a poster-sized copy of a book jacket over the bed, were the room's only decoration. The poster showed the laughing face of the author, Richard Feynman, positioned so that his eyes seemed to be looking at the pillows.

"He was Martin's hero," Kitty said, noticing me staring at it. "Martin read everything he wrote, which gave him the idea he ought to go to some fancy science school, like the one in California where Feynman taught. We fought about that."

Feynman's name was familiar. "A scientist, right?" I guessed.

"A physicist." Kitty bit off the word, as if it were something despicable—a symptom of degeneracy, like her daughter's drug abuse. "He won the Nobel Prize, so I guess he was smart, but what good does that do you? He's dead like all the rest of them, but Martin doesn't see it like that. Martin always says Feynman's work made him immortal."

Her jaw worked; she kept staring at the photograph. "Of course, Feynman died before Martin was born, but he started reading about him when he was still in junior high, and then he collected everything he could, books and so on. Martin's first science project, when he was twelve, was trying to show how Feynman figured out what made the space shuttle blow up.

"Martin made six rockets, three with faulty O-rings and three without. He tested them; he wanted the faulty one to crash at the science fair, but he couldn't make it happen because the atmosphere this near the ground isn't cold enough, as any fool would have known. So then he tried doing the experiment in dry ice, which Len thought was such a wonderful idea he went out and filled the garage with it. Toby Susskind, one of the neighborhood boys who came around to stare at the rockets, he passed out from the dry ice, and his father acted like I'd murdered him."

She waved a hand at the models above his workstation. "Those are the last two. Martin kept them after he saw he had to give up the idea. He was that upset, as if it was the end of the world. Len took it seriously, too, even though I told them to forget about it. Rockets. Rockets do nothing but kill people, I said, but that didn't worry either of them for one second."

Poor Martin, growing up in this desert. At least his grandfather had entered into his enthusiasms. It must have seemed like a wonderful adventure to the old man, trying to fill a room with enough freezing air to bring down a rocket. And then they'd come inside to Kitty and her bitter, biting comments, colder than a garage full of dry ice.

I changed the subject abruptly, saying I wanted to look through Martin's papers, and get a look at his computer. Kitty wasn't happy about that. First she told me it wouldn't do any good, but when I said, "You never know," she insisted on pulling up a chair near Martin's computer monitors to watch me.

"I know Charlotte trusts you, but I never saw you before, I need to watch what you're doing."

I couldn't fault her for her caution with a stranger in her house, but when I warned her it might take some time, she merely clutched the edges of the chair, as if she thought I would carry her out.

In fact, it took no time at all. When I tried to power up the computers, nothing happened. I stared at the screens for a long moment. Martin had a kit of small tools in a tray on his desk. I unscrewed the backs of both CPUs. When I had them open, I saw he'd removed the drives.

Whatever he'd discovered that didn't add up, he was concerned about it enough that he didn't want anyone getting a look at his files. I'm not a computer whiz, but Martin was: he must have figured that even if he zeroed out the drives, a pro could reconstruct his files.

When I told Kitty what he'd done, she gave me the vacant look that was starting to get on my nerves. If she'd been my age or younger I would have shouted at her to wake up, be alert, but she was an old woman, she was in trouble, she didn't need me arguing with her.

In as many ways as I could think of, I tried to get her to remember what else Martin had said his last weeks at home. Nothing else when he left the house that final day? Nothing about friends, or coworkers, or projects he'd been assigned to over the summer? Nothing at the meals they'd shared those last few weeks?

No, it was like him to be withdrawn. He liked to torment her by think-ing about equations when she could have used a little company. Didn't Martin see how lonely she was since Len's passing?

I finally gave up on it and started looking through the desk draw-ers. Like the rest of Martin's monastic space, these were almost empty. He'd kept his notebooks from high school, which included printouts of his history and English essays. He'd written a number of times about Feynman's life and work. The essays were filled with red ink and com-ments like, "You need to learn to construct a paragraph and an argu-ment," or, "See me if you want to rewrite this."

Other binders contained problem sets, with Martin's answers writ-ten out in a tiny, careful hand. From long-ago calculus classes, I vaguely recognized some of the symbols—derivatives, integrals, polynomials. On one problem set, a teacher wrote, "You might find it easier if you took the following route," and then included a different series of equa-tions. Almost all were marked "100," and twice, "Bravo, Martin. Be-yond amazing."

Those comments seemed to be the only thing in his room that showed a connection to the outside world. He had a photo of a rough mountainside tucked into one notebook, but there were no pictures of friends, no remnants of camping trips. A couple of ribbons from cross-country meets where his team had finished second or third, that was it.

For a gregarious boy, this beautifully built hideaway would have made the perfect hangout. For Martin, the isolation must have added another layer of painful loneliness to his life.

"What about his friends?" I asked Kitty.

Kitty started plaiting her fingers together again. "He doesn't have a lot of friends. There were a bunch of rich kids his age who had summer jobs at the place Martin works; they got on his nerves, thinking because they went to Harvard or places like that, they could look down on him, and then he had to fix their mistakes. That made him plenty mad. But for some reason, they invited him to a barbecue the night their summer jobs were ending. Martin went, but he came home early. I thought it was because the kids were such snobs, but it was that weekend that he started brooding over, well, whatever he was brooding over."

"Do you know the names of the kids he went to the barbecue with?" I asked. "Maybe he talked to one of them."

Kitty didn't know their names; Martin never talked about them, just told her there were seven college kids who'd all worked together. One of the girls lived in a place with a beach and her folks had agreed to let her have a party there, but Kitty didn't know her name or where exactly the parents lived.

"Did he ever have a girlfriend? Or boyfriend?"

"Martin isn't a homosexual," she protested.

Martin could be a Martian who slept with a space squid and his grandmother wouldn't know, but I kept that remark between me and the model rockets. "Girlfriend, then."

"Martin didn't have much luck with girls. I told him it was because he took himself too seriously; girls like a boy to loosen up, not always be talking about theories and whatnot. Believe you me, when you carry on like that, nobody can stand to be around you."

You hear a lot these days about helicopter parents who can't stop hovering over their offspring's every movement. Kitty was more like a mole, burrowed so deep underground she was almost unaware of her grandson.

"There isn't anyone you can think of who he talked to regularly? What about the boy Toby who passed out in the garage? Did you ask if he knew where Martin had gone?" I said patiently.

"It wouldn't have done any good."

Her voice was so low I barely made out the words.

"Ms. Binder, do you know what happened to your grandson?"

She shrugged. "He could be dead, or he just ran away."

"What aren't you telling me?" I cried.

She looked at me blankly. "People die or they run away. If you haven't noticed that, it's because you're not paying attention."

I opened my mouth to protest, then shut it again. Her husband had died, her family was killed in the Second World War, her daughter had run away. Now Martin. From her perspective, she was right.

I asked about her husband's family, wondering if Martin might have gone to visit them.

Kitty wasn't in touch with Len's sisters; they'd never gotten along, they all thought she was a gold digger who married Len to get an American passport. "They even blamed me for bringing Len to Chicago, instead of back to Cleveland where they all lived!"

"Why did you come to Chicago?" Personal curiosity took me off track. "Was it because Lotty was here?"

"Charlotte Herschel, one of the princesses of the Renngasse? Don't make me laugh! No. After the war ended, I went back to Vienna with the British Army to see if anyone was still alive. I heard a rumor at a place my mother used to work that she and my father were in Chicago, so Len and I came here. That was a mistake, but Len got a good job at a big garage, so we stayed. Anyway, what business is it of yours?"

"This is where we started, Ms. Binder. It's because of your daughter and the ugly murder down at the house where she was living. She thought her life was in danger, and it turns out that ten days ago, her son disappeared. Do you think that's a coincidence?"

"Yes. Yes, I do," she snapped. "Judy is a drug addict and a loser, she had two abortions and then when she had Martin, she couldn't look after him. If it hadn't been for Len and me, where would that boy be now? I think it's a total coincidence."

"Perhaps Martin wouldn't go out of his way to be in touch with her, but Judy might have tried calling him, you know."

The lines in her face deepened. "No!" she shouted.

"Who else would your daughter reach out to, besides Lotty, if she was really frightened?"

"You mean who else could she con? After all this time, I'm happy to say I don't know!"

I hesitated for a moment, then pulled out the photo of the metal pod on stilts.

"Do you know any of these people? I found it in the house where Judy's been—"

She snatched it from me. "That—oh! So she stole that after Martin's bar mitzvah, along with my pearl earrings and forty dollars in cash. What was she doing with it?"

"What is it, Ms. Binder?" I asked. "Lotty said the people looked familiar, but she couldn't remember their names."

"Of course she couldn't: she was a Herschel. The rest of the world was beneath her notice. Just go! You've hurt me enough for one day." She thrust the photo inside her sweater, her face squeezed into a tight knot of misery.

I put one of my cards next to the rockets. "If you change your mind about your daughter, or if you want me to help you find your grandson, let me know."

5

COMPUTER GAMES

I **BRUSHED PAST KITTY** and left Martin's room, but before I reached the basement stairs, she called to me. "Ms. Detective! Don't run off."

I went back to Martin's den. After a certain amount of backing and forthing, she decided she wanted to hire me to find her grandson. I told her I'd get her a standard contract, but that my rates were a hundred dollars an hour. She backed and forthed some more, but in the end, her worries about her grandson trumped her worries about money and contracts. She told me she'd pay for two full days' work and then we'd see how I'd done. I also managed to dig out the name of the company where Martin had been working: Metargon, some ten miles north of the house.

When I got back outside, my body felt as though someone had tied me to a wall and thrown rocks at me. I wanted to go to bed for a year or two until my muscles stopped aching, but after slumping in my car for a time, I pulled away from the curb. As I left Kedvale Street, I saw the blinds twitch in Kitty's front window.

Since I was already north, I decided to go to Metargon first, to see what they knew about their missing computer tech. Before I turned onto the expressway, I looked up the company on my iPad. I'd heard of them, of course, because their game box, the Metar-Genie, was an industry leader, and their search engine, Metar-Quest, was coming up the ranks as a rival to Google. I hadn't known, though, that Metargon was big in energy technologies. They were defense contractors, they had plants in seventeen countries around the world. Martin had worked in their computer research lab, just the place for a young man with a passion for rockets and computers.

I had an easy drive at this time of day, but once I got to Waukegan Road, it was difficult to spot the building. Every big-box retailer on the planet has an outlet along Waukegan. Sprinkled among them are giant fast-food outlets. Their signs flash and dazzle in a muscular competition for notice, but Metargon didn't draw attention to itself. I finally parked outside a Kentucky Fried and made my way down the street on foot, looking for street numbers.

Metargon had wrapped itself in a forest of evergreens. I found the sign and the address on a small plaque attached to a set of high rolling gates. On the left, at driver's-window height, was a phone. I picked it up and told the scratchy voice at the other end that I was hoping to speak to someone about one of their computer techs. The voice asked me to spell Martin's name, then put me on hold.

While I waited, the gates rolled open and a few cars came out; a UPS truck pulled up behind me and got buzzed through. I was tempted to walk in behind it, but I continued to hold and in another minute my virtue was rewarded: the voice was replaced by someone who announced himself in an incomprehensible squawk, but added he'd meet me in the lobby in twenty.

The gates rolled open and I walked into an industrial park totally at odds with the clamor on the street outside. The lab looked like the latest thing in functional modernity, steel and glass, solar panels on the roof, white screens at the windows to minimize the heat. Beyond the drive, a pond surrounded by marsh grasses created a completely different mood, contemplation, peace. As I crossed the parking lot toward the main entrance, I saw a man emerge from a copse on the pond's far side. He stopped to stare at the water.

Since I had twenty minutes to fill I went over to stare at the water myself. I could see carp lazing about under the surface. Ducks were hunting for food in the reeds, and the ubiquitous geese, the rats of the urban parkscape, were waddling along the bank. If you had to come up with an idea for a new kind of energy or rocket, the water and the birds might bring you to that calm interior space where creativity lives. Staring, thinking about nothing—my neck muscles began to relax from Kitty's battering.

I finally made my way back to the research building. A burnished sculpture of indeterminate shape stood outside the entrance, next to a metal sign that read "Metargon: Where the Future Lies Behind." I wondered how much they had paid a branding company to come up with that cryptic slogan.

The entrance doors were locked; I announced myself again through an intercom and was buzzed into a small lobby. A semicircle of tan leather chairs and hassocks made up a waiting area. Two people sat there, one thumbing through a magazine, the other typing on her laptop. On the other side of the lobby stood a glossy wooden counter, where a woman handled an intercom and phone bank. I gave her my card, told her someone had promised to talk to me about Martin Binder.

"Oh, yes, that would be Jari Liu. I'll let him know you're here."

I wandered around the small space, looking at awards and pictures or models of machinery: the Orestes booster rockets which had sent up modules to probe the reaches of the galaxy (Metargon photovoltaics powered the space probe); a mock-up of a nuclear reactor (Metargon's first plant, designed with a unique core, still powering southern Illinois); the Presidential Freedom Medal, awarded to Metargon's founder by Ronald Reagan.

"V. I. Warshawski, is it?"

I jumped and turned around. Jari Liu had come up behind me on such soft crepe soles that I hadn't heard him. He was a stocky man in his thirties with lank black hair falling over high cheekbones. In the old days engineers wore white shirts and ties, but Liu had on jeans and a T-shirt that proclaimed "In God We Trust, All Others Show Data."

He shook my hand and propelled me toward the doors that led to the interior. "I'm Martin Binder's boss, assuming he ever resurfaces and that we take him back. Normally we prefer people to phone in advance for appointments, but I happen to be free right now, so let's go into the back and talk. I need to take your cell phone and your iPad—we don't like anyone surreptitiously taking pictures while they're pretending to talk about AWOL employees."

I took my cell phone out of my pocket, but removed the battery pack before I gave it to him. "I don't like anyone copying my files while they're pretending to answer my questions." For the iPad, I'd have to hope my encrypted lock would keep snoopers at bay, although it probably wouldn't hold off anyone as sophisticated as the Metargon team.

Liu led me quickly to the inner doors. The two people who'd been in the holding pen when I arrived looked at me sourly as we sailed past: they'd been here longer, why did I get priority?

Liu bent to press the security card he wore around his neck against a control panel and the doors opened with a pneumatic hiss. We were in a long, high room filled with machine tools and banks of computer consoles. Liu zipped me along too fast for me to have more than a confused impression of a giant magnet lifting a piece of metal that looked like an outsized Frisbee, of men in safety glasses bent over a lathe, a woman in a lab coat and hard hat checking the dials on something that looked like a vat of witches' brew.

We passed a room labeled "Decontamination," another with the familiar inverted triangles announcing radiation, and moved through a corridor to the second section of the building. Everything in here was quieter.

Liu took me to the corner of a room that held several dozen computer monitors, some with the traditional screen most of us know, others with the transparent glass that wowed me in the Bond movies with Judi Dench.

Liu looked me up on the Internet, using one of the glass screens so I could see exactly what he was doing. My website came up. Liu pressed a switch on the rim of the screen. There was a tiny flash, and my face suddenly appeared on the monitor next to my website profile. He dragged the image onto the photo I use on my home page.

He grinned as he saw my eyes widen. "Yep: you're the same person. Whether you're really who your website claims, that I can't tell. Now you tell me why you're here asking about Martin Binder."

"He's vanished," I said bluntly. "The last time anyone saw him was ten days ago, which you must know: someone from your office called his home last week, looking for him. He lives with his grandmother, but he didn't say anything to her about where he was going. He's not answering e-mails or his cell phone. I know he went out with some college kids who were summer interns here. I'd like to get their names so I can see if he told any of them what was in his head, why he took off."

Liu leaned back in his chair, pursing his lips into a gargoyle frown. "I don't think I can give you names. I was the mentor for the summer fellows—they aren't interns, by the way, they're too grand for that. It would be an invasion of the privacy of the kids in the group. What I can do is send an e-mail to them and ask them to get in touch with you if they feel like talking."

I pushed on him, stressing the urgency of asking questions now, before the trail got any colder.

"How about Martin's phone number and e-mail?" I asked when it was clear he wasn't going to budge. "I didn't get those from his grandmother."

Liu finally decided he could give me those in good conscience. He put them into an e-mail that I'd be able to read as soon as I got my cell phone and iPad back from him, but he also sent an e-mail to Martin explaining what he'd done. He didn't stop my looking over his shoulder while he typed. He finished with "If you're reading these, Martin, give me a shout. Jari."

I returned to my chair. "Did Martin talk to you about anything that bothered him during his last week here?"

Liu shook his head, slowly. "He was a very focused guy. One of the most creative we've worked with. But he was also very private. The kids we take on for summer projects were his age. That's why Martin was put in my group—there's a theory around here that I connect with Millennials, but it wasn't a good fit this time. Martin's been here almost two years. He was a full-time employee, with a different background and mind-set. The fellows looked down on him for going to night school, so they couldn't cope with his being better at logic and math than they were. He resented them for—I don't know—the sense of entitlement they exuded.

"Frankly, I'm surprised that he got asked to their end-of-summer barbecue. Might have been one of the women in the group—once or twice I thought they might have had something going on."

I pounced on that, but Liu wouldn't give me her name.

I asked what Martin was working on. "For that matter, what do you do here that involves big lathes and gantries and radiation and a gazillion computers?"

Liu gave a mock-wounded look. "It's the same old story: everyone knows about Bell Labs, but no one's ever heard of Metargon. We're as big or bigger, we've won almost as many prizes, and we're turning energy on its head in the way that Bell turned communications upside down with the transistor. That's what Metargon means: beyond energy. Watch my face and watch the screen at the same time."

He turned the glass monitor around so I could see his face and the screen together. He blinked four times and my face and website disappeared. He blinked twice and the screen filled with icons. He looked at an icon with a sword on it and the application opened—a video game that began with a movie of a woman in shimmering turquoise armor. She was locked in combat with five large men. Liu moved his eyes around, and the woman's arm changed directions, changed movements.

"It's clumsy; Princess Fitora still dies in five minutes, although Martin could keep her going for eight. He designed some of the software that runs her, but it's set up as a computer game because that makes it more fun, more engaging if you're working on it. Ultimately, when we have it refined, a person who's completely paralyzed will be able to use those eye blinks to tell a computer to bring him or her a drink, or move their wheelchair to the bed, or change a catheter bag."

"Sounds quite wonderful," I said honestly. "When I looked at the plaques in the lobby I thought you were involved in nuclear power."

"We have a nuclear design section, but old Mr. Breen started in computers; it's where he made his money after World War Two. Metargon also works in energy; we're ahead of the game in solar, but this location is focused on electronics."

Princess Fitora was lying on the ground, her sword-arm moving feebly as her attackers converged on her.

"That's what Martin worked on for us: how to use voice, or even tongue clicks, to mimic using a mouse or touching the screen. Anyway, Martin was focused, he was creative, he moved this project along well, but if he had a personal life, he didn't talk about it. I didn't know until you said it that he lived with his grandmother, for instance."

I asked Liu if he had gone to the fellows' barbecue, but he said it was something that the group had organized themselves. "They were done for the summer; it wasn't a place for management to butt in." A bell chiming on his computer drew his attention back to the screen. "My next meeting's in five minutes; I've got to take you back to the lobby."

As I got to my feet, I looked back at the glass screen. Princess Fitora was lying on the ground with five swords through her chest. The men

around her were giving each other high fives. The image was profoundly disturbing: as Liu escorted me back to the main lobby, I found
myself pressing my hand against my heart.

When we passed the machine shop, three men were positioning the
Frisbee over something that looked like a wellhead, but Liu hustled me
along too fast to stare. At the exit, he handed me back my phone and
my iPad. I walked down the drive to the gates, where I stood until the
receptionist saw me on her monitor and rolled them open.

AUSTRIA, 1943
The Mother's Heart

IT'S COLD ON THE TRAIN PLATFORM. The station signs have been taken down because of the war, but Martina thinks she must be in Vienna. Somehow you feel a big city, even when all you can see are the necks of the hundreds of other people pushed into a tight herd around you.

Of course, when she left the mountain lab they told her nothing, just the kick in her side to wake her.

"Get up, you're leaving, we've no further use for you." The insolent "*Du*" delivered by a pock-faced guard who would be butchering hogs if the war hadn't given him a uniform and a boot.

How fortunate that I travel light. She kept the ironic thought to herself. Nothing to pack, the grimy dress she sleeps in the same that she wears in daytime. With the rest of the slave laborers she was prodded at riflepoint out of the cave onto a small train along the siding.

There had been rumors for weeks that the lab would shut down. They hadn't produced results, which wasn't surprising, given the sloppy quality of the work. Several times the scientist in her had rebelled; she tried to suggest a different experimental design, but that earned her a beating twice, a kicking once, a day without rations all three times. After that she shrugged every time she saw another waste of hard-to-find minerals.

The train was a small one, two freight cars. The guards made sure the prisoners watched as the cars were filled with fruit and meat from the local farms, extra torture for people close to death from privation. After standing for several hours, while the peasants joked with the guards, the prisoners were shoved into a carriage whose seats had been removed. Boards had been nailed across the windows so they couldn't see out.

For the limbo of time that the journey lasted they stood, unspeaking, like sheep knowing they are bound for the abattoir. Now and then the train stopped, flinging the sheep against each other and into the car walls, and then some timepiece clicked and they lurched forward again. Einstein's clock, Zeno's paradox, the train departs Innsbruck for Vienna, and for the inmates the journey lasts both forever and the blink of an eye.

When she'd made the reverse journey fourteen years earlier, leaving Vienna for her glorious year at Göttingen, she hadn't slept the night before out of excitement, not this near-dead state she inhabits now. *As if you were going to a lover,* her mother commented sourly all those years ago, even more sour on Martina's return because her passion was reserved for matrix algebra and quantum mechanics, not the father of the child she was carrying.

At first, realizing she was pregnant, Mama had thought she understood Martina's excitement at going to Göttingen: physics had been an excuse for meeting a lover. But when she realized that the child was an afterthought, something that happened when a shared passion for particle decay spilled over into bed, Mama became even angrier. Papa was dying, who was going to look after him and a baby, if Martina was going to work at the Radium Institute?

When she returned to their tiny flat on the Novaragasse, Martina had been shocked at how frail Papa had become during her year away. His eyes still were filled with life, though, and he annoyed Mama by demanding all the news of the elusive atom. When the baby came, he kept her next to him in bed, showing little Käthe the play of light on the ceiling through the prisms he had brought home for Martina after she'd first seen the rainbow in Sophie Herschel's nursery.

Locked now in this dark train, Martina finds her one source of thankfulness a deep irony: Papa's tubercular lungs, weakened by gas attacks in the trenches of the Great War, allowed him to die at home in bed, with Martina holding his frail hand. *Spectral lines.* Mama incensed that those were his last words.

Her tired, fevered mind is still a jumble of Papa's death, Heisenberg's matrix, when the train lurches to a halt once more. This time the doors are unlocked. Guards and dogs order them onto the platform where they are pushed into the midst of a pack of people as worn down as themselves.

No one bothers to ask a neighbor where they are going, how long they have to stand in the cold. As long as they are standing here, they aren't being shot or shoved headfirst into lime pits or gas chambers. No need to think further ahead than this.

Next to Martina, an old woman keeps grabbing her arm, scrabbling at the sleeve of Martina's threadbare coat so that it falls back, revealing how thin her arms have become. Those little bony twigs that used to be round, muscled, now end in thinner twigs covered with radiation burns.

The old woman is distressed. "Where is Joachim? He said he was going out, just for a moment, but he hasn't come back. Have you seen him? He's never late." Joachim could be a husband or son or brother, it's impossible to know.

Most of the crowd is silent. Too many years, too many humiliations, too many losses have taken away their voices. Martina has had her losses, too. Her mother and her aunts, for instance: they stood on a platform like this a year ago, disappeared into a train like the one she and her fellow sheep are waiting for. The thought of those three women twists her diaphragm with a sharper pang than hunger.

She has a panacea for pain and starvation, and she turns to it now, imagining differential equations for electric fields. From there it's not much of a jump to quantum mechanics. For a time she doesn't hear the whimpers and barks around her, doesn't feel the anxiety of the woman next to her still fretting for Joachim, doesn't feel the painful throbbing in her feet, which are swollen from cold and ill-fitting shoes. She puts a hand absently into her pocket, feeling for a pencil—Maxwell's equations for free space are eluding her—and then remembers that all her papers and pencils were confiscated—stolen—when she was put on the train outside Innsbruck.

Perhaps it's true, as Benjamin always said, that she is too aloof to feel the passions and griefs most people experience. Her own mother, after all, often said the same thing, only in an angrier, shorter way. If she had real human feelings, for instance, at this moment, when she is almost certainly going to her death, shouldn't she be thinking of her child, not free space? I should write you a letter, my daughter.

Dear Käthe.

She imagines the paper, the ink, the pen.

My daughter, we have had so little time together that I hardly know you. Not just because you left for England over three years ago, but all your little girlhood I was at the Institute day and night. Your grandmother saw you take your first steps and it's she who has cared most for your fate.

The day they got the news from the Cavendish labs that announced the discovery of the neutron, Martina was so excited she could hardly choke down a piece of cake with her afternoon coffee. Long after Professor Meyer left the Institute for the day, she and Benjamin stayed talking with some of the students, pondering the implications. Benjamin's tidy equations covering one side of the chalkboard, her own diagrams filling the other, her student, Gertrud, crying out with excitement that this explained the effect that Irène Joliot-Curie and Frédéric Joliot were finding in Paris. Although it didn't speak to the odd half-life of one of the radium isotopes.

The Stephansdom clock struck eleven and Benjamin looked around with a guilty start: his wife would long since have gone to bed, his dinner would be cold and dried out by now. Not spoken: his wife's resentment, her suspicion that more than quantum mechanics kept her husband late at the Institut für Radiumforschung.

When Martina herself reached home, she quietly stowed her bicycle in the service entrance and tiptoed up the stairs: no one in Vienna stayed up so late unless they were at the theater. And there her mother sat at the kitchen table, mouth pinched in anger. *Käthe said her first sentence today,* her mother announced: *"Oma, Käthe needing milk."*

When Martina responded, *How lovely,* her mind only vaguely absorbing the news, her mother slapped her. "That piece of pike on the sideboard has more feeling than you. You don't deserve a bright young child like Käthe. Why did I let your papa talk me into allowing that trip to Göttingen? Your education has destroyed you as a woman."

Was Käthe a bright young child? She always had seemed petulant, but perhaps that was my fault, not yours, my little daughter. You wanted something from me I wasn't able to give you. I wanted you to share my excitement over the innermost secrets of nature; you wanted me to be at home with you instead of your *Oma,* or Frau Herschel's *Kindermädchen.* On the days Martina's mother still worked for Frau Herschel, Käthe and Frau Herschel's granddaughter, Lotte, played in the light, bright nursery in the big apartment on the Ring, but when Martina would ask Käthe, *Did you see the rainbow of light on the nursery floor?* the child would only stare at her sullenly.

Right before the Anschluss, she had taken Käthe and Lotte on a skiing trip in Tyrol. She tried to interest Käthe in the stars, in the mystery of the explosions inside them that made those jewels twinkle and glow in the night sky. It was Lotte whose eyes grew round with wonder, Käthe who gave the pinched scowl of disapproval she'd learned from her *Oma*, announcing it was too cold to stand outside at night.

Birgit, the *Kindermädchen*, appeared from the shadows and swept the girls away with her. Past their bedtime, too much excitement for them, anyway. And then a month later, the Anschluss, the new laws, and Birgit looking at them with contempt. *I'm not picking up after your children anymore. You do some work for a change.* Addressing even Frau Herschel with the familiar *du*, and all of them powerless to respond.

The memory is too difficult, but before she can lose herself once more in statistical mechanics, the noise around her suddenly increases; the soldiers are barking like their dogs, compressing her even more tightly against the old woman, who is still crying for Joachim. The train, staining the dawn sky black with its puffs of coal smoke, is entering the station. No whistle, no lights, just the relentless thudding of axles, so that the proper Viennese burghers, sleeping on the other side of the station, are protected from the sight of cattle cars filled with, well, whatever they're filled with. Not citizens, because citizens wouldn't be treated like this. And not people, because they've been labeled as vermin. But—it's a conundrum—because if they're not people, then there's no need to protect the rest of Vienna from seeing them packed up, shoved, heels nipped by the dogs, the old woman still crying for Joachim.

If I didn't look after my daughter when she wept, over all the un-accountable things that made Käthe weep, why should I look after you? Martina thinks, but she nonetheless puts a gentle hand under the old woman's elbow and helps lift her into the boxcar.

6

ARITHMETIC PROBLEMS

I T WASN'T QUITE FOUR when I got back to my office. I yearned for a nap, but with only an hour left in the business day, I needed to answer calls and messages from my clients. Before I started, I put Martin Binder's phone number and e-mail into my database and wrote him a note, explaining who I was and how distressed his grandmother was at his absence.

"If you want to get in touch, I promise that I will keep anything you say completely confidential," I finished.

I also looked him up in the social media universe. He played some complicated math game in the Facebook world and had made a killer move in early August, right before he disappeared—that was his last update. He had one photo of himself, taken outside a tent in a snow-drift. He was wearing a T-shirt and cutoffs and was grinning at the camera, proud of standing half-dressed in the snow. Unfortunately, he had on sunglasses and a baseball cap, making it hard to see his face. I uploaded it to my own system, but for a good search I'd need a better head shot.

Martin also had a Twitter account, which showed a few tweets from the summer, mostly on music, but he was a uniquely silent member of his generation.

I logged into LifeMonitor, a subscription database that hacks into people's financial history. Martin had told his grandmother that something didn't add up. Maybe he'd discovered that his mother was stealing from him. Just in case, I started a search for Martin's bank account. After that, I turned to my real business.

Among all the client calls and complaints was a message from Doug Kossel, the Palfry County sheriff. I waited until I'd responded to my most urgent client demands before returning his call. Kossel was out in his cruiser, the Palfry dispatcher said, but I could reach him on his cell phone.

"Hey, PI V.I. Wondered if you'd make the time to talk to us downstate hicks. We got an ID on the body you found in the field. Ricky Schlafly. Name mean anything to you? No? He's a local boy, but he lived in Chicago for about fifteen years."

"Sorry, Sheriff, I lose track of a few of our locals every now and then."

"Don't get sarcastic on me. You're in law enforcement, even if you're private. That means you see your share of scumbags, so it's always possible Schlafly crossed your radar. He left here before he graduated high school, figuring if he wanted big money he should go where people had money. Anyway, it was his mom's family that owned the house, and when her mother passed two years ago, Ricky came back and took possession. Turned it into the health resort and spa it is today."

"Was Judy Binder with him when he moved back?" I asked.

"From what people are saying, she showed up about a year ago. At least, that's when folks in Palfry started noticing a gal around town who sounds like her. She'd be at the local coffee shop, or sometimes panhandling in front of the Buy-Smart out west of town. Even came in for a hairdo when she had extra cash. No one's seen her since the house got shot up, so she may have landed on her feet somewhere else."

A year ago, that was a bit after Len Binder had died. Len might have kept slipping his daughter money over Kitty's objections, or without Kitty knowing. When he was gone, Judy would have been desperate for a place to live.

How Judy hooked up with Ricky Schlafly wasn't important: druggies find each other by some system of smell or twitches, although for meth users the rotting gums are a giveaway. Judy and Ricky could have shared some dump in Chicago before Ricky returned to his roots.

I didn't agree with Kitty Binder's vehement assertion that Martin stayed away from Judy—children want to find some proof that their mothers care about them, especially mothers who abandon them when they're babies. I could imagine Martin slipping silently out of the house, going to visit Judy without Kitty's knowledge. He might have met Ricky Schlafly when he was still living in Chicago.

An arithmetic error, Martin had said to Kitty, something that kept him brooding in his basement for more than a week. If his mother had hacked into his bank account, he could have bicycled down to Palfry to confront her—although why wouldn't he have driven?

"You still with me, Ms. PI?" Kossel demanded. "I got a traffic accident I'd better get to."

"Judy Binder's son disappeared over a week ago," I said. I explained Martin's situation. "Can you ask if anyone noticed him? He might have come down by bus, or hitched down. He's a skinny kid, dark curly hair, narrow face, a bit James Dean–looking. I could probably find a photo and e-mail it to you. The basement to Schlafly's house—it had a dirt floor."

There was a pause at the other end. "Crap, PI. You thinking I should dig up that floor?"

"I'm thinking someone with a hazmat suit could tell if it had been dug up recently. They could also climb into the pit in the backyard. I didn't have the gear with me yesterday to poke around in it."

After another pause, the sheriff grunted. "The boy comes down a week ago to see if his ma has been stealing from him, Ricky shoots him, buries him, but she's still around until two days ago? Hard to picture. Still, who knows what a woman full of meth might do. Hell, maybe she shot her own kid her own self."

I used to represent women who sold their ten-year-old daughters to pimps for a single pipe of crack. It's not the only reason I left the public defender's office, but it was high on the list.

Kossel said, "If I look at the basement, there's something you can do for me. See if you can find any of Ricky's old pals in Chicago, see if someone up there wanted him dead. I've got my eye on a couple of rival dealers down here, but they all have pretty good alibis for when Ricky likely was shot."

So that was why the sheriff had called, all cooperative with a private eye in a way the law usually isn't. "I've been hoping I could get through the rest of my life without looking at another drug user," I said.

"Told you you'd seen your share of scumbags," he mocked.

"How about we trade? I'll get a hazmat suit and rake through that garbage pit in Ricky's backyard, and you come up here and start hanging out with local drug dealers."

"Big-city gal like you can't handle a little heat? Just wear a bullet-proof vest and make sure your will is up-to-date and you'll be fine." The sheriff laughed heartily and cut the connection.

He called back a second later. "Ricky's short for Derrick, not Richard."

I drew little circles on my desk with my forefinger. If I wasn't careful, I was going to let other people move their problems into the center of my stage. I did not care who killed Derrick Ricky Schlafly. I did not care what had become of Judy Binder. My only involvement in the Binder world was to give Kitty sixteen hours of hunting for her grandson.

I turned back to my own investigative issues. It was when I'd made my third mistake, confusing a bookstore's problems with those of a completely unconnected yoga center, that I realized Martin Binder's face was coming between me and my clients.

Kitty Binder had mentioned a boy who'd been Martin's high school friend. She was one of the more unreliable narrators I'd listened to in decades of hearing dubious stories, but if she was telling something close to a fact, I could find him.

I hadn't made any notes when I was with Kitty, but the friend's name had made me think of television. Not David Sarnoff or Aaron Spelling. David Susskind. Martin's friend was something Susskind. Toby.

I found three Susskinds in the Skokie area. LifeStory, another sub-scription search engine, came up with a family that included a Tobias the same age as Martin. They also had a daughter three years older and another son starting high school. Jeanine Susskind was a social worker with the Cook County Department on Aging; her husband, Zachary, worked for a big accounting firm.

It was almost six now. I reached Jeanine at home, but she was not going to share any confidential information with a stranger on a phone.

"I think you're wise, ma'am," I said, wishing she weren't. "Can we meet for a cup of coffee or a glass of wine this evening? Martin Binder has disappeared, and I'd like to talk to someone who knows him. Kitty Binder said your son and Martin are friends."

I heard grease sputter: Jeanine had the phone tucked between head and neck while she stirred something into a pan. Mushrooms and broccoli, I imagined, feeling suddenly hungry.

There was a muffled conversation in the background. Jeanine came back on the phone and asked for more information, first about Martin, then about me. After another consultation, she decided I could come to their house when they'd had supper. She wasn't enthusiastic, but who could blame her—a strange woman claiming to be a private eye, wanting to talk to her son, calling at the end of a long workday—I wouldn't be enthusiastic, either.

I had about two hours to get home, walk the dogs, and eat my own mushroom broccoli surprise. Instead, I picked up the phone and dialed an old friend at the public defender's office. Stefan Klevic had stayed on long after the rest of us gave up in despair.

Stefan wasn't any more excited than Jeanine Susskind at hearing from me. "I'm on my way home, Warshawski. Can't it wait until morning?"

"A guy named Derrick Schlafly was killed down in Palfry yesterday morning," I said.

"I'm fascinated. Especially since I never heard of Schlafly or Palfry."

"A hundred miles down I-55. Schlafly was a meth maker."

"If the killer is arrested in Cook County, I'll put up a spirited defense of whoever shot him," Klevic promised. "Now, Doug has dinner waiting for me, so if you don't mind—"

"Schlafly operated around here for fifteen years or so. I need to find some of the scum he knew then, to see if any of them can help me find a woman who was living with Schlafly. About the time he was killed, she called up crazy scared, then vanished."

Klevic sighed audibly. "Leave her to the police, Warshawski. Turn over the details to them. If she shot Schlafly, it's the Palfry County PD's job to look after her, not mine, assuming their budget extends to public defenders."

"The missing woman's name is Judy Binder," I continued. "That's B-i-n-d-e-r. She's a protégée of Lotty Herschel."

Lotty had saved Stefan's sister's life several years ago. I heard him grind his teeth, but he muttered that he'd see what he could find out.

"Thanks, Stefan," I said. "I knew I could count on you."

"You know you're no better than a frigging blackmailer, V.I."

"Am too," I said. "A frigging blackmailer doesn't get nearly as good results as I do. Say 'hey' to Doug for me."

I checked my e-mail one last time before I left. My note to Martin had bounced back with the long message about "fatal errors" you get from sending to a nonexistent mailbox. I double-checked Jari Liu's message, but I'd entered Martin's address correctly. I tried the cell phone number Liu had given me. I was not astounded to learn that the number was not in service.

I forwarded my fatal-error message to Liu. "Any more recent address you want to share? Any other cell numbers? The one you gave me isn't answering."

As I locked up my office for the day, I wondered if I should call one of my contacts in the Chicago police as well. If Schlafly had a sheet, which was probable, they'd have his pals listed. Kitty Binder had been so insistent about not talking to the police that I hesitated: her daughter probably had a sheet, too. I could picture the tormented evenings when Judy was a teenager, the calls from the police, the fights with the daughter coupled with anger at the police. I'd wait to see what Stefan Klevic turned up before going to the boys in blue.

On my way home, I took a detour to the emergency vet to check on my waif. They'd done surgery to remove a ruptured spleen; while they were inside they took out her ovaries and uterus. She had some sepsis in the wound so she was on high-dose antibiotics for that. She had heartworm, which required a special regimen all its own. At some point in her short life—the vet reckoned she was about three—she'd broken a leg that had healed on its own.

"For all she's suffering, and considering the abuse she took, she still has a pretty sweet disposition," the vet said. "A little nervy, but she hasn't tried to bite anyone, so you may be able to take her home."

"Maybe," I said doubtfully. "I have two dogs already and a full-time job. If she recovers in good shape, I'll help find the right family for her."

The receptionist asked me to pay the bill to date. Forty-eight hundred and counting, but I handed over my credit card without complaint. So many of the humans I work with have a tendency to bite no matter how well they've been treated that it seemed like a good expenditure to rescue an uncomplaining Rottweiler.

My own dogs—a golden retriever and her half-Lab son—greeted me as if we'd been separated for twelve months instead of twelve hours. I hadn't been able to give them a proper workout the past two days, so

I took them over to Lake Michigan for a long swim. My downstairs neighbor, who shares them with me, rode over to the lake with us. I floated in the lake for a bit, letting the cool water ease away some of the stresses of the day.

Back on land, while I threw balls for the dogs, Mr. Contreras and I caught up on each other's lives. He was less reproachful than usual over his exclusion from my adventures: he had received a long e-mail today from my cousin Petra. He adores her and was bereft when she left Chicago for the Peace Corps. Her remote El Salvadoran village doesn't often get an Internet connection, so today's e-mail had pepped him up.

When he heard my story, his main focus was on the Rottweiler. "What do you think we should call her, doll?"

"'My Own True Love,'" I said brightly. "As in, 'Fare thee well, my own true love.'"

Mr. Contreras looked at me reproachfully. "That ain't right and you know it, cookie. It seems like it was meant, you going down there to find Dr. Lotty's gal and saving this dog's life along the way. We got two dogs already, how much trouble can a third one be?"

Mr. Contreras is almost ninety, with the energy and personality of a pile driver. Even so, his days of running big dogs are behind him.

I put an arm around him. "We'll make a budget. We'll see whether we can afford a full-time dog-walker, and whether Mitch and Peppy will welcome a half-feral outsider into their pack. For now, the Rottweiler has to be in segregation until she stops shedding heartworm larvae."

Mr. Contreras's lips were moving; I wasn't sure he'd been listening to me. "We'll call her Mottle, for 'My Own True Love.'"

7

ROCKET SCIENCE

J EANINE AND ZACHARY SUSSKIND met me at their front door together. Sort of together. Zachary was a bulky guy. Even though Jeanine was slim, she couldn't fit herself quite next to her husband in the doorway.

Before I finished announcing myself, Zachary demanded to see my ID. Something about Skokie gave its residents a mania for inspecting my credentials. I handed him a card and showed him my PI license. He frowned over it but reluctantly decided I could be allowed inside.

"What's this about? Why does Kitty Binder think my son should talk to a detective?" Zachary said.

His gut was pushing me against the edge of the open door. I leaned forward into him and he backed up a step.

I had my spiel about Martin's disappearance down to a thirty-second sound bite. "Your son is the one person Ms. Binder says Martin was friends with," I finished. "I'd like to talk to Toby to see if he knows where Martin was heading."

"He doesn't," Zachary said flatly.

"Did you ask him? Did you know Martin was gone?"

Zachary scowled. "If Martin took off to do something illegal or dangerous, Toby is smart enough to stand clear. I don't—*we* don't—want you harassing our son."

"I don't want to harass him, just ask him if Martin talked to him." I was tired. I'd ended up not having time to eat more than a few bites of Mr. Contreras's mac and cheese—sans broccoli and mushrooms—before heading north again. It took an effort to keep my voice level.

"If Martin turns up dead in a ditch and a few words from your son could have brought me to him in time, I won't be a happy detective." I decided not to put in the effort.

Jeanine Susskind said gently that we would all be more comfortable in the living room. "And we'll all be more comfortable not threatening each other," she added.

The Susskinds lived on the street behind the Binders, in a house that was bigger and airier. We went into a front room whose beige couches and armchairs made a suitable backdrop for a wall-sized abstract painting in blues and golds. A tray with coffee cups and a thermos sat on a glass table in front of a gas fireplace.

"Look," Zachary said, when his wife had finished the coffee ritual. "Everyone knows that Martin Binder's mother has a serious drug problem. When Martin and Toby were ten or so, she showed up one day and took them off to Great America without talking to Jeanine or to Kitty. She ended up driving her car into a streetlamp on Skokie Highway. It's a miracle that everyone walked away from that outing, and she's goddamn lucky we didn't sue her behind to hell and back.

"I told Toby he was never to go anywhere alone with Martin again unless he talked to me or his mother first, and he's been good about that, even when they got to be in high school. They went camping together a couple of times, but I was on the phone with Toby every day making sure that addict wasn't anywhere near them."

I rubbed the crease between my eyes. "Mr. Susskind, are you saying that Martin talked to Toby this past August and told him he wanted to visit his mother?"

"I—no." For the first time, Susskind paid attention to what he was saying; when he spoke again the belligerence level in his voice had gone down. "But if Martin had talked to Toby about doing anything alone, Toby would have told me."

"Zach, they're twenty now, not ten. You can't be sure of that," Jeanine said.

"I don't think Martin's any less reckless or dangerous now than he was ten years ago," her husband said. "Since Len died, there hasn't been anyone to balance Kitty's lunatic ideas. For all I know, she persuaded Martin to find the people she keeps claiming are following her."

"That's a persistent fear, is it?" I asked. "I wondered this morning if it stemmed from her childhood experiences, or if it had roots in something more recent, such as her daughter's drug problems."

"That's it in a nutshell," Zachary said. "With that kind of stepmother, or grandmother, I guess, it's no wonder Martin grew up to be such a lone wolf. Jeannie feels sorry for him, but even she has to admit, some of what he got Toby involved in was downright dangerous."

The coffee was weak for my taste. I took a few sips to be polite before putting my cup back on the tray.

Jeanine laughed softly. "It wasn't dangerous, not in that way. Martin wanted to re-create the Challenger disaster. When he was around twelve or thirteen he got fascinated by the history. He and Len built a series of rockets; Martin wanted to see if he could replicate what went wrong and Toby couldn't stay away, not when the boy across the alley was launching rockets!"

"He could have put out Toby's eyes, or his own," Zachary grumbled. "But you know darned well, Jeannie, they came close to suffocating when Martin filled the garage with CO_2."

"Ms. Binder told me how much that episode distressed you," I said.

"Zach," Jeanine said. "Please. You're giving Ms. Warshawski a very distorted picture here."

She turned to me, leaning forward over her coffee cup. "Martin idolized Richard Feynman. Do you remember him showing us all on national television how the O-ring in the rocket broke when it froze in outer space? Martin's enthusiasm infected Toby, who brought the story home to us."

"It was the rockets," Zachary said dryly. "No twelve-year-old boy could resist those rockets that Len was helping Martin build."

"That's true," Jeanine admitted. "All the kids in the neighborhood who'd been calling Martin names all those years, they crowded around, they wanted to go to the lakefront when Martin and Len were going to fire them off.

"Anyway, Martin was trying to get his rockets to freeze, so he got Len to buy a huge vat of dry ice. They filled the garage with it and Martin left his rockets in there to freeze, that was all. He and Toby got a little light-headed, but nothing came of it."

"And nothing came of the rockets, either, except one of them landed on the Tubman roof and set it on fire," Zachary said.

"It was so cool!"

We all three jumped at the words: none of us had noticed the younger Susskind boy standing in the doorway. He had a mop of the thickest, reddest hair I'd ever seen on a boy.

"Voss!" Jeanine said. "Don't you have homework?"

"I'm mostly done, honest, just history and physics left and—"

"Upstairs now," Jeanine said. "I don't want another night of you in bed after midnight."

"Voss," I interrupted, "do you know where Martin Binder was going when he took off last month?"

"Don't question my son without my—" Zachary began, but his wife silenced him with a head shake.

"Voss, this is Ms. Warshawski," Jeanine said. "She's a detective, she's trying to find out what happened to Martin."

Voss nodded: he'd been listening ever since I arrived. He shot an uneasy glance at his father, who told him petulantly to go ahead.

"Me and Sam Lustic were—"

"Sam and I," Jeanine interrupted.

"Sam and I, we were going over to the pool and Martin came out of the garage with his camping stuff strapped to his bike. You know, he has that cool tent that folds up like a kite, so I guessed he was going camping. Only not with Toby."

"Would that have bothered your brother?" I asked.

"I doubt it," Jeanine said. "Toby has a lot of friends; he always did, whereas Martin was, well, he was kind of a one-friend person. If he went camping without Toby, it's because Toby didn't want to go. They haven't been as close since Toby started college, anyway."

"Martin's been gone almost two weeks," I repeated. "I've got to tell the police, even though Kitty feels very strongly that they not be involved."

Voss was listening, mouth agape. "Has Martin been killed?"

"I doubt it," I said with a heartiness I didn't feel. "If he'd been killed someone would have told his grandmother by now."

"Are you still here?" Jeanine said to her son. "This conversation is not for you or about you."

When she'd shooed Voss up the stairs to his room, I asked about her earlier statement, the kids in the neighborhood who'd been calling Martin names. "What was that about?"

Jeanine looked troubled. "Kitty is so strange. The house was a difficult place to be in, so the kids wouldn't go there, not even for Martin's birthdays. Len tried a few times—he went around the neighborhood and invited everyone personally. No one showed up, except the little Gluckman girl, but she was even more desperate for friends than Martin.

"Of course, everyone knew some garbled version of Judy Binder's life, so the kids would say things, especially because when he was in kindergarten, Kitty used to send Martin to school in some of Len's old clothes, cut down, but still very much not children's clothes. We talked seriously to Toby about not joining in the taunting, but it wasn't until the rockets that he and Martin spent any time together."

She broke off to offer me the coffeepot. "Anyway," she continued when I'd hastily declined, "I suppose Martin took refuge in his experiments and computers to avoid thinking about his loneliness. In high school he turned out to be quite a good cross-country runner, and a computer whiz, so the kids laid off him, but I don't think he had real friends. Although I have to say, the senior project Toby did with Martin is probably what got him into Rochester—his math SATs weren't anywhere near as good as Martin's."

"Since Martin's were perfect they couldn't have been," Zachary put in. "That was a surprise to everyone, probably to Martin himself, since he was an odd man out in high school. Kitty thought he had a future as a bookkeeper. The only time she's ever talked to me, I mean sought me out to talk to me, was to see if I could get Martin a job at my firm."

"Did you try?" I asked.

"If Martin had been interested I might have gone through the motions, but a computer whiz and an oddball loner to boot—I'd be more afraid he'd hack into client accounts."

That opened up a different line of thought: Martin had been hacking and the FBI was on his trail.

"Do you think he was a hacker? Would Toby know that?" I asked.

Jeanine made a face. "I don't think Toby and Martin saw each other more than twice all summer. If Martin started doing something illegal—I don't know. Toby's days of running after Martin to be close to his rockets are long gone. It's hard to know what a boy like Martin might do, though. It's too bad Kitty wouldn't let him go to college. She kept saying blue-collar work was the foundation of a good society, and that her father and her husband were wonderful examples of that. She said if Martin went off to college, he'd turn into a scientist, turn arrogant."

"What's that about?" I asked. "Is she a fundamentalist, or did a scientist let her down?"

Zachary gave a crack of unkind laughter. "Can you imagine a guy getting close enough to her to let her down?"

Jeanine shook her head reprovingly. "We only knew her when she was already old. We've lived here since Toby was two, but we don't know anything about her. I think it was something that happened in the war, World War Two, I mean. We have a lot of Holocaust survivors in Skokie, or used to: they're getting old, they're dying. Kitty's odd behavior—it doesn't seem impossible that it's connected with the war."

"She grew up in Vienna," I said, "but she went to London with the Kindertransport when she was about nine."

Jeanine nodded. "If she lost everyone she'd left behind, if one of those people was a scientist, she might translate that into a feeling of betrayal by science. She isn't a fundamentalist, but she still grumbles if there's something about climate change, or even medical research, on the news. She'll go out of her way to make sure that everyone around her knows that scientists make things up just to make the people around them feel uncertain about the future."

"I wondered if her childhood in Vienna explains why she was so insistent about my not talking to the police about Martin."

"That's because of Judy," Zachary said. "We weren't here in those days, but the Lustics and other families have told us what *that* used to be like—cops on the block every night, Judy coming home coked to the gills, Judy arrested for dealing drugs on the high school grounds. If Kitty doesn't want you going to the cops it's because she knows Martin is with Judy."

"That's possible," Jeanine conceded. "But that doesn't mean Martin's in a safe place. He might have thought he could handle his mother and her associates and gotten in over his head."

Someone outside the room sneezed. I went to the doorway and found Voss hovering on the stairwell. Jeanine joined me in the hallway.

"You are a pest, aren't you?" I said before his mother could scold him. "What did Martin say when he rode off?"

"First he said, *'Hasta la próxima.'* That's because when I was little he used to play Mexican bandits with me."

"And then?" I prompted when Voss stopped.

He looked sidelong at his mother. "He asked if I'd take a book back to the library for him, in case he couldn't get home before it was overdue, so I said sure, and he went inside and came out with the book."

"And did you?" his mother asked.

He scuffed the stairwell carpet with his bare foot. "I kind of forgot."

"Then remember now and bring it down here. You know if there's a fine, you have to pay it."

Voss ran up the stairs. We heard thuds as he sorted through his room and then silence. Behind us Zach demanded to know what was going on.

"Back in a minute," Jeanine called to her husband, then yelled up the stairs to Voss to bring the book down.

"I don't know if it's teenage boyness, or too much gaming and texting, but he has the attention span of a gnat. Voss! Now!"

We heard a few more thuds and some rustling, but after another minute went by, Jeanine went up the stairs. She came down, exasperated.

"He's lost the book. I don't want to solve Martin's library problems, but I wish Voss could remember what he did with it."

"Does he know what it was?" I asked.

Voss appeared behind her. "I don't know," he said unhappily. "The cover was weird, it showed someone stabbing the Statue of Liberty."

Bookstore and library staffs' favorite way to find a title: The cover was red. There was a picture of a shark/puppy/Statue of Liberty.

Jeanine shooed her younger son back to his room. I waited until I heard his door shut before I told her what I'd found yesterday in Palfry.

"I really need to talk to Toby, or to someone Martin would have confided in. It was a mess down there—"

Jeanine looked back into the living room at her husband. This time it was he who gave his head a minatory shake.

"We don't want you bothering Toby," Zachary said flatly. "We'll call him and let you know what he says."

Like Jari Liu. What was it about my face that made people feel I couldn't talk to their staff or their children?

"I can't promise not to talk to your son. I have to find someone who knows what was on Martin's mind those last weeks he was home. Even if Toby doesn't know, he could give me names of some of the other people they both know."

"Toby's a minor," Zachary said. "It's against the law for you to talk to him without our consent."

"I'm not a cop, Mr. Susskind, I don't have powers to arrest or try anyone, so that particular law doesn't apply to me."

Jeanine murmured an apology as she escorted me to the door.

"I'm used to it in my work," I said. "If the book Martin handed to Voss turns up, will you call me and let me know the title?"

Jeanine promised. I could see her thinking that if she found the book it would make up for her husband's brusqueness.

8

DINNER WITH THE KING OF SWEDEN

I T WAS PAST NINE when I left the Susskinds', but I drove down to Lotty's place anyway. We'd spoken briefly when she got home from the clinic. She hadn't heard anything new from Judy Binder, but she wanted to know what I'd managed to learn.

"Is the Binder house still dripping in lace?" Lotty asked when we were sitting on the balcony overlooking Lake Michigan.

I'd found the lace oppressive myself but something in Lotty's voice made me perversely want to defend Kitty Binder. "It's beautiful work. She told me her grandmother taught her."

"Yes, Käthe's grandmother was a skilled seamstress. Embroidery, lace, all those things, besides making dresses and drapes and mending my grandfather's socks. I used to look down on her, attitudes I picked up from my grandmother, I'm afraid, although of course every woman of my *Oma*'s generation could embroider and even knit. When we all had to survive as best we could in the ghetto, Frau Saginor's skills were in much higher demand than my grandmother's gift as a hostess." Lotty's voice was tinged with bitterness.

"I was maladroit with Ms. Binder about her family. She had a snapshot of herself with her two sisters—"

"She told you she had sisters?" Lotty interrupted. "She was like me: an only child."

I felt a lurch of uncertainty. "They were all in bathing suits," I insisted. "Her parents and the three girls."

"What did they look like, these *soi-disant* parents?" Lotty demanded.

"I didn't get that close a look. Plump, jolly. The man had dark hair that was thinning in the middle, the woman, hard to say, she had a big straw hat on."

"I knew Käthe's mother. I can remember the fights at Käthe's home because her mother never remembered to come home in time for dinner. Food didn't interest Fräulein Martina—Käthe's mother. She was thin, with an angular, intense face. Anyway, Käthe was like me in another respect. Neither of us had a father on the premises.

"Käthe and I used to have stupid quarrels about whose papa was better. Käthe hated that I at least knew my father, could visit him when my mother chose to live in the tiny flat he shared with his parents and his sisters. Käthe retaliated by making up fantastic stories about her own father."

Lotty gave a harsh laugh. "We both knew my papa was a street musician, so hers had to be something grand. Käthe used to bore me to tears with her boasts about how he had met Albert Einstein, how he ate dinner with the King of Sweden. Who is this big shot? I would ask, but she couldn't even put a name to him! One morning I got so sick of hearing about him that I slapped her, and then my *Oma* made me apologize. *I sympathize with the sentiment, Lottchen, but not the method of expression,* she told me."

"Dinner with the King of Sweden, friends with Einstein—that sounds as though her father, or the man she thought was her father, won the Nobel Prize," I said.

"Yes, my dear, it didn't take Einstein himself for me to figure that out," Lotty said dryly. "My point is, Käthe didn't have sisters. She has a snapshot of herself as a child with two other girls and their happy parents, so she's made up a story about that, just as she used to make up stories about a scientist. Now she believes it's true."

"You're sure of this?" I said. "I know you don't like her—"

"That wouldn't cause me to make up my own fairy tales about her!" Lotty snapped. "Her mother taught science in the girls' technical high school in Vienna, that's probably why Käthe's fantasy father was a scientist. I think her mother did research at the Radium Institute there. Maybe Käthe had a crush on one of the masters, or perhaps on someone who visited Fräulein Saginor from the Institute."

I frowned. "Ms. Binder told me that her father was a builder. She said she didn't want her grandson going off doing theoretical work because it only leads to trouble. Which story is correct? The Nobel laureate or the builder?"

Lotty made a helpless gesture with her hands. "We were so young when we left Vienna, and the trauma of it all—I can't begin to tell you what her real history might have been. The family she lived with in England could have been builders—I don't know anything about them."

"She said her family had all been killed," I said. "But she also said she came to Chicago after the war because someone in Vienna told her that her parents were alive and in Chicago. The whole story is so confusing I can't make head or tail of it, but one thing does seem clear: Kitty's grandson has disappeared. Also she's afraid of the police. I'm going to have to go to them, but it will be against her wishes."

"Oh, this constant harping on the police!" Lotty exclaimed. "Käthe always has to cloak what she's doing in drama and mystery. It's the same as pretending her father won the Nobel Prize: she's so important that the FBI pays attention to her comings and goings. It's not surprising that Judy went off the rails, living in that madhouse. How Len stood it all those years I can't fathom."

"According to the neighbors, the police came to the Binders' quite a bit during Judy's adolescence," I said. "Ms. Binder has probably had enough of their involvement with her family."

"Yes, but this has been the bee in her bonnet since she first arrived in Chicago. I wasn't ever to talk to the police about her, because that could get her killed. I put it down at first to survivor paranoia: as you know, I have my own allergies to people in uniforms. Once you've seen police beat your own grandfather—never mind that. What's frustrating about Käthe is that she'd rather not take the trouble to differentiate between the past and the present. Between real threats and imagined ones."

Lotty was breathing hard. I waited, watching the running lights of the boats on the inky sea beyond. Lotty poured herself another cup of coffee. I'd reluctantly declined a cup of her rich Viennese coffee, such a contrast to the Susskinds' tepid brew: caffeine is starting to interrupt my sleep at night, but it never seems to bother Lotty.

"What are you going to do?" Lotty asked at last.

"Find the one friend Martin seems to have had in high school. I met his parents tonight; they let drop that their son is in Rochester, so I ought to be able to track down what college he's attending. I'll also try to locate some of Judy Binder's associates. Do you know anyone besides yourself she might have turned to when she was so frightened yesterday morning?"

"I don't know her well enough for that," Lotty said. "I'm the person she comes to when she's in trouble, which started when she was in her teens. I was astonished when she appeared at my clinic the first time, but after that, it became chronic—she had STDs, she was pregnant, she turned up one evening in the middle of a terrifyingly bad drug reaction. She landed in a locked ward for a month that time.

"After that, I didn't see her for years, really, until the day she showed up pregnant with Martin. I thought then she'd turned her life around: she stayed clean throughout the pregnancy and for four or five months after. It didn't last, though."

"Do you know who the father was? Would she have stayed in touch with him?"

Lotty lifted her arms in a helpless gesture. "I was her doctor, not her confidante. Besides, Judy slept around so much that she probably didn't know which particular man was responsible for the pregnancy. The miracle to me is that Martin has turned out to have a brilliant mind. If a drug addict was the responsible, or rather, the irresponsible man, the risk of brain damage was high."

"Yep," I said. "Kid got perfect math scores on his SATs. Not too much brain damage there, just a lot of psychic damage from living with your old friend."

"Victoria, please. You're hurting me in a sore point." She hesitated, twisting her coffee cup in her fingers. "Judy asked if I would adopt Martin when she realized she couldn't look after him. I told her I'd help her find a good family for him, but I had an active surgical practice; if I'd taken him, a nanny would have raised him."

I reached across the metal table to squeeze her hand, but she pulled it away.

"Don't tell me I did the right thing. A nanny would have been better than Käthe, but before I could do anything, Judy had given the baby to her parents."

In the dim light coming from the living room I saw her mouth twist in a bitter line. "She felt I betrayed her: I've only seen her twice since that day. She and I both appeared at Martin's bar mitzvah, and again at Len's funeral. She didn't look well, either time. She must be around your age, but she looked worn and old enough to be your mother. At Len's funeral, she said she was going to live on a farm, to see if life in the country would help her get clean and sober. I wanted to believe her. Of course I was deluding myself, the way one does when confronting someone whom you feel you've let down. You hope their problems will solve themselves without you. I hope she hasn't dragged her son into her unhealthy world."

"I don't think so. He's twenty—if he'd been going down that road someone would have seen signs by now."

I told Lotty what Martin had said to Kitty about uncovering an arithmetic error, and my speculation about whether Martin thought his mother had been stealing from him.

"I'm thinking he rode his bike down to Palfry to confront her. But why did he and Judy both disappear? I don't think he was with her when she screamed at you for help."

"What can you do?" Lotty asked.

"I have someone in the public defender's office tracing any associates of the man whose body I discovered. Martin disassembled his computers, so there's no way to hack into them to find a trail there, but if I can get a working e-mail address I may be able to find out where he's been logging in from. And then, I guess I'll see if I can find out whether there's any possibility that Kitty Binder's parents were here right after the war. Martin probably heard tales about them when he was growing up—he might have tried to track them down. What was Kitty's birth name?"

"Saginor," Lotty said. "But remember, that was her mother: we don't know her father."

"It's easy to get a list of Nobel laureates," I said. "Someone who won the prize between 1920 and 1939, that should fit the bill. Unless her father was a builder. Perhaps he was a builder who dined with the King of Sweden, though: he wasn't a Nobel laureate, but simply the king's carpenter."

Lotty laughed at that, but her face remained worried as she ushered me through her apartment to the elevator.

As I drove home, I remembered, a bit belatedly, that I'd promised Kitty Binder I'd keep her affairs confidential. I also remembered vowing not to let other people put their problems into the center of my stage. One more day, I vowed: one more day on the Binder-Saginor mystery and then I'd turn my back on them.

It was close to eleven when I got home, but I stayed up another hour to talk to Jake Thibaut, the bass player I've been seeing for the last few years. One of the chamber groups he belongs to was on tour along the West Coast. They had started in Alaska and were working their way south to San Diego. They'd made it as far as Victoria on Vancouver Island.

His absence made my schedule easier in some ways, but it also meant I was lonely at the end of a long day. I waited up until his concert had ended, so we could exchange news of the day. His had definitely been more fun than mine: the concert, held in a refurbished church, had been a major success. Tomorrow, on their day off, a friend was taking them out deep-sea fishing.

"If I catch a salmon I'll send it home to you."

"I'll prop it up at the dining room table and talk to it over dinner; that will make us both forget we miss you."

I casually mentioned the dog I'd rescued from a meth house, and he groaned. "No more dogs, V.I., please. Peppy's mellow, but I can only just tolerate Mitch; a third dog and we're going to do some serious talking."

"A third dog and I'll be in a witness relocation program," I assured him. "Don't you care that I was risking life and limb in a meth house?"

"Victoria Iphigenia, what can I do about that? If I told you to steer clear of them you'd do your cactus imitation. Anyway, I'm three thousand miles away. Even if I were right next to you, I know you're the person on our team who takes down meth dealers, not me. I'd be worrying about my fingers and you'd have to protect both of us."

I had to laugh. I abandoned the effort to extract worried cluckings from him and moved on to Kitty Binder and her missing family.

That did get his attention. "You say Lotty told you this Kitty's birth name was Saginor? Was she related to a Viennese musician named Elsa Saginor?"

"I don't know." I was surprised. "Who is that?"

"She was one of the Terezín musicians. She played flute, but she composed, also; some of her music was in the scores from the camp they discovered several years ago. We perform it from time to time. It's rather intricate, fugal but in a serialist style. The fun thing, if it isn't sacrilegious to talk about having fun with death camp music, is to lay about ten tracks of the recording over each other and then play live against the backing. It's exhilarating to concentrate so hard."

I wondered if mentioning a musical aunt would make Kitty Binder unbend with me, or if she would purse her lips still further and utter some pithy condemnation of people who had their mouths on their flutes instead of their eyes on the prize.

Before we hung up, Jake said, "Don't get in over your head, V.I. I miss you. I'd hate like hell to spend the rest of my life missing you instead of just the next three weeks."

9

SHADOW OF THE THIN MAN

I N MY DREAMS, Jake was playing his bass for the King of Sweden, who said he would perish in the death camps if he didn't build a new kitchen for him by morning. "Keep your head in the clouds," the king cried, "or I will cut it off."

I spent a strenuous night, fighting the king, hiding Jake's bass, getting lost in the clouds. When I got up in the morning, I was almost as tired as when I'd gone to bed. I went for a long run, on my own, without the dogs, to clean out my head.

Jake's response to my poor rescued Rottweiler had rankled a bit, but it also hit home. It was a strain to look after two big dogs, even with Mr. Contreras's help; I didn't often have enough time to do the meditative running I enjoy. A third dog would make it impossible.

After four miles, I was moving in an easy rhythm that made me want to keep going all the way to the Indiana border. It was hard to turn around and face a day in a chair, but I was one of those people who keep their feet on the ground, their shoulder to the wheel, their nose to the grindstone. What a boring person I must be.

While I showered, I mapped out a program for the day. Track down Martin's friend Toby Susskind to see if he could tell me anything about where Martin had gone. Library work on Nobel Prize winners to guess a father for Kitty Binder: Martin Binder might have gone hunting his putative family. I'd round out this fun-fest by following up with my pal from the PD's office, to see if he'd unearthed any of my dead meth maker's associates.

It would have been easier to find Toby if I'd had his cell phone, but I finally learned he was a student at the Rochester Institute of Technology. The school wouldn't give me a phone number for him, but they let me have his college e-mail address, since that was essentially public information. While I waited for him to answer my e-mail, I started my search through the list of Nobel laureates from the 1920s and thirties.

It wasn't the slam-dunk search I'd been imagining. I went down to the University of Chicago science library so I could use their reference support, assuming I'd be in and out within an hour. That wasn't my biggest mistake of the day, just the first.

By digging deep I found some mentions of Martina Saginor in an essay—in German—on women at the Institut für Radiumforschung in Vienna. I didn't want to wait for Max or Lotty to translate the article for me, so I took the file to the reference desk, where they called up a kid from the back who read German. With his wire-rimmed glasses and white shirt under a sweater-vest, he made me think of William Henry, the young wannabe criminologist in *The Thin Man*.

He said he was Arthur Harriman; I said I was V. I. Warshawski. When I explained that I was a detective, trying to machete my way through seventy or so years of undergrowth to the trail of a dead physicist, Harriman became even more like William Henry. "We're hunting a missing person? Was she a German spy? Do I need to know how to use a gun?"

"You need to be able to read German, which I don't." I handed him my laptop, with the German essay on the screen.

"This sounds interesting," Harriman said after he'd scrolled through part of the article. "The Institut für Radiumforschung, that was the Radiation Research Institute. Vienna wanted to compete with Paris and Cambridge and Copenhagen in the quest for the secrets of the atom. What's amazing is that forty percent of the Viennese research staff were women, compared to practically none in the U.S. or the rest of Europe—even including Irène Curie's lab, which hired a lot of women."

He scrolled down the page until he got to Saginor. "Your lady taught chemistry and math in the Technische Hochschule for girls from 1926 to 1938. In between she went off to Germany, to Göttingen, to do a Ph.D. in physics, and then she became a researcher at the IRF. Göttingen was where Heisenberg developed the special algebra of quantum mechanics. Everyone in physics came there at some time or other. Oppenheimer, Fermi, everyone."

"Does it say anything about Saginor's personal life?" I asked. "Did she have children, a husband, any of that kind of detail?"

He read through to the end of the essay. "Nothing about her personal life. After Germany annexed Austria and imposed the Nazi race laws, Saginor lost her high school teaching job, but for some reason the IRF didn't fire its Jewish staff right away. Not clear why. Then in 1941 Saginor got detailed to the Uranverein."

"Which was?"

Harriman clicked on a couple of links. I waited while he read some other documents, his lips moving as he translated to himself. "It means 'Uranium Club' literally, but these were the research locations where Germany tried to develop the physics and engineering to build an atom bomb. There were six Verein labs in Germany, one in Austria; your lady got sent to one in the Austrian Alps."

He read some more, still muttering to himself. "So. In 1942, with things going badly on the Russian front, Germany was running out of money for its bomb project. Besides, Hitler never really believed splitting the atom was possible. Shows why it's a mistake to let your research be dictated by a dictator."

He gave a half-grin at his little pun, but became serious again as he finished reading. "Sorry to say, but Saginor got shipped east in 1943, after the reactor in Austria was shut down. Saginor was sent first to

Terezín, then put on a forced march going east from there, probably heading for Sobibor. She must have died along the march route, since that's the last record of her."

I squeezed my eyes shut, trying to push away the image of a poorly clad woman dying in the snow. "Does that mean that before she died, she worked on the German equivalent of the Manhattan Project?" I asked. "I didn't know they had one."

"Oh, yes. It was a mad global arms race," Harriman said cheerfully.

"But—was she doing weapons work in Vienna, at this IRF place?"

"No, no." He put down my laptop. "She was like everyone else doing physics in the thirties: she was trying to understand the interior of the atom. In the essay you found, the one about women at the Radiation Institute, one of her old coworkers says Saginor was a dedicated researcher."

He looked at the screen again and clicked back to the first article. "She used to come into the Institute at the end of her high school teaching day and start running experiments. The woman they quote in the article says that Saginor never seemed to eat—they served coffee and cakes in the common area, but Martina could hardly bear to leave her lab. This other woman thought Martina's main interest had been in neutron interaction with heavy nuclei, but thirties physicists, chemists, geologists, they all crisscrossed each other's interests all the time."

He tapped the screen. "I can see why she was drafted into the Uran-verein, although it was as slave labor. Saginor may have been one of the early believers in fission, because already in 1937 she seemed to be experimenting with different materials, trying to come up with a way to capture the resonance cross sections of uranium and thorium without a lot of background noise."

I tried to nod intelligently, but internally I groaned: Why hadn't I paid more attention to Professor Wright's lectures when I was an undergraduate here?

I got Harriman to write what he'd just said and put it in an e-mail to me. When he'd obligingly finished that, I asked him about Nobel Prize winners Martina Saginor might have met, either in Vienna or Göttingen. "It has to be someone who would have been in Chicago around 1955 or so, because Martina's daughter came here looking for him."

This, too, turned out to be a complicated search. Physicists in the 1930s were like migratory birds, flitting from Copenhagen to Cambridge, from California to Columbia, stopping en route in Göttingen or Berlin and Paris.

Harriman said, "You know, science didn't get the kind of government research money in those days that we poured into it during the Manhattan Project or the Cold War, but these guys—and gals—must have received money from someone to travel the way they did."

We looked at the list of Nobel laureates in physics and chemistry from the twenties through 1950. Any number of the laureates might have been in Germany or Vienna when Kitty Binder was born. Most of the European laureates had fled either to England or the U.S. during the war; Harriman said that any of them might have spent time in Chicago. Some, like Fermi, joined the University of Chicago faculty. Others worked here on the Manhattan Project, or had stints in Chicago as visiting scholars.

"Chicago was the hot spot for physics after World War Two. Fermi, Teller, they attracted the next generation of phys whizzes. Would the nationality matter?"

I shook my head. "Saginor had her baby in 1930 or '31, so the father is someone she met either in Vienna or Germany in '29 or '30. From what you're saying, it could have been anyone from Werner Heisenberg to Robert Oppenheimer."

"Yes," Harriman said, "but Heisenberg wasn't here after the war, so it's not really such a wide net."

I didn't add my private fret: that Kitty's fantasies about her father might mean he hadn't been any kind of scientist at all, let alone a Nobel Prize winner. He might really have been a Viennese builder who already had a wife and two other children. The snapshot on Kitty's credenza could have shown a day at a beach where the wife had been generous enough to include her husband's lover's child.

Harriman handed me back my laptop. I was closing the windows he'd opened when I saw the photograph. In the middle of one of the German articles Harriman had found was a copy of the print I'd found in the meth house down in Palfry, the giant metal egg on a tripod with serious men and women staring proudly at the camera.

"What is this? Who are these people?"

Harriman stared at me, my voice was so strangled, but he took back my computer. "An early proton accelerator designed at the Institut für Radiumforschung. What's so exciting about it?"

"I just saw a print of this picture, in a place where I would bet good money no one ever heard of a proton accelerator, let alone cared about it. Who are the people?"

"There isn't a caption," Harriman said, "but they were all at the IRF. I suppose your Martina must be one of the women; that shouldn't be too hard to work out. The second man from the right, I know his face. I think I've seen it in our archives."

He looked at the clock on the wall. "I have to get to a meeting, but I can do a little checking after lunch. Even if you won't let me carry a gun, I might be able to track these people down."

I thanked him profusely: it was a relief to offload even one task. While he vanished into the bowels of the library, I found an empty carrel and sat down to check my messages.

Jari Liu had written back to say that was the only e-mail he had for Martin. He'd tried it himself and gotten the same error message.

Martin's friend, Toby Susskind, had written me. He didn't know where Martin was, but he included his own cell phone number. When I called, Toby talked to me in a halting, troubled way about why he and Martin had lost touch.

"Martin wanted to go to college, but his grandma, she was so against it that he ended up staying in Chicago and getting a job. That made it hard for him and me to talk. I mean, I probably wouldn't have gotten into Rochester if Martin hadn't helped me write my high school senior project; and, well, it kind of made it hard, if you know what I mean."

I murmured sympathetically: I could imagine Martin's hurt, Toby's embarrassment, the strain on a relationship that had never been close to begin with. I asked Toby whether he knew who might have hosted that August picnic.

"I need to talk to someone who saw Martin around the time he disappeared," I explained, but Toby said he and Martin had barely seen each other all summer, and anyway, Martin had never talked about his coworkers.

"What did Martin tell you about visiting his mother?" I asked.

"He never mentioned it. Of course, everyone knew she was a drug addict. Some of the kids rode Martin pretty hard about it, so I guess if he went to see her, he kept it to himself."

Martin must have learned to put up a shield at a young age; maybe his grandfather was the only person who ever really got behind it. I thought of the two of them grinning at Martin's first-place science fair exhibit.

Toby was edgy: he needed to get to class, he needed to take another call, he couldn't really tell me anything. He didn't have a cell phone number for Martin. Ms. Hahne, who taught AP physics over at the high school, might know Martin's plans; Toby thought Martin had been close to her.

Nadja Hahne was in class. The receptionist took a message, promising that she would get it to the teacher. While I had a sandwich and a surprisingly good cappuccino at one of the little cafes near the campus, Stefan Klevic, my old pal from the PD, sent me an e-mail: he had found Ricky Schlafly's Cook County sheet and scanned it for me.

I read it, trying not to drip hummus on my keyboard. Schlafly had

been arrested a number of times for possession, for dealing, for breaking and entering. He'd taken part in a botched armed robbery of a
convenience store. No one had been seriously hurt, but he bought himself five years in Stateville that time.

Schlafly's last known Chicago address, right before he headed back
to Palfry, was in Austin, at the far end of the city's run-down West
Side. The lease was in the name of a man named Freddie Walker.

Stefan closed his e-mail by saying, "Walker doesn't have a record
but Oak Park and Chicago PDs both say he's the muscle behind a lot
of the coke moving around that part of town. You now know everything I do, but if you plan to go visiting, I'd put on my best Sunday
Kevlar."

Not only did I return home for a vest and my handgun, I even mentioned my expedition to one of my acquaintances in the Chicago PD,
although Conrad Rawlings's district, down on the southeast side of the
city, where I grew up, was at the opposite end of the map from Austin.

We'd been lovers for a time in the misty past. Our breakup hadn't
been happy, especially since Conrad took a bullet in the process, but in
some deeply buried chamber of his heart, Conrad still cares if I live
or die.

"I hope you don't imagine I'm going to escort you to a meth house,
Ms. W. If you want that kind of thrill, you can come down to my turf
any old afternoon."

"I wouldn't dream of taking you from the Latin Cobras, Conrad. I
thought you might let some of your buddies in the Fifteenth know I'm
coming so they don't arrest me when they see me going into that address on Lorel. Also, I'd like someone to look after my dogs when I'm
gone."

"I'll say the tear-jerkiest eulogy you ever heard, at least if you were
alive to hear it, but I will not take those damned dogs. The male,
what's his name? Mitch? He's come way too close to my manhood way
too many times. What's this really about, Vic?"

I told him about Derrick Schlafly's death, and Judy's cry for help. "I'm trying to find where she ran to when she couldn't reach Lotty."

I could hear Conrad tapping a keyboard at the other end of the phone. "Missing person in a drug murder case, don't you dare go into that apartment, Warshawski. I'm sending a message to Ferret Downey; he'll get a warrant to check out the place. *You* leave it alone. This is why they pay us cops the big bucks. You got that?"

"Aye, aye, Sergeant," I said.

"Don't be a wiseass, Vic, it isn't becoming at your age. If I find you've gone in there on your own, I will shoot you myself."

10

IMPULSE CONTROL

I **TOOK MY GUN** into the kitchen to clean it. I hadn't been at the range since the beginning of summer. If I was going to be butting heads with drug lords on a regular basis, I'd better start taking target practice every day, and invest in Tasers and automatic pistols as well.

There's no end to the armory I could get by hanging out in the right bars, but I seldom carry the one gun I do own. Having a weapon makes you want to use it, and if you use yours the other person wants to use theirs, and then one of you gets badly hurt or dead, and the one who survives has to spend a lot of time explaining herself to the state's attorney. All of which takes time from more meaningful work, although you could argue that killing a drug dealer constitutes meaningful work.

Conrad's warning had been a prudent one. Only a wiseass who behaved in a way unbecoming to her age would disregard it. I put on a leg holster, easiest for me to reach if I was ducking or rolling away from an attack. Ferret Downey, I wondered as I left my apartment. That had to be a nickname that Conrad had used inadvertently.

I considered stopping at Mr. Contreras's place to pick up Mitch so I had a little backup, but then I remembered the dead Rottweiler at the meth house in Palfry. Besides, if I told Mr. Contreras what I was going to do, he'd insist on picking up a pipe wrench and joining me.

"'She travels the fastest who travels alone,'" I announced grandly to myself. Although she shouldn't travel so fast she plunges over the edge of a cliff.

As I got on the expressway, I tried to estimate times. Say Ferret Downey read Conrad's message right away and took it seriously. Applied for a search warrant. Or overlooked that formality—the Supreme Court has been giving the police alarming latitude in breaking into people's homes, cars, and even our brassieres merely on suspicion.

I was guessing that even if everyone cared enough to move at warp speed, it would take at least four hours for the police to arrive at Freddie Walker's building. My worry was that no one would bother to check for a day or two. Police are stretched thin, they have a routine, a missing junkie wasn't likely to generate heavy interest, either in the district or with the state's attorney.

When I reached the stretch of Lorel where Walker operated, there were no signs of blue-and-whites, or of much else. The street had the exhausted air of too much of Chicago's West Side. Weed-filled vacant lots, boarded-over doors and windows, a handful of emaciated men sitting on curbs, staring profoundly at nothing.

Walker's six-flat looked as run-down as the rest of the block, the brickwork badly in need of remortaring, the paint on the window frames peeling, chunks of the concrete sills crumbling. The windows were intact, though, and had thick bars across them. The front door was solid. A camera in the lintel surveyed the front walk. The intercom by the door held only one button; no names or numbers were listed.

I stared at the entrance, trying to imagine what kind of sales pitch would not only get me inside, but back out again as well. I pressed the buzzer. No answer. I pressed again.

One of the men on the curb was watching me. "You buyin' or sellin'?"

"Does that affect whether I can get in?"

He blinked, slowly, like a tortoise. The whites of his eyes were yellow, streaked with red—he'd been buying for far too long.

"Don't make no difference. Nobody been answering all day. But if you're selling, I might could arrange a buyer."

I looked over the heavy front door. It had two locks, dead bolts of the kind that take a certain amount of effort to undo.

"Camera's a fancy unit," I said to my companion. "Wireless. Freddie must do a good business."

"I guess he does okay," the man agreed.

I don't usually perform for an audience, but I didn't think this yellow-eyed man would be able to describe me to anyone who asked. I went back to my car for my picklocks and a roll of duct tape.

My new friend followed me back up the walk, offering to hold the tape or my picklocks or do anything I needed. After tearing off a small piece of tape, I handed the roll to him. His hands shook badly; he kept dropping it, but watched with keen interest as I covered the camera eye.

As if he'd sent out a wireless signal himself, a few more people trailed up the walk behind us, a couple of guys and a heavyset woman about my age who was gasping for air by the time she reached us.

"What she doing, Shaq?" the woman asked. The harsh rasp in her lungs sounded painfully like my father, who'd ended his smoking life with emphysema.

"Don't know, Ladonna," Shaq grunted. "She breaking in, I guess. Look how she cover up the camera, simple as pie."

Not only did I not want an audience, I didn't want an escort, but I couldn't think of any way to hint to my quartet to leave. I lugged over an abandoned car battery to use as a stool and started work on the top lock.

"Freddie ain't gonna like this," one of the other men said.

"Freddie ain't gonna like what, Terrell?" Someone had come around the corner of the building so fast and silent he took everyone, including me, by surprise. The .45 in his hand made my entourage back away.

"Told her she shouldn't be doin' this, Bullet," Shaq said, nervously sticking the roll of duct tape into a trouser pocket. "She's like, I gotta get into this place, and I'm telling her, 'Worth your life. White girl like you got no business here,' but she in—"

"Yeah, Shaq, you're a hero," Bullet growled. "We been watching your parade of losers coming up to the door all day, but you know Freddie's policy, man, no credit! We know when you get your Social, so you fuck off until the first of the month. You, too, Ladonna, Terrell. And you, white girl, you better explain to Freddie what you're doing, messing with his camera and all."

He waved the gun at me. I stepped down from the car battery. Impulse control. When would I ever learn?

Bullet pushed the buzzer, once short, twice long, and someone inside released the lock. He poked the gun into my back, the spot where the T-1 vertebra connects the neck to the torso. The hairs stood up on my neck. Fear—another impulse I couldn't control.

"I don't suppose your mother called you 'Bullet,'" I said as he pushed me to the stairwell.

"Shut up!" He shoved the gun harder against my spine.

"If she thought you were special, she would have used a special name," I mused. "Lancelot, or Galahad, or—"

"Shit-Face," he shouted. "She used to call me 'Shit-Face,' which you are going to be when Freddie finishes with you. He don't like bitches coming around messing with his business."

"That explains a lot."

I tripped on the stairs, twisted and shoved my shoulder into his diaphragm. He fell backward, tumbling down, hitting his head on the edge of the riser. His gun went off as he fell. The shot echoed and re-echoed in the stairwell.

Footsteps pounded on the floor above me. Shouts, "Bullet, what the fuck? You kill the bitch?"

A man leaned over the banister at the upper landing, saw Bullet, shouted for help. "Freddie! Bullet, he's—it looks like he's dead, man!"

"Shit, Vire, bitch shoot him? Get her, you fuck-up!"

Bullet's body blocked most of the stairs behind me. I couldn't get around him without exposing my back to Vire's gun. I slung a leg over the banister and slid down to the next landing, just as Vire fired. I had a tiny edge; Vire took time skirting around Bullet on the stairs, pausing to fire wildly down the stairwell.

I reached the front door, but the locks were sealed from the inside. I pulled my gun from the leg holster, took cover as best I could in the dark at the back of the entry hall. Someone had left a bicycle. I tripped and fell heavily over it and lost my gun. I fought free of the bike and hurled it at Vire as he came up the hall toward me.

The bike caught him in the face. I scrabbled on the floor for my own gun, found it just as all the stairwell lights came on. A moment later Freddie himself appeared. He was a big, rangy guy with a scraggly beard and black hair flopping over his forehead. He picked up the bike and flung it to the ground in front of Vire.

"Who the fuck left the goddamn bike in the hall? Morons, do I have anybody but morons working for me? Who are you, bitch, and what the fuck you doing picking my locks?"

"I'm looking for Judy Binder." I was winded; my words came out in gasps.

"Judy Binder? You kill my man Bullet looking for that wasted bitch?"

"Is Bullet dead?" I said. "I didn't shoot him; he fell down and hit his head."

"Yeah, you tell that to judge and jury, bitch."

"Bitch. Fuck-up, fuck, bitch. You'd be more interesting if you developed your vocabulary." Freddie had a semiautomatic in his right hand, but I kept my own gun pointed just below his belt buckle; this made him unconsciously put one hand over his crotch.

"I'm not talking to you to be interesting, b—whoever the fuck you are. What do you want with the Binder ho?"

"You remember Ricky Schlafly?" A moral person would just shoot Freddie and get it over with.

"Ricky? Yeah, of course I know the dude. We do—" He cut himself short. "What about him?"

"Haven't you heard? Ricky won't be doing business with anyone anymore. I found his body in a cornfield. Crows had plucked out his eyes. They ate his balls, too. It was an ugly sight. Makes a person think about mortality and all those things."

"Ricky dead?"

Vire kicked the bike away and took a step toward me. I kept my own eyes on Freddie's eyes. The wilder they got the more likely he was to start shooting.

"Ms. Binder was down there with him, but she ran away. I'm trying to find her; she's a material witness."

"What? You a cop?"

"A lawyer," I said, thinking it might be marginally safer than admitting to being a detective. "We need to find Judy. Is she here?"

"She's trouble, Freddie, told you not to let her in the door. I'll go upstairs and take care of her."

"Take care of this one first." Freddie's gun hand came up.

I hit the floor, rolling, firing, ducking behind a wedge of wall under the stairwell. Eight bullets in my clip; three gone. Freddie marching toward me, firing.

Over the ferocious noise, a bullhorn: "This is the police. Put your weapons down and come out with your hands in the air."

11

CHEMISTRY SHOP

Y OU'RE THE PI CONRAD RAWLINGS TRUSTS? One of you is going to have to explain why that makes sense."

Ferret Downey was talking to me in an empty apartment across the hall from Freddie's drug shop. As soon as he'd come up the front walk, with two patrol officers in his wake, I'd known who it was: with his long nose and drooping mustache, he looked exactly like a ferret. He only showed after I'd been cuffed to Vire for over half an hour.

Vire turned out to be short for Virus, which turned out to be a nickname for Erwin Jameson. Erwin. Such a weeny name for a bodyguard.

My legs were wobbly: shock, too much exertion. All the gunfire in the hall had left me with a loud whining in the ears; I had a hard time hearing what any of them, cops or robbers, was saying.

"We wasn't doing nothing," Freddie said to the first responders. "This bitch comes and starts picking my locks, can you believe that? In broad daylight?"

"You a user or a dealer?" one of the officers asked me.

"My name is V. I. Warshawski; I'm a licensed investigator. You can see my ID in my wallet. A woman who disappeared two days ago is in this building. These goons threatened to shoot her. We need to look for her *now*: she may still be alive."

The officers were not interested. They were so sure I was in the drug business that they only made a pretense of looking at my license. When it became clear they weren't going to ask the crime scene crew to look for Judy, I stopped contributing to the conversation—even after Freddie claimed I had broken in, killed his main man, Bullet, trashed his building by shooting it up. Basically, he added, he was just a man trying to live a peaceful life; he only started firing a semiautomatic in self-defense.

Various officers wanted to know if someone sent me to take out Freddie. Who was my Mexican contact? Where was I standing when I shot Bullet?

I didn't say anything, just stared at the street, silently cursing myself for not following Conrad's advice. At one point an ambulance arrived; a stretcher crew brought Bullet down. His face was uncovered; they had him strapped in a neck restraint, which made me believe he wasn't actually dead.

"He's still breathing," I said to Freddie. "If you've got good health insurance for your playmates he should be back in the lineup before long."

Freddie spat in my face. What a prince.

When Lt. Downey finally arrived and learned who I was claiming to be, his face did not light up in ecstasy. "Yeah, we got a heads-up she'd be coming out here. What's been going on?"

The first responders said they'd been alerted to gunfire on Lorel, found the three of us shooting at each other. Freddie started his pitch about self-defense, that I'd broken in, blah, blah.

"You a deaf-mute, Warshawski, or you going to give your version?" Downey asked.

I twisted my neck to look at my cuffed hands, but didn't speak.

"Oh, release her," Downey said to one of the officers in a voice of long suffering. "Rawlings over in the Fourth vouches for her, although damned if I can see why."

When my hands were free I rubbed them slowly, massaged my shoulders, did some neck rolls. "Judy Binder is or was on the third floor." I still was having trouble hearing and wondered if I was actually speaking. "I came to see if she was hiding here, which I told your team; so far I don't think they've bothered to look for her. When I got here, Freddie and his buddies didn't answer the bell."

"That why you were picking the lock?" Downey's sergeant asked me.

Bullet had taken my picks before shoving me into the building; the techs had found them on their way in.

"Man, we saw her breaking in, watched it on the monitor," Vire blurted. "Bullet went down to stop her!"

"That why you broke Bullet Bultman's neck?" the sergeant asked me.

"He had a gun stuck in my spine. I didn't like my odds if we got all the way to the top of the stairs, so I ducked and gave him a hard shove. I didn't shoot him. If there's a bullet in him, it came from Erwin. Erwin was pretty hysterical. He flew down the stairs, shooting like a maniac. I don't know how he missed me."

"It's 'Virus,'" Erwin hissed.

"Is there a bullet in the Bullet?" Ferret Downey turned to survey his squad.

"Don't think so, Looey." One of the SCI team stepped forward. "They'll be able to tell at the hospital."

"Take me inside; we'll have a look-see. Warchosi, or whatever your name is, you come along. We'll find you a place to sit that doesn't contaminate the evidence."

"Erwin here said Judy Binder was in the building," I repeated. "He offered to kill her if Freddie wanted, but Freddie told him to shoot me first. I want to find her before another of Freddie's punks tries to kill her."

Downey blew on the ends of his droopy mustache. "I know you're God's gift to Conrad Rawlings, but I've managed to stagger my way through crime scenes without your help for twenty years. It's hard to believe anyone would waste time and money looking for a junkie, but if we find one hiding on the premises, I'll be sure to let you know."

His sergeant snickered appreciatively. I took a deep breath: I reminded myself that a clever response would bring me only a brief reward. What I really wanted most was not to have the last word, but to leave soon. With my gun and without being charged.

A tech came along with shoe covers and gloves for Downey, his two acolytes, and me. There were six apartments in the building, but no signs of any inhabitants, unless you counted the bicycle in the lobby that Virus-Erwin and I both had fought with.

The drugstore was open on the third floor. A TV was on: Sox up by three in the eighth. The feed from the camera watching the street showed only streaky lines: no one had taken off the strip of duct tape. A grinding rap beat came from a room somewhere in the back. It grated on my ear, but I was pleased that I could hear it. The ringing from the gun battle was beginning to fade.

Downey told his sergeant to try the apartment across the landing. The door wasn't locked, another sign, if one needed it, that Freddie controlled the whole building.

"You go in there," Downey told me. "We'll get to you when we get to you."

The sergeant pushed me into the room. I stumbled again and couldn't avoid landing on his left foot.

"Sorry, Sarge," I said. "Gunfight and standing cuffed for so long, my coordination isn't too good right now."

He eyed me measuringly, fingering his revolver. "You want me to stay in here with her, Looey?" he asked Downey.

"She won't go anywhere as long as we're holding her gun," Downey said.

Sad, but true. The sergeant shut the door and left me alone with a dirty beige armchair and a portable TV on a metal TV table. My legs were genuinely unsteady as I lurched over to look at the chair. It was filled with cigarette burns and ash and had stains whose origin I didn't want to contemplate. Discarded butts and roaches had fallen into the crevice between cushion and armrest.

I would have welcomed a rest, but not in an armchair that held an arsenal of lethal bacteria. I wandered into the back of the apartment and found a room with a narrow bed, the sheets smelling sweet-and-sour, a faint smear of blood on the pillow. On the floor, a bra, once white, now gray and stretched out of shape; some wadded-up tissues with dried blood on them. Under the bed, a thick layer of dust that made me sneeze.

I squatted on my haunches, unwilling to sit on floor or bed. The bra belonged to some woman who had no money or no interest in her appearance. A junkie most likely. Judy Binder, for instance. The motto on the T-shirt Jari Liu had been wearing yesterday at Metargon popped into my mind: *In God We Trust, All Others Show Data.*

I had limited data: just Vire's asking Freddie if he should kill the "bitch" now or later, but I guessed Judy had been sleeping here.

I got to my feet and went into the kitchen. A couple of used dishes stood in the sink, where a bunch of cockroaches was enjoying a pre-dinner snack. Another party scurried away when I opened a cupboard. All it held were high-sugar cereals, a box of microwavable popcorn, and a couple of greasy glasses.

There were two doors, a new one that must have been put in to connect this place with the temple of doom, another that stood ajar. I pulled it all the way open and saw a back staircase. I tried the temple of doom door, but it was locked.

I picked up one of the glasses to use as a crude amplifier. When I put my ear to it, I gagged, imagining what was on the hands of the last person to touch it.

Real detectives do not suffer from germ phobia, I lectured myself. Think of Mickey Spillane. Think of Amelia Butterworth. Neither of them ever shied away from a dirty job. With the glass pressed against the keyhole, I could hear the cops in the other apartment, but couldn't make out individual words. Judging by the commotion, more units had arrived.

If Judy Binder had been here, she would have heard the shoot-out between Vire and Freddie and me. She would have scampered, just as she did when someone shot Derrick Schlafly in the cornfield two days ago.

I handed the greasy glass over to the cockroaches in the sink and went to the back staircase. There was a light switch on the wall, but no bulbs in the overhead fitting. I pulled out my phone and tapped the flashlight app.

Halfway down, I found a beat-up loafer, probably a size six. Some-one had been racing so fast, with so much fear, that she couldn't stop for a shoe. At the bottom, a door opened onto a weed-filled yard. The door didn't have a handle or a lock on the outside. I shone my phone around the area floor and found a broken chair to use as a doorstop.

The yard seemed to be where Freddie dumped his old beer cans and tequila bottles. The nettles and sow thistle were tall enough that I kept tripping on bottles on my way to the high metal fence that surrounded the yard. A gate was heavily crossed with chains. I worked my way around the perimeter. At the south edge, soil had eroded enough that a slim or desperate person could slide underneath. The second worn-out loafer was here. Judy, or whoever had been in the fetid bed upstairs, had gone out this way. Barefoot across the broken rocks and glass.

Where had Judy scampered next? If drug dealers got killed or broke their heads wherever she appeared, none of her old associates would welcome her.

It would have been a squeeze for me to follow her, but I could have done it. Unfortunately, as the ferret had said, I wanted my gun. I went back inside and slowly climbed the stairs, massaging my calves every few steps. When I reached the kitchen again, one of Downey's crew was waiting for me. He didn't comment on my side trip, just told me that the lieutenant was ready for me.

Downey was in a room that Freddie apparently used as an office. Computers, ledgers, locked cabinets—now opened to display an impressive amount of heroin, unless it was cocaine, as well as old-fashioned apothecary bottles filled with pills—a fifty-inch TV screen, a stack of license plates, a Bose iPod player, and an armchair covered in a black-and-red upholstery that made my eyes hurt.

Downey was sitting in the chair. Easier than looking at it, I guess. I rolled a desk chair over to face him.

He stared at me for a long moment. "I'm going to believe your story. For now. Looking at the video footage, we saw you ringing the bell, then Freddie and his doofuses filmed themselves laughing at you and calling you names. Then the screen went blank, so if you were picking the lock, there's no way of knowing."

It seemed prudent not to respond.

"What about the junkie you came looking for?" he asked.

"Judy Binder. I'm thinking she might have been a guest in the apartment next door. I found where she, or some woman, anyway, slid out the back door and under the fence. She fled another drug murder downstate two days ago."

That got Downey's attention. We spent a good ten minutes going over the Palfry murder, the connection between Freddie Walker and Derrick Schlafly, between Judy Binder and both men. I gave him Sheriff Kossel's cell phone number down in Palfry, but added that I knew very little, that I was looking for Judy as a favor for her elderly mother.

"Thought you said a doctor was involved, Warchosi."

So he'd been listening all along. "Warshawski," I corrected.

He stared at me. "You related to the auto-parts people?"

"No." I sighed, repeating my standard line, including the Yiddish writer. "Going back to Judy Binder, she called her doctor. I heard the message on the answering machine. Judy was terrified. The doctor sent me to Judy's mother. Sheriff Kossel down in Palfry asked me to check on Freddie Walker."

I paused, but Downey only fingered his mustache. I added, "Judy Binder has a son, kid of about twenty, who's also gone missing. I didn't see any sign of him next door. Did you find anything to say he might have been around?"

"Warshawski the Yiddish-Writing PI, you know what it's like in a drug house: guys and the occasional gal have been camping out in some of the empty apartments downstairs, shooting, smoking, snorting, leaving crap behind that I don't want to touch with six pairs of gloves on. If the three Wise Men had been here we wouldn't be able to tell except by the camel droppings. If you have prints from the kid, or a DNA sample, we'll sort them out when the techs finish with the scene. I can tell you this much for nothing: someone broke into one of these drawers"—he gestured at the desk—"and helped themselves to a fistful of dollars. We found twenties and hundreds floating around. The sarge and I were sorely tempted, weren't we, Rodman?"

Sergeant Rodman grunted, but didn't smile. You don't joke about tens of thousands of dollars in drug loot, I guess.

Downey kept me for another fifteen minutes, just because he was frustrated, but in the end he told Rodman to give me back my Smith & Wesson.

When the sergeant pulled my pistol out of his pocket, my picklocks came with it, jangling to the floor.

"If we keep these, you going to buy another set?" Downey asked me.

"More than likely."

"Give 'em back," Downey told Rodman.

"Looey—they're crime scene evidence," his sergeant protested.

"Nah, they're evidence of some Yiddish-writing detective's stupidity. I still don't know what Rawlings sees in you," Downey added as I stuck my picks into a vest pocket.

"I look better in the fresh air," I said.

"I'll take your word for it." His phone was ringing; he pressed the talk button and forgot about me.

It was past five now, glue-time on the expressway. I stuck to the side streets. They took just as long, but weren't as hard on the nerves. Kids were out playing, people were sitting on their porches talking. I passed boys shooting hoops and prayed that none of them would ever go through the door of a place like Freddie Walker's apartment.

I swung by the emergency clinic to check on my waif and learned that Mr. Contreras had already been in. They'd let him visit the dog; he'd shelled out the seven hundred dollars they needed for her continuing care. The vet thought if all went well, we could take her home in another week, which made me realize life can always become more complicated.

Back in my own place, I took another fumigating shower, washing off the greasy glass, the cockroach eggs, the sight of all that spattered blood and bone, the sound of Ladonna's racking cough. I was hoping to slip out for the evening, but I'd forgotten texting a reporter friend when I decided to go into Walker's building.

Murray Ryerson arrived as I was putting on a black sundress and sandals.

"I thought your boyfriend was on the West Coast. You getting some action on the side?" Murray asked.

"Just when I'm feeling sorry for you, you remind me of why I shouldn't," I said, pushing past him to the door.

"Sorry, Warshawski, sorry!" He held up his hands, traffic cop style, to stop me. "Let me have the highs or lows or whatever of the shoot-out in Austin. I picked up the main points on the TV feeds, but you had a front-row seat."

By the time I'd finished describing Palfry, my search for Judy, the gunfight I'd been in this afternoon, Mr. Contreras had shown up. He'd heard about the shoot-out on the six-o'clock news, so I had to go through the story all over again. Mr. Contreras doesn't like Murray, so he was annoyed that I hadn't told him first. He spent ten minutes chewing me out for not taking him out to Austin with me. That was a good reality check: I hadn't believed things could have been worse, but at least I'd been spared Mr. Contreras trying to intercept Freddie's and Vire's bullets.

The three of us went out, not for the lovely dinner at a slow-food trattoria I'd been imagining, but to the local cafe where Mr. Contreras and Murray could have the big burgers they were craving. After a day of guns and blood, hamburgers dripping red turned my stomach. I left the two men eating in uneasy silence and went home to cook up a pot of pasta. I had some good cheese, a half-drunk bottle of wine. I sat on the back porch with the dogs, listening to a CD of Jake's High Plain-song group, and slowly felt some peace return to my spirit.

Jake himself called a little later. He hadn't caught anything in his deep-sea expedition, but he'd had a lot of fun. I'd caught someone, but had had no fun at all. Which proves something, I'm not sure what. Still, while I sat on the porch, he played me a lullaby on his bass. I went into bed a happier detective than I'd been an hour earlier.

12

DON'T DO ME ANY FAVORS ANYMORE

M Y SLEEP WAS FILLED with unquiet dreams, with Freddie, Vire and Bullet chasing me through a cornfield filled with dead bodies, while Judy Binder played hide-and-seek behind the cornstalks. She was giggling, taunting me: *You'll never find me, you'll never find my son.*

I got up early again, but this time drove the dogs to the lake for a swim. When I'd showered and changed, Mr. Contreras offered to buy me breakfast at the Belmont Diner.

"I'd love to," I said, "as long as we don't talk about Murray or the abandoned Rottweiler."

"Yeah, doll, but you know, that dog has to live a quiet life until she gets rid of her heartworm, which means I could—"

I cut him off ruthlessly. He managed to make it all the way through a plate of French toast without a word about the Rottweiler. It was only when I ordered a BLT to take along for my lunch that he brought her up again.

I brushed his forehead with my lips. "I'm on my way downtown. Later, my friend. Thanks for the breakfast."

My first appointment was with my most important client, Darraugh Graham. I parked at my office and took the L into the Loop. It was the morning rush hour; all the seats were taken, so I leaned against a pole, my briefcase wedged between my feet. I pulled out my phone to check my messages, joining the other commuters in focusing on a world far from the one we were looking at.

I wondered if any of the other passengers were getting furious texts from police sergeants, demanding that they call at once. That was not only the first message on my phone, but the fifth, sixth and ninth. I knew it would be a stressful conversation, so best get it over with before Conrad Rawlings had a whole day to create a head of steam. As it was, he'd already built up plenty:

Had he or had he not told me not to go into that apartment on my own? He'd had to do major damage control with Ferret Downey, to assure him that if I'd killed Bullet, it had been a complete accident.

"Do not call me again for favors, Warshawski. I am fed up to my back teeth with your recklessness. The next time you want to go up against a West Side drug lord, take that weedy violin player you're dating."

"Understood, Sergeant. No more favors. Got it. Although Jake plays the bass, not a violin."

"Violin, ukulele, what difference does it make. He's still weedy, but you are a goddamn piece of work." Conrad cut the connection.

There was something pleasing about knowing Conrad was jealous of Jake. I went back to my in box. A law firm I work for wanted an investigation into an imbalance in their receivables; a wine retailer wanted to know if merchandise was disappearing from deliveries before or after they reached their store.

Nadja Hahne, Martin Binder's high school physics teacher, could see me today after three-thirty; she'd leave my name with the high school security department if I could make it. I e-mailed back an acceptance. The librarian at the University of Chicago had found names for all but one of the eight people in the photo of the metal egg on a tripod.

I called him at once. Even with the way cell phones flatten the emotions in the voice, I could tell Arthur Harriman was excited.

"Do you have the picture in front of you?" he asked.

"I'm standing on the L," I said. "I can't get at my computer."

"Okay, try to visualize it. Remember the five guys who are standing? The one in the middle is Stefan Meyer, who was head of the IRF in the thirties, at least until the Nazis came to power. The lady in the middle, sitting directly in front of him, is a Norwegian physicist who did a lot of experiments with Meyer. Your Martina is on the Norwegian's left, and Gertrud Memler, one of Martina's students, is on the other side.

"But I'm sure the man you want is the one standing on Meyer's left, Benjamin Dzornen. He won the Nobel Prize in 1934 for his work on electron states in transuranic elements, but the point is, he left Vienna in 1936, went to the University of Wisconsin, and then, in 1941, got involved in the Manhattan Project. After the war he spent the rest of his career here, at the University of Chicago."

"And he obviously knew Martina Saginor, since they're in the picture together," I said.

"They all knew each other back then," Harriman said. "But Dzornen supervised Martina's thesis. She went to Göttingen the summer of 1929 to start work on her Ph.D. He was there at the same time and agreed to supervise her so she could finish her work back in Vienna."

I saw with a jolt that I'd ridden past my L stop; I was heading west alongside the Eisenhower Expressway. Inattentional blindness, a growing affliction in the wired world. I thanked Harriman with more haste than grace and raced up the stairs to cross over to the inbound side.

I was almost ten minutes late to my meeting, which is inexcusable. Worse, I couldn't resist entering Dzornen's name into my search engine while I was supposed to be listening to questions about three candidates to head Darraugh's South American engineering division. I promised to have a report back to the executive committee within five days, but when I left the meeting, I saw I'd written down "Martina Dzornen" instead of one candidate's name. I had to go back to get the correct name from the internal security chief, who was not one of my fans.

By the time I returned to my office, my search engines had created reports on Benjamin Dzornen. He'd been born in Bratislava in 1896, attended school there, served in the Austrian Army during the First World War. After the war, he'd left Czechoslovakia for Berlin, where he came under the spell of Einstein, Max Planck and their circle.

In Berlin, Dzornen married a German woman, Ilse Rosenzweig, who came from an affluent cultured family. In the 1920s, he moved on to Vienna to work at the Institut für Radiumforschung. He and Ilse had three children, two daughters born in Vienna in the twenties, and a much younger son born after they arrived in the United States.

I scanned down the report: sure enough, he'd been in Göttingen in 1929, working with Heisenberg on matrix algebra and quantum mechanics. Among the students involved in the project was one M. Saginor, sex not specified.

If Dzornen and Martina had been lovers, then Kitty's claim that her father dined with the King of Sweden was true. But how could I possibly find out? I imagined creeping into Kitty's bedroom in the middle of the night for a DNA sample, then darting up to one of Dzornen's descendants at a party to stick a Q-tip in her mouth. There had to be an easier way.

I sat back in my chair. The question wasn't whether Dzornen was Kitty's father. It was whether she believed he was. The family romance, that was what Freud called the belief that you'd been separated at birth from your real parents, who were special, perhaps royal. My Granny Warshawski believed she was descended from Queen Jadwiga of Poland, and that those genes made her superior to every other immigrant working on the killing floor of Chicago's stockyards.

Kitty wouldn't have kept her belief in her own royal lineage secret from her family. I could imagine her bragging to her husband, or her complaints to her daughter: *My father won the Nobel Prize, you must get your weak genes from your father's family*.

If Martin was on the trail of something that didn't add up, was it something he'd discovered about his mother? His grandmother? What if it had nothing to do with drugs or money, but rather that he feared he had symptoms of a genetic disorder? He'd have gone to his father's family in Cleveland, but he'd also have tracked down the people he'd been raised to believe were his mother's family.

Dzornen died in 1969; Ilse survived until 1989 without remarrying. I looked at where their kids had landed. The son had never married, but the two daughters had. They'd produced children and now grand-children. I counted them: five grandchildren for Benjamin and Ilse, eleven great-grandchildren. One of Dzornen's daughters had died, but that still left eighteen people who might know something about Mar-tina Saginor and her daughter. They were far-flung—two were in South America, three in Europe, the others spread out across North America.

None of Dzornen's three children had gone into science. The son, Julius, didn't seem to have gone into anything. He was about seventy now, living in a coach house near the University of Chicago, without any assets to speak of. In contrast, the surviving daughter lived on the Gold Coast with a tidy portfolio of bonds and a winter place in Arizona.

The computer turned up an old photo of Ilse, Benjamin and the two daughters standing in front of a frame house in Madison, Wiscon-sin, in 1937, with Ilse visibly pregnant. I tried to remember the snap-shot on Kitty Binder's credenza: Had the girls looked anything like these?

Kitty said her family had all been killed in the war. She also said she had come to Chicago because she'd learned her parents were here. Had she said parents or father? Maybe she tried to find Dzornen, but he rebuffed her: he was an important player in the post-war American scientific world; he wouldn't have wanted an inconvenient reminder of a protégée/lover who hadn't survived the war. Or he wasn't Kitty's fa-ther and she was a nuisance.

Dzornen's children might know something about Kitty, or Martina, or even Martin. Julius Dzornen's coach house was on University Avenue, not far from where I'd been yesterday. It seemed odd to me, the more I thought about it: he didn't have any visible means of support, he hadn't strayed far from his parents' house. It would be quite a detour to visit him before seeing Nadja Hahne at the high school, but I could just fit it in if I really hustled with my to-do list.

I did an hour's worth of work with the wine retailer, agreeing to help him buy and place discreet surveillance cameras. I talked to the law firm about their receivables, then set up a phone date with a mining company in Saskatchewan. Two hundred dollars of billable hours duly entered in my spreadsheet.

On my way south, the odometer in my Mustang rolled over the hundred-thousand-mile marker. If I was ever going to afford a new car, I'd have to stop racing around the city like this. I suppose some detectives might bill the way lawyers do, for every six minutes spent even in thought on a particular client, but I didn't think poor Kitty needed to pay for the time I spent driving, let alone my fracas at Freddie Walker's drug house.

It was still early enough in the day that I made good time to Hyde Park. Julius's coach house lay behind a square frame house on University Avenue. The top of an ash, its leaves already yellow, towered over the house from the back.

I wondered if I should cross the lawn to get to Julius, then noticed a flagstone path that bordered the fence. I followed it past the big house to a large yard that held a swing set and a badminton net, although the giant ash had sent out so many knobby roots that it would be a challenge to run down stray shots. The coach house stood behind the tree, its windows so covered with ivy that I couldn't tell if any lights were on inside.

Shrubs along the fence were hung with bird feeders. The birds squawked off at my approach, reminding me unpleasantly of the crows around Derrick Schlafly.

I pounded on the door: there didn't seem to be a knocker or a bell. Behind the door I could hear faint noises, a radio, perhaps. After three or four minutes of knocking, when I was beginning to wonder if Julius might have died, he suddenly opened the door. He was a short, stocky man with his mother's high-domed forehead. He had a two-day growth and his eyes were red: too much beer, not enough sleep.

"Mr. Dzornen? My name is V. I. Warshawski. I'm a detective—"

He started to slam the door on me. "No cops without a warrant."

I stuck my flashlight into the jamb and pushed against his weight. "I'm private, not with the cops."

"Then there's no way you can get a warrant, so fuck off. I don't talk to detectives."

"Is that the cornerstone of your faith?" I asked. "You made a bedrock decision fifty years ago to eschew all detectives and nothing has ever happened to make you change your mind?"

The door reopened so quickly that I lost my balance and fell into him. For a moment we did a tangled tango of arms, legs, briefcase and flashlight, until he backed up and I fell onto my right side. As I got back to my feet, I saw his face looked white and gluey, as if he had suddenly smeared himself with Crisco.

A worn tan jacket was hanging on a hook behind me. I draped it over his shoulders and led him into his sitting room, where I pushed him down into a frayed armchair. The room was heavy with stale cigarette smoke; an ashtray on the coffee table was overflowing with butts. Other than that, the room wasn't really untidy, just in need of a good vacuuming. Not that I should judge.

What was surprising was that the walls were covered with photographs and maps of migratory birds. His own observations were written in a finicky script on strips laid across tracking maps. Several binocular cases stood on a ledge next to one of the tiny windows, a worn leather case with "Carl Zeiss" stamped on it and a bigger, more modern case from Nikon.

When Dzornen's color started to return to normal, I asked, "What happened fifty years ago, Mr. Dzornen?"

"I dropped out of school."

"Was that because of something a detective did?"

His mouth twisted in a sneer. "Because of something a detective didn't do."

I thought this over. "A crime was committed but a detective never solved it and you were framed so you had to quit school?"

"Interesting guess, Detective. Where were you fifty years ago?"

"Lying in my crib, probably. You want to tell me what the detective didn't do fifty years ago?"

He gave a ferocious grin. "The detective never showed up. Unlike you. You're incredibly late. What do you want?"

"Did this non-arriving detective have something to do with Kitty Binder?"

"Oh, Kitty." He made a dismissive gesture. "You been talking to Herta?"

"Not yet," I said. "Should I?"

"My sister's always had her undies in a bundle over Kitty. Herta considers herself the guardian of Benjamin Dzornen's memory. She has a shrine to him in that mausoleum she lives in. She's always imagined Kitty wants to desecrate the shrine—Herta doesn't understand Kitty is like her and Ilse, just one more fucked-up refugee from Hitler's Europe."

I wasn't sure what he was talking about. "Does Herta think Kitty Binder wants to attack her?"

"She may worry that Kitty will attack her bank accounts. Did Kitty hire you to pry money out of Herta? Tell her from me that Herta clings tightly to her hoard, only opening her wallet on rare and special occasions."

"Like when she bought you those?" I gestured toward the binoculars.

He spread his lips in a parody of a smile, showing teeth stained gray by cigarettes. "Not even then. The Zeiss was something my father left me. Social Security paid for the Nikon."

"Kitty hired me to find Martin, her grandson," I said. "I thought he might have called on you or your sister before he disappeared."

"You keep thinking, Detective. It may win you the Nobel Prize, like it did for my old man. But believe me, all those thoughts, and all those prizes, they don't save you from being really stupid in the end. I try not to think, just watch the birds. They keep you far away from human muck."

"Very likely." He was watching me warily behind the patina of world-weary chatter, thinking like mad, but about what? "Did Martin come to see you this summer?"

"Why would he do that?" Julius said.

"Because he saw something that didn't make sense to him, and I wondered if it was connected to his family's history, which is possibly also your history."

"You wonder away, Detective, because, like they say on the TV cop shows, this conversation is over." He leaned back in the armchair and put on an ostentatious pantomime of a man asleep.

I watched him for a bit, but he didn't budge: eyes drooped shut, jaw slack, short loud snorts coming from his nose. When I got to my feet and started poking about among the drawers on an old desk, he was up in a flash. He was seventy-something, but he was strong, and he grabbed me hard enough to make me wince. I broke away from him, but didn't retaliate: he was in the right—I didn't have any business looking at his papers. And, as he'd said at the outset, I couldn't produce a warrant.

13

THE DZORNEN EFFECT

T HIS IS MY SIXTEENTH YEAR of teaching. I've had a number of bright students, but Martin Binder is one who stays with me. Such a combination of native talent and poor direction."

Nadja Hahne was talking to me in a corner of the faculty lounge,
where we had to lean our heads almost touching so we could hear each
other: at the end of the workday, teachers were blowing off steam, some
more loudly than others. Dressed in jeans and a white shirt, with her
brown hair falling in unruly wisps around her face, Hahne didn't look
old enough to have been teaching for sixteen years.

"In what way, Ms. Hahne?"

"Nadja," she said. "I'm 'Ms. Hahne' eight hours a day; I need to be
a person at the end. They sent Martin into my AP physics class when
he got a perfect math score on the PSATs. He should have been in the
gifted program from the outset, but some idiot put him in our UTG
track."

I looked blank, and she gave an embarrassed smile.

"One of those horrible private acronyms: Unlikely to Graduate.
Martin's grades were mediocre, because expectations of him had been
low both at home and at school. His grandmother had this incomprehensible opposition to his becoming an academic. Anyway, Martin
came to me already in love with physics; he saw the shape of it, if you
know what I mean."

I shook my head.

"Physics can be just equations and formulas and graphs: the Maxwell equations for light, the Feynman diagrams for electron spin, that kind of thing. We get plenty of bright kids at this school who understand them. But physics is also a place where you send your mind chasing after the infinite, searching for the harmonies that lie at the heart of nature. That's what Martin saw.

"He played catch-up for a couple of months, but he was already asking the best questions I got that term. And then, when he'd mastered the background, his mind began leap-frogging ahead of mine. I'm just good enough at what I do to see where he was going. I was able to teach him a few things, but mostly I sat back and enjoyed watching him explore and grow.

"He was my only student ever to score a five on the physics C exam, which only a few kids take, but his grandmother wouldn't budge on letting him try for a top-tier school. I tried assuring her that Martin would thrive at a good college. I think the grandfather agreed, but he was quite ill and Ms. Binder was adamant that Martin not turn into a, I don't know what, time-wasting dreamer, I think is what she said. Nothing could budge her. It was unbearably frustrating. Painful, really." Nadja pounded her fists on her thighs, the frustration still infuriating her.

"What is he like as a person?" I asked. "I talked to the parents of one of his friends; they said he was socially awkward."

Nadja gave a sad smile. "He talked very little about his home life; I think he disappeared from it into physics. He was a bit awkward, but he had a sweet streak, and he was good-looking in that brooding way that makes girls think they can save a boy."

"Any girlfriends?" I asked hopefully.

"I don't think so," Nadja said. "In high school, anyway, he couldn't see how to connect to other people's lives."

I fiddled with a pencil that was lying on a nearby table. "He's been gone without a trace for about ten days. It's not a secret, but his mother is a drug addict. I've been worried that he's gotten involved in some mess she's part of; a man was murdered downstate in the house where she was living."

"Murdered? Oh my God. Was Martin—" She broke off the sentence, her face contracting with worry.

"I don't know. I followed his mother to the home of a drug dealer on the West Side and ended up in a firefight over there. She disappeared before I could get into the building. I hoped Martin might have talked to you this past summer, told you what was on his mind before he disappeared. His grandmother said something had upset him several weeks before he actually took off, but she doesn't know what."

Hahne shook her head unhappily. "After it became clear he was not going to university, Martin stopped talking to me. My guess is he felt ashamed and thought I might be criticizing him. While he was a student, before his college dreams got broken, we'd talk a lot, but it was mostly about abstractions, music sometimes, or heredity. He was so obsessed with questions about hereditary abilities that I asked why he didn't focus more on biology, but he said wanting answers to one specific question wasn't the same as being in love with a whole subject. Anyway, I thought he was probably worried about whether he would become an addict, like his mother."

"It may have been more than that," I said. "His grandmother was an illegitimate child in Vienna, and she offers conflicting versions of who her birth father might have been. In the version she used to repeat as a child, he was a Nobel Prize–winning scientist—Benjamin Dzornen."

"Oh!" Nadja's eyes opened wide. "He discovered the Dzornen-Pauli effect; the equations are remarkable."

I grinned. "I'll take your word for it. Anyway, Kitty Binder seems troubled enough about her parentage that Martin likely grew up with a lot of questions about his own background. Not to mention the fact that there seems to be no way of knowing who his own birth father was."

Hahne played with the wispy ends of her hair. "Martin's mother did phone the school a couple of times, asking about him, or wanting to talk to him. The principal told me, since he knew I was the teacher who was closest to Martin. I guess his mother was pretty high every time she phoned. The two of us had to inform the grandmother, since she was Martin's legal guardian. She said not to let Martin know."

I nodded. "The grandmother thinks Martin obeyed her and never saw his mother, but I'm betting he did; kids need to see their parents. They keep hoping they'll get love, even if the parent is as unstable as Judy Binder."

"Did Ms. Binder, the grandmother, I mean, hire you to find Martin?" Hahne asked.

"At least for today," I said. "First Kitty—Ms. Binder, the grandmother—told me to leave Martin alone, but then she asked me to find him. I have a dozen wildly incompatible theories, but one of them is that Martin might have gone off the skids and started killing people he imagines as corrupting his mother."

"I refuse to believe that!" Hahne flushed to the roots of her mousy hair. "He wasn't that kind of boy. Socially awkward, but not—not unstable!"

A couple of people chatting nearby looked at us curiously, wondering what I could be saying to upset her. I didn't challenge Hahne: Martin was her special student.

"If he didn't disappear to hunt for his mother, where else could he be?" I asked. "His grandmother says something happened his final weeks at home that upset him. The last thing she remembers him saying was that something didn't add up. He left for a few hours in the morning, came home for a short time, then took off for good."

Hahne frowned. "That sounds as though he was analyzing a

problem, not planning revenge. He used that phrase when he couldn't make sense of a problem or a theory, if he thought his approach was off-base, or if he thought the theory wasn't right."

"Martin hasn't been in touch with you? If he has, if you know he's safe, I won't pry, but—here he's disappeared, while his mother is jumping from one drug house to another with a posse of furious meth makers behind her." I leaned forward in my intensity; Hahne shrank back into her chair.

"Sorry," I said. "It's just that the people she hangs with are absolutely ruthless. If what doesn't add up in Martin's mind has to do with her or them, I need to know."

Hahne spread her hands helplessly. "If I knew, I'd tell you, but honestly, Martin hasn't talked to me since he left high school."

We talked a little longer about Martin, his infatuation with Feynman, his gift as a musician—he played bassoon, although he sometimes fooled around with bongo drums just because Feynman had.

"I always told him the ugly duckling turns into a swan," Hahne said, escorting me to the door. "I still believe it. If he's in trouble of some kind, if you find him and he needs any kind of support, legal, financial, anything, you must let me know at once."

I promised, but drove away from the school more worried than when I'd arrived. An arithmetic problem. Something he couldn't make sense of, but in an intellectual way? Of course, Hahne felt a maternal protectiveness toward her gifted awkward student; she might not want to recognize a fissure in him that would break under the wrong pressure.

Still, there was the fact that he'd emptied his computers. Something didn't add up, but he couldn't bear for anyone else to know about it? But who would look at his machines, besides his grandmother? She might make a scornful remark about people who waste their time on theories, but I couldn't picture her hacking into his files.

I was equally puzzled by Julius Dzornen's behavior. He'd stonewalled me completely about whether Martin had come to see him

before disappearing, which made me believe that he had. To ask him—
what? What could Martin have said that would make his great-uncle—
if Julius was, indeed, Kitty's half brother—clam up?

Just as baffling was what had derailed Julius fifty years ago, so
much that he'd dropped out of school and almost fainted at the sight
of a detective. He was seventy-three or -four now. Something in his
teen years, or his early twenties.

I pulled over at a gas station on Irving Park and found his sister
Herta's phone number. Herta Dzornen Colonna. I started to dial the
number but hesitated; I wanted her to see me and it's so easy to say no
and end the conversation when you're on the phone. Besides, a cell
phone with the trucks roaring down the nearby expressway was a recipe for unsuccessful communication.

I drove down to the Gold Coast, thirty miles of bumper-to-bumper
traffic. I found a parking space near Herta's building, one of the grand
duchesses of Chicago apartments that line Lake Shore Drive East.
They face the lake and Oak Street Beach, with mortgages that would
take a blue-collar woman like me a hundred thirty-five years to pay off.

I was stiff from my long drive. After feeding quarters into the ticket
machine—twenty-five for an hour—I went to the little garden that
separates the duchesses from the beach and stretched my shoulders.
And thought about how to get past Herta Dzornen's doorman.

INNSBRUCK, 1942
Pebbles in a Bottomless Well

AFTER MONTHS OF COLD AND STARVATION, all the prisoners hallucinate. Platters of beautiful food appear just out of reach. Parents and old lovers blur with the faces of other prisoners or even guards. Old enemies appear in the shadows on the cave walls.

One day Martina thinks she sees her high school mathematics professor, Herr Papp, examining her work.

"But you are blind," she says out loud.

A guard pulls out the short whip that they all carry and snaps it hard enough to produce a whistle. "I see you perfectly, you lazy cunt. No talking to the other prisoners."

She's trying to measure the purity of a piece of carbon, but her hands are weak from hunger. The cold and damp in the cave also affect the balances so that it's almost impossible to get the weight correct. As she returns to the task in front of her the last time she saw Herr Papp comes to her.

She had visited his shabby three-room apartment near the Volksgarten when he finally answered her letter. It had taken him so long to respond that she wondered if he had died, or thought she was writing as a prank: he had been a sarcastic professor, belittling the girls in his classes. In response, several of the students in Martina's year had sent him flowery love letters signed with the names of cabaret singers or dancers at the opera.

By the time she wrote him, she was a full-fledged researcher at the Institut für Radiumforschung, although she couldn't afford to quit her day job, teaching physics and mathematics at the Technische Hochschule.

When she arrived at Herr Papp's apartment, a housekeeper waited at the top of the stairs. The woman didn't acknowledge Martina's *"Grüss Gott,"* except to gesture to the open door, disapproval lines dug deep around her mouth.

Herr Papp didn't stand when Martina went over to greet him. Out of old habit, before sitting in a chair near his own, she curtsied to him—really no more gracefully than she'd done for Frau Herschel twenty-five years earlier.

Herr Papp's thin voice with its sarcastic inflection hadn't changed. "Ah, yes, you were the young lady who always worked out her problem sets so thoroughly. I remember that you sat so upright I sometimes wondered if your mother had tied a backboard beneath your jacket. And you are still upright. Please sit down so that your voice is at my level."

It wasn't until she sat that Martina realized he was blind. After the housekeeper poured tea for them both, the woman sat next to him, guiding his hand to the cup, placing a piece of cake on his fork, making sure he had control of the fork before releasing her hold, wiping the front of his frayed jacket when he spilled tea or cake.

It must have been the housekeeper who had written the reply for him: Martina had been surprised by the round, careful letters, not the spiky script in the notes that used to show her a more economical way of solving a problem.

"I never thought of you as the kind of young lady who paid visits to the elderly or the infirm," Herr Papp said. "You struck me as the kind of single-minded person who is rather like the hypotenuse, taking the shortest distance between her present location and a goal."

His words echoed her mother's in such an alarming way that

Martina was silenced for a moment. Not that Frau Saginor would ever refer to a hypotenuse, but her rages against her daughter's obsession with mathematics and science always had this at their core: Martina was selfish, thoughtless, what she wanted came ahead of the needs of anyone around her.

Frau Saginor used to keep up a stream of hopes that Martina might fail her exams, a barrage of demands that she quit her studies and get a job as a bookkeeper or a shop assistant. "That would help put food on the table and pay for Papa's medicines."

This was when Martina was seventeen. Papa had been in the early stages of tuberculosis, coughing up so much blood every day that it was hard to know how his body was able to produce more. But even in his weakness, Papa told Martina over and over that he wanted her in school. On the table next to the bed, he kept those of her essays and problem sets that had been marked "100 out of 100," or "First Prize in the mathematics section." Until the last few days of his life, he read them in the long watches of the night when he couldn't sleep.

Martina used to work out her math problems sitting next to him, and if he was still awake when she finished, she would play for him: her flute had also won her a prize. She often played at three in the morning, making the neighbors pound on the thin walls between the tenements.

"Even in Vienna, Mozart has enemies," Papa used to joke.

It was Papa who had learned about the Technische Hochschule for girls. He was a carpenter who'd worked on the building when it went up in 1912. After Martina had come home dazed by the rainbow in Frau Herschel's nursery, Papa brought back bits of leaded glass left over from a job site so that he and Martina could make prisms. He brought home books on light and color that he found in secondhand shops. When Martina was seven, the two of them re-created Newton's experiments with sunlight, making a rainbow out of one prism, using a second prism to turn the rainbow back into white sunlight.

Mama watched, tight-lipped, then dragged Martina to the table to work on her embroidery. Martina always bunched the thread, broke it, split it. Her practice work on scraps of linen made Mama fume.

Papa suggested to Martina that she learn to sign her name in embroidery stitches: something special, that she could use when she signed her school papers. Martina created a design that used Newton's prisms as a symbol of herself, but the result when she sewed it was as abominable as the rest of her work. Mama wouldn't let her stop sewing, but she gave up on any idea of Martina ever helping her in the workshop.

Papa learned about scholarships to the Technische Hochschule. He and Mama argued late into the night about fit jobs for girls, and whether Martina was becoming conceited because of her schooling, but when Martina was twelve and Austria was losing the war, she sat the scholarship and entrance exams. She was first in the city in mathematics. The next year, the first year after the war had ended, Papa escorted her to the lofty stone building on Elisabethstrasse.

Martina was wearing the uniform of the school, sewn by her mother with meticulous care: anger over husband and daughter for reaching above themselves was one thing, but none of the wealthy burghers' daughters would ever taunt Martina for her clothes.

The streetcar was jammed with people going to work or looking for work, but when Papa helped Martina down from the high step, they had to pass clots of unemployed men who gathered daily on the streets. Many were still in their Imperial uniforms, ragged from four years on one front or another, and now the only clothes they owned. Like most Viennese, they were bewildered at losing the war, bewildered at loss of empire and emperor in one stroke of the French, American and British pens. A skinny Jewish girl in an upper-class school's uniform would be an easy target for rage.

That was when Martina learned to hold herself so erect that she herself looked like the Empress: aloof, untouchable. Better than a backboard in her jacket.

Even now in the cave in the Austrian Alps, her posture infuriates the guards, who want her to bow her head, to grovel to them. She has been beaten more than once for her unbreakable arrogance.

In that visit to Herr Papp, his blindness seemed to give him a sixth sense for the emotions. Although Martina sat still, spine straight, he knew his words about her behaving like a hypotenuse hit a mark.

He laughed softly, a sound like dry leaves rustling underfoot. "Single-mindedness is not a crime, Fräulein Saginor. They say that the great Newton could go days without sleep, holding a problem in his mind like a kaleidoscope, turning it over until the array of colored pebbles showed him the pattern he was seeking in nature. So it is not a crime, Fräulein, for you to come here because you want something. I just question what an old blind mathematics professor can offer you, since you don't even want Frau Werfel's cake."

It was true: Martina seldom thought about food in those days, and the cake looked unappetizing. For form's sake she ate a bite, but it was so rich she quickly washed it down with tea.

"Leibniz," she said.

"Leibniz?" Herr Papp echoed, incredulous. "You surely have not come here to discuss a seventeenth-century mathematician, not when you have the University of Vienna and the Institut für Radium-forschung available to you."

"Do you see English—does anyone read English journals to you?" Martina asked.

"An old student reads French to me sometimes but no one who knows English comes to visit."

"An Englishman named Turing wrote a paper last year on comput-able numbers and how they relate to the *Entscheidungsproblem*. He's contradicting Professor Hilbert's paradigm, which seemed like heresy. Recently, though, I've been wondering how to determine the structure of an atom when you can see electron scattering but have no idea what atom is scattering them. The computations can be done, in theory, but in practice—" Martina spread her hands, an expression of exhaustion that of course Herr Papp couldn't see.

"In practice the work might take you years," he finished for her. "And why did this make you think of Leibniz, and of me?"

"You told us one day in class how deep his works were."

This was actually a diplomatic recollection of Herr Papp at his most biting: *My dear young ladies, I know that the word "philosophy" makes your lovely eyes turn to glass, where you reflect back to me what I'm saying without absorbing more than a glancing ray of light. Therefore, when you hear the name Leibniz, I know that I am not even throwing pebbles into a bottomless well, just shying them off a glass wall. But his was the deepest mind of the German Renaissance.*

"You told us that besides inventing the calculus, Leibniz thought on many mathematical problems, including how to express all computations in binary numbers. And you showed us a photograph of a medallion he made with a design for a computation machine engraved in it."

Herr Papp's wandering blind eyes focused on her face. He turned abruptly to Frau Werfel, demanding that she lead him to a bookcase by the window.

Frau Werfel spoke for the first time. "Herr Papp, you are too tired; this woman, she is importuning you for her own gain."

Martina was about to protest, but Herr Papp forestalled her by telling Frau Werfel she was speaking nonsense. "If a young lady who cares about electron scattering remembers a lecture of mine from fifteen years ago, I am almost immortal. Take me over to the bookcase, the mahogany one."

The housekeeper, shooting Martina a venomous look, led the professor to the case. He wouldn't let Frau Werfel touch the papers, but felt among them, shelf by shelf. In the end, he brought back a document whose title was in the elaborate script of the seventeenth century: *De progressione dyadica. On binary progression.*

"Return it to me when you've read it, Fräulein Saginor. It's a facsimile copy, of course. A high school mathematics professor cannot afford an original of Leibniz."

She had curtsied again on leaving, a gesture that Herr Papp sensed, since he gave her an ironic half-bow in return. Martina had rushed back to the Institute, completely forgetting that she had promised to retrieve Käthe from the Herschel apartment at six.

She stayed at the Institute library until past midnight, making slow going of the old Latin. It took her over a week of late nights to translate the most significant passages into usable German: she had won no prizes for languages in high school. In the end, she had made a good enough effort to share the excerpts with her students.

When she returned to the Prater to give the manuscript back to Herr Papp, Frau Werfel told her the professor was resting and had no need to talk to her further.

"The old cow is jealous of you," her student Gertrud Memler crowed when Martina told her team about the incident.

"Don't be vulgar, Fräulein Memler," Martina said, although she wondered if Memler's comment might be true. Was this another instance of what her mother and Benjamin both accused her of? Blindness to ordinary human emotions?

The students on her team couldn't find a way to make Leibniz's theoretical computing machine a reality. Martina had them experiment with different tubes that could store a charge, to see if they could use the signals to replicate the mechanical gates and registers Leibniz had imagined, but the war came before their research amounted to anything. Martina drew a number of careful charts of her own, showing the way in which she imagined electron capture could be used to make an automated computing machine.

Fräulein Memler had been a hardworking scientist, lacking in imagination but willing to stay long hours testing vacuum tube signals with Martina. After the Anschluss, though, it turned out she had been a secret member of the Nazi Party since 1935. It had been outlawed in Austria until the German annexation, but once the Nazis were in power, Memler refused to take orders from a Jew.

By that time, Martina had abandoned vacuum tubes as a way to store computation results. A study of Onsager's work on oscillation in magnetic fields took her in a different direction: she saw that, among other things, Onsager's studies meant a ferromagnetic surface might be used for data storage. Martina couldn't get materials to build anything, but she was able to do imaginary experiments. She continued these until the day she was forced to leave Vienna for Innsbruck.

Martina thought she had seen the last of Fräulein Memler the day in 1939 when Memler ordered her out of the Institut für Radium-forschung. A month after Martina was sent to Uranverein 7, though, the Memler arrived, assigned to head the fissile materials unit.

The Memler has forgotten none of Martina's criticisms of her vulgar manners. The Memler delights in tormenting Martina, and in addressing her with the familiar *du. You thought you were something important, you thought a Jew could critique my methods. Well, see where that has brought you, Jewess Martina.*

Martina has suggested that an automated computing machine could aid in the calculations their group is making. Fräulein Memler bristles: Martina was brought here to see whether carbon could be made pure enough to substitute for heavy water as a fissile material, not to question the methodologies of the high command. Martina argues, once only, in exchange for a beating and twenty-four hours with no rations.

Martina knows that any success she helps Uranverein 7 achieve will support Germany's war effort, but she can't help it: the problem of whether you can harness the energy released in the fission of an atom is so absorbing that she can't help studying it. It's her weakness, her strength, to burrow so deep into the understanding of nature's secrets that she forgets the world around her.

14

EYE ON THE PRIZE

"Y**OUR BROTHER SAID** you were the person who knew the most about your family's history."

Herta Dzornen Colonna eyed me warily in her doorway. I'd sent the doorman up with one of my cards and a note that said I was investigating a matter that involved her father. That simple message got her to agree to let me in, but the doorman lingered in the entryway, making sure I wasn't going to assault her or smash any of the highly polished statues that dotted the apartment.

Herta was at least ten years older than her brother. Her white hair stood out from her head like a medieval wimple, showing the same high forehead as her brother, the same round pale eyes. Her khaki dress was cut in a boxy, bush-jacket style, but the fabric was soft, the kind that drapes nicely and sets you back a couple of grand at the nearby Oak Street boutiques.

"I'll be all right, Gordon," she said to the doorman. He left reluctantly, telling her he wouldn't shut the outer door so he could hear her if she needed help.

Limping slightly, Herta led me through an archway into her sitting room, the one with the view of the lake. It was dusk now; you could see running lights on the boats out on the water. Herta seated herself on a nubby white couch. Only a very clean and tidy person could sit on furniture like that.

She darted a glance at me, uneasy, almost fearful, then looked away, at a glass étagère whose shelves were filled with photographs. It was an involuntary sideways look, as if she was afraid for the safety of the pictures. Of course, that made me stop to inspect them before I sat down.

Most were contemporary, children, grandchildren—a daughter with three children who'd all inherited the family's high-domed forehead. A son who looked like the sandy-haired man in Herta's wedding photo. There were a number of older pictures as well, several showing two little girls in the short, cap-sleeved dresses popular in the 1920s and 1930s, the little girls sitting on ponies, the little girls and a giant hound following their mother. Both girls and the mother were carrying rifles. I glanced at Herta: she might be lame and elderly now, but she knew how to shoot.

A photograph of Dzornen in white tie bowing to the King of Sweden caught my eye. His actual Nobel medal, mounted on navy velvet in a shallow box, stood next to it. I bent to stare at it. There's an aura to that prize, not because of the gold, although it glowed in the darkening room. I supposed this was the shrine that Julius had mentioned.

Herta coughed loudly behind me. "You said you had been talking to Julius about our family."

I straightened up and joined her near the window. There was a tubular chair, black leather, chrome arms, in one corner. I pulled it over near her—I didn't want to leave mud or sweat or something human on the white upholstery.

"Yes, I went to see him about Martin Binder. Martin's grandmother has hired me to find him, and I know you knew her in Vienna. Back when she was Käthe Saginor."

She sucked in a breath. "Why did she tell you to come to me? To us, I mean?"

"She didn't," I said. "But your families' histories intersect; her mother was your dad's student. Ms. Binder thinks he was her father."

"Has she been telling you that lie?" Herta knotted her fingers in a way that reminded me of Kitty twisting the cabling in her heavy sweater.

"Is it a lie?" I asked.

"Of course it is. Käthe was a horrible child. She would do anything to gain attention, and as an adult she turned out to be much the same. It's true her mother was one of Papa's students; he thought very highly of her work, at least he did at first. But Käthe—Kitty, I guess she calls herself now. My sister Bettina and I couldn't stand her. We had to play with her sometimes, when families from the Institut für Radium- forschung got together for outings or the New Year's party. Käthe was younger than us, so we wouldn't have wanted to play with her, anyway, but she was such an angry girl, so prone to temper tantrums that we ran off into the park whenever we saw her coming."

She stared at me with fierce eyes. "Before the war, when we were living in Vienna, Papa troubled himself sometimes over Fräulein Sagi- nor's sad fate. I think he tried to look after Käthe because he worried about her mother, not having much of a stipend and being a single mother. And Käthe twisted that into thinking he was her father!"

"I was told that Ms. Binder came to Chicago to see your father, that Ms. Binder thought he knew where her mother was."

"Fräulein Saginor did not survive the war," Herta said stiffly. "If Julius told you otherwise, it's because he enjoys mocking people."

"Julius didn't mention Fräulein Saginor at all," I said. "He did say you've always been upset by Ms. Binder's presence in your life."

"The war had been over for ten years," Herta whispered. "We were sure Käthe was dead. When she suddenly appeared here in Chicago— Papa was away, of course. He always was, going off to Washington or Berkeley, even though his health was not good."

"When was that?" I asked.

"I remember it like yesterday. Probably when I am finally dying, that day will be my last thought, not my wedding or my grandchil- dren, but Mama phoning me, telling me that Käthe had arrived and was creating the most alarming scene all over the neighborhood. Julius lived at home, but he was in class over at the university—University of Chicago. It was before he dropped out, although he probably would have been thrown out because he was failing everything."

"So it wasn't Kitty Binder's sudden arrival that made Julius fall apart?" I said.

"He never minded her," Herta said bitterly. "He'd been *falling apart* for a number of years before she showed up to ruin our lives. He's always made fun of Bettina and me for what he calls overreacting to Käthe. If he'd been home that morning, he might see my point."

"What did she do?" I asked.

"Mama was home alone. By then Bettina and I were both married, but Bettina was living in Los Angeles, so it was up to me; Mama called me and I took a taxi down to the house."

Herta shook her head, still upset by a scene half a century old. "I knew Käthe at once, even though I hadn't seen her since we left Vienna in 1936. She was looking for Papa, of course, because—well, of her strange ideas about him and her mother. Käthe was going around the neighborhood, ringing doorbells, telling people that Papa—it was sickening! Even though everyone told us they didn't believe her, you could tell from the pitying glances they gave Mama that they thought, 'No smoke without fire.'"

"How long did this go on?" I asked. "I was told she even made a scene at the university's physics department."

"Papa made her go away," Herta said.

"How?" I asked.

She shook her head. "I don't know, but when he got back from wherever he'd been that time, he said he'd take care of it. For one week she showed up every day, at the house, or the university. She made a scene at the physics department. She even drove out to the national lab in Argonne, where they'd built the new pile, and tried to fight her way past the guards. I moved back down to the house on Greenwood

Avenue, so that Mama didn't have to be alone during the day. I was pregnant with my first child; except for worrying about Käthe, it was lovely to be back in Hyde Park, with Mama looking after me, instead of having to keep house myself." Her face softened, her youth in front of her eyes.

She looked up at me. "Anyway, whatever it was that Papa did, Käthe stopped coming around, and after another week, I felt it was okay to leave Mama on her own. For years, Käthe kept quiet, she didn't bother us, but we always felt she was a, oh, an unexploded grenade. Sure enough, her horrible daughter arrived out of the blue one day, disgustingly drunk, or drugged, that's what Stuart—my husband—said it was. And now here you are."

I nodded: Kitty might have stopped pestering the Dzornens, but she had talked about them in front of her daughter. Junkies know no shame; Judy would have seen the Dzornens as a potential revenue stream.

"Judy tried to get money out of you," I said.

Herta nodded, her mouth pursed into a tight rosebud. "More than once: first when she was young, around twenty. She came back several times. She tried—never mind that. My husband was a lawyer; he sent her about her business very quickly."

"You said Ms. Binder's mother didn't survive the war," I said. "Do you know what became of her? What made Ms. Binder think her mother was still alive and working in Chicago?"

"Oh, she likes to dramatize herself!" Herta flung up her hands in a contemptuous gesture. "I don't know specifically what became of Fräulein Saginor, why she didn't leave Austria when it was still possible."

"But you heard your parents discuss her situation," I suggested.

"Oh, often," Herta agreed. "Papa was always rather softhearted. Mama had to look out for the welfare of the whole family."

"Your father wanted to bring her with him?" I said. "And your mother wouldn't allow it?"

Herta's face was heavily powdered, but I could still see her cheeks redden. "Fräulein Saginor was not a family member; there was no way the Americans would allow her to come on our visa. Papa wanted to bring her as a research assistant, but what would she have lived on, even if the visa had been issued? *He* didn't have independent resources to pay a stipend, the way the head of the Institute did. You do understand that there were many more Jews trying to leave Europe than there were countries willing to take them in."

"Yes, but the great scientists all found homes; look at your own father," I said.

"That's the point," Herta said, her tone contemptuous. "My father was a great scientist. Martina Saginor was not. As sad as her fate may seem, it wasn't possible in that climate to find a lab willing to offer her a place."

"Maybe she was a great scientist who had a gender handicap," I suggested.

"Yes, that's what Käthe wanted to believe, too," Herta said, "that my father abandoned Martina Saginor because he was jealous of her abilities, or my mother was jealous of her for this imaginary affair. The drug addict daughter said the same thing when she showed up. She said Papa owed it to her because Mama's jealousy murdered her grandmother!"

She added savagely, "My father was not the father of this stupid Binder woman. Martina Saginor lived in a ghetto filled with poor Jews from Eastern Europe; likely she spent the night with a vagrant junk dealer or some such, and wanted to pretend it was a more glamorous story. Benjamin Dzornen never betrayed my mother, and he was far too honorable to have an affair with one of his students. If you put anything out in public suggesting otherwise, my husband's law firm will file a suit of libel against you!"

"Yes, of course," I said. "It's a comforting tale, anyway. But Martin Binder, Kitty's grandson, has he been in touch with you?"

She eyed me with a wariness that made me think of her brother.

I added, "I know he visited your brother, but Julius wouldn't tell me what they discussed."

"Then there is nothing further for me to say to you on the subject," Herta said.

It was meant as a conversation ender, but I ignored it, asking instead about Julius's strange comment. "Your brother said a detective should have come fifty years ago and didn't. What did he mean?"

Relief that I was abandoning the subject of her father and Martina Saginor took the anger out of Herta's face, replaced by a look of sorrow, or puzzlement. Perhaps both.

"Something went wrong between him and Papa, but neither of them ever said what. That happened before Käthe showed up, about three years earlier. Julius had followed Papa like a duckling before that, loving science in the same way Papa did, and then, suddenly, it was over. Julius started making ugly remarks to Papa at the dinner table, and Papa would sit there, not responding. Mama tried to make Julius stop, but Papa would only shrug his shoulders and disappear into his study. I'm sure the change in Julius hastened Papa's death."

I got to my feet, handing her a card. "Call me if you remember why Martin Binder came to see you."

On my way to the door, I stopped again to look at Dzornen's Nobel medal. "I'll never be this close to a Nobel Prize again," I said.

Herta came over to stand next to me. She picked up the shallow box and unhooked its glass lid so that I could touch the medallion. I ran my fingertips over the figures on the coin's reverse side, two women draped in the robes of classical antiquity. *You were there when the King of Sweden handed you to him,* I addressed the medal in my head. *What was in his heart? Was Kitty Binder his daughter?*

I handed the prize back to Herta. Thinking again of the snapshot in Kitty Binder's living room, I said, "You hated the times you had to play with Kitty, back when you were girls in Vienna. Do you remember ever taking her to the beach on an outing with your parents?"

Herta laughed scornfully. "There are no beaches in Vienna, just the Danube running through it. Since the end of the Habsburg Empire, Austria has been a little landlocked country."

"A trip to the park, then, you, Bettina, and your parents."

"I don't know what you're implying, perhaps that my father let Käthe into our family, but I assure you, we never took her on any private outings. And anyway, I don't remember Papa going anywhere with us, even when we went to Mama's family's summer home in Sumperk. The Institut für Radiumforschung, that was his life, not his wife and daughters."

Her tone changed from contempt to bitterness. I might be a vulgar American who didn't know the map of Austria, but it was her father who'd let her down. As I rode to the lobby, I tossed a nickel. Tails, Benjamin Dzornen had never slept with any of his students. Heads, he was Kitty Binder's father. Three times in a row, I lifted my hand and saw Thomas Jefferson's profile. Conclusive proof.

15

THE DOCTOR'S DILEMMA

I CALLED LOTTY when I got home. "I just left Herta Colonna's apartment," I said. "You might have met in Vienna when you were eight or nine and she was Herta Dzornen. She and her sister Bettina were Benjamin Dzornen's daughters."

"I don't remember them," Lotty answered. "Dzornen—that name is familiar. Isn't he a scientist?"

"Nobel Prize, Manhattan Project. Martina Saginor's thesis adviser back when he was part of some radium institute in Vienna."

"Oh!" I heard Lotty suck in a breath. "He was Käthe's—Kitty's—father?"

"She thinks he was; Herta says her father was an honorable man who would never have had affairs, least of all with a student. Herta repeated what you said, that when Kitty first came to Chicago, she made a royal nuisance of herself. She pestered the Dzornens, she had a tantrum at the University of Chicago; she even went out to the lab in Argonne to a new pile, whatever that is, and made a fuss. Benjamin put some sort of pressure on her; Herta claims not to know what, but after that, Kitty left the family alone.

"Judy arrived years later as Act Two, trying to extort money from Herta, maybe from the sister Bettina as well, although she had moved to the West Coast. I'm pretty sure Martin went to see both Herta and her brother, Julius. Neither will admit it, but their body language is talking loudly. And Julius is an odd duck."

I was disappointed that Lotty didn't know the family—I was hoping she might know why Julius thought a detective should have shown up fifty years ago.

"He feels guilty about something," Lotty said. "You don't need to be Oprah's tame psychiatrist to realize that, but it could be anything. Did he see his father do something unspeakable? Or was his father unable to protect him from assault? Hyde Park was a dangerous community in the 1950s. Can you uncover violent crimes from that era?"

"Only with more blood, sweat and whatever than I can provide. Maybe not even then—the police don't create files for all the nonproductive calls they respond to. That's more in the nature of communal knowledge at the district."

"Would knowing what happened fifty years ago help you find Martin?" Lotty asked.

"How can I say? I had one idea that may be really far-fetched, but what if Julius discovered that his father's Nobel Prize was bogus?"

"Bogus?" Lotty's voice crackled across the line. "These prizes are genuine, it's not like saying you served with the Navy SEALs, thinking no one could check the story. You are one person, the eyes of the world are on you."

"Bogus is the wrong word," I conceded. "Herta was very belligerent about Martina Saginor not being a good scientist. But Martina was Dzornen's student: What if he took credit for work that she really did? Dzornen let Martina and Kitty languish in Vienna while he spent the war safely in the U.S. Julius was apparently another gifted math and science student. If he went back through old research papers and found that his father stole Martina Saginor's work, that would completely end his respect for his father. It also explains why Dzornen never discussed the matter with his wife or daughter."

"I suppose Martin Binder might have stumbled on the same evidence, if it were available," Lotty said doubtfully, "but why would he then disappear?"

"Maybe Herta killed him to preserve her father's memory," I suggested flippantly. "She has a photograph of herself as a kid in the mountains carrying a hunting rifle."

"All the wealthy Jewish women back then aped the rich Gentiles. They stalked deer, they shot rabbits. My grandparents had a place in the mountains where friends used to come to shoot, although my grandparents didn't. My *Oma* Herschel didn't like blood sports."

I brought the conversation back to Martina. "Do you remember something, anything, from your childhood, an argument you overheard, that might show Martina was angry or bitter over her professor's award?"

"Oh, Victoria, I was eight or nine the last time I saw her. That she was in love with science I remember because she used to take Käthe and me to her laboratory. At home she was awkward, but at the Institute, her eyes came to life. Whether she was as gifted as she was enthusiastic, how can I possibly know? What attention did you pay to adult conversations when you were that age?"

I had to admit she was right: children sift out the things that aren't essential to them.

"It must have been Professor Dzornen who sent the money for Käthe to join Hugo and me on the Kindertransport to London," Lotty said. "The decision for her to go came at the very last minute. My grandfather would not have sent Käthe at the expense of my cousins: he had money only for my brother and me, and then suddenly Käthe was part of the journey. If Professor Dzornen was her father, he did at least save her. Maybe that's how he ended her pestering when she came to Chicago eighteen years later: he told her he'd saved her life and that was all she got from him."

We talked it over for several fruitless minutes, but we had to agree in the end that the Metargon slogan applied to us. We had no data, we couldn't prove any of our speculations.

"It's my bedtime, Victoria. My alarm rings at four tomorrow morning."

Before I hung up, I asked if she had any idea where Judy might have gone.

"All I can say is that if she's running from one drug dealer to another, you must not chase her: your next encounter with one of them may not end as easily for you as yesterday's did."

I agreed soberly as she hung up. The last epitaph any of us wants is for our friends to be standing over our grave saying, "I told you so."

I needed to work smarter, harder, faster. Any trail Martin had left was all but obliterated. The older and colder that trail grew, the more unpaid time I'd be spending trying to sniff it out. Trouble was, I couldn't think of any smarter, faster, harder angles to follow.

In the morning, my fears diminished, as they often do in sunlight. The dogs and I loped over to the lake without interference. After we'd all swum, I put on my old cutoffs. I had no meetings scheduled—it was a day for digging in the data mines, and I could dress for comfort.

Before I started work for my bread-and-butter clients, I couldn't resist calling Arthur Harriman, the German-speaking librarian at the University of Chicago. When I suggested my theory that Benjamin Dzornen might have stolen his student's work, Harriman became quite excited: Nick and Nora come to life for him. He said his physics wasn't strong enough to analyze the work, but he had a friend who was writing her dissertation on Dzornen; he'd ask if she'd ever seen any sign of Dzornen stealing his students' work.

I settled happily into research that I was knowledgeable enough to analyze: no Dzornen-Pauli effects, just garden-variety fraud. It was ten-forty, when I was in the middle of a long conversation with a project manager at a Saskatchewan mine, that my computer began to chime at me. My answering service, which picks up calls when I don't

answer, had an incoming one that they thought was urgent. I looked at
the monitor. Cordell Breen wanted to talk to me ASAP.

I clicked a box on the screen so the answering service would know
I'd seen the message. While I finished my Canadian call, which took
another fifteen minutes, Breen called again. Twice.

I typed up my notes before I forgot them, then looked up Breen. Of
course: I was getting too old for this work. When I'd been at Metargon
labs three days ago, I'd seen a picture of Edward Breen accepting an
award from President Reagan for some fancy reactor design. Cordell
was his son; he'd taken over Metargon after Edward died.

I called Cordell Breen at once, hoping the urgent messages meant
he knew where Martin was. His secretary apologized, but the shoe was
on the other foot: Mr. Breen wanted to know if I'd found Martin
Binder. He hadn't realized Martin was missing until his daughter told
him about it. Mr. Breen would appreciate it if I'd come to his office as
soon as possible so we could discuss what I was doing.

I felt so let down that I replied rather stiffly that I didn't have any
time today, unless he wanted to talk on the phone. The secretary put me
on hold; in another moment a man's warm baritone came on the line.

"Ms. Warshawski? Cordell Breen. I know it's an inconvenience, a
major one, for you to come out to Northbrook, but I'm hoping I can
persuade you. My problem is that everything we do at Metargon is
sensitive. We have hackers and snoopers trying to eavesdrop on us or
break through our firewalls twenty-four/seven. Even when I think my
phone lines are secure they may not be; I'd like to be free to speak to
you frankly."

When he put it like that, of course it was hard not to be persuaded.
I muttered gracelessly that if I could move my lunch meeting to the
afternoon I'd be able to get there around one-thirty.

"Terry!" I heard him shout. "Get me clear at one-thirty and give
Ms. Warshawski directions."

Terry, Terry Utas, the secretary, came back on the line and explained that their headquarters were on the west side of the lab I'd visited the other day. Ms. Utas's main instruction, besides telling me which access road to take, was to make sure that the name she gave to security exactly matched what was on my photo ID.

I went back to my report on the Saskatchewan project manager, but in the back of my mind, I was hoping Breen wanted to hire me. I wondered, too, about his daughter, how she'd come to tell Breen that Martin had disappeared.

As soon as I'd finished the report, I went to one of my subscription databases for a quick rundown on the family. The entry was meager; I suppose Metargon's computer resources combined with their security fears meant Breen could do a good job of keeping most of his personal information personal.

All I learned was that Breen had apparently married late, or at least started his family late: he was seventy-four, but his only child, Alison, was twenty. Alison was taking a gap semester from Harvard. No word on what she was doing. He and his wife, Constance, lived in an eighteen-room shack in Lake Forest.

There was a little background on the early days of Metargon, when Edward Breen had done highly classified work in rockets and weapons. He'd been in Europe at the end of the war, working for something called Operation Paperclip. This seemed to be the code name for a program that brought Nazi rocket and weapons personnel into the States; when I looked it up, I discovered we apparently had let in some notorious war criminals without questioning their backgrounds, just to keep them out of Soviet hands.

It was Edward Breen's early work on computers, more than his rocketry, that moved his little company forward. Just at the time that John von Neumann was bringing the first big computer online at Princeton, Edward Breen came up with a relativistic model for the matrix that altered the mechanics of core memory. I read that last sentence three times and decided that English might not actually be my first language.

I was so happy in my cutoffs that I hated to change into work clothes, but Breen would treat me more seriously, and I'd behave more professionally, in a jacket and trousers. I drove back to my apartment to change, pulling on my soft Lario boots, which always made me feel like a million dollars—perhaps because that was what I'd paid for them.

16

SOURCE CODE

SINCE I'D MADE such a song and dance about my limited time, I skipped lunch and headed straight to Northbrook. Metargon's corporate offices were behind the research lab I'd visited earlier in the week. For once in a blue moon, the traffic was moving fast. I reached the electronic gates surrounding Metargon Park with ten minutes to spare—I could have eaten lunch after all.

The Metargon security team whisked me through with surprising speed, but after the gates had opened I realized I was being photographed. Computer screens in the guard station showed all the traffic on the access roads, including close-ups of license plates and occupants. I hadn't noticed this when I'd been to the lab because I'd entered on foot.

Once I was inside the park, I followed a drive that curved around the lab's south side, away from the pond. While the lab was a severely functional structure, the limestone headquarters building managed to create an aura of both prosperity and tranquillity. A thicket of trees blocked any view of the lab but this part of the campus had its own pond, where a pair of swans was swimming. Much classier than ducks.

Breen and his staff were prepared to respect my time. As soon as I reached the receptionist, a poised young man appeared to escort me upstairs. *Traffic was good? Had I had a pleasant summer? He'd hand me over to Terry Utas, Mr. Breen's secretary; she'd take good care of me.*

Terry Utas, with her pearl earrings and salmon-colored dropped-waist dress, made me feel dowdy, even in my Lario boots. Her makeup had been put on with a sure hand, whereas I'd forgotten even to run a lipstick over my mouth. She stopped in the middle of whatever she was doing to tell an intercom the good news of my arrival.

Breen himself appeared a moment later, a tall man whose broad shoulders and flat waist showed a rigorous attention to the workout room. His thick hair still had some dark streaks in it.

"Ms. Warshawski, thanks for interrupting your day for me. I only learned this morning that Martin Binder had gone AWOL, and it's a source of concern." He put a hand between my shoulder blades to nudge me toward his office. "Terry, let's have some coffee in here, or tea, if you'd rather?" he added to me.

I murmured that coffee would be fine. Breen gestured toward a corner where a glass-topped table stood underneath a big painting of purple squares. Rothko's name was on a discreet plaque for ignorant people like me. When I sat down, I saw an array of wires embedded in the table's top.

Breen smiled at my look of surprise. "The team made this for my father on the fortieth anniversary of the Breen Machine. We all knew, including him, he wouldn't live for the fiftieth."

"The Breen Machine?" I said politely.

"Yes, yes, the machine that made Apple and the Cloud and all the rest of it possible. My dad wanted to call it the BREENIAC, sort of flipping a finger at Johnny von Neumann and the MANIAC at Princeton, but his lawyers persuaded him it wasn't worth a court fight. I was sixteen at the time it came onstream; Edward took me out of school so I could be there. Everything at Metargon grew out of that afternoon."

The young man who'd escorted me to Terry Utas came in through a side door with a tray. The coffee surprised me: it was creamy and rich. Breen nodded approval at my enjoyment.

"Yes, yes, I see you have a good palate. Adam, tell Terry we'll need about twenty minutes without interruptions."

He waited until the door had shut again before adding, "Now, let's hope you have an equally good investigator's palate. Tell me what you know about Martin Binder."

I rolled Breen's words and the sideways glance from under his thick-knit brows around on my investigator's taste buds. I saw no reason to lie, especially since I knew so very little. I repeated my shopworn tale of Martin's mother's flight, the visit to his grandmother, the fact that he was a loner and that no one had heard from him.

"Ms. Utas told me you learned about his disappearance from your daughter," I added. "Not from Jari Liu."

"Yes, yes, I talked to Jari about that; he's a brilliant engineer, but sometimes brilliant engineers can't put two and two together. My daughter, Alison, was part of the college crew that worked at the lab this summer, so she got the e-mail Jari sent out after he saw you on Tuesday. She called me this morning, very concerned, as well she should have been."

He paused, shaking his head, his daughter's behavior still troubling him. "Jari said he showed you a demo of the system that young Binder was working on, right? We don't let anyone take code out of the building. We also monitor outgoing messages to intercept anything they might be uploading from our systems, but Binder is an odd young man, a kind of idiot savant in some ways. He could have memorized, oh, not a million lines of code, but the broad outlines of the system. It's far better than anything else being done in that arena, even at Israel's Weizmann Institute. It would be worth a lot to any number of competitors, in and out of the defense industry."

"I assume you do a background check on anyone you let into your lab," I said.

"Of course, but we overlooked some things about Binder."

"Like what?" I drank some more coffee; tone casual, puzzled, a mistake always to betray eagerness.

"We knew he lived with his grandparents but we didn't realize his mother was an addict. We also didn't realize he'd wanted to go to college but his family vetoed it: we thought he was one of the computer cowboys. You often find them in this business—they're self-taught, uninterested in formal education. According to Liu, Martin had a chip on his shoulder with the kids from the Ivies who worked on the Fitora project with him. If he sold our system, he could afford to spend the rest of his life taking classes at Caltech or MIT. The thing that alarms me is that he's gone dark."

I shook my head.

"Binder unplugged himself from the Net and from cellular systems." Breen's tone was impatient: my palate was proving mediocre. "He canceled all his ISP connections, he isn't sending or receiving e-mail or texts, at least not under any address that Jari's team can find, and they are skilled hunters. That's what's making me fear he could be re-creating my system for another company, or even another government."

So Jari Liu hadn't been spinning me around by giving me the wrong details for Martin, as I'd feared.

"I've never met Martin, so I can't give you an opinion," I said. "Everyone I've met agrees he's both brilliant and a bit awkward socially, but that doesn't tell me whether he's poised to become another Unabomber, or another Feynman."

Breen made a sour face. "Sunny—Alison—thinks he'll be a second Feynman. Jari says he'd be astonished if Binder was selling our secrets, but frankly, after almost fifty years in this business, I've seen even the most socially balanced people sell out their companies if the stack of cash in front of them is high enough. What bothers me as much as anything is that Alison let him into our home."

"They weren't dating, were they?" That surprised me—I pictured Breen's daughter as too sleek and sophisticated to be attracted to an awkward nerd. I remembered Nadja Hahne's description of Martin—

those brooding good looks, his aloofness—perhaps a sleek and sophisticated young woman would see that as a challenge.

Breen paused. "Alison seems to have some romantic ideas about Binder, as if he might be a Horatio Alger hero. While my wife and I were at our place in Bar Harbor, Alison held a picnic for all the fellows in the summer program. She included Martin, even though he wasn't one of the college crew, because he was their age, worked on the same project. And she felt she could do something for him."

He made a face that was part sour, part proud. "I love my girl, but she's always been the kind that brings stray kittens home with her. Anyway, she let the kids explore my dad's workshop. Edward used to do a lot of his drawings or build his prototypes in his third-floor workroom; he liked the view of Lake Michigan. Sunny let Martin and the others wander around in there. No telling what he might have made off with."

The first sour taste on my palate. "I would imagine all your father's inventions would be here, in the Metargon labs, not lying around the house for your daughter's stray friends to pick up." I poured more coffee and leaned back in the chair to look at him over the cup rim.

"Yes, yes," Breen said. "You're right, up to a point."

He fidgeted with his own cup, then said, "My father was involved in some top-secret work after the war. Defense work, you understand. He was proud of his signed letters from presidents and Nobel Prize winners. He also had things on his desk that ought to be in a vault.

"I never got around to putting them away after he died; frankly, I never thought about them; they were just part of the background of my life. It was only when Alison told me she'd let the kids explore the workroom that I remembered the letters. Metargon's code, coupled with any of those letters—well, just say that my father played a part in thermonuclear weapons development, and you'll see that it would be better that we didn't let outsiders read some of those letters."

"Without seeing them, I can't judge, but surely all that history is in the public domain by now," I said.

"Not all of it," Breen said sharply. "That's my point."

I didn't believe him: there was something in his father's workshop that he was ashamed of an outsider seeing, but I didn't have any hunch of how to probe for it. I changed the subject.

"Your father knew Benjamin Dzornen, didn't he?"

"How did you know that?" Breen sat up straight, his voice still sharp.

I widened my eyes, naive detective. "You said he liked to display his signed letters from Nobel laureates. Dzornen worked on the Manhattan Project; your father did defense work. It's not a stretch."

Breen relaxed again. I obviously hadn't found the danger spot.

Something didn't add up, Martin had said. Had he seen a letter in Edward Breen's old workshop that told him something about his family history? Or that suggested my own theory about the stolen Nobel Prize?

Breen and I spoke, or fenced, a little longer; we were both feeling rumpled when I got up to leave.

"Martin left his home to talk to someone the morning he disappeared. Was that your daughter?"

"Unlikely," Breen said. "She flew out to Mexico City right after the summer fellows left. She's been there almost six weeks now."

"Mexico City?" I echoed. "What, is she doing a junior year abroad?"

"It's a gap year, or semester," Breen said sourly. "She's helping build a tech lab for some high schools in Mexico City. Metargon is supplying computers and Metar-Genie game boxes. It's all well and good to want 'to give back to the community,' but not when you're an heiress who's connected to a firm like Metargon. You don't go to kidnap central. Her mother and I couldn't talk her out of it, though."

"Any chance Martin is down there with her?" I asked.

That did startle Cordell. He started to rap out a denial, but then he sat back, fingers steepled together.

"Someone is supposed to be keeping an eye on her for me, but I suppose Alison could have worked her way around that; she has a trust fund. I'm going to get the FBI to start hunting Martin. If he is in Mexico with my girl, they'll sort that out pretty fast. In the meantime, if you get any whiff of where he is, I want to know at once."

"Are you proposing to hire me, Mr. Breen?" I asked. "If you become my client, I'll certainly report my findings to you—as long as working for you doesn't conflict with my existing client."

He paused again, then gave a smile that must have opened a lot of cookie jars for him. "Yes, yes, I see your point. I doubt a solo operator who doesn't have great computer skills can track down a computer-savvy guy like Martin, but if you do, I would be prepared to offer a, well, call it a reward. A reward for knowing where he is."

"I'll think about it." I got up. "As I said, I can tell you nothing without my client's permission, but with that proviso, I'll let you know when I've located Martin. Assuming the Feds don't shoot him, or anything drastic like that."

Breen thought that was amusing enough to tell me I had a good investigative palate, after all, but we both knew he thought I had as much chance of finding Martin as I did of explaining relativistic models of matrix theory to a kennel of Chihuahuas.

17

V.I. CAN'T TURN TRICKS

I PASSED A FOREST PRESERVE on my way to the expressway and pulled into it. The trees were starting to turn; despite the continued warm days, summer was over. Ahead lay Chicago's winter roulette: last year's mild one or the previous year's endless snow and bitter cold?

Sitting in my car, watching the squirrels and birds without really seeing them, I tried to parse my conversation with Cordell Breen.

Martin Binder had gone dark. Breen thought that was to keep anyone from finding where he'd absconded with Metargon's precious code. Call that possibility A. I started to type it into my iPad, then thought of Breen's boast about Metargon's hacking skills. If Breen believed I knew where Martin was, he'd sic Liu on my computer.

I pulled a pen and a legal pad from my briefcase—change is good, but old-fashioned ways still have merit. Possibility A: Martin Binder was in Shanghai or Tehran, or even Tel Aviv, reconstructing a million or two lines of the code that allowed Princess Fitora to fight off five attackers.

Liu had touted the system as a breakthrough for people with stroke or spinal cord damage. Breen had suggested the project had defense applications. I tried to imagine what those might be.

My mother had hated guns and weapons of all kinds. My father's service weapon had to be locked each night in a high cupboard, away from my cousin Boom-Boom's enterprising fingers. No toy weapons could be used in our yard or house, but Boom-Boom would grab a doughnut and fit it in his hand like a gun. Humans can turn anything into weapons.

If Metargon was a world leader in computer design and applications, they could easily design a cyberwar virus; perhaps that was what really lay behind blinking at Princess Fitora's sword-arm.

Which led me to possibility B: far from trying to sell Metargon's code to the Chinese, Martin had realized he was actually helping design a cyberwar system, some kind of advanced Stuxnet worm. He had vanished until he could come up with a WikiLeaks style of publicizing what the company was doing.

Martin was at that age, the cusp of adulthood, where idealism runs strong. Someone like him, who didn't have friends to give him ballast, might go in any direction—join a jihad or the Peace Corps, or drop out of sight in a monastery.

I'd been alone in the parking area, sitting so still that rabbits were hopping close to my car. I know they destroy gardens, but their soft brown fur and dark liquid eyes make them seem innocent, helpless.

"What do you think?" I asked through my window. "Unabomber or ultra-idealist?"

They didn't stop nibbling. I was overlooking something obvious, they seemed to be telling me.

A third possibility lay in whatever Martin had seen in old Edward Breen's workshop. It had to do with Benjamin Dzornen, because that was what had made Cordell Breen tense up. But if it was something shameful, Edward wouldn't have put it up on the wall. Or he had pulled a fast one on Dzornen; Dzornen had written in protest and Edward framed the letter to remind himself that even if he didn't have that beautiful gold medallion, he was smarter than a Nobel laureate.

If I could find Alison, would she tell me whether something in the workshop had upset Martin? There were only twenty million or so people in Mexico City; it shouldn't be too hard to locate her.

I drummed my fingers on my steering wheel. I needed to know whom Martin had gone to see right before he vanished. It couldn't have been Cordell because Cordell was in Bar Harbor. It might have been Jari Liu; Liu could have put on a good show of feigned astonishment or worry when I saw him at the lab three days ago.

I was certain Martin had tried to contact Julius and Herta Dzornen, but I had no way of knowing if it was before or after he'd been to the Breen mansion. He could have been wanting them to admit their father was also his great-grandfather, and that they needed to fork over Dzornen's prize money. The King of Sweden gives you a million or so dollars; if Dzornen had invested it wisely there should have been a substantial inheritance. Not, of course, judging by Julius Dzornen's coach house.

I drew some rabbit ears and whiskers on my legal pad. Lotty thought Dzornen must have paid whatever fees and bribes it took to get Kitty Binder out of Vienna in 1939. That meant he acknowledged her paternity and his children knew it. But so what? They wouldn't have done away with Martin. Unless Martin had proof that the prize was bogus. I was going around in circles.

Whatever awful secret Martin saw in Edward Breen's old workshop couldn't have been a blatant statement from Dzornen that he'd faked his research. That was a big "if," anyway. It also couldn't have been a photo of Dzornen's wife shooting Kitty, since Kitty was still alive. Or she'd shot and only hit an arm or a leg. *Basta*, Vic! I admonished myself. No wild fancies here!

Edward Breen worked with all those Nazi rocket scientists after the war. Pre-war physics was a small world; even Nazi physicists would have known Dzornen; that photo from the Radium Institute in Vienna showed him and Martina, with Norwegian and German scientists. Those Nazi rocketeers Edward Breen helped bring into the States, they would have known Martina, too. I could imagine the gossip. *Oh, Dzornen, he saved his skin but he sacrificed his student. Yes, she died doing slave labor for our rocket program.* And then Breen rubbing Dzornen's face in it.

I tried to picture young Martin seeing a letter about his great-grandmother. Is that what hadn't added up for him? Nothing to do with his work at Metargon, only the nagging questions about his family?

In that case, maybe he'd trundled downstate to the meth house where his mother was pretending to be in rehab. Look, Mom, we could blackmail the Dzornen family, after all. Not over Dzornen's research, but over their paternity. Her drug pals liked the idea of easy money; they started blackmailing Herta Dzornen, and she sicced some thugs on them.

I flung my pen onto the seat in disgust. Speculation, speculation, with no knowledge of anything, including Martin Binder's character.

The rabbits fled into the underbrush, but not because of me. A gray-haired woman had roared into the area, driving my dream car, a red Jaguar XJ12. She let a pale-gold retriever out of the back; the two of them headed for a creek that runs through the woods. That's what I should be doing, making enough money to spend my days driving my dogs around in Jaguars, not second-guessing someone who understood relativistic principles.

I, too, fled the park. Not for the shrubbery, but for Skokie. I rang Kitty Binder's doorbell with an aggressive finger. After five minutes, I saw the front window blinds part the width of her fingers. Time passed. I rang again, and finally she opened the door the width of the chain bolt.

"Ms. Binder, has your daughter been here?" I asked, before she could speak. "I found the place where she'd been staying on the West Side of Chicago. When I went there, her pals shot at me. Maybe you saw the story on the news—one of her old friends was arrested, another seems to be badly injured. Judy is pretty toxic right now. If you've heard from her, or she's here, this would be a very good time to call the police."

She stared at me through the crack in the door, her face frozen in a stew of uneasy emotions: fear, anger, misery. "I told you, no police. The police come and I get killed."

"Is Judy here?" I said. "Or one of her friends? Have they threatened you? If you let me in, I can help."

"I don't want you in my house again," she said harshly.

"Martin," I said, desperately trying to keep the conversation alive. "He's cut off all communications with the world. His boss at Metargon said they haven't been able to find any ISP—Internet service—addresses he may be using. I talked to Herta and Julius Dzornen yesterday. Martin went to see them but they won't tell me why. Do you know?"

At that, anger blazed uppermost in her. "Those vermin! Worse than rats or cockroaches, lying, stealing—!"

"What did they lie to you about?" I asked.

"They know, but they pretend that they don't. It's been the same story for more than seventy years now."

"They know what? That Benjamin was your father as well as theirs?"

She turned her head to one side, to hide the tears that had started to well. I was not supposed to see her as weak. "My father, my real father, was a builder. I told you that before."

"Then why did you go to see Benjamin Dzornen when you got to Chicago?" I asked.

Her mouth worked. "My mother. That's what I wanted to talk to him about. He had been her professor, she revered him. Not me, not her child, I was never important to her. Only those invisible particles she spent day and night with. She saw atoms, but she couldn't see me. Even the last time we were alone, up in the mountains right before Germany took over Austria, she didn't care when I tried to show her how I could dance. She wanted me to look at pictures of something invisible in the atmosphere!"

"That must have been very hard." I spoke with sincerity: for mothers, balancing between domestic duties and private passions is harder than standing on one toe on the point of a pin. It's impossible to do it perfectly, but some women get it more wrong than others.

"My grandmother raised me," Kitty said fiercely. "She was tough but she cared about me. She made my mother beg for the money so that I could go to London with Charlotte and her brother. And then my grandmother was killed. Phfft, like that! First off to Terezín, then off to Sobibor, then—no record but most likely dead. I found all this out when I went back to Vienna as an interpreter in 1952."

"Your mother begged the money to send you to London?" I interrupted. "She got it from Professor Dzornen, didn't she?"

Kitty stared at me as if I had wizarding powers. "He said never to tell. He told me when I saw him here, in Chicago, but he made me promise to say nothing to nobody. Anybody. How did you know? Did that smug witch Herta tell you?"

I smiled sadly. "It was a lucky guess. The war hadn't started, your mother could still get mail from America."

"If you talked about me to Herta, I will fire you at this minute. They were a thousand times more stuck-up than the Herschels. Those Dzornens, to them I was always the seamstress's granddaughter. When Herta and Bettina were left alone with me, I was supposed to run their errands. They expected me to do up their hair or deliver their little love notes to the stupid boys they dated. They even thought I should clean their shoes, so I threw those into the cesspool."

"I didn't discuss you with Ms. Colonna," I said. "What did Benjamin Dzornen tell you when you went to the physics department back in 1956?" I asked. "That Martina was dead?"

She stared at me. "You think you can trick me, Miss Detective? You can't. All that chapter in my life is finished, I never discuss it. I never talked about the great professor paying my fare to London, you tricked that out of me. For the rest, if anyone asks you, the police, Princess Charlotte Herschel, the FBI, anyone, you can tell them I never discuss it."

I had been bending over with my ear to the door to hear her. I was getting a crick in my neck, but there was no way she'd open the door for me, as angry as she was now.

"But Judy did discuss it, didn't she," I said.

"Judy is crazy, I thought you knew that already. There's no telling what she might do."

"And Martin?"

"Don't start telling me lies about Martin. He would never talk to those Dzornens, not for any reason, so stop trying to spread muck on him."

"If I'm going to find him, I need a good photograph," I said, pretending I hadn't heard her. "Something I can show to people who might have met him. Can you get me a good shot of him?"

"Do you listen to anything I say?" she hissed. "You and your detecting, you're as bad as Martina and her atoms! Leave me alone, leave Martin alone. If you want to go into drug houses with Judy, you're welcome to them!" She slammed the door.

Did this mean I was fired? It certainly meant I wasn't going to be paid. A smart woman would have walked away from the whole mess then and there.

18

DIARY OF A COLD WARRIOR

B ACK IN MY OFFICE I had a message from Doug Kossel, the Palfry County
sheriff. After my conversation with Kitty Binder, I expected the
worst, that he had found Martin's body in the cesspit behind the meth
house.

"Warshawski!" He sounded unnecessarily energetic for the end of a
workday. "You big-city gals know how to act. Your police buddy, what's
his name"—there was a pause while he wrestled with paper—"here it
is, Downey. He called to talk to me about Schlafly, who definitely did
not make a good scarecrow. When I told the Wengers—they farm that
cornfield—what the body looked like, even Frank Wenger turned
green around the gills. I'm not sure but what he'll leave that little bit of
corn where you found Ricky Schlafly go this year."

He laughed so merrily that my eardrums vibrated. "Anyway,
Downey told me you created a situation in Chicago, neutralized one
bad boy and got two others arrested. What do you do on your day off?"

"Pitch short relief for the Cubs," I said, halfheartedly entering into
the spirit of the conversation. I regretted it when Kossel erupted in
another ear-shattering laugh.

"Did your guys look at that pit behind the house?" I asked.

"Couldn't find anyone who wanted to gear up and wade into it," he
said. "But we raked through it. No bodies, just a lot of empty ether
cans and etcetera."

And etcetera? Maybe that was an expression unique to Palfry County. "What does Lieutenant Downey reckon?" I asked. "Do you two think that Freddie Walker killed Schlafly?"

"Not likely. We hoped it could be a falling-out of thieves, but Walker was on his way back from Mexico at the time our ME says Schlafly was shot. Not that Walker wanted to tell us where he'd been, but when he saw it was that or a murder rap, he produced the manifest that showed him on a private plane leaving Juárez at four that same morning. Our ME says the deed was did by six A.M. at the latest, and likely earlier. Kind of hard to tell with the birds pecking out his pecker."

I held the phone from my ear just in time to avoid another hearty guffaw. Maybe Kossel was a psychopath who had shot Ricky Schlafly himself and now was enjoying jokes about the dead man's organs. Pecked his pecker, kayoed his kidneys, beaked his brains. Or the sheriff was merely one of those nerveless people who can fly bombing missions.

"Of course, it could have been one of Walker's boys doing the deed on his behalf. Your lieutenant will look into that; could be the guy whose brains you beat out. Pity, in a way; can't get a confession out of a man who can't talk."

I was tired of explaining how I'd come to knock "Bullet" Bultman down the stairs. Let Murray and the Palfry County sheriff imagine I'd carefully executed a move that got Bultman's head to hit on the edge of a stair. Maybe it would make the next punk more hesitant to act when he saw me. Or the next punk would be so freaked he'd shoot me on sight.

I missed a couple of lines from Kossel, but heard his sign-off line: "We'll be sending you a subpoena for the inquest, Warshawski, so don't you go too far away."

"I love you, too," I said, but he'd already hung up.

I looked at my notes. Freddie Walker had been in Mexico;

Metargon heiress Alison Breen was down there helping set up a computer lab. Mexico was a big country, but could they have met? Could she be a spoiled rich drug user? She wouldn't be the first young person whose parents didn't know she had a habit.

I called Jari Liu at Metargon. I started to tell him I'd met his boss earlier in the afternoon, but he already knew.

"Cordell told me to give you any help you need; we're very anxious to locate young Martin."

That made it easy: I wanted a photo, and I was sure they had a good head shot, given the way he'd quickly added my face to his database. Liu said it would be in my in box by the time I hung up.

"Anything else?" he asked.

"A crystal ball," I said. "Someone who understands Martin Binder's personality. Mr. Breen thinks he could be reconstructing your Princess Fitora code for the Chinese, or just for Microsoft or Apple."

"Yeah, I know," Liu said sourly. "He chewed my ass pretty hard for not telling him myself that Martin had vanished. It's so commonplace for cowboy programmers to leave without warning that I didn't think I needed to do anything more than report it to HR and my own department head. I'm supposed to have guessed if Martin was missing that there was a danger he was selling our secrets to the highest bidder."

"You think that's a real possibility?" I asked.

"Money didn't seem important to Martin, but he might be motivated by revenge. Not against Metargon per se, we had a good rap, or I thought we did, but he might want to show the richer, cooler kids that he could grab the spotlight in ways that would be beyond them."

"You think he could rebuild your code?"

"There's a story about Mozart my old man told me, when he thought I could be another Yo-Yo Ma," Liu said. "It was a big disappointment when I had a tin ear. Anyway, Mozart, the boy genius, is sitting in the Vatican chapel listening to a mass. The music is jealously guarded: only Vatican musicians get to see the score. Mozart hears it once, goes home, writes out the score."

"Even if Martin has that kind of mind where he lays it all out in his head and sees it, Mr. Breen said it would be millions of lines of code," I objected.

"We only let people work on a few aspects of a program to avoid the temptation to share it with a bigger world. But with someone like Martin, if he mastered the underlying architecture, he wouldn't need the whole code to reconstruct a big piece of the program. That's what Cordell is worried about, but nothing on any of our nerve endings suggests that a third party has seen the code."

"You'd have heard?"

"High-end computing is like any high-stakes game. People are always spying on each other, trying to figure out or steal what the competition is doing. We don't always hear everything, but especially after talking to Cordell this morning, we're very much on the watch for it and nothing is bubbling up."

I saw that I'd added some razor-edged teeth to my earlier cartoon of a rabbit. Bugs Bunny's evil twin, ready to eviscerate someone's viscera. "Mr. Breen says that Princess Fitora has defense applications."

Liu sucked in a breath. "If the old man is going to talk out of school, he has a heck of a nerve—never mind, forgot what I was about to say."

"To chew you out for dropping the ball on Martin's disappearance," I finished for him. "He told me his daughter is in Mexico; a drug dealer who's connected to my inquiries was down there four days ago. Did you see any signs that Alison might be—"

"Drugs? Alison? No way. And don't you dare suggest that to Cordell—you'd be in court so fast your body would be a mile behind your feet. What's Martin's connection to drugs?"

"I didn't say he was connected to drugs; I said that there's a dealer connected to my inquiry into him. No one is telling me anything, Mr. Liu; I have to ask whatever questions I can to get a handle on this investigation, even if they annoy you or Mr. Breen."

"If you have any evidence that Martin is a drug user—"

"You're sure that Alison Breen doesn't do drugs, but after spending almost two years as Martin Binder's supervisor, you don't know whether he does? Something isn't computing here."

Liu paused, then said stiffly, "I'm sure Martin never came to work high, but he's a very guarded young man. He could conceal a drug problem pretty easily."

"You're a bright computer wizard, Mr. Liu, but you're also a skilled corporate ball player. I'm sure as soon as we're done, you'll be shooting an e-mail to Cordell Breen, suggesting he alert the FBI to Martin's possible habit."

I added a machine gun to my razor-toothed rabbit. "If it turns out you've slandered Martin, I won't threaten to take you to court so fast your clothes will leave your body, but I might find another way of reminding you that everyone in this country has a right to privacy. And a right to be thought innocent until proven guilty. We may wake up tomorrow to find the Bill of Rights applies only to the one percent, but until that happens, Martin gets the same benefit of the doubt as Alison."

"You're right, of course," Liu said quietly. "I'm sorry, but I've known Alison since she was twelve. I only met Martin two years ago. Of course I'm biased, more by my long relationship with her than by her family's money."

I sort of apologized—I didn't trust his judgment about Alison any more than I did about Martin, but I couldn't afford to cut off communication lines to Metargon. When he hung up, I clicked on my e-mail. Sure enough, Liu had sent me a head shot, in which Martin looked sober, even anxious. His face had matured but he hadn't filled out much from the skinny kid at the science fair with his grandfather. Jari Liu had included a second, informal shot of Martin demonstrating something to his other team members. With his high cheekbones and dark curly hair, he looked exotic, like a Cossack, perhaps, certainly erotically appealing. Maybe Alison Breen had tucked him into her suitcase and carried him to Mexico City with her.

I printed out a dozen copies of both pictures. I'd start tomorrow at the commuter bus stop near Martin's home, go to the Skokie Swift, see what else I could see.

I turned my attention back to Darraugh Graham's assignment. I was in the middle of a complicated conversation with a uranium mine manager when Jeanine Susskind called on my other line. Martin Binder's friend's mother, I remembered, missing a couple of sentences from my Canadian contact.

I called Jeanine back as soon as I finished with the miner.

"We found that book that Martin gave Voss to return; you wanted to know the title—it was *The Secret Diary of a Cold War Conscientious Objector: Arnold Zachny and the American View*. We owed five dollars in fines on it and they tried to make me pay for the damage that Martin had done to the book. Never have a teenager, Ms. Warshawski."

I could safely promise everyone that there was little likelihood of my taking on that particular challenge. When Jeanine hung up, I looked up the title. I could see why Voss had found the cover startling; it showed the Statue of Liberty, her mouth taped shut and a hammer and sickle plunged into her heart.

I dimly remembered the *American View*, one of the few national publications produced in Chicago. Like *The Atlantic*, it had been a monthly with a mildly liberal opinion page, publishing short fiction and essays on people or current events. My parents didn't subscribe to magazines, but I used to read the *View* sometimes in the law school library when I was working on my JD.

The Chicago Public Library had a copy of *The Secret Diary* at their main branch. I was meeting Max and Lotty for dinner at the Pottawattamie Club downtown—Lotty had asked Max to see if any of his old refugee networks had any information on Martina Saginor—so it was easy to stop at the library on my way.

Since I found myself at the club before Max and Lotty, I sat in the reception area, thumbing through the book, looking for what had interested Martin in it. *The Secret Diary* wasn't as much a biography of Arnold Zachny as a history of the *View* against the background of the Cold War. Zachny had been an early supporter of disarmament; he published a collection of letters from Japanese women on the damage that radioactive fallout had done to their husbands and sons caught in the Pacific when the U.S. exploded hydrogen bombs in the Marshall Islands.

As I flipped through the pages, a familiar name jumped out at me.

One of the most curious incidents in the history of the View *was its publication of a letter from a woman named Gertrud Memler. Memler had been a high-ranking Nazi engineer brought to the United States in the great Russian-American talent grab at the end of the Second World War. She was a controversial figure: she was the highest-ranking woman employed by the Germans in their nuclear weapons work. In fact, although hard evidence is difficult to find, as a member of the Uranverein (Uranium Club), she was probably in charge of the reactor program near Innsbruck.*

When Memler came to the States after the war, she was assigned to projects at the Nevada Proving Grounds under the aegis of the Nobel Laureate Benjamin Dzornen. She disappeared in 1953 and was never seen again. However, from time to time, she would write letters to learned journals or to newspapers. These letters were vehemently anti-nuclear in content. Her about-face, from Innsbruck overseer to anti-nuclear activist, was extraordinary.

The FBI tried unsuccessfully to trace her, since she was privy to U.S. nuclear secrets. She may have defected to the Soviet Union; one of their embassy attachés could have posted letters for her. A letter that Memler wrote to the View *and the FBI's response show their futile efforts to track her down.*

May 1962
To Arnold Zachny
Editor
American View

Re: Edward Teller and *The Danger of Fallout*

Dr. Teller is widely known as the "Father of the Hydrogen Bomb." In his recent essay in your magazine, he assures us, as a good father should, that his child poses no threat to the well-being of other children on this planet. He writes that radioactive fallout from nuclear tests is no more dangerous to our long-term health than being a few ounces overweight. The fear of radiation is irrational, Dr. Teller concludes, and has led Americans to the dangerous place of ending the thousands of tests of hydrogen and atom bombs that we have detonated on the ground, on the sea and in the air.

Like many parents whose children behave mischievously, Dr. Teller has either been too busy or too blind to see what damage his little darling is doing. Perhaps all the time he spends in Washington, fighting to continue nuclear testing, means he hasn't had time to go to the Nevada Proving Grounds to see the impact of his child on human and animal life.

I, to my sorrow, spent some time in these proving grounds. This is what I saw: it was routine for the United States Army to expose its soldiers to bombs being detonated less than a mile away. They were given no protective gear, not even sunglasses, just told to put their hands over their ears and stand with their backs to the blast.

It was routine for the United States Navy to put pigs, sheep, and dogs, chained in cages, at Ground Zero of these tests. Animals at Ground Zero are obliterated. Those chained in cages further away come back to U.S. Navy labs with the skin ulcerated and peeling from their bodies.

The data on the health of humans, both soldiers and civilians, exposed to this much radiation is a secret jealously guarded by our government, but I saw the burns on their skin myself. If Hiroshima and Nagasaki did not give us enough data on the high (60 percent) probability of developing bone or blood cancers for survivors of an atomic bomb, one test at Nevada should have told us all we need to know about Dr. Teller's baby's tremendous destructive power.

The first time we slaughtered dogs should have been the last. They were guilty of no crime except their inexplicable love for humans, which let them follow us into cages where they were left to die in terrible fear. But we could not stop with one test, we continued to do many hundred others, with dogs, sheep, pigs, whose screams will follow me to my grave, as much as the screams of prisoners at the Uranverein weapons and reactor plant.

Civilians as far as 135 miles away have begun developing terrible cancers in numbers disproportionate to their population. We see this, but we continue to build bigger bombs, enough now to obliterate the entire human race many times over.

If I had produced a child this dangerous, I would not go around the world bragging about being its father.

Sincerely

Gertrud Memler, Ph.D., Physics

July 16, 1962

Telegram from: Cal Hooper
Special Agent in Charge
Washington
To: Agent Luke Erlichman
Chicago Office
Federal Bureau of Investigation

Luke: How in hell did a letter get published in a national magazine about animal testing at the Nevada Proving Grounds? And who the fuck is Gertrud Memler? Congress has received thousands of letters demanding hearings, or an end to using animals in nuclear tests and we're catching heat. Even RFK is demanding to know who this Memler is and whether she's a reliable source.

Find out soonest how this leak happened. The Boss is not happy.

Cal

July 28, 1962

Letter from:
Agent Luke Erlichman
Chicago Office
Federal Bureau of Investigation
To: Cal Hooper
Special Agent in Charge
Washington

Cal: Magazine produced letter and envelope for Gertrud Memler, return address in Ft. George, Utah. Dispatched agent Titheredge to find and silence her, but no record of a Gertrud Memler in any phone books, churches, etc. The return address was a local cemetery.

Looked up Memler in our files. An Austrian scientist by that name entered the country in 1946, was assigned to weapons and rocket development at Nevada

```
because of WW II experience with German proto-atomic
bomb work. Find nothing in her file after 1953. Was
she civilian-relocated? Did she marry?
```

The Secret Diary included a long passage from Arnold Zachny's diary, where he wrote about the day the FBI came in to seize his files and to order him never to print any letters he received from Memler. The passage ended with a photocopy of another telegram between FBI agents in Chicago and Washington.

```
August 2, 1962
Private letter from Cal Hooper
Washington, DC
Luke Erlichman
6937 S. South Shore Drive
Chicago

Cal, for your own good as well as mine, do your fuck-
ing damnedest to find Memler. From now on, set up a
mail intercept for both American View and Zachny's
home correspondence. Can't have a loose cannon pub-
lishing secret signals to Uncle Nicky* on our watch.
```

My librarian at the University of Chicago had identified Gertrud Memler as one of the women sitting around the pod in the old photo I'd found in Palfry. Memler worked with Martina Saginor and Benjamin Dzornen, both of whom were Jews. Then she'd become a Nazi, overseeing a weapons lab, and had ended her life in the United States, a deeply and skillfully hidden anti-nuclear activist. If she was still alive, she'd be at least a hundred, probably more, so it was a safe bet she'd made it to her grave without FBI detection.

If Martin was hunting for a connection between Dzornen and his

---

*Nikita Khrushchev.

great-grandmother, he would have tried to find Memler. Had he seen something at the Breen house that made him think he could find Memler where the FBI had failed?

I was so lost in thought that I gave a strangled cry when Max tapped me on the shoulder. Lotty was with him; we exchanged the usual greetings and went into the private dining room Max had reserved.

When I'd gone through the different scenarios I was imagining, Max groaned and clutched his head. "Victoria, you're making me dizzy. Is Martin murdering drug dealers who got his mother in trouble? Is he avenging his great-grandmother for having her work stolen? Or is he selling secrets to the Chinese or the Israelis or perhaps Google? No wonder you can't make any headway. You need to pick one path and follow it."

"Yeah, if I could get a single reliable fact out of anyone I would," I snapped. "I have two facts, call it three. After going to a barbecue at the home of Metargon's owner, Martin announced that something didn't add up. His high school physics teacher says he said that when either his answer, or the problem itself, seemed wrong. He stayed at work for few weeks after the barbecue, then he disappeared, giving a book on Gertrud Memler and the Cold War to a neighbor kid to take back to the library. The other fact is that his mother's on the lam. She's run from two drug houses and has also disappeared. Are the drugs and the Cold War connected? Are he and his mother connected?"

A waiter was hovering; Max interrupted me long enough to put in our dinner orders.

"My semi-fact is that Martin went to see Benjamin Dzornen's two surviving legitimate children. To top it all off, this afternoon Kitty all but fired me. I can't keep up an expensive search if she's fired me, but I can't leave Martin to hang out to dry, either. Just in case it's drug dealers he's messing with, not century-old missing scientists."

I showed him and Lotty the passage about Gertrud Memler that I'd just been reading. "You said you might be able to work some of your old refugee networks. Is there any way you could track down the Memler woman?"

Max rolled his eyes. "When Lotty talked to me, I was thinking more of Martina in Vienna, seeing where she might have gone when the Innsbruck facility was shut down. None of my networks is better than the FBI, believe me."

"Okay. Find out what happened to Martina. That might bring some comfort to Kitty, anyway."

My phone rang as he started to ask for more details. I looked at the screen. "Kitty Binder," I mouthed, and turned away from the table to take the call.

"Is this the detective?" she demanded, without preamble. "They're stalking me again."

"Who is, Ms. Binder?"

"The people who always do. I want you to come over."

"I'm almost an hour away, Ms. Binder: it's best if you dial 911."

"Don't you understand?" she screeched. "The police are the problem. You keep saying you want to help. I need your help now." She hung up.

"Käthe is paranoid," Lotty said when I repeated the conversation. "I keep telling you that. If she won't call the police, you must do so yourself."

"You know what the guy says in *Catch-22*: just because you're paranoid doesn't mean they aren't following you. Someone killed Judy Binder's housemate five days ago; if they think Judy's gone back to her mother, then Kitty is in real trouble."

"All the more reason to phone the police!" Lotty said.

"She thinks they're part of the problem." I got to my feet.

"The problem they're part of is her paranoia," Lotty cried. "I told you that earlier, this has been her song and dance since she arrived in this country, that the police or the FBI were stalking her."

"Lotty, this is how I get to where you become furious with me. I can call the police, but I can't leave her quaking in terror behind those dead bolts."

Lotty's eyes were filled with pain. "I do understand that, Victoria. But can't you take five minutes to ask if there is a better way, an easier way, to solve the problem?"

My own face contorted in lines of misery, but I left the club. Half a dozen times on the road, I started to dial 911 and stopped. Kitty Binder was paranoid. There was nothing to be lost in calling in the pros, except any fragile confidence she might be feeling in me.

19

BLEEDING OUT

WHEN I PULLED UP in front of the Binder house, lights were on in the basement and the top floor but not the ground level. I took the flashlight out of my car and went up the walk to the front door. It was shut and locked. I leaned on the bell but didn't get an answer.

I didn't like this. This afternoon, she'd parted the living room blinds, and that was when she wasn't expecting me.

I ran to the back of the house. The kitchen door was swinging on its hinges. I took the extra seconds to call 911. *Home invasion on Kedvale in Skokie,* I reported.

"The Binder residence?" the dispatcher said. "We just sent a squad car past and they didn't see anything."

"Back door," I said. "It's been forced open."

The dispatcher promised to send another car, but her tone lacked enthusiasm. I didn't have my gun, but I didn't want to wait for the posse. I made myself as small a target as possible and edged into the kitchen. Crouching, I fumbled for light switches, slipped on something and fell. I turned on my flashlight. All the books and papers that had been stacked on the kitchen table were strewn across the floor; I'd slipped on a loose sheet of paper.

I found the light switch and started calling Kitty's name. No one was on the ground floor, but in the front room the lace had been ripped apart, the little knickknacks smashed. In the bedrooms on the upper floor, the same savage hands had undone the bedding, slit the mattresses, upended the bureau drawers.

I stumbled back down the stairs, to the basement, to Martin's suite. Kitty lay on the floor, next to her grandson's bed. She'd been beaten about the neck and arms; her head was bleeding heavily.

Her eyes fluttered open when she felt my fingers on her neck. *"Oma?"* she whispered. *"Oma?"*

"It's the detective, Ms. Binder," I said gently. "Hold on; I'm calling an ambulance."

I kept an arm around her while I once more called 911.

"We're sending someone," the dispatcher said, "but it will be a few minutes."

"An ambulance," I snapped. "To the basement. A woman has been badly beaten, she's close to death. Make it happen."

"Oma, wozu das alles?" Kitty whispered.

I turned on the recorder on my phone, still holding her; the German might be important.

Her breathing grew harsher. *"Das war ja alles sinnlos."*

The ambulance came a moment later, but the EMT crew shook their heads grimly; Kitty was already dead. I moved aside as they shifted her body onto the stretcher, but couldn't find the strength to get to my feet. While I sat, head on my knees, I watched blood spool from under the bed. It took me a long instant to realize there was another body under there, but when I finally alerted the crew, they lifted the bed away from the wall.

A scarecrow of a woman lay there, her breath coming in shallow raspy bursts. Her dark curly hair was streaked with gray, her skin dry and flaking. Blood oozed from her abdomen. Judy Binder. Kitty had died protecting her daughter.

20

WHAT DID IT ALL MEAN?

A ROUGH HAND SHOOK my shoulder. "Doll, wake up! Sorry to bust in on you in bed, but here's the doc, worried sick about you."

I woke up slowly, from a great distance. I'd been deep in sleep, back in a scene from my early childhood, when my mother had made cocoa to comfort me after an attack by some neighborhood bullies. Mr. Contreras was staring down at me, his faded brown eyes anxious. When I turned my head on the pillow, I saw Lotty behind him. I shut my eyes, hoping to recapture my mother's face, but it was gone.

I opened my leaden lids again and pushed myself up in the bed, pulling the covers up to my waist so I could sit cross-legged without embarrassing Mr. Contreras.

"Have you come to tell me you were right?" I spoke past Mr. Contreras's shoulder to Lotty. "If I had called the Skokie police, Kitty Binder would still be alive."

Lotty pushed past Mr. Contreras to stand next to me. "I came to make sure you were all right," she said. "It was a long and painful night. I heard about it from Helen Langston at Glenbrook."

"I don't know her," I said. "She must be the one person who didn't interrogate me last night."

I had spent hours with the Skokie police, and then Ferret Downey from the CPD had shown up, wanting his own rundown. Murray Ryerson had picked up the story on his scanner; he'd been waiting by my car when the cops finished with me. He went with me to Glenbrook Hospital to see if they would tell us anything about Judy Binder's condition, but she was still in surgery. In the waiting room there, I recited my lines for the third time. The only good thing about going over my bad decision so often was it started to feel remote, as if I were just reporting a movie plot.

"Helen—Dr. Langston—is the surgeon who repaired Judy's intestines," Lotty said.

"She survived?"

"She had so many drugs in her that they protected her from shock. Cocaine, meth, but mostly oxycodone. The anesthesiologist had a tough job figuring out what he could safely administer." Lotty's mouth flattened in an angry line. "The police talked to Judy when she finally left the recovery room, but she could remember nothing, not who had been in the house, not why they shot her or bludgeoned her mother. All she could do was laugh like a little girl and say, 'Duck and cover, she never believed in duck and cover, but it works, it's the best.'"

"Duck and cover?" Mr. Contreras repeated, bewildered. "Is that a hunting slogan? Is this Judy saying someone was stalking her ma?"

"Judy's conversation is so unfathomable that I'm afraid I stopped trying to understand it many years ago." Lotty produced a bleak smile. "I need to talk to Victoria alone."

I saw the hurt in my neighbor's face and squeezed his hand. "It's okay. It's better if we're alone when she gets what she has to say off her chest. Do you want to wait in the living room?"

"I'll take the dogs out, doll." Mr. Contreras made a gallant effort to maintain his equanimity. "The doc didn't want me bringing 'em upstairs."

When he'd left, Lotty and I stared gravely at each other.

"I should have listened to you," I said. "Anything you want to say about my hotheadedness, or pigheadedness, go ahead: I deserve it."

Lotty sat on the edge of the bed. There were lines in her face I had never noticed; she was getting old, another thing I was powerless to stop.

"After you left the Pottawattamie Club last night, I did call the Skokie police," she said. "They promised to send a car by the house, but when I checked back, they said they hadn't seen anything. Apparently because of Judy, neighbors have called them a number of times over the years, but the family never let them in. Last night, when the police rang the bell and no one answered, they assumed it was another false alarm. I don't know if Judy's life is worth the time and skill and money we're investing in her, but she would be lying there dead next to her mother if you hadn't acted with your usual rash—your usual spiritedness."

"The end justifies my means?" I said, my voice cracking. "I don't know, Lotty. Right now I feel as though I should retreat to a cave above Kabul and eat twigs until I die."

"You would do it for two days, then you would get tired of seeing women assaulted for going to school, or burned for running away from a forced marriage. You'd go out and break open some Taliban heads and then it would get ugly very quickly, I'm afraid," she said with a flash of wry humor.

She played with the fringe on the bedcover. Not like Lotty to be nervous enough to braid and unbraid threads. "Kitty and I were almost the same age, with almost the same history, I told you that. Illegitimate daughters raised by our mothers' parents. My grandparents adored my mother and treated me as another little princess, but Kitty's grandmother, Frau Saginor, had no patience with Martina—her daughter, you know, Martina Saginor. Frau Saginor looked after Kitty, but I don't think she was a warm—"

Lotty interrupted herself, shaking her head. "That isn't what I wanted to say. The truth is, I knew nothing about them. Frau Saginor sewed for my *Oma*, my granny, along with other wealthy families in our quarter. I looked down on Kitty because my *Oma* looked down on Frau Saginor. Probably I brought out the worst in both Kitty and her grandmother.

"Fräulein Martina, that's what we called Frau Saginor's daughter, Fräulein Martina fascinated me. I'm sure it was partly because Kitty and Frau Saginor despised her. But also, Fräulein Martina would show us the wonderful apparatus she built at her Institute. She showed me the way light broke through the prism in my nursery windows, and explained spectral lines and the photoelectric effect to us. Kitty would react almost violently when Martina started talking about experiments with light."

Lotty gave a tight, bitter smile. "If the two were to come into my clinic today, I would tell Martina that her daughter was desperate for the affection and attention Martina was lavishing on prisms and gamma rays, but at eight and nine, I just knew I could outshine Kitty in nature studies, so I was a bit of a show-off, and a bit of a little bitch, grabbing her mother's attention to myself. Still, it was Fräulein Martina who first made me interested in the mysteries of the universe."

Lotty bit her lips, angry with herself. "What I'm trying to say is that I carried my old Viennese class attitudes against Kitty with me to London, and then to the New World. When she showed up again, I couldn't listen to her story. She may have been right when she accused me of responding to Judy's cries for help as a way of snubbing her."

She took a deep breath. "Victoria, will you put aside any thought of a cave until you have found Martin Binder? I need you to do this for me; I will pay your fee. I delivered Martin. Also Judy. On those grounds alone Kitty never forgave me. She came to me because she was frightened; someone told her I had exceptional skill, but it's not a good idea for your childhood nemesis to see you splayed and bleeding in a delivery room."

I held her hand, as I had done with Kitty Binder last night. "I'll do my best, Lotty."

We sat quietly for some minutes, then she asked awkwardly whether Kitty had been dead when I reached the house.

"I don't want a description of the mayhem, but I hope she died in peace," Lotty said, "not in great pain."

"She spoke in German." During the long night that followed Kitty Binder's death, I had forgotten those terrible last minutes with her. "I recorded her in case she was saying something that would help track her assailants."

I got out of bed, pulling on a pair of jeans so that I wouldn't embarrass Mr. Contreras, and retrieved my bag from where I'd dropped it on my way into my home this morning.

Lotty took the phone from me and played the recording several times. "This isn't anything to do with who killed her. She's saying, 'Granny, what did it all mean?' Then she adds, 'What was the point of it all?'"

She turned my phone over and over in her hands. "It's so painful, Victoria. Kitty had a difficult life, and then to die like that, thinking her life had no point! If you've lost everyone, and then you give birth to a drug addict and your only grandson has run away, perhaps to become a terrorist or a traitor—life would feel meaningless!"

"My reaction is less cosmic," I said dryly. "First, Kitty thought she was with her granny, so she died feeling comforted. Second, what if it's not her life she's asking about, but something specific—what it was her home invaders came hunting for—why did it matter so much to them?"

Lotty put my phone down. "I hope you're right. It would be a help, to me, anyway. How can you find out?"

"Cordell Breen, who owns the company where Martin has been working, doesn't think a solo op like me is much use, but I am willing to do legwork. People who rely on technology sometimes miss the small and obvious. I had been thinking of canvassing for Martin at bus stops, but it's been two weeks; the trail is cold up here. I'm going to drive back to the place Judy was living, and see if anyone in the town remembers Martin."

VIENNA, 1938
Teddy Bear, Teddy Bear, Turn Around

L ITTLE CHARLOTTE IS WRAPPING her teddy bear's head in bandages. "He fell from the building, *Opa*, and hurt his head," she explains to her grandfather.

"It burst open like a rotten pumpkin," Käthe laughs. "Juice and seeds all over the ground."

Frau Herschel frowns. "Language, Käthe!"

"That's what happened to this man who got pushed off the building yesterday. Everybody who was there laughed and one man said that, that his head was a rotten pumpkin, a rotten Jew pumpkin head. I can take a knife and slice open Teddy to show you."

Ever since the Germans attacked Austria, Käthe has been talking back to Frau Herschel. It's as if seeing the rudeness of Austrian Christians to the Herschels makes her feel that she can attack them as well.

"Where was that, Lotte?" Grandfather asks his granddaughter.

"By Fräulein Martina's lab. She took us there yesterday for science lessons. It was fun. We got to see the films she made of the insides of atoms, you know, the ones she took when we all went to the mountains for the Easter holiday. But Käthe got bored, she's so *stupid* that sitting through science class bores her own pumpkin-seed head."

"You're the pumpkin head," Käthe shouts. "I'm smart enough to know that science gets you nowhere. You have to have money to get away from the Nazis, or show them your titties. Science will only get you killed."

"Charlotte! Käthe!" *Oma* says sternly. "I will not have this language from you. We may have to live in the ghetto, but we will not speak like the ghetto."

Little Charlotte apologizes to her grandmother with a curtsy, but Käthe bends over her knitting, her lips pressed in a furious scowl.

They have been doing a literature lesson with Grandfather Herschel, reciting lines from Schiller that neither girl understands. Herr Herschel is teaching the children German and literature now that the schools have expelled Jewish students. Fräulein Martina is supposed to teach science and mathematics, but she often forgets how young they are. She talks to them about alpha particles and electrons. She wonders aloud about the instability of the uranium nucleus, and has the girls count scintillations in her lab.

Frau Herschel, "Big Charlotte," doesn't like it; she doesn't like her granddaughter coming home with stained fingers, her pinafore smelling oddly of chemicals and the stink of the cigars that the men in the Radium Institute smoke. Herr Herschel agrees that with water scarce and laundry soap almost nonexistent, it is a nuisance, but working in the lab keeps little Charlotte from worrying too much.

This evening, after the literature lesson, they are waiting for Käthe's grandmother to get back from trying to trade her embroidered napkins for food.

Grandfather takes Teddy from little Charlotte. "I'm sure your bandages will make him well very soon, Lotte. So Fräulein Martina took you to her lab yesterday and let you play with atoms?"

"It's not like that, *Opa*. Atoms are too tiny to see, and then they have tinier things inside them. You can't play with them, not like they were Teddy, but you can study them; then you know how sunlight is made. Fräulein Martina showed us on a piece of paper, black lines from the sun. See, there's this atom in the sun called helium, and when you make it on earth you have radiation. Then you see the lines it makes on a piece of paper, it's like a ghost, so they call it 'Spectral.'"

"Those lines won't keep you warm in the winter when there's no coal," Käthe says. "So what's the point?"

A laugh from the doorway startles all of them; they turn to see Käthe's mother standing there.

"Lotte, *Liebling*, the lines are from a spectrum of light that the sun and the stars emanate, that's why they're called spectral, but I like the idea that the ghost of the sun's explosions makes them. And you, my little daughter, you've been listening too hard to your own *Oma, nicht wahr?*"

Fräulein Martina comes forward to her daughter and tries to smooth the wisps of hair that have escaped from her braid, but Käthe jerks her head away.

"*Oma* is right," Käthe says, small chin at an obstinate angle. "We can't eat your atoms."

"Everything you eat is made up of atoms," Fräulein Martina says, "but I understand what your *Oma* is telling you. Still, they pay me a little stipend at the Institute; that helps put some atoms in your bellies."

"What did the girls see yesterday?" Frau Herschel pulls Fräulein Martina back to the doorway to ask in an undervoice. "Käthe said something about a man falling from a building?"

Fräulein Martina looks at the two girls. In the tiny room where the Herschels now live, it's impossible to have a private conversation: the same thing is true in her own flat, across the hall. She thought, growing up, that her parents' four rooms were tiny and squalid compared to the large light flat where the Herschels lived on the Renngasse. Now the new government has moved three other families into her home. She and her mother mourn their lost rooms just as much as Frau Herschel grieves for her ten rooms and private baths.

"A man was pushed off a building," Käthe says loudly. "We told you on the way home, but you wouldn't listen. We saw it. These other men picked him up and threw him off, just as if he was a doll, and they laughed. They said he'd been an ugly Jew when he was alive and now he was pretty because he was a dead Jew! And your stupid atoms won't save you from someone doing that to you."

"That's enough coarse talk to your mother," Frau Herschel says sharply, adding to Fräulein Martina, "Your own mother is frightened; we all are frightened, so Frau Saginor says these things. I tell her that Käthe repeats them, and that perhaps she shouldn't complain about you quite so much, but—"

Fräulein Martina smiles as Frau Herschel breaks off, mid-sentence. "I know what Mama says: that if I loved my child as much as I love physics, Käthe wouldn't complain about my work. I'm sorry that I didn't notice the man who was pushed yesterday. What a terrible thing for the children to have seen.

"The trouble is, we had to leave the lab early on account of the curfew, but my mind stayed in the library, not with what was happening on the street. My mother is right: that's my biggest fault, not seeing what's in front of me. Or second-biggest."

The biggest, according to Frau Saginor, being Martina's coldness, but even as she speaks to Frau Herschel, Martina's mind scurries from her daughter and the dead man, back to the Institute library.

"I hadn't been able to find a reference I was looking for," she tries to explain. "It was an old paper by a German chemist, Ida Noddack; I finally tracked it down this afternoon. No one paid attention to it when she published it, because she criticized Fermi's study of uranium decay, and his work is supposed to be beyond criticism. Still, when I first read it, I did wonder if we should redo Fermi's experiments, and go down to elements below lead. When I suggested as much to Professor Dzornen, he said we didn't have the resources and that we had to accept Fermi's results. Anyway, there's no better experimentalist in physics today. But Noddack suggested that U-235 doesn't decay into trans-uranic elements, but into—"

Käthe interrupts her mother with a loud scream. She grabs the teddy bear from Herr Herschel, darts to the window and hurls the bear down to the courtyard. "Now he's dead, and a good thing, too, ugly Jew bear. No more useless *klatsch-klatsch-klatsch* from his stupid mouth!"

The shock in all the adult faces makes Käthe run from the room, trailing her knitting. Little Charlotte, stunned only for a second, leaps up and follows her. The adults hear the two girls kicking and shouting in the hall.

Herr Herschel goes out and separates them. He speaks with a sternness that is unusual for him. "Käthe, you must go to your own home now. We will see you again for lessons when you can behave in a civilized fashion."

He pulls his granddaughter away from the Saginor child, shocked to see her small face contorted with such hatred. It's not enough that the Austrians hate us, we have to hate each other, he thinks. The antipathy between little Charlotte and Käthe seemed to date from birth, long before the Nazis took over Austria, but the way they all have to live now, five or more people to a room, makes everyone edgy.

The Matzo Island, Frau Herschel used to call the Leopoldstadt where the Saginors live. Like most people of her age and class, she'd been contemptuous of the slum which poor Jews from the eastern reaches of the Habsburg Empire had flooded in the days after the Great War. She doesn't use that phrase now that they are living there themselves.

On the Matzo Island, their daughter flirted and pouted and danced and sang with Moishe Radbuka, a violinist. No one could resist Sophie when she acted irresistible, least of all a Matzo violinist. The violinist gave Sophie Herschel a baby, whom she called little Charlotte, an olive branch to her mother, who seized on the infant with glad hands. When Martina Saginor had a baby only a few months later, no one knew who had given it to her.

"Martina, such an odd child, an odder woman, one wonders how the child Käthe was conceived," Frau Herschel used to say. "Perhaps some explosion in the lab produced a baby."

Tonight, instead of punishing little Charlotte for fighting like a ghetto cat, as her grandmother wishes, Herr Herschel carries her down four flights of stairs and out into the courtyard. They find Teddy, dirty from the mud and the slops on the cobblestones, but otherwise intact.

Herr Herschel picks up a scrap of paper torn from a magazine and wipes the bear with clumsy fingers. Perhaps his wife can clean Teddy with one of the mysterious concoctions she is able to manufacture out of their minute rations.

He pulls Lotte to him. She trips and stumbles on one of the loose cobblestones, but bites back a cry because she knows Käthe is watching, ready to make fun of her for her clumsiness.

Herr Herschel bends to replace the loose stone. The ground underneath has subsided, leaving a sizable hole; all the stones in this section of the courtyard are loose. Courtyard—what a grand name for a small circle that has nothing courtly about it at all, just dead trees and bare glass-shard-filled earth where grass once grew. Only the stench of rotting waste connects it to a medieval court.

He puts an arm around his granddaughter and leads her back into the building.

21

DOWN ON THE FARM

PRIVATE EYES ARE REQUIRED to tell local LEOs when we're about to start
stalking or staking out on their territory. In Chicago, I don't bother:
the cops would either snarl at me to get out of their hair, or tie me up
for hours in useless interrogations about my investigations. In Palfry,
though, I began my day at Doug Kossel's headquarters. In a county
like this, everyone knows everyone. If the first person I questioned
didn't rat me out to the sheriff, the second would for sure.

"Your funeral," he said. "No one's talked to me about the boy, but
if he's putting the same things up his nose as his ma, he likely sneaked
in and out when the farmers were sleeping. This is an early-to-bed kind
of place, you know."

I nodded meekly: there was no point in offering the sheriff my version of Martin Binder. The sheriff's office was in the city-county
building at the south end of Main Street. I'd found a parking space
without any trouble: the Buy-Smart outside town had decimated Palfry's stores even before the economy collapsed. Now there was just a
handful of survivors: a small drugstore that did a brisk business in al-
cohol and lottery tickets, a dusty furniture store, and a few diners.

I'd left Chicago at six, covering the hundred miles down I-55 in
under two hours, but as the sheriff had said, this was an early-to-bed
town. People had been working their fields since before sunrise. At

eight-thirty, they were taking a break at Lazy Susan's Coffee Shop, which looked like the one lively place on the street.

When I walked inside, heads turned. Strangers were rare enough down here to merit a second look, but I was merely another woman in jeans whose dark hair showed flecks of white, nothing out of the ordinary. Conversations resumed.

Lazy Susan's was a no-frills kind of place. Padded red banquettes along the walls, tubular chairs around Formica tables in the middle, paper placemats, and a couple of waitresses who dashed around far too quickly to be called lazy anything. Most of the tables were filled, but I found an empty stool at the counter.

"What'll yours be, hon?" A waitress appeared out of nowhere, pouring coffee into my mug without asking.

The flimsy placemats had the menus printed on them. Eggs, hash browns, waffles. I'd had coffee before leaving Chicago, but I realized I was famished.

"A short stack and OJ," I said.

She didn't write it down, just hollered it to the griddleman behind her and zipped off to her next battle station.

"How's the dog?"

I turned to see a woman in uniform standing behind me. Jenny Orlick, her badge read. One of the deputies who'd come when I found Ricky Schlafly's body in the cornfield. She'd done a better job than me—I wouldn't have recognized her again.

"She's on the mend, Deputy. Would you like her when she's shed her heartworm larvae? She seems to have a sweet disposition."

"No dog from that hellhole can have a sweet disposition," Orlick said. "Anyway, I have three cats who would rip her to ribbons within a week. Is that why you came down? To find her a home?"

I pulled Martin Binder's picture out of my briefcase. "I'm hoping someone around here might have spotted him. I need to find him."

"Is he a Chicago kid? Why would he be down here?"

"He's the son of a woman from the meth house." I gave Orlick a quick thumbnail of Martin's disappearance, his grandmother's murder, the drug house in Chicago where I'd flushed Judy Binder earlier in the week.

Orlick frowned over Martin's face. "I think I'd remember him, he looks so, well, New Yorky. We only have two Jewish families here in Palfry, so he'd kind of stand out, if you know what I mean. If you want, I'll take it over to the Buy-Smart, put it up on their bulletin board. At the County office, too, if you have an extra."

I pulled a half-dozen copies out of my case and printed my cell phone number on the bottom of each one. My short stack arrived as Jenny's partner, Glenn Davilats, came over to clap her on the shoulder and tell her it was time to roll. Both of them looked better than they had when we'd met at the cornfield.

"This here's my number," Orlick said, handing me a card from the Palfry County sheriff's department. "I'll call you if I hear anything, but you get in touch if anything gets squirrelly, or if you find another druggie with his pecker getting pecked."

"Pecker pecking" must be a local idiom, not a sign that the sheriff was a psychopath. Jenny and her partner took off, but my waitress and one of my counter-mates had heard our conversation, which meant it spread through the coffee shop at warp speed. While I ate my pancakes, most of the people in Lazy Susan's stopped by to look at Martin's picture. None of them admitted to having seen him before.

As the diner cleared out, the waitresses took a breather. Two went outside for a smoke, but the third perched on the stool next to mine.

"You really a detective?" she asked.

I nodded. "These pancakes are delicious. Housemade?"

She grinned. "You flattering me because Jenny Orlick told you I'm Susie Foyle?"

I shook my head. "Lazy Susan? How come? Stevedores on the waterfront don't work as hard as you."

She was pleased by the compliment, but said, "Oh, you know, it's how the two words come together. When I was a kid, my brothers used to tease me, calling me Lazy Susie. How come you want to find this Martin kid?" she asked.

"His granny raised him," I said. "He disappeared two weeks ago. His granny died in my arms night before last. I owe it to her to find him."

Susie nodded soberly. "A lot of that going around. Not grandmas dying in your arms, I mean, but grandmas having to raise their own kids' children. We see it down here as much as you do in Chicago. It's hard."

She picked up the picture and stared at it. "I haven't seen the boy, but I'm sure he was in town, even though everyone's saying 'no,' to you. One of those rumors that zips around, you know how that goes. If I was you, I'd talk to the Wengers. They have the farm closest to the Schlafly place."

"The sheriff told me it's a quarter mile away, that no one there saw anything."

Susie grinned again. "Don't know why he'd say that. If you think every farmer in the county doesn't keep track of the comings and go-ings of the neighbors up to a mile away, that only proves you're a city girl. I should know—I grew up on one of those farms. The gossip could crush a combine. By the way, you never did tell me if you were really a detective."

"Private." I took my license out of my wallet to show her, and handed her one of my cards.

"Well, V. I. Warshawski, good luck to you. If you're still around at lunchtime, I bet you've never tasted as good a BLT as what I serve here."

She sketched a map on the back of one of her placemats, showing me how to get to the Wengers' house. She also told me to put Martin's photo on the corkboard by the front entrance. I found a place in be-tween ads for a used tractor, an offer to exchange haircuts for fresh vegetables, and an announcement of the Palfry County haybale-throwing contest.

In my car I studied Susie's map. East of town, toward the Schlafly place, then right at a crossroads, left to a county road that ran parallel to the one in front of Schlafly's. I took a minute to look up the family on my iPad. Frank and Roberta, early fifties; one child, Warren, a high school senior, still at home; two daughters who'd moved away, one to St. Louis, the other to Columbus, Ohio.

Before going to the Wenger farm, I detoured past the Schlafly place. There were no crime scene tapes, either at the house or the field, just the broken stalks to show where the county van had driven in to collect Ricky Schlafly's body. The house looked abandoned, but I walked around the perimeter, checking for any movement behind the windows that weren't boarded over. I hoped the sheriff had gotten someone to remove the dead Rottweiler from the kitchen.

The road to the Wengers' was a badly pitted gravel track. I went slowly, to preserve my tires. I had to pull over to the verge a couple of times as pickups roared past me, covering the Mustang with a fine white dust. As I bumped along, I passed a hand-painted sign telling me that the Wengers' Prairie Market was straight ahead. Fresh eggs, flowers, tomatoes and "notionals," whatever those might be.

The corn on either side of the car looked brown and tired, signs of the terrible drought gripping Illinois. Blackbirds and crows were darting through the stalks, even though I couldn't see any ears worth harvesting. Unless there was another body in there.

When I'd been down here before, Frank or Roberta had been on a tractor in the distance, but the fields were empty this morning. I was in luck when I pulled into the yard: a man was working on a tractor parked in front of a dilapidated outbuilding. Beyond him was another building with a bit of a parking lot around it, a large picture window, and a sign proclaiming "Wenger's Prairie Market."

I don't know the etiquette for visiting a working farmer in the middle of the morning. I walked across the yard and watched at a respectful distance—close enough to talk, but not breathing down his neck. He wasn't working on the tractor, but a piece of machinery attached to it, something with wide, sharp teeth. One of the teeth had broken and he was having a hard time getting it out of its slot. He kept slamming at the bolt with a hammer, not bothering to look across at me.

"Need a hand?" I asked politely.

He looked up. "You a mechanic?"

"No, but I can hold the bolt in place while you whack it with your hammer."

"Can you, now? You ready to get grease all over those fancy clothes?"

I was wearing a jacket and a blouse over my jeans, but I had a T-shirt in my car. I went back and changed under cover of my open car door, draping the jacket and blouse across the passenger seat. As I returned to him, I saw movement behind the picture window in the Prairie Market. A woman about my own age, with skin sunburned a reddish brown, was hurrying out to join us.

"The market isn't open on weekdays once the school year starts," she said.

"I didn't come for the market; I came to talk to you and your husband, if you're the Wengers."

"Who are you, anyway?" she said.

"V. I. Warshawski," I said. "Are you Ms. Wenger?"

"You out here selling something? We have all the insurance we need."

Frank Wenger, as I assumed he was, said, "She's set to help me undo this bolt, Bobbie. If she's selling something, wait until we're done before you throw her off the land."

I squatted next to the machine. The ground was baked hard, with deep ruts from all the big wheels that had come through when the soil was wet. I made sure I had both feet planted in one of the ruts before taking the bolt wrench from Wenger. I kept my arms bent so that my biceps would absorb most of the shock. Even so, it took every ounce of strength I had not to let go when he whacked it. Five furious strokes, and I felt the bolt turn.

"Okay, got it," he said. "You're stronger than you look. You a farm gal?"

"Nope. City all the way. I don't even know what this thing is we're working on."

"Disc harrow. Need it to chop and mulch the stalks, such as they are, once we've got the corn harvested—such as it is. What can we do for you, city gal?"

I sat on the edge of one of the deepest ruts, rubbing my arms. "I'm a detective, from Chicago. I'm the woman who found Derrick Schlafly's body in the cornfield."

"You tell Doug Kossel you were out here?" Frank asked.

"Yes, sir. I stopped at his office first thing. Of course, we've been speaking on the phone off and on since I found the body. He sent me to find one of Ricky's old Chicago playmates, which I did, but now I'm back here, looking for a missing person."

"Only missing persons in our lives are our daughters," Frank said.

"Oh?" I pretended I hadn't looked up his family. "How long have they been gone?"

"Since we saw them at Easter," Roberta said sharply, while Frank laughed. "We don't know anything that can help you, and I'm in the middle of making up Halloween displays."

My hands were covered with grease, but Frank had a roll of paper towels near him. I wiped off as much as I could and went back to my car. Using one of the towels I kept for the dogs, I pulled a photo of Martin out of my case and walked back to the Wengers.

"His mother was one of the people living in the Schlafly place," I said, holding it out with the towel still in my hand. "He's been gone for some weeks now. I'm wondering if he came down here to see her."

"You look across the field here and tell me how much you see, then ask me again what I notice about my neighbors," Roberta said.

I followed her finger to where she was pointing at the Schlafly house, a small gray structure in the distance. People like to be thought above nosiness and gossip. City or country, the ones who protest most about it are the ones who are probably the nosiest, but I murmured sympathetically.

"You farm these fields, Sheriff Kossel told me. It must have been a worry, all those chemicals Schlafly and his pals were cooking with."

"Oh, yeah," Frank said. "Couple-three times they blew out some windows. First time, I thought Al-Qaeda was attacking us. And the dogs—I went over there once to ask them, nicely you know, to cover up that chemical pit behind the house. You can smell it over here when the wind's blowing. We have a kid; we don't want him breathing that stuff." He hammered the bolt again for emphasis.

"Anyway, they had that gate all locked up. When I rang the bell, they didn't even bother to answer, just saw me on their video camera and sent out the dog from hell, pardon my French. They released the gate by remote and the dog tore through. Got back to my truck right before it took my throat out. After that, I never went out without my shotgun in the truck, tell you that much for nothing."

I thought of the dog I was supporting in Chicago. Maybe not such a sweet disposition after all.

"You told Sheriff Kossel?" I asked.

"What, big-talking, do-nothing Kossel?" Roberta said.

I didn't speak, just cocked my head hopefully.

"Come on, Bobbie," Frank protested. "I told Doug, but it's not like Ricky's is the only meth house in the county. There are three over by Hansville."

"And when does he ever shut down any of them?" She glared at him.

"Is Kossel getting a piece of the action?" I asked.

"Of course not," Frank said. "He's not that kind of man."

"No, he's not corrupt, he's just lazy. He was a lazy tackle back when you played football at Palfry High, which is why you never got the scoring numbers that might have won you a scholarship. He hasn't gotten any more energetic just because he's a glad-hander who gets people out to vote for him. Look how he got this woman here—what did you say your name was? Warshawski, look how he got her to track down one of Ricky's drug dealers in Chicago."

I let the argument run another few minutes, but didn't hear anything that made me believe Kossel might be on the take. Before Roberta got so angry she stormed off to her Halloween displays, I held out Martin's picture again.

"His mom was one of the people living in Schlafly's place, so it was his grandmother who raised him. I was holding her when she died two nights ago. I need to find Martin, to tell him about his granny, and to make sure he's okay. Any of those times you were disking or harrowing or whatever it is you do with this lethal thing"—I nudged the broken tooth with my toe—"near Schlafly's place did you see him?"

Frank looked at his wife, who turned redder under her sunburn. He seemed to be waiting for her to speak, but all she said was that she never worked the big fields. "I do the greenhouses and the truck farm out on the other side of the house; it's where we grow the organics for the Prairie Market. I've got to get back to work; you wouldn't believe it in this heat, but Halloween's just around the corner."

She turned back to the building that housed the market. In a city woman, I would have said she scuttled, but in her case, I suppose she was only hurrying back to her displays.

I asked Frank, but he said when he was on the tractor there was too much noise and dust to notice much of anything. "All I can tell you is people come and go there all the time, although since they shot each other the place has been empty."

He busied himself with the bolt I'd helped loosen. When he spoke, he kept his head down as if he was talking to the harrow tooth. "Go check out the market. Roberta does amazing things in there."

22

THE PITS

IKE THE OTHER OUTBUILDINGS, the market was made out of unfinished wood that was showing rot at some of the joins. This made the interior all the more startling. It was a clean, bright space, with wide windows that overlooked the fields to the north and the Wenger house and barns to the south. One side was filled with refrigerated shelves for the produce. The rest of the space was taken up with "notionals," everything from "locally sourced organic goat's milk soap," to birdhouses, baby blankets, lavishly decorated flowerpots, even quilts, all guaranteed handmade in Palfry County.

Roberta was busy at a long worktable. She glanced up when I came in, but she was intent on her work, inserting a series of tiny figurines into a dried gooseneck gourd. A large wicker basket filled with gourds was on the floor next to her; two completed ones sat in front of her.

She had cut squares in the side of the gourds and filled them with witches dancing around a cauldron. They had tiny cats and pumpkins at their feet, while a harvest moon festooned with bats hung overhead.

"These are amazing," I said. "How on earth do you make the witches?"

"Pipe cleaners wrapped in gauze. The faces are the hardest because I paint them on fabric. They go on sale this weekend. Eighty-five dollars if you want one now."

I wandered over to the window that faced the Schlafly place. I heard her suck in a breath; when I looked over at her, she was staring at the shelf next to the window, but she quickly returned to her work.

The shelf was filled with packets of dried herbs, but next to the window a blue baby blanket covered something lumpy. I lifted it to find a pair of binoculars. When I picked them up and looked across the field at Schlafly's, the whole ugly yard behind the house rushed forward to greet me: the deep pit with its toxic brew, the broken gate, the back door hanging on its hinges. I could even make out wasps circling under the eaves.

Roberta glared at me. "You can't come in here and dig through my things; this is private property."

I put the binoculars back on the shelf. "If I had a house full of crazed dopers that close and a sheriff who couldn't get here fast in a crisis, I'd be keeping an eye on the place, too. You see whoever shot Ricky Schlafly?"

The flush underneath her sunburn died away. "I heard a shot as I was starting to get up, but it wasn't five o'clock yet, which is still dark this time of year. I went down to put the coffee on, then I heard another shot. Of course, like Frank said, there were always explosions and such coming out of the house, but a gun doesn't sound anything like a window blowing out. I slipped out and came into the market here."

She gave the ghost of a smile. "Frank and Warren, Warren's our son, he's a senior over at the high school, they think it's wrong for me to be looking at the neighbors. Spying they call it."

"Could you see anything?" I asked.

She shook her head. "It was still too dark. If I'd known they were murdering Ricky, of course I would have called the sheriff, but I guess they killed him out in the north field. I didn't even hear the shot, with the Schlafly house being between us and all. The only thing I did see that early was a car taking off. SUV, I'd guess, from the height of the headlights. I know now it must've belonged to the killers, parked by where they cut the fence out when they went in. I suppose the gal took off in it, because I heard all this shouting, and more shots."

She started twisting a pipe cleaner round and round in her fingers. "I told Frank when I went back in to make breakfast, but he said not to get involved, if drug addicts were shooting at each other they wouldn't thank me for interfering. Of course, he was right. If I'd driven over, like I had half a mind to, they would have murdered me just like they did Ricky."

"Very likely," I agreed: whoever had torn that house apart had been way more savage than Ricky's poor dead dog.

"Ricky Schlafly was bad news from day one, but I went to school with his older sister. She died of breast cancer three years back, or the house would have gone to her. I hate to think of how she'd feel, knowing Ricky had lain out in that field all day getting eaten by crows."

The pipe cleaner broke in her fingers, but she kept twisting the ends around. "All day long I kept looking over there. One time I saw this woman—" She broke off and the flush returned to her face. "That was you, wasn't it? I thought you looked familiar. You have any idea what happened to that gal who'd been living there, the one who took off in the SUV? She didn't go through town, or someone would have told us."

"She drove up to Chicago, to a drug house on the city's West Side," I said, "but she ran from there to her mother's place. Whoever was after her caught up with her there. They shot her, but she's still alive. Her mother, Martin Binder's grandmother, died protecting her."

Roberta's face softened in pain. "The things we do for our kids, even when they keep breaking our hearts. I know that story, beginning to end."

"Did you see Martin over there?" I asked, pointing toward the Schlafly place.

She picked up a fresh pipe cleaner and started to wrap a piece of gauze around it. "I may have done. So many kids came and went there, buying drugs, you know, that I didn't pay attention to one more than another. Still, a couple of weeks ago, about the time you say this Martin disappeared, there was a kid out there got into a fight with the woman. Judy, you say?"

"Physical fight?"

"Not exactly. They were arguing over some papers, an old envelope full of papers. He was pulling them away from her and she was hanging on to them. He ended up with them and took off." She paused. "I don't know if it's any use to you, but a couple of 'em fell into that waste tank they've got dug out back."

I groaned. The last thing I wanted to do was climb into that pit. Besides which, after thirty minutes in that stew, paper would dissolve. Would anything be left after fifteen days?

After watching me silently for a moment, Roberta put down her pipe cleaners and left the market. She came back about ten minutes later. She was carrying a bundle that opened up into a set of waist-high waders, arm-length rubber gloves and an industrial face mask.

"We used to keep cows, until it got to be too much work. I kept these from when I went in to clean out the waste tank. You're a bit taller than me, but these things are built generous."

I thanked her, without feeling any real gratitude. Still, I knew if I didn't go into the pit, I would be haunted back in Chicago by the thought that I'd let an important clue go begging. I tried on the waders, just to be sure. She was right, they were built to cover layers of clothes and shoes. They went on over my jeans and running shoes with room to spare.

When I carried them out to my car, Frank was waiting for me. "You know how to drive a stick? Figured you would. Take the pickup. It's got a winch, case you need to haul up something heavy."

I looked at him narrowly. "You got something specific in mind, like a body?"

He laughed, a rusty, hooting sound. "Nah, but Bobbie saw 'em throw chairs and such in there from time to time. They'd get high, who knows what they thought it was funny to toss around."

He climbed into the passenger seat of the pickup and watched while I fumbled with the clutch and the stick. The truck was old and the gears were well worn. Even so, I killed the engine a couple of times before I got it going.

Frank rode with me to the end of the drive. I thought he was checking on me, but he wanted to show me a path across the field that lay between his house and Schlafly's.

"Not that it matters, with the corn crop destroyed by the drought, but there's always a track alongside a field so you can drive equipment across without hurting the crop. You follow that, you'll get to Schlafly's back fence. The hole the killers cut is wide enough to drive the truck through."

He pulled an old receipt out of the glove compartment and found a pencil stub. "This here's my cell phone. You'd best not drive the truck into the tank, since it's got my winch on it. If you get in any other kind of trouble, give me a shout. Leave me the keys to that little Mustang of yours and I'll drive over to get you."

I bumped the truck along the track he'd pointed out and drove through the hole in the fence behind the Schlafly house. Before putting on all the heavy rubber gear, I pulled out my gun and made a tour of the house. I'm not often afraid, or even very squeamish, but it took a lot of effort to go inside. I was sweating by the time I'd forced myself over the kitchen threshold, but the Rottweiler's body was gone. All I found were cockroaches and a pair of starlings who'd taken advantage of the open door to build a nest on the light fixture in the front room.

I did up the bolts to the front door so that anyone wanting to interrupt me would either have to break down the door or come up the side to the hole in the fence. Leaving my gun on the floor of the truck, with the door open next to me, I pulled on the waders, hooked the suspenders around my neck so the pants would stay up, and pulled on Roberta's industrial shoulder-high gloves.

The drought had mostly dried the bottom of the pit, which was about the only good thing to be said about it. I kept on the high waders, though, not just because my feet still sank into sludge patches, but to protect my legs from the ether, Drano and the rest of the revolting soup.

Whoever had given the crime scene a once-over had tossed the murdered Rottweiler into the pit along with the towel I'd used to cover him. Insects had eaten most of the flesh; fur and bones fell out of the grappling hook as I tried to use Frank's winch to lift him.

"I'll bury you later," I promised him. "Even if you did go for Frank Wenger's throat, you were only trying to please the people you were unfortunate enough to love."

I'd forgotten to bring my water bottle from the Mustang. After an hour in the September sun, I was thinking more about water and less about the stink and the toxins I was handling.

As the morning wore on, I pulled out enough empty jugs and ether canisters to fill a large tarp that I'd found under the porch. As Frank said, the Schlafly menagerie had also tossed in chairs (two), two-by-fours (eleven), beer kegs (three) and dressers (one).

I kept cooling my head and neck under a garden hose, but I couldn't bring myself to drink any water connected to the meth house. Around one-thirty, I took off Roberta's gear and drove the truck into Palfry. I stopped at a convenience store on the outskirts of town for two gallon jugs of drinking water. I sat in the car, resting, drinking, then remembered Lazy Susie's BLT. Just what I needed to restore my salt balance.

The lunch crowd had taken off; only one other person was at the counter.

"You want that BLT?" Susie asked. "How's it going at the death pit?"

"And you know this because I stink like a chemistry lab?"

"Just showing you that we all know what we're all up to here in Palfry. You want fries with that or slaw?"

I chose slaw, not from an obsession with health but because I could imagine the weight of all that starch in my stomach when I went back to work. Susie was right about her BLT: I'd never tasted better. I had a cup of her thin coffee before pushing myself off the stool. Susie gave me directions to Herb's Hardware, where I bought more tarps and a fine-toothed rake.

Back at the meth house, I used the rake to cull the bottom of the tank. I brought up a mass of rotted leaves. When I raked through it, I uncovered syringes, cigarette butts, the remains of a dozen or so KFC buckets and pizza cartons and a large collection of condoms, but no documents, at least none in any condition I could recognize.

And no human bones. All afternoon long, as I'd shifted through the muck, I'd been terrified that I'd find some trace of Martin.

I took off the gloves and finished my second gallon of water. My arms and legs were wobbly from exertion and salt loss. Pulling off the waders, I climbed into the pickup, where I tilted the passenger seat as far back as it would go. As I slumped there, my feet up on the dashboard, I figured at least I could head to Chicago knowing that I'd left no condom unturned.

A blast from a car horn jerked me awake. I remembered where I was and reached reflexively for my gun. Frank and Roberta had pulled my Mustang up the track outside the Schlafly fence. I hastily slid the gun back to the truck floor.

"You look like the sorriest piece of leftover detective I've ever seen," Frank said. "We came over to see how you were doing. Also, Warren, our boy, is playing football tonight. We need the truck to go watch him, unless you want us to take your car."

I swung my legs over the side of the truck and lowered myself gingerly to the ground. My legs still wobbled, but at least they didn't give way on me. "I've raked through that whole sludge heap and I didn't see anything that looked like the papers Martin fought over with his mother."

Frank inspected the three tarps I'd covered. "I'd say you got just about everything that could be got."

"They threw this in?" Roberta had walked over to the dresser. "This was Agnes's piece. She was Ricky and Janice's grandmother, the lady who left the house to Ricky. This was an heirloom. Her great-grandmother brought this with her when they moved to Illinois in the 1840s, and she always said that it was the grandmother's great-grandmother who brought it to Pennsylvania from Germany back in 1750 or so. This is terrible. Those beautiful inlays all damaged, and the drawer pulls—they were gold. I suppose Ricky tore them off and sold them and then dumped this in the pit because it wasn't any use to him anymore."

Frank walked over and put an arm around her. "We can take it back with us, see if we can do anything to restore it."

He found a blanket behind the driver's seat of the pickup and placed it on the truck bed. When he lifted the dresser up, the drawers fell out. I lumbered over to help Roberta pick them up. And found paper sticking to the undersides of two of them. I laid the drawers, bottom sides up, out on the baked clay of the backyard and squatted on my sore haunches to inspect them.

Time with drain cleaner had taken a toll on the paper, but we could see that it was several layers deep. The top layer included fragments of unpaid bills, shreds of an ad for Pizza Hut, bleached-out photos that looked as though they were torn from a porn magazine. Roberta stuck out a hand to pull off the top layer, but I jerked the drawer out of reach.

"We need something like forceps; otherwise we'll destroy what's underneath."

Her sandy eyebrows lifted in surprise, but she said, "I'll drive over to my workshop. Got plenty of little tools there."

She climbed into the truck, saw my gun on the floor. "Were you planning on shooting your way through the trash in that pit?"

I took the gun from her, smiling feebly. "I found Ricky Schlafly's body, and that poor dog over there. I didn't want to die in a meth pit."

23

TRUNK SHOW

ROBERTA'S EXPERIENCE in making miniatures had given her a sure touch with delicate material. Within an hour we had lifted most of the paper from the two drawers and laid it on a clean sheet of plastic that she'd brought from her workshop.

There were only two items that might have been what Martin and his mother had argued over. One had bonded so tightly to the drawer bottom that we didn't risk peeling it off, but it looked like the remains of an old savings passbook.

I held my magnifying glass over it. "The address is something on Lincoln, I think."

Roberta looked over my shoulder. "Lincolnwood?"

"It could be. That puts it close to where Judy Binder grew up. Her passbook, or her mother's."

I thought of Kitty Binder's outcry over the picture of Martina at the Radium Institute: Judy had stolen it along with Kitty's pearl earrings and cash. Judy might also have stolen her mother's savings book and drained the account.

The other interesting paper was a photocopy of a government document, partly redacted. Roberta and I both hunched over it. The header was from an "Office of Tec . . . al Serv . . . es, Of . . . Ins . . . al," in the "United St . . . De . . . n . . . Co . . . rce." The date was illegible.

"Technical Servers?" I said dubiously.

"Services," Roberta suggested. "We get memos from the Department of Commerce, so I'm thinking that's the third line."

I thought that made sense, but neither of us could figure out "Of-Ins-al." We studied the text together. Between the redaction and the Drano damage, we could only make out bits of it.

"city of Inns . . . he . . . a chemical engineer . . . duct underground te . . . She was a member . . . if she was to work . . . luded a major bomb . . . orking and living co . . . Nor did [*redacted*] ever witne . . ."

Frank coughed. "Kickoff's in forty minutes, gals. Can you put that aside?"

Roberta and I got reluctantly to our feet. We folded plastic sheets around the papers we'd loosened, including the redacted document, and laid the packet in one of the drawers to protect it. The drawer with the passbook welded to the bottom I wrapped in a blanket. I placed both in the Mustang's trunk.

Roberta protested. "Those were Agnes's. I'd like to refinish them, find some new drawer pulls."

"I'll get them back to you," I promised. "I want to take the papers to a forensics lab in Chicago, to see if they can bring more of the letter or the bank book back to life."

Roberta frowned unhappily, but Frank put an arm around her. "Bobbie, that chest of drawers would have rotted away if this Chicago detective hadn't spent a day in the pit. As for you, Detective, you look like the bad side of a dead cow. If you're planning to drive back to Chicago tonight, you need to think that through a few more times. What you ought to do is find a motel, get a shower. In fact, you ever go to a high school football game?"

"I played basketball; my cousin played hockey," I said.

"Tell you what: you check into the motel other side of town and come watch my boy play against Hansville."

When I shut my eyes to think it over, the world started spinning; if

I looked even close to how I felt, bad side of a dead cow was a generous description.

Roberta pulled a T-shirt advertising the Palfry Panthers from her bag. "You borrow that. You can wash it in Chicago and mail it back to me."

I took it meekly and followed them into town. Frank honked and pointed at the high school stadium, then to the road leading to the motel. When I'd checked in and showered away the worst of the stench, I longed to lie down and pass out, but Frank and Roberta had more than extended themselves for me today: I needed to drag my weary bones to the football stadium to watch young Warren.

In the end, I was glad I'd gone. The September air cooled as the sun went down. The crowd was loud but friendly. When I made my way through it to Frank and Roberta, I found I was part of the entertainment.

In a town suffering from a disastrous harvest, a Chicago detective who had found not just Ricky Schlafly—good riddance, was the general sentiment—but a version of buried treasure was better than a TV crime show. At halftime, while Frank stood in line for pizza, fifteen or twenty friends of the Wengers came by for a firsthand account of digging through the meth pit. Roberta was happy to add the embellishments of the missing gold drawer pulls.

I stayed long enough after the game for an introduction to their son, Warren. I had dutifully cheered him during the game: he was a middle linebacker who made an interception and caused a fumble. Even though Hansville won on a late field goal, he was a cheerful junior version of his father, checking in with the family before heading out for burgers with his buddies.

Back at the motel, I stayed awake long enough to send an e-mail to the Cheviot labs, the private forensic lab I use. I wanted to drop the drawer and the fragment of letter off when I got to the city tomorrow; their Sunday skeleton crew could book them in and keep them safe.

I tuned the app on my iPad to the Midnight Special, streaming from WFMT in Chicago, which made me feel that I was at home. I fell asleep in the middle of Gordon Bok singing "The Golden Vanity." The music played through my sleep, and my dreams were pleasant, not the nightmares that had dogged me lately.

Leg pains were what woke me, shooting across the feet and up the shins. As I massaged my calves, I heard noises in the parking lot. Four-eighteen, an odd time for people to be coming back to their rooms in a town whose bars all closed at midnight on Saturdays. I parted the curtains. Two men were taking a crowbar to the trunk of my Mustang.

I pulled on jeans and a T-shirt and was in the hall, gun in hand, without bothering to find my shoes. I sprinted down the hall to the door that overlooked the parking lot, pushed it open just enough that I could see the men.

The two froze briefly, then turned more energetically to my car. I dashed barefoot across the lot, but they had the trunk open before I got to them. They grabbed the drawers and were bolting toward their own waiting car when the papers I'd wrapped in plastic fluttered to the tarmac. I got to them first, but one of the punks ran back and tried to grab them from me. In the tug-of-war, the paper disintegrated.

I slugged the thug across the jaw with the handle of my gun. He yelled in pain, his hands clutching his face. His partner had gotten into their car and swung it around for him. I tried grabbing him by the shoulder, but he broke free and made it into the car.

I fumbled in my jeans for my car keys, but I'd left those inside along with my room key and my shoes. My trunk was open and empty. I had caught their car model, a Dodge Charger, but I'd been fighting so hard that I didn't get the license plate. I was too angry with my own stupidity even to swear.

Several people appeared in the doorway, shouting out confused questions. I stuck the Smith & Wesson inside my waistband at the small of my back.

"Someone was breaking into my car out there," I said. "When I called out, they dropped their crowbar and took off."

My fellow residents streamed past me, looking for damage to their own cars. I went to the front desk, where I had some trouble rousing the night clerk. I explained what had happened, but that in my haste to drive off the intruders I'd locked myself out of my room.

The clerk wanted proof of my identity, which was also in my room, but she finally agreed to come with me to open the door. She stood in the entrance and told me to describe what was in the room.

"I left a beige jacket and a rose-colored silk shirt on a hanger in the closet. The briefcase on the desk has my iPad and my wallet in it, and I have the code to unlock the iPad."

Now that I'd gotten her up, she was determined to be zealous: she watched me unlock the iPad, which was now playing a Haydn sonata, incongruously enough, before returning to her desk to call the sheriff.

The night deputies, two men I hadn't encountered before, met me at my Mustang. By then I was dressed again in my silk shirt and jacket and had my gun in my tuck holster. I'd double-checked all the surfaces in the room for my belongings. I didn't have much—iPad, phone and Roberta's Palfry Panthers T-shirt. I packed those into my briefcase, along with odds and ends like my picklocks.

When I told the deputies what had been taken from the trunk, they didn't roll their eyes or give the blank stares I'd expected.

"Oh, yeah. You're the Chicago detective who found buried treasure at Schlafly's. How valuable was it, you think?" The taller, older deputy felt compelled to lean into my face, which meant I could read his name badge in the dim light: Herb Aschenbach.

"I don't think it was valuable at all," I said. "It had sentimental meaning for Roberta Wenger because the dresser once belonged to Agnes Schlafly."

"Not what we heard," Herb said. "Talk was about gold."

I sighed. "Ms. Wenger said the drawers used to have gold handle pulls. If someone passed that story along I suppose it could have grown into a stack of gold, but all I found were chicken bones, ether cans and tampons."

As I'd hoped, the word "tampon" made Herb back away from me. "What were you looking for, anyway? Why did you take the drawers?"

"I'm not the one who committed a crime here," I said. "I'm the victim. The punks drove off in a Dodge Charger, in case you have one zooming around the country connected to B-and-E's."

The two deputies looked at each other, startled. They knew the Dodge.

"You must have been looking for something," the younger deputy said. "We went and took a look at that pit out back of Schlafly's. You got it pretty well cleaned out."

"Since you know everything I've been doing, Jenny Orlick must have told you I'm looking for a young man named Martin Binder. He was at the Schlafly house a few weeks ago. He might have dropped some papers in the pit which could shed some light on where he went next."

"Seems like a lot of trouble for not much to me," Herb said.

"Hard to argue with that, Deputy, especially since I also have a smashed trunk lock on top of not much. You can talk to Ms. Wenger in the morning, which is right now, come to think of it, and get her version."

The night clerk came out through the back of the hotel. "Kyle, I got a whole bunch of nervous guests in there, wanting to know if their cars are going to be vandalized. Can you come talk to them?"

Kyle and Herb looked at each other, looked at the Mustang, nodded.

Kyle said, "Yeah, Tina, we'll be right in. We can't do anything for you here, Miss. I mean, we could dust the trunk lock for prints, but frankly that's a waste of time, no matter what they say on those TV shows. We'll file a report and tell the team to be on the lookout, case anyone hears anything about these drawers. I'm guessing someone who heard the talk at the game last night got carried away, thinking you'd dug up gold, and went and helped themselves to it."

Herb added, "We'll send Jenny Orlick over to Wenger's in the morning, see if Roberta remembers anything else. How long you fixing to stay here?"

"Not long, Deputy."

"You stop by the station to sign a complaint before you head back to Chicago, okay? And don't go leaving the jurisdiction without letting us know."

"Right you are, Deputy."

I watched while the two men followed Tina into the motel. I picked up the crowbar by one end and laid it in the trunk. I doubted it would show any prints or DNA, but you never know. The punks had damaged the lock so badly it wouldn't stay shut; I had to fasten it with a bungee cord to keep the lid from swinging open.

Like the deputies, I didn't think there was any point in doing anything else, such as signing a complaint, or getting permission to leave the jurisdiction. I slipped out the back exit, my lights off, gun on the seat beside me. Only when I was clear of the motel did I consult my iPad for advice on a route to Chicago. I wanted the old state highways and county roads. I was tired, my legs still hurt, I didn't feel up to driving eighty on the interstate in the dark. I also wanted to make sure I was alone.

Night creatures skittered away from my headlights, raccoons, foxes, rat-like creatures. Now and then a tractor would rumble across the road to get on one of the tracks alongside the fields. Sunrise was still two hours away, but lights were on in many of the farmhouses I passed.

I didn't think my punks were looking for buried treasure; I thought they wanted the bleached-out documents Roberta and I had found. Judy Binder and her son had argued over some papers, Roberta said: she'd watched them through her binoculars, but she hadn't heard what they said. Invaders had torn Kitty Binder's house apart, searching for—what?

I shifted uneasily in my seat, rubbing my driving leg. Was I ruling out the obvious because I wanted the subtle? Judy and Martin could have been fighting over her drug habit. They could have been fighting because he was furious that she'd rather be with crack and meth than him. Ricky Schlafly, that death had all the earmarks of a falling-out among drug dealers. And drug dealers were a wild, unstable bunch. Roberta and Frank Wenger had said there were a number of drug houses in the county. Other meth makers would have heard about my find at the football game: they could easily have believed a tale of buried treasure.

Even if that was the correct analysis, it didn't answer one big question. Where had Martin Binder gone?

24

PAST DUE

DAWN WAS JUST BREAKING when I reached my apartment on Racine. Early to bed, early to rise, leaves me cranky with rings under my eyes.

Mr. Contreras was up, puttering around his kitchen. I described yesterday's drama to him, including the theft of the dresser drawers. It was a long narrative because the old man kept interrupting, partly to see if I was all right, partly indignant I hadn't taken him along for protection.

When we'd finally hashed it over as much as I could stand, he went with me to the lake. I swam out to the far buoy with the dogs and floated in the water for a time, watching the gulls chase each other, until I got so cold I had to swim back at high speed. In a way, the hour in the water was more refreshing than a night in bed. Only in a way.

Back at the apartment, while Mr. Contreras and I shared a plate of French toast, we argued over the theft: Had it been dopeheads in search of gold, or someone more sinister in search of documents?

I thought again of Jari Liu's slogan about God and data. The only data I had were two stolen drawers, a passbook to a bank that might have been in Lincolnwood on Chicago's northwest edge, and a report from an Office of Technical Services.

I helped Mr. Contreras do the washing up, then went to my own apartment to do some work on my laptop. The Department of Commerce website didn't list an Office of Technical Services. Roberta and I might have misinterpreted the headers; after all, we'd merely been guessing.

I shut my eyes, slowed my breathing, tried to picture the redacted, bleached page. Bombs had been mentioned. A chemical engineer. A redacted name hadn't witnessed something. A city of Inns. I couldn't remember anything else.

I looked up "City of Inns." Many towns advertised themselves as "cities of inns," but Innsbruck popped up on the second results page. Innsbruck is in Austria. Martina Saginor, Lotty, Kitty Binder and Martina's student Gertrud Memler had all come from Austria. And during the Second World War, according to the young librarian at the University of Chicago, the Nazi war machine had tried building nuclear reactors near Innsbruck. I liked it.

I found an article on the Innsbruck weapons site in the *Journal of Science and War*. In 1940, no one knew if you could have a self-sustaining chain reaction, which apparently was essential for turning atoms into bombs. Physicists like Heisenberg in Germany and Fermi in America built nuclear reactors to see if they could create a chain reaction. As we all know now, Fermi could do it; Heisenberg couldn't.

Japan and England had also been trying to build a bomb; our history books never mentioned that. Every war room everywhere wanted the most devastating way to obliterate as many women, children, men, dogs and trees as they could.

Herta Dzornen said Martina had been dragooned into weapons work during the war, probably at Innsbruck. I knew I was creating a monumental pyramid without straw, but I wondered if Martin filed a Freedom of Information request about Martina. No, that didn't make sense; she died before the war ended. The U.S. wouldn't have files on her. If anything, Martin would have searched for her in the Holocaust

Museum. He must have been looking for Gertrud Memler, Martina's Nazi student-turned-anti-nuke-activist—he'd learned about her in the book about the Cold War.

But if the Commerce Department document was something Martin had gotten through the Freedom of Information Act, he wouldn't have been fighting his mother over it. Unless he brought it with him to show her, to demand what she knew about Memler or Martina. I could see Kitty, bitter toward both Martina and science, stonewalling her grandson. He'd had a last-ditch hope his mother might know something, drug-addled though she was.

More guesswork. I had a whole five pages in the Binder file devoted to "useless speculations."

The bank book was more promising. It had been an old-fashioned passbook, created long before the Internet. I can still remember going every week to the Steel City Bank and watching my mother carefully push across the stacks of quarters she'd earned from giving music lessons. The teller would count them and enter the amount by hand in her passbook. My favorite part was the red date stamp that went next to the entry.

An old passbook from a Lincolnwood bank could have been Kitty's, stolen by Judy. It was possible that Benjamin Dzornen had set it up to buy her silence back when she was creating such a stink on the South Side. The notion was a stretch, but a tempting one.

I put on a pair of good trousers, a knit top and a red-and-gold scarf and headed out. My first stop was the garage on Lawrence Avenue I use. Even though it was Sunday, Luke Edwards, who must be the most lugubrious mechanic on the planet, was in the shop, taking a transmission apart. He looked at the trunk as if I personally had taken a crowbar to the lock.

"Why'd you go and do that, Warshawski?"

"Just one of those fits that overtakes me sometimes, Luke, where I feel like taking an ax to my ride. How long do you reckon to fix it?"

"Depends how long it takes me to find the replacement parts. You know these older Mustangs, the fittings are different, can't just order them from Ford."

"But you'll shake a few branches and see what falls out. I can't lock the car with the trunk open. Any way to set the alarm on the door with the trunk lock broken?"

Luke gave me a withering look. "Of course not, Warshawski: anyone can get into the car through the trunk, so what would the point be? I'll call you next week. It ain't the car your old Trans Am was, but I'd still like to see you take better care of it."

I grinned ferociously, in lieu of popping him one, and drove down to the Gold Coast. I called Herta Dzornen Colonna's apartment while sitting in my car across the street from the entrance.

"Ms. Colonna: it's V. I. Warshawski. We met last week."

"Met? You call barging in on me 'meeting me'?"

"I'm about to barge in on you again. I know that your father created a savings account for Kitty Binder. Can we talk about that?"

She was silent for a moment, then whispered, "What is it you want? Are you trying to get money out of me?"

"No, ma'am. All I want is information. Can I come upstairs to talk to you in person? Or do you want to continue this on the phone?"

"You're outside my home," she cried. "Oh, don't do this to me!"

"Ms. Colonna, I don't want to torment you, and I certainly won't broadcast your secrets to the world, but if you told me what really went on between your father and Kitty Binder, it might put some old ghosts to rest."

"Nothing went on between my father and Kitty Binder."

"What about the bank account in Lincolnwood?"

"How did you know—oh, what are you doing?"

"I'm coming upstairs, ma'am. This is too difficult a conversation to hold over the phone."

I put my car flashers on and walked over to her building entrance.

The doorman called to announce me, most unwillingly: my careful grooming didn't make me look any more trustworthy than I had on my first visit.

Herta was waiting in her doorway, one hand at her throat. She was using a cane, which she leaned on heavily as she led me to the living room—sighing equally heavily. When she had carefully lowered herself onto the white couch, I again pulled the tubular metal chair over near her.

"When did you find out about the bank account?" I asked.

"When Papa was dying," she whispered. "I used to go down to Hyde Park two or three times a week to help Mama. Julius was useless, you've seen him, by that time he was just sitting in his bedroom playing the guitar and smoking—marijuana. He wouldn't even come down the stairs to help Mama lift Papa to change his sheets."

She was letting herself be distracted by old grievances, shying away from the hard part of the narrative. I sat very still, not an intrusive person at all, just one of her photographs, listening, not judging.

"One morning when Mama was at the grocery, Papa told me he needed my help. He wanted me to look after the bank account, but not to let Mama or Julius or my sister Bettina know about it."

"Did he say why it had to be a secret?"

"He was afraid if I talked to Julius, he'd try to get the money, and he thought Bettina would tell Mama. She suffered so much from all those rumors about Käthe Saginor, he didn't want to add to her pain. Better that she think she would never be bothered by the Saginors again."

"Did he tell you why he'd set up the account?" I asked. "If the stories about him and Martina Saginor were merely rumors . . ." I let my voice trail away suggestively.

"Of course they were just ugly stories," Herta said, indignant. "He felt terrible that Martina had been stuck in Austria during the war. Papa said that after the war, when he learned what had become of Martina Saginor, he owed it to her memory to do something for her daughter. I protested that he owed Käthe nothing: she was married, she had her own life. And if Mama found out, she would have thought all the rumors were true, you know, what the neighbors said when Käthe came to the house back in 1956. But he said that was how he got Käthe to leave us alone, by giving her some money."

Maybe that's what Dzornen told his daughter Herta, but I didn't think it was true, and I wasn't convinced she believed it, either.

"Was the bank account for Kitty herself or for her child?" I asked.

"He gave Käthe a little money when she first showed up, so she and her husband could afford a down payment on a house, then when she had her baby, Papa put more in the account so Judy Binder could go to university, or get business training, whatever she wanted when she grew up. He could only put a little money in every quarter, otherwise Mama would have noticed, so he wanted me to promise to keep adding to the account. He gave me the account number and deposit slips. You know, it was before ATMs and everything."

"And did you keep putting money into the account?" I asked.

Herta was twisting the cane round and round, digging a hole in the Chinese carpet at her feet. "No," she finally whispered. "Stuart—my husband—he said Kitty was a blackmailer. Stuart sent one of his law firm's investigators over to see what the Binders were like, so that we could decide whether Judy was worth supporting. Judy was thirteen but she was already, well, precocious if you know what I mean."

I hadn't heard the word used in that way for a long time. Precocious as in sexually mature for her age, not musically or mathematically.

"And we had three children, that wasn't cheap, braces, you know, college education."

"So you took the money out of the account and used it for your own children?" I tried hard to keep anger and judgment out of my voice, but I must not have done a good job because Herta flinched.

"It was our money," she cried. "Papa was taking our money and giving it to Kitty and her drug-addict daughter. And then the daughter

found the passbook. She actually came down to the Greenwood Avenue house when Mama was still alive! It was terrible—she was drunk
or on drugs. Mama called the police, she called me, it was such a shock,
the first she knew about Papa stealing money out of her own children's
mouths. And Julius, he was *still* living at home, and he was almost
forty by then! He asked if Mama thought it was worth murdering Kitty's daughter. He sat and laughed and said he could do it for a fee."

Herta's face turned alarmingly red. I squeezed my eyes shut, knowing I shouldn't blurt out the first thoughts in my own mind: How
could you keep pretending after seeing the bank account that Kitty
wasn't your sister? And what happened to all that Nobel Prize money?

"When was that?" I asked instead. "When Judy was thirteen and
already precocious enough to guess something was up with her mother
and your father?"

"Not then, a few years later. Judy found the bank book and tried to
get money from the bank. I don't know how she found out that Papa
had put money into the account—I wouldn't put it past Kitty to tell
her she should come down here and ask us for it. Judy came three
times, I think it was: that first time, when Mama was still alive, and
then when she saw the news about Mama's death! She showed up at the
funeral, oh my God, that was terrible!"

"Then Martin came, what a month ago? And you thought he was
going to pick up where Judy left off."

"He kept asking about Martina," Herta whispered. "What did I
know about her work? He was implying that Papa stole work from her!
I knew then he wanted me to say the Nobel Prize should have been
Martina's! He was going to demand that we give the prize money
to him."

"Is that what he said, or what you were scared he would say?"

"I told him the police would be coming if he said one more word!
The idea that Papa would steal, let alone that the ideas of a sewing
woman's daughter were worth stealing!"

This time I couldn't stop myself blurting out, "What, the fact that Martina's mother sewed for a living meant Martina wasn't capable of creative thought? If your father's ideas were as embalmed as your own, I imagine he did have to steal from his students."

Not surprisingly, that ended our conversation. I tried to regroup, but Herta picked up the phone to call the doorman. I left before he came up to escort me out.

25

HIGH SHERIFF AND POLICE, RIDING AFTER ME

OVER AT MY OFFICE, I tried to piece together what Herta Dzornen had said with what I knew about Martin's disappearance. When he went to Palfry, he found the bank book, which made Martin visit Herta and Julius Dzornen. Herta said Julius once offered to kill Judy Binder. Had that been a tasteless joke, or was that how Julius afforded the birdseed for all those feeders? Anyway, Judy was still alive, so if Julius was a hitman, he was singularly ineffectual.

I slammed my pen against the desktop in frustration. It was high time I started paying attention to my other clients. I jotted my notes from Herta into the Martin Binder case file and closed the folder.

True, it was Sunday, but equally true, I was days behind on my work. Around one-thirty, when I broke for lunch, I remembered that I'd sent an e-mail to the Cheviot labs, telling them I'd be bringing the drawers and the paper in. I left a message on my account manager's voice mail to say the job was off.

I stopped a little before six, feeling incredibly virtuous with the amount of work I'd cleared. The most important report, for Darraugh Graham, was done and e-mailed. Most of the others were close to finished. I'd be able to send out invoices on Monday and end September in the black—if I didn't count the six-figure legal bill I was paying down.

One of my friends plays on a tag football team on the South Side.

On an impulse, before going over to the park, I drove to Julius Dzornen's coach house. A couple of kids were playing on the swing set, arguing in shrill voices. They stopped to watch me bang on the coach house door: I was a novelty, a visitor to the sullen recluse who lived behind them.

Julius again took his time answering, but finally opened the door. He was wearing baggy khakis and an old T-shirt, but no shoes or socks. "Herta told me you'd been over there bugging her about the Binder woman's money. If you think you can get any out of me, you have the power to squeeze blood from a rock."

I leaned against the jamb so that he wouldn't be able to slam the door on me. "Nope. I'm not here about the money. Herta spent all Judy's money on her kids' orthodonture and I know you don't have any. Herta told me you offered to kill Judy because she'd upset your mom so badly. Is that what happened fifty years ago? You killed someone but the detectives never arrested you?"

Julius's face turned the color of putty and he swayed. For a moment I thought he might be going to fall over, but he held on to the doorknob.

"Fifty years ago," he repeated. "Is that what I said? Maybe I meant sixty. Could have been seventy. I lose count. Fifty years ago, I was a dropout and a loser living in my mother's house while my two sisters screamed their heads off about finding a job. When our mother died—and believe me, no one ever called her 'mom': Ilse definitely was not a 'mom' kind of woman. When she died I was disappointed to learn that she wore old-fashioned corsets: I always thought she had an exoskeleton that she'd bequeathed to Herta. I was softer, like our father. Prone to panic in a crisis. I doubt I could have killed Judy Binder, even if Ilse had ordered me to."

"Did you think your father stole his Nobel Prize research from one of his students?" I asked.

Julius gave a crack of unpleasant laughter. "From Martina Saginor, for instance? That would make a fine Dan Brown novel, wouldn't it, conspiracy, death, Martina disappears so no one can check on who did the work. No. In his youth, Benjamin was a brilliant scientist. The record is there for anyone to see."

"Is he the person you killed? Is that what the detectives who never came were supposed to investigate?"

His face contorted into a terrible sneer. "You could say Benjamin and I killed each other. He wasn't a Nietzschean *Übermensch*, and neither was I. When we had to face disagreeable realities, we both collapsed. Unlike Edward and Cordell Breen, who flourished like that famous biblical tree. Tell that to Herta, and Martin, and anyone else who wants to ask. Good night."

I moved out of the doorway. He'd pulled himself together; he wasn't going to crack again, not until I had a better hammer and chisel to attack him with.

I went over to the park in time to cheer my friend through the final minutes of her football game, which entitled me to join the team for a vegan barbecue. It was past nine when I got home again, as happy as if I'd never heard of Binders or Dzornens or Nobel Prizes.

Mr. Contreras had been in the pocket handkerchief of a park up the street, giving the dogs their last outing of the day. We walked inside together, but Mitch insisted on pushing past me up the stairs. Peppy joined him, her tail waving like a red flag.

I called to them sharply, but they didn't respond. I ran up after them. At the second-floor landing, I managed to step on Mitch's leash, but he gave a short bark and broke free.

"You got mice, or a steak or something he's smelling?" my neighbor said, stumping up behind me.

The two dogs were at the top by the time I reached the last landing. Mitch hurled himself against my front door, snarling and growling. Peppy began to bark in loud, sharp repetitions: beware, danger!

"Get downstairs," I cried. "Call 911. Someone's in my place."

The old man started to argue with me: he wasn't leaving me to face—

"Just go, just do it, I don't want you shot." I yanked the dogs back.

My arms were still weak from yesterday's work. All I did was move the dogs into a potential line of fire. I let the leashes go and the dogs attacked the door again. I stood with my back flush with the wall, gun in my hand.

On the second floor, the Soongs' baby began to wail. A newcomer to the building, a woman who sold bar appliances, appeared at the second-floor landing. "Those dogs are a major nuisance to everyone in this building. I'm calling—"

"Do it!" I shouted. "Call the cops! Someone broke into my apartment; that's why the dogs are crazy."

"Yeah, stop being a pain in the you-know-what," Mr. Contreras added. "We'd all be dead if the dogs hadn't—"

"Get out of the line of fire," I screamed at him.

I pulled my cell phone from my hip pocket to dial 911 myself. "Home invasion." I croaked out my address, repeating it twice over the dogs' noise.

"Stay on the line, ma'am; we'll get someone there as fast as possible. Keep talking, tell us what's happening."

My door has a steel core. You don't hear much through it, but over the dogs' noise, I could tell the locks were being rolled open. I made another desperate grab for the leashes, but I had to drop the phone.

A gun muzzle appeared through a crack in my door. I backed against the wall again, screaming at Mr. Contreras to get down.

Mitch broke from me and made another dash at the door. His weight forced it open. The gunman fired, but the shots went wide. Mitch knocked the man to the ground and stood with his forelegs on his chest, his muzzle near the man's throat. I flung myself in after and squatted with my own gun next to the thug's head. His eyes were rolling wildly.

A second man appeared in front of me. "Call off the dog or I'll shoot him."

The downstairs doorbell began to ring.

"That's the police," I said. "You can leave through the back. Or you can kill us all and then let the cops shoot you. Or you can put down your gun and come quietly."

"Or you can call off your dog and then look at twenty years in Leavenworth for assaulting a federal officer," the second thug said.

"Yeah, right." I kept my gun pointed at the man on the floor.

Someone let the cops in. They pounded up the stairs, phones crackling, shouting questions. The woman who sold bar supplies was putting in her furious two cents, Peppy was barking. Mr. Contreras was shouting instructions to the cops. In another instant the room was filled with people in riot helmets and flak jackets. I backed away from the thug on the floor, grabbed Mitch's leash and managed to haul him off the man's chest.

For a moment all was confusion: guns, shouted questions, dogs, neighbors, the Soong baby's howls. The police made me and the two thugs hand over our weapons and then demanded an accounting.

"We're federal agents—" the second thug began.

"I live here," I interrupted. "I just got home. My dog sensed an intruder and when the guy on the floor opened the door to shoot us, my dog jumped him and knocked him to the ground. They're pretending to be federal agents in the hopes you won't arrest them."

"We shot because you were attacking—"

"Shut up!" I snapped. "You do not break into people's homes and shoot them when they return home. Not unless you are drug dealers pretending to be Feds. If you are Feds, you produce credentials, and even then you'd damned well better have a warrant, and even then you don't break in. You wait for the homeowner to return."

"Okay," the police sergeant said. "Let's take this one at a time. Who is the homeowner?"

"She is," Mr. Contreras said. "Like she just told you, she just got home—"

"Do you live here, sir?" the squad leader asked.

"On the ground floor, but her and me, we share the dogs, see, and when we got in from their last walk—"

A woman in the unit came over to Mr. Contreras and asked him to join her on my couch. "Let's let the sarge sort this out, okay, sir?"

The sergeant decided to start with the intruders. "What were you doing here?"

The man who'd been on the floor had joined his partner over by my piano. I saw that they'd opened the back and had been searching in the strings and I felt my blood pressure start to rise.

"What were you looking for in my piano?" I said. "If you've damaged the strings, I don't care if it's Janet Napolitano or Pablo Escobar you're working for, you are paying for every dime of repairs—"

"Ma'am," the sergeant said, "I understand you're angry, but let's sit down and talk this through quietly."

"I want to search the apartment first," I said. "If they broke down the back door I need to call an emergency service. I also want to see if there's anyone else lurking in here."

The sergeant thought that was reasonable; one of his officers escorted me through my four rooms. I took Mitch with me; every time one of the thugs spoke, his hackles rose. I didn't think Mr. Contreras could hold Mitch if the dog thought they needed another lesson in manners.

The goons had pulled my old trunk out of my hall walk-in closet. They'd tumbled music and papers onto the floor, including Gabriella's hand-marked score of *Don Giovanni*. Three or four pages had been torn in their carelessness. I blinked back tears of fury and grief.

In my bedroom they had dismantled my dresser drawers, they'd searched the books on my bedside table. I glanced in the closet. They hadn't stumbled on the safe behind my hanging shoe holder, that was one mercy.

In the kitchen they'd dumped ten days' of recycling onto the floor.

I looked at the back door. All the locks were in place. They'd come in through the front, with some pretty sophisticated tools.

In the dining room, where I use the built-in china displays as bookshelves, they'd pulled off most of the books and left them open on the table. A number had fallen to the floor. I squatted next to the cupboard where I keep my most precious possession, the red wineglasses my mother brought with her when she fled Italy in 1941.

The glasses were safe; the rest of the wreckage I could deal with. I picked up the books and realized that my work papers were gone.

"All the papers I was working on at my dining room table are missing," I said. "I can't tell at a glance if they've taken anything else—the chaos is too horrible," I told the officer.

The officer texted the information to her sergeant. We returned to the living room, where we found that the thugs had produced federal credentials.

The sergeant looked sourly at the two men. "These may be legitimate, but I'm going to call to verify them. You were in here without a warrant and without the homeowner's knowledge."

"We are conducting an investigation connected to our national security. This gives us certain warrantless rights." This was the thug whom Mitch had knocked over. What a good dog.

"And among those rights is the right to shoot the homeowner on her return?" It took a major act of will, but I kept my tone conversational.

"We were acting on information and belief that you have documents that affect our national security." That was Thug Two.

"So you broke into my home and ripped up my mother's music?"

"We didn't rip it up, we were looking for documents. It was a logical hiding place."

"And then you stole my work papers—"

"We confiscated them," Thug Two snapped. He had a nice mop of wavy brown hair that he clearly spent a lot of time tending.

"Ooh, good one, Curly, confiscation. When I was with the public defender, a lot of my clients had confiscated cameras, jewelry and so on. I wish I'd known that we could have been pleading national security. 'Your Honor, we held the plaintiff up at gunpoint and confiscated his belongings because we believe his wallet affected national security.' I still have colleagues in the PD's—"

"That's enough," the sergeant said. "I don't know who's right and who's wrong here, but even if you two are federal agents, firing a gun in a populated apartment building is a recipe for a disaster. There are babies in this building. There are old people."

He got a squawk on his cell phone, exchanged a few words, turned to me. "Looks like they are really federal agents, not scam artists, Ms. Warshawski. Beats me why they don't have a warrant, but the local federal magistrate ordered us to stand down."

He looked at the thugs, or Homeland Security agents as they liked to be called. "You going to give the lady a receipt for those papers?"

"When it's an issue of national security with a potential tie to terrorism, we don't have to have a warrant or give a receipt," Mitch's agent said. Moe, for short.

"I'll include that in my report," the sergeant said. "Ma'am, could you give me a list of what papers they've taken? If they're valuable, and they show up somewhere, at an auction or something, we can produce a police report stating they were taken from you during a home invasion."

"It's not a home invasion," Curly said. "We had—"

"Yeah, I know, I know," the sergeant said. "Do you want to tell me how you got access to the lady's apartment? I looked at the locks. You'd need safecracker tools, not just street-grade picklocks."

"Why are you so bent on obstructing our investigation?" Moe asked. "You verified our IDs, you know we have good reason to be here—"

"That's what I don't know," the sergeant said. "I don't know why you think this lady's ma's music needed tearing apart. I know that this lady's father trained my dad when my old man joined the force, and that Mrs. Warshawski, her ma, was quite a singer, according to my old man. There wasn't a better officer in Chicago than Tony Warshawski, ask anyone from the old days. When I was a boy, my dad always quoted him to me: Tony used to say the only end that justifies the means is laziness. A lazy cop is as bad as a bent cop, that's what Tony Warshawski taught my dad, and I'm betting he taught this lady here the same. Am I right?"

I sat up straighter, blinking back tears. "Yes, Sergeant." I'd cheated once on a social studies quiz. When Tony found out, he got me out of bed an hour early every day for a month to run errands for a housebound woman on our street. *Your mother and I have been letting you get lazy. You run these errands for Mrs. Poilevsky and you'll work the lazy out of your system. Don't let me hear of you cheating a second time.*

The sergeant gathered up his unit, bent to scratch Mitch under his chin, and took me out into the hall. "They're going to take you down to question you. I'm leaving your gun with your downstairs neighbor. I don't want you making your problems worse by shooting one of those *federales*, however tempting it seems."

He handed me his card: Anton Javitz, Town Hall Station. "You need anything, you give me a call, okay?"

He was gone before I could do more than stammer out my thanks.

26

MIDNIGHT RIDE

SPENT SEVERAL HOURS talking to Curly and Moe, while a federal magistrate hovered nearby. As they were carting me off, Mr. Contreras promised to call my lawyer. Partway through the interrogation Deb Steppe, one of my lawyer's associates, showed up.

It was good that I had Deb with me, because when I learned that the federal agents had been in my office before they came to my home and that they'd taken the hard drive from my big computer, the room turned red in front of my eyes. Deb had a hand on my shoulder as I started to my feet.

Curly warned me for a second time that I could have the charge of assaulting a federal agent added to anything else they chose to charge me with. I whispered to Deb for a few minutes.

She turned to the agents. "You apparently watched Ms. Warshawski's office until she finished work for the day at five-forty-five. You then entered, using advanced electronic technology. We haven't had time to inspect her office, but if it resembles the condition of her home, you acted without restraint in searching for material that you refuse to identify."

Curly started to repeat his worn-out slogan about national security, but Deb held up an authoritative hand. "You took Ms. Warshawski's hard drives; it would be easy to pretend you cared about national security, but you used that as a cover for theft. Ms. Warshawski is well known in Chicago. If she's working on a case that overlaps a federal investigation, it would have been simpler for you to come to her with a warrant and an explanation. What were you looking for?"

It was their turn for a sidebar, this time with the assistant federal magistrate catching weekend duty. Deb and I couldn't hear the conversation, but the magistrate looked startled, then angry. She said a few sharp words to the agents, then called Deb and me back to the conference table.

"Ms. Warshawski, you came in possession of some documents yesterday in Palfry, Illinois, that these agents are anxious to retrieve. If you can produce those documents, the agents will return your computers and proceed with their investigation."

I could feel my eyes growing large. "My investigation has nothing to do with terrorism. It's a sordid story of drug users and dealers."

I gave a précis of Judy Binder's story. "I went back to the meth house yesterday, hoping there might be something that would tell me why she was shot. I found an abandoned dresser with papers glued to a drawer; I was bringing them to a private forensics lab to see if they could restore any of the text. Someone broke into my car in the motel parking lot at four this morning and stole the drawer and the documents. The local sheriff's police came out; you can talk to them to see if they've turned up any leads."

"Pretty convenient," Moe sneered. "It's a great story."

I ignored him and spoke to the magistrate. "If the agents had any inkling that the meth pit held secrets about terrorism, they had a week to go down there and excavate. Since they broke into both my office and my home, I assume they are the same guys who broke into my car."

The prosecutor asked Moe and Curly what they knew about the theft from my car.

"Nothing. It's a great story, but she had all day to dispose of the papers," Curly said. "Of course we went to the Cheviot labs, but they claimed the perp—"

"The what?" Deb Steppe interrupted.

"The suspect," Curly corrected sulkily.

"How about, 'the detective'?" Deb said.

"How about, 'Ms. Warshawski,'" the magistrate said dryly. "It's midnight. Let's adjourn this episode of 'he said, she said.' If the lab doesn't have the documents, and Ms. Warshawski doesn't have them, they are most likely in the possession of whoever took them from her car. If she scanned them into her computer, it should be easy to inspect the hard drives and sort out what's there. I'll talk to Judge Frieders, but I'm sure he'll set a time limit on how long you can keep the drives."

"Your agents have walked away with my client's entire work life. They are destroying her livelihood for a fishing expedition," Deb said sharply. "I'll be in front of Judge Frieders first thing tomorrow morning myself to demand the return of the hard drives and the documents that they admit taking from Ms. Warshawski's home."

"We need the machine for at least a week," the agents protested.

"Your computer division must be pretty pathetic if you can't copy my drives and give them back to me right now," I said. "Not that I want my confidential client information in your grubby—"

"Vic!" Deb rapped out warningly. "I thought we agreed that I would do the talking."

The magistrate shut her eyes and rubbed a circle in the middle of her forehead. She was tired and she wanted this case to go away.

"I'll talk to Judge Frieders, but Ms. Warshawski has a point: if you want to inspect the drives, just copy them."

Deb hustled me out of the magistrate's office before Moe or Curly actually charged me. Just as well: I was feeling pretty Mitch-like over the theft of the drives from my big office computer. I still had my laptop. At least, I hoped it was still in the briefcase I'd dropped on my way up the stairs tonight, but it couldn't hold all my detailed reports and client data.

Deb waited with me while I flagged a cab. Time was starting to blur. Was it day or night, was I in Palfry or Chicago, had Homeland Security broken into my car at the motel early this morning, or had it been random punks, as the sheriff's deputy wanted to believe?

The downtown streets were empty. I didn't think anyone was tailing the cab, but I was too tired to pay close attention. And really, what difference did it make? The important question was how Homeland Security knew I'd found the bureau drawers, but didn't know they'd been stolen from me soon after. Either the right hand didn't know what the right fingers were doing, or a second party cared about the papers Martin Binder might have dropped in the meth pit.

I dozed in the cab. When the driver pulled up in front of my building on Racine, I woke with a jolt. "They read my e-mail," I said out loud. "That's why Martin went dark."

"It's eighteen dollars, Miss, whether you e-mail it or text it, and whether it's dark or light."

I fished in my pocket for my wallet before I remembered it, too, had been in my briefcase. I hoped it was Mr. Contreras who'd found my case, not Moe or Curly, or the angry second-floor tenant.

At least my keys were in my pocket. The cabdriver cursed me, but he had to wait while I went inside for some money. My first piece of good luck: Mr. Contreras had left a note saying that he had my briefcase. I found it inside his own front door, with my wallet and laptop still inside. By the time I got back to the cab, the meter was at twenty-one dollars. Homeland Security is not cheap, but then, what worth having is?

Back in my own apartment, it wasn't just the damage Homeland Security had done that got me down, but the sense of vulnerability, that they had let themselves into my home, touched my things, touched my mother's music, even her concert gown. I took the keys to Jake's apartment from a dish in my kitchen cupboard.

Jake's place looked as tidy as when he'd left. I rinsed off federal agent dirt in his bathroom and crawled thankfully into his bed.

My dreams were turbulent, but I slept deeply and didn't waken until almost noon on Monday. I remade the bed, tidily, the way my mother had taught me, corners squared off. My own bed I usually don't bother with, but the squalor in my place had given me an urge to be neat.

I'd gotten a five-figure bonus from a case I'd worked in the summer. Part of it had gone to a high-end home cappuccino machine. While the boilers heated, I cleaned up my kitchen. Why had Moe and Curly been so destructive? Usually when the law sneaks in without a warrant, they're careful not to leave a trace behind, so why had this pair been so wanton? Were they hoping I'd think street punks had broken in?

I fussed around with the machine, discarding shots until I pulled a couple of perfect ones. I couldn't bear to have anything second-rate right now. I took my cappuccino with me while I worked on my home: folding my mother's concert gown back into its protective tissue paper, replacing the score to *Don Giovanni*, putting books back on shelves.

If Moe and Curly knew I'd e-mailed Cheviot Labs, announcing the arrival of the dresser drawers, they had hacked into my server and were helping themselves to my correspondence. That meant the confidential report I'd sent Darraugh Graham yesterday was government property.

My temper was rising again. I wanted to act, to sue the government or blow away Moe and Curly, or—don't do it, I counseled myself. Anger is the surest route to making terrible mistakes. Calm down, think it through.

Question one. Why was Homeland Security reading my e-mail? We all know that various government agencies, from local up through the National Security Agency, troll through e-mail looking for some set of dangerous words. Which ones had I been using that made them care about the meth house in Palfry?

I sat at my dining room table, a copy of Sciascia's *Il Contesto* that I'd

been about to reshelve in one hand. It wasn't the meth house. It was
Martin Binder that they wanted. Homeland Security had learned I
was looking for him, probably from Cordell Breen: he'd told me he was
going to sic the FBI on finding out if his daughter was hiding Martin
down in Mexico City.

Roberta had spread the story of our inspecting Agnes Schlafly's
bureau drawers far and wide at the football game. Anyone could have
passed the news on. Homeland Security knew I'd found the drawers
because they were monitoring my e-mail—they'd read my message to
Cheviot Labs.

Since Homeland Security didn't have the news that the drawers had
been stolen, that meant two sets of people were looking for Martin. Set
One broke into the Mustang while the Feds were waiting to intercept
the drawers when I got back to Chicago. So Set One were drug dealers.
In that case, the sheriff's deputies who'd come to the motel at four
yesterday morning were right—meth heads thought I'd dug up treasure and they wanted it.

If Cordell Breen was tracking Martin, he could have bribed anyone
to let him know whether they found anything at the meth house. My
head ached from chasing my ideas in circles. I could see drug dealers
murdering Ricky, I could see them thinking that Judy had run from
Palfry with a chunk of Ricky Schlafly's money. And then imagining
that I'd found gold in the meth pit when the stories began circulating
at the football game.

"DTs," I printed in block capitals, short for Drug Thugs. "DTs
killed Schlafly and Kitty (probably). HSTs—Homeland Security
Thugs—are monitoring my e-mail because Cordell Breen has asked
FBI to find Martin Binder. Cordell thinks Martin is selling Metargon
secrets, but there's been no whiff of buyer or seller."

The DTs probably would just trash the bits of paper on the dresser
drawers. In fact, they'd trash the drawers, too, when they realized that
the only treasure there was fool's gold.

What did the HSTs imagine I'd found? Not the bank account. The document from the Department of Commerce about Innsbruck? But that was something obtained through the Freedom of Information Act; anyone could read it.

I pulled my laptop out of my briefcase and started to power it up, but stopped. If the HSTs were monitoring my e-mail they could be embedded right in my accounts, looking at every search I made. They'd see the laptop's ISP and come trundling along looking for me and my machine. I needed a computer where someone wouldn't be tracking me. I put *Il Contesto* away, but left the rest of the books on the table.

27

DERRICK, KING OF THE DAMNED

A GOOD FRIEND OF MINE had died in a bad fall earlier this summer. I'd put her private documents into my safe while she lay unconscious in the ICU. When she died a few days later, trauma and grief put any thought of her papers out of my mind. I came on them when I was checking my safe, to make sure Homeland Security hadn't been inside it.

Leydon Ashford had been not just a loving and energetic friend, but a risk-taker who enjoyed thumbing her nose at authority. I figured she would applaud my borrowing her identity for a few days.

I took public transportation down to the South Side so I could use the University of Chicago library. Before I went, I checked in with Mr. Contreras. He started to ask me what had happened to me last night, but I put a finger over his mouth and took him outside with the dogs. While we stood on the beach throwing balls for them, I told him what had happened last night with the federal magistrate. I asked him not to discuss any aspect of this current case when we were at home or in my car.

"Those Homeland Security guys have got me nervous. If they've hacked into my e-mail account, they might easily be bugging my phone, or the car or our building."

The warning made my neighbor angry: this wasn't what he'd risked his life for at Anzio all those years ago. Far as that went, it wasn't why he'd worked hard at Diamond Machining for forty years, creating struts for B-52s.

I couldn't offer him any consolation. It wasn't what I'd worked all my life for, either. "The trouble is, they seem to think I know something about our nuclear policy, or weapons or something, and until I figure that out, I don't have a way of getting them to leave me alone."

Back at home, I took the battery out of my phone so that its GPS signal wouldn't betray me. I left my iPad and laptop with Mr. Contreras so I wouldn't be tempted to check my e-mails.

I wasn't going to drive, in case someone had bugged my car. On my way to the L, I stopped a couple of times, to tie my shoes, to buy a paper, but I didn't see any obvious signs of tails. Either the HSTs were too subtle for me or I was exaggerating my importance to them. Still, it would reduce my carbon footprint to ride the L: I felt virtuous as the train made its languid afternoon run into the center city.

That was about the one positive in the day. Until I knew for sure why Homeland Security was focusing on me, I wasn't going to be a very happy detective. A government audit had shown that Homeland Security monitors e-mails and phone calls from Americans without even trying to connect us to terrorism. They don't have a budget, they just do what they want. The problem is that once the government starts monitoring you, they invade all aspects of your life, not just the little bit they think they need.

I needed to talk to Judy Binder. She surely told her son about the bank account Benjamin Dzornen had set up, but I bet Martin didn't care about that—it would have been ancient history to him. He'd gone to his mother because he thought Judy had some documents about the significance of Martina's work, something neither Judy nor Kitty had recognized or cared about.

I liked that, because it meant that was why Ricky Schlafly was murdered. Ricky overheard mother and son arguing. He figured Judy was sitting on valuable documents. For any dopehead, something was valuable if it could be sold or bartered for drugs.

Ricky tried to sell the documents. I'd never met him alive, but I assumed he was as lazy and greedy as the addicts I used to represent. He wouldn't have done anything subtle, like gone to archivists with offers of important papers. He'd have gone straight to eBay or Craigslist, and then anyone would have known about the documents: Julius Dzornen, some other drug dealer or even Homeland Security, come to think of it.

Downtown, I left the L to ride a bus down to Hyde Park. If Chicago really had rapid transit, I wouldn't drive so much: the fifteen-mile run from my home down to the university took eighty minutes.

At the library, they let me inside with Leydon's driver's license. I couldn't borrow books, but I could use the collection, including the computers.

I logged on first to the online auction site Virtual-Bidder. I tried to imagine how Schlafly might have thought. He probably hadn't known Martina Saginor's name, but I started with her, anyway, tried Benjamin Dzornen, moved to physics in Vienna, and finally hit pay dirt, so to speak, with "Nuclear Weapons," where there were hundreds of thousands of hits: manuals from the Nevada Proving Grounds, photos from Hiroshima and Nagasaki, videos of old movies with names like *Atomic Bomb*.

A seller named King Derrick had been offering "Authentic Nazi Nuclear Secrets." King Derrick, ruler of the Empire of the Damned. I saw his decimated body again, the eyeballs gone, the crows circling, and shivered.

Starting bid for his authentic secrets was suggested at a hundred dollars, but the auction had been shut down. A large red-and-black banner covered most of the page, announcing that the auction had been in violation of Virtual-Bidder rules. Behind the banner, parts of a screen shot that King Derrick had called "Proof of real Nazi weapons secrets" were visible.

> If k_{eff} = 1, then . . . is critical. If neutrons . . . added . . . by . . . external . . . and if the system is not quenched by a strong . . . absorber, they can trigger an explosion. An external Ra-Be neutron . . . at Innsbruck emitted S_0 = 10^6 neutrons/second . . . know the neutron-mul . . .

At the bottom of the page was a small circle with a kind of design in it. It seemed to be interlocking triangles with another symbol that was too blurry on the screen image to make out. I wondered if it might be some symbol of authentication that collectors of Nazi memorabilia looked for.

The part of the text visible behind the banner meant nothing to me, except that it concerned the weapons facility where Martina had spent part of the war. A weapons expert would know whether it proved they'd been building the bomb in Innsbruck. Was this why Homeland Security was on my case? Not because of Martin and the Metargon code, but because they thought I knew something about nuclear weapons?

I stopped looking at auction sites and began searching the Web. Homeland Security had access to all my log-in information, which meant if they were in fact monitoring me, they'd know when I went to one of my subscription databases. That limited me to the standard search engines, Yahoo, Dogpile, Metar-Quest. Once again, I started with my Viennese scientists.

I got too many hits on Benjamin Dzornen to bother with them. There was nothing for Martina Saginor, except for a mention in tandem with Memler in a book on women at the Radium Institute in Vienna during the 1920s and 1930s. The library had a copy. I closed my search: the library periodically wipes the buffers clean, but I didn't want to leave any of my pages open.

The book was in the science library. I was curious enough to trudge across the campus to the science quad. Arthur Harriman, my young science librarian, was working the desk when I stopped to get permission to go into the stacks.

"Nora! I wondered when you'd come back," Harriman said. "Have you found the missing warheads?"

"Like the purloined letter, they were right out in the nuclear stockpile where anyone could see them." I tried to get into the spirit of the joke.

"You know, I told you I'd ask this friend of mine who's writing her dissertation on Dzornen about whether he'd stolen your lady's work, and she pooh-poohed that. Dzornen's prize was for work he did before your Ms. Saginor became his student."

Another blind alley, then. I thanked him for remembering to ask, and got a day pass from him. After a few more tedious Nick-and-Nora jokes, I went into the stacks to read about women in Viennese physics.

I sat cross-legged on the floor with the book, checking only the pages where Martina was mentioned. I found a brief bio: she'd been born before World War I to a working-class family, won a scholarship at a new Technische Hochschule für Mädchen when she was twelve. (With the highest mathematics score in the city. I thought of Martin with his stratospheric test scores.) She taught at the same school from 1928 to 1938, did a Ph.D. in physics at Göttingen in 1929–1930.

In another section, detailing Martina's career, I read:

Saginor's unpublished work was nearly all destroyed in a purge of the Institute's files during the Nazi era, probably at the command of her onetime student, the Nazi weapons expert Gertrud Memler, so we can rely only on a few surviving notebooks and the articles Saginor published between 1931 and 1938.

Saginor was like Fermi in believing in her strong intuitions about physical phenomena. The effort to downgrade her abilities stems partly from L. F. Bates' troubling visit to the Radium Institute in 1934, and partly from Memler's efforts to extinguish her former professor's memory.

I put the book back on the shelf and leaned against the metal divider. Lotty said Kitty resented her mother's absorption in physics; would knowing that someone rated Martina's abilities highly have pleased Kitty? She was more likely to have been anguished: the bio made no mention of a child. It wasn't because Martina had kept Kitty's birth a secret—not only Lotty, but Dzornen's two daughters had played with Kitty when they were little girls together. Whatever stigma might have attached to illegitimacy in 1930s Vienna, Martina hadn't tried to hide the child. Any more than Lotty's grandparents had hidden her.

The real interest in the story, at least for me, was Gertrud Memler. Kitty's murder had made me forget the book I'd been looking at right before she called for help, *The Secret Diary of a Cold War Conscientious Objector*. Memler had figured in that, as well.

Memler had survived the war intact, coming to the States with Operation Paperclip after the war, working on nuclear weapons, and then she suddenly vanished, reappearing under cover to attack U.S. nuclear policy. Perhaps watching actual bombs explode in Nevada, doing actual damage to dogs and people, had given Memler a Saul-like conversion.

I'd been sitting too long; my brain was turning to glue. I got up and stretched, bending backward in the stacks, undoing the knots in my spine one at a time.

Outside, we were having one of those golden afternoons that Chicago sometimes gets in September. I walked several miles before going to a bus stop at the northeast end of the neighborhood, near the expressway and the lake. While I waited, I put my phone back together.

I had seven messages, one from Jake, wondering where I was; he'd missed talking to me the last few nights. Lotty had called to say that

Judy Binder was in a stable enough condition to be moved out of intensive care.

I phoned Jake while I stood on an overpass looking at Lake Michigan. Calm seas, lover's voice, I felt happy. The bus came while we were talking. I hung up, not wanting to share my private words with a bus full of strangers.

Once we got downtown, I flagged a cab home. Enough carbon-saving virtue. I called Lotty from the taxi. The driver, speaking into his own phone in a language I didn't recognize, certainly was paying no attention to me, and very little to the traffic on Lake Shore Drive.

"Can I see Judy?" I asked Lotty.

"You can if you want," Lotty said, "but she's apparently in a rather ugly frame of mind."

I said I wanted to see if Judy could remember anything about the attack.

"Helen Langston, the surgeon who treated her at Glenbrook, says Judy doesn't remember it. Helen doesn't think it's trauma-induced amnesia. She thinks it's because Judy had so much oxycodone in her system that she couldn't process anything going on around her."

"If I ask her about her 'duck and cover' remark, maybe it will trigger something," I suggested.

"I'll go with you," Lotty said. "I haven't been able to bring myself to visit her alone; I'm angry with her, for the wreck she's made of her own life, and, really, for putting Kitty in death's path, and there is no point in going into her hospital room and upbraiding her. Are you at home or in your office?"

"Heading home." I'd have to face my office, to see what Homeland Security had done to it in the name of protecting America, but that could wait until morning.

"I'll pick you up in half an hour."

Lotty hung up before I could protest that I would drive. I'd had so many life-threatening adventures in the last week that I supposed riding with Lotty might seem tame. Lotty had a kind of "stand your ground" approach to other drivers: if she didn't intimidate them first, they might force her from the road. One thing about letting Lotty drive, she'd give anyone tailing me a workout.

I noticed that since Kitty's death, Lotty had stopped calling her "Käthe." It was a kind of indirect apology, I supposed, for the decades of contempt she'd confessed to me after Kitty's death.

Lotty was driving a silver Audi these days, a little coupe that I coveted. It closed around me like an eggcup when I climbed inside. I didn't know if that meant it would protect me or make me more vulnerable in a crash. As Lotty zoomed up the Edens, she tried to ask me about the state of the investigation. I answered in monosyllables, yelping each time we came within scraping distance of another vehicle.

When she turned into the Glenbrook Hospital exit in the face of an oncoming semi, I said, "Lotty, this is a beautiful car. Give it to me and drive my old Mustang if you want to wreck something."

She pulled into a space reserved for physicians, put a placard on the dashboard, and got out of the car. "You fuss too much over trivial things, Victoria. The important thing is whether you have found a way to discover what happened to Martin."

"Even if I had, it wouldn't do me much good if I were in traction," I grumbled, following her into the hospital.

28

DUCK AND COVER

JUDY HAD LEFT intensive care, but she was still in serious condition. The ward head warned Lotty and me that she was screaming a great deal, demanding morphine or oxycodone for her pain.

"It's hard to know how to regulate her meds, because of her addiction. We've been weaning her from her morphine drip and switching to channel blockers, but it's hard to tell if those are working since she keeps demanding more morphine. We've had to put her in restraints because she was scratching her arms open."

"I was afraid of this." Lotty frowned.

The ward head took us to Judy Binder's room. She was attached to machines that monitored her fast-beating heart, administered fluids, checked her breathing. Her eyes were shut, but I didn't think she was asleep. Her cloud of gray-streaked curls moved on the pillow as she twitched and groaned. Her face was red and puffy, her lips swollen.

"Is she allergic to something in her medications?" I asked.

Lotty and the ward head exchanged sour looks. "Opiate withdrawal," the ward head said. "She's got a very long rehabilitation in front of her. She isn't going to make a good recovery from the bullet wound if she doesn't take drug rehab seriously. Once we get her physically stable here, she's got to go into a good residential program."

Lotty went up to the bedside and put two fingers on Judy's pulse. I could see the raw welts on Judy's arms where she'd been clawing herself. Her eyes fluttered open at Lotty's touch.

"Dr. Lotty! I knew I could count on you. I'm in terrible pain, I need morphine, or oxy. Vicodin will do if the dose is strong enough. I can't sleep, my gut is on fire. Get me back my morphine pump."

Lotty ignored her demand. "This is V. I. Warshawski, Judy. She saved your life."

Judy barely looked at me. "Thanks, I guess, for saving me for this torture chamber. Dr. Lotty, I need my morphine, I need it now, you can't come here and not help me."

"I'm not your doctor here, Judy, I'm just a visitor. Ms. Warshawski needs to ask you—"

"That cunt, that bitch, she told you to say no, didn't she?"

Judy's voice rose. I was taken aback briefly, thinking she meant me, but then realized she was looking past us to the ward head.

"She's one of those women from Belsen, isn't she, pretending to be a nurse, but she's really a Nazi and a torturer. You know, you're a Holocaust survivor, don't side with her. Get her fired, you're a surgeon, they'll do what you say. Fire her fucking mean ass and get me my pump."

"Ms. Binder," I said, "I'm sorry to intrude when you're in pain and when you're grieving."

"Damn straight I'm in pain. And grief, too."

"Because of your mother?" I asked.

"Anyone with a mother like that would grieve over it," she snarled.

"You don't remember seeing her get shot? I'm afraid she wasn't as fortunate as you: she died of her wounds."

"Batty Kitty has gone to God? I'm sure He'll be thrilled. And her real father, he'll be ecstatic when she shows up. Who the fuck are you and why can't you mind your own business?"

I wanted to yank the IV lines out of her and throttle her, but I kept my voice even. "Duck and cover. The night you were shot, you said that duck and cover worked the best, even though she never believed in it. Was that your mother who never believed in it?"

"I'm in pain," Judy screamed. "I'm in pain and you want to interrogate me. You're not a fucking cop. I don't have to tell you fucking anything." She thrashed in her restraints so violently that she knocked the oxygen tube from her nose.

"Of course you don't," I said. "You were very smart to get under your son's bed like that. 'Duck and cover' saved your life. Who told you it was a bad idea?"

For a moment, Judy stopped tugging at her restraints. I couldn't read the expression in her eyes, the pupils were so dilated, but when she spoke, her voice was soft and dull.

"Did I really say that? Is that why you won't give me my morphine?"

I tried to assure her that no one was punishing her, that I admired her creativity hiding from her attackers, but her restless twitching began again. She shied from the "duck and cover" topic, and couldn't or wouldn't say who had shot her and her mother.

"You were pretty amazing back in Palfry," I said, "getting away from the guys who killed Ricky Schlafly. That took real guts."

Judy focused on me for the first time, her dark eyes large circles in her emaciated face: the Palfry debacle was something real in her mind that momentarily made her forget her desperate need for narcotics. "Not guts, I was terrified," she whispered. "They shot Bowser. I was asleep and suddenly Bowser started barking. Ricky yelled that he was tired of the damned dog barking at nothing, but I looked out the window and there was this black SUV. I yelled at Ricky to wake up, get his shotgun. These men got out of the SUV and shot out the camera. Then they cut a big hole in the security fence and broke down the back door.

"Bowser tried to jump them but they shot him, Ricky and I were sitting on the stairs watching, it was so terrible. Delilah, she was always a 'fraidy-cat, Ricky used to kick her for running away, or kick me for loving her, she took off when they shot Bowser."

Delilah, that was the waif Mr. Contreras and I were supporting.

Judy started gasping for air. Lotty put the oxygen tube back in her nose. After a bit her breathing became less labored.

"Delilah is going to be okay," I said. "I brought her back to Chicago; she's in the hospital right now."

Judy's eyes opened, a startled expression that turned wary: Was I trustworthy, or was I using the dog to con her?

"How did you get away?" I asked.

"When Ricky saw them shoot Bowser he undid the locks in the front door and ran outside. They chased him into the cornfield and I got in their SUV and drove up to Chicago."

"Very cool head," I said. "So you drove up to Freddie Walker's place in Austin. Where'd you leave the SUV?"

"I gave it to Freddie. It was a Lincoln, brand-new, but he said it was too hot to sell as a whole car, so he had his boys strip it for parts."

That was why Freddie had let her crash, I guess, and why he let her get high on his product. A brand-new Navigator's parts would bring a nice little chunk of change.

"The people who shot Bowser and Ricky, were there two of them?"

She nodded vigorously. "I didn't know them; they weren't any of the local meth heads who Ricky sometimes fought with. This is too hard, remembering all that, I'm in pain, I'm giving you shit for nothing. At least Freddie gave me oxy for the SUV."

"Yeah, you're in a hard place," I said, putting as much sympathy as I could into my voice. "I went back to Palfry and found the old dresser that Ricky tossed into the meth pit. I found the bank account that Benjamin Dzornen set up for your mother."

"Those Dzornen shitheads? Are you working for them? That goddamn bitch Herta stole my money. Her daddy wanted me to go to college but she took that money and gave it to her children. If you're working for her you can fuck yourself and her in the bargain."

"I'm not working for the Dzornens. The last time I tried to talk to Herta Dzornen, she threw me out because I called her out for disrespecting your mother's family."

I spoke loudly and slowly. Judy eyed me warily.

"How did Martin find out about the money?" I asked. "Did you tell him, or was it your mother?"

"Oh, no, you don't. Meds, meds, meds, meds," Judy chanted. "You don't get something for nothing. Get me some oxy, get me morph, and I'll get you answers."

Lotty and I exchanged looks and head shakes, which Judy saw.

"Yeah, you two bitches, you think God left you in charge of the planet, but He didn't."

"Ms. Binder," I tried one last time, "your son came to visit you down in Palfry a few weeks ago. You argued over some documents. I know you had the bank passbook, the photo of Martina in the lab with Dzornen and Gertrud Memler. Wasn't there also some document about the work Martina was doing at Innsbruck? You took those when you came to Martin's bar mitzvah seven years ago—"

"It was *my* heritage," Judy yelled. "Kitty hated Martina, she hated her science, I was the person who kept her name alive. I named my child after her to keep her memory green. Taking those papers was *not* stealing; it was preserving!"

Judy "preserved," Homeland Security "confiscated." All these pretty names for theft. You hear more euphemisms for lying, cheating, even pedophilia, on the news in a week than you hear truth in a year.

I changed the subject. "Martin used to visit you without Kitty's knowing back when he was in high school."

Judy didn't say anything, but her mouth twitched in a sly smile.

"Martin saw the picture of Martina in her Vienna lab when he was younger," I persisted, "but something happened that made him come down to Palfry to get the picture and the other papers you'd, uh, preserved after his bar mitzvah. What made him want them?"

"It's your story, you tell me." Judy flounced on the pillows, at least as much as she could with her arms in restraints.

"He argued with you over the papers. He tried to take them, you tried to grab them back, some of them fell into the meth pit where you let them lie. That was when you realized that these papers had more than sentimental value. And then you and Ricky tried selling them online. You thought you had Nazi nuclear secrets, always a popular item. Someone saw the auction and came to collect the papers."

"It wasn't me," she said quickly. "Just Ricky. He saw Martin arguing with me and came down to see what was going on. I told him they were my granny's heritage, she died in the Holocaust, but Ricky didn't have any respect. He even sold his own grandmother's drawer handles, like he thought they were really gold when they were just polished brass. I never would have sold my own granny—"

"Of course not," I said soothingly. "Who were the buyers? Did Ricky ever actually get any money, or did they just drive up in their Lincoln Navigator and try to collect the papers at gunpoint?"

"You're so smart, you know everything, you should know that, too." She began weeping. "I'm in pain, you won't leave me alone, you won't help me. I'm supposed to do all the work around here, my mother's dead, my daddy's dead, the Dzornens stole my money, and all you want to do is talk, talk, talk. Go away, I hate you, I hate you!"

Lotty tried to put in a few questions of her own, including what Judy wanted us to do with Kitty's body, but Judy began screaming loudly for meds. "Put old batty Katty in the ground, I don't care, just get the fuck out of here if you won't help me."

I looked at her thin, tormented face, her mouth one large pain-filled gash in her head. She'd worn me out. I looked at Lotty and jerked my head toward the door.

Lotty stayed in the room a bit longer. She came out a few minutes later, looking grim. We didn't talk on the way back to the parking lot. As I strapped myself into the Audi's passenger seat, Lotty said she wanted to go to Evanston, meaning to Max's house.

For once, Lotty drove at a normal pace, didn't weave around slow-moving cars on the clogged streets, didn't race the lights as they turned red. We got to Max's around seven-thirty. His lovely old home, where he and Térèz, his long-dead wife, had raised their two children, is across the road from Lake Michigan. While Lotty filled him in on our stressful meeting with Judy, I wandered over to the lake.

The sun had set; there were a few families out on the private beach, but no one could really see me. I took off my clothes and folded them on a bench. The water was still warm from our long hot summer. I waded out and let it envelop my naked body. The lake seemed to fold arms of love around me. Jake's long fingers caressing me, yes, but I thought more of my mother, whose love for me had been both fierce and tender.

Kitty and Judy Binder never had that bond. The invective Judy spewed had been her withdrawal speaking, but a painful wound underlay it. Kitty herself had drunk a toxic mix of worry, anger, loss—her real father, the builder, whoever that was, dead in the war; her birth father refused to acknowledge her; her mother cared more for protons than for Kitty; the grandmother who raised her was murdered in the Holocaust. There'd been precious little love for Kitty to pass on to her own daughter.

I swam to shore and fumbled my way in the darkness to the bench where I'd left my clothes. I found a towel on top of them. Max, or Lotty, had noticed I was swimming.

I dried off and joined them in Max's rose garden, where he had set out cold roast duck and salads. He and I drank one of his bottles of Echezeaux. We talked of Jake's West Coast tour and other musical matters.

It was only as Lotty and I were helping him clear the table that I went back to our visit to Judy. "It was my question about 'duck and cover' that got through to her. It frightened her. Why?"

"Do you think so?" Lotty said. "All I remember is her cursing me."

"She was quiet for an instant, and then wondered if I was punishing her because she'd mentioned it. What's so important about that?"

"It was the slogan of the Civil Defense movies in the fifties," Max said. "Térèz and I were furious when we saw them. They had a turtle who laughed and was very jolly, telling children if they crawled under their desks, they would be as safe from fire falling from the sky as a turtle in his shell. Meaning, not safe at all."

I shook my head, baffled. "I know about the movies, although they'd stopped using them by the time I was in school. What I don't understand is why Judy thought she was being punished for saying it."

"That isn't what Judy said," Lotty said. "She was laughing because 'duck and cover' had worked for her, despite someone—probably Kitty—telling her it was nonsense. Kitty would have ordered Judy not to repeat any of her views on American defense policy at school. You didn't spend time in Nazi Austria without learning to keep very quiet if you opposed government policies. Not to mention the intense anti-Communist hysteria here during the fifties. If you opposed nuclear weapons you were labeled a Red or Red sympathizer."

I pictured Judy as a little girl, her mother warning her not to repeat any of the family's subversive opinions in public, warning her so sternly that in her adult, drug-eaten brain, she thought some terrible punishment was meted out for trumpeting "duck and cover" as a survival strategy.

"It's as good an explanation as any," I said. "It's just—I don't know—her reaction made me expect something deeper. Maybe it's because of Homeland Security being on my tail, or Metargon thinking that Martin has absconded with their version of the Stuxnet virus. Is this story about family secrets or nuclear secrets?"

"It could be both," Max said. "His great-grandmother died when Benjamin Dzornen could have saved her. Edward Breen brought Martina's Nazi student to the States to do rocket and weapons work. Those connect Martin's family to nuclear secrets."

I took a handful of silverware from Lotty to dry. "I feel like I'm in the middle of that old Dylan song: *Something is happening here, but you don't know what it is, do you, Warshawski-Jones?*"

To the Editor
Physics Today

July 1985

Not since the days of "Duck and Cover" have we seen so much time, money and energy spent on something as futile as President Reagan's "Star Wars" plan. The Great Communicator knows that money talks: 500 million in immediate cash has gone to the top ten defense contractors to spread across the United States. This doesn't include some hundred billion in multi-year appropriations for space lasers, secure ground communications, and many other expensive fantasies. I was glad to see Edward Breen's Metargon company in the top ten: Mr. Breen and I are old collaborators, and I know he will do whatever it takes to make his contractual obligations come true.

Despite the beautiful graphics in your June issue, this initiative is more an exercise in expensive science fiction than in achievable physics and engineering. So far, the only tests of laser weapons in destroying incoming targets have worked within a margin of error for stochastic excursions only, but notwithstanding this, appropriations are happily escalating.

The program is destabilizing, both for our delicate relations with our European allies and with the Soviet Union, thus leading us closer to the preemptive first strikes so dear to defense hawks.

It has only been a short two years since we got to see a leaked Pentagon report, claiming that the U.S. could survive a "protracted," i.e., five-year-long, nuclear war. Defense Secretary Weinberger's undersecretary for Strategic and Theater Nuclear Forces has said that if the United States had a good civil defense policy, we'd be back to normal within five years of total nuclear war.

Last year on the anniversary of Hiroshima, the United States Energy Secretary went to the Nevada Proving Grounds where he witnessed his first thermonuclear test. He said it was "exciting," and that he remained committed to a winnable nuclear war.

I had the dubious privilege of spending time at the nuclear weapons proving grounds in Nevada. The ground water there is still undrinkable, the cattle who stray onto the land to graze suffer terrible deformities, and towns a hundred miles away suffer from rare cancers even to this day.

Star Wars apologists have no idea what would happen if we started detonating our weapons on human populations, but the Roman historian Tacitus must surely have seen their vision when he wrote, "They ravage, they slaughter, and call it 'empire.' They create a desert and call it 'peace.'"

Sincerely

Gertrud Memler, Ph.D., Physics, University of Vienna

July 2, 1985

To: All Field Agents
From: Barney Montoya, Senior Agent in Charge

Locate Gertrud Memler. This search has highest priority. She is an embarrassment to the President of the United States and it is a black mark on our Bureau that we have failed to find her during the last twenty-five years.

Our file on her shows she was a Nazi sympathizer or supporter brought into the U.S. in 1946 to help build weapons & rockets, vanished from Nevada 1955. She has a deep cover, surfaces briefly with letters or articles on weapons, but always uses false return addresses.

Stressed with *Physics Today* urgentest that they not print further letters from her without Bureau

approval, but editor uncooperative. Resisted search
of premises, forced us to produce Federal search warrant. Have put watch on all incoming/outgoing mail
from *Physics Today*, but Memler seldom strikes the
same publication twice.

Memler moved seamlessly from Nazi collaborator to
Communist supporter. She has access to classified
documents. Attached is last known photo, with our forensic specialists' work-up on how she might look today, at age 73. Advise all immigration staff to look
at passports; if she's living outside the country
she's probably traveling under a different name.

29

NIGHT CALLER

I HAD LOTTY DROP ME under the L tracks at Belmont and Sheffield, four blocks from my home. If someone was watching me, I didn't want them to put her Audi on their list. Neither of us said much during the ride from Max's house, but as I opened the passenger door, Lotty spoke.

"Judy's dramas cause a great deal of damage in the lives around her. Her mother, her son, now it's your turn to get burned in her fires."

"Was there any joy, ever, in that household?" I asked. "The picture of Leonard with Martin at the science fair made him look happy and proud of his grandson. Did he feel that way toward his daughter?"

Lotty spoke slowly, thinking back. "When Judy was born, Leonard was as delighted as if someone had handed him a winning lottery ticket. Of course I never was part of the day-to-day life of the family: I can't tell you what he did when she brought home a C in math, or wasn't interested in playing the piano. My guess is he didn't mind; he didn't care about credentials, or achievement."

Someone honked behind us; Lotty pulled over to the curb. The fluorescent lights around the station turned her walnut-colored skin green.

"I think Kitty was rather different," she said. "For all she whined about her real father being a builder, and claimed she didn't want academics or scientists around her, that was a case of the lady protesting too much. She wanted her real father to be the Nobel Prize winner. At least, that's what I believe; I don't know the secrets of her heart."

"Poor Judy," I said, "although poor all of them, really. Sometimes the pain I encounter in my job is more than I can rightly handle."

Lotty squeezed my hand. "Yes, for me as well."

As I got out of the car, I could see tears shining in her eyes. I walked home slowly, not worried about tails, just weighted down. So much red wine at the end of a long day hadn't been a good idea. It makes you mellow for an hour, then it brings you down.

When I got to Racine Avenue, I walked up the opposite side of the street from my building, scanning cars, looking for anyone who was out of place among the dog walkers and homebound bar crawlers. They all seemed innocuous, so when a young woman suddenly appeared on the sidewalk near my front door, my heartbeat spiked. I ducked and rolled without thinking. When she called my name in a soft, doubtful voice I got to my feet, feeling like an idiot.

"Yes, I'm V. I. Warshawski. Who are you?"

"Alison Breen. I was hoping to see you." Her voice was even more doubtful: a detective who rolls under the boxwood when she's startled must not seem very stable.

"I thought you were in Mexico, Ms. Breen, setting up a tech lab for local high schools."

"I am, but—but—I wanted to see you, I need to talk to you."

This was getting to be an annoying routine, strangers arriving late at night to talk to me. At least she was asking, instead of breaking into my apartment.

"Right. Let's go inside where we can speak with a bit of privacy." I unlocked the outer door and held out an arm, gesturing her to enter.

As we came into the entryway, Mr. Contreras was opening his door. Mitch and Peppy, barking and whining, ran out to greet me and to inspect the newcomer.

"They heard you talking out on the front walk, doll, and wouldn't give me no peace until I opened the door." Mr. Contreras lied shamelessly. "This young lady was here earlier, looking for you. I tried to call you, but you wasn't answering your phone."

Seen under the foyer light, Alison was plainly a child of affluence. Her clear tanned skin, even white teeth, the glossy brown hair pulled away from her face and clipped to the top of her head with some kind of Mexican pin, but above all, the confidence with which she bent to pet the dogs, and to offer a hand to Mr. Contreras—all these added up to someone secure in her place near the front of the line.

"Alison Breen, Salvatore Contreras. Can we come into your place to talk?" I asked my neighbor. "I'm not sure whether Homeland Security is bugging my apartment."

The old man's eyes brightened: he's pined for someone young and energetic—and female—since Petra joined the Peace Corps. "It ain't much to look at," he warned Alison, "but it's clean enough and we'll take good care of you, the dogs and Vic and me, so you come on in, rest yourself. You want tea or coffee or something? I have beer and grappa, too."

"Stay away from the grappa," I warned Alison. "Mr. Contreras makes it himself and it has been known to topple strong men."

She smiled politely, but said water would be fine. She dropped her backpack on the floor and perched on the edge of the old man's sagging armchair.

I sat on the couch, facing her. "Do your folks know you're here?"

"I—no one knows I'm here. My plane got in at four; I've been waiting here off and on since five. Mr. Contreras came to the door when I rang; he said you were in town and should be back soon, so I've kept returning every hour or so."

"I doubt very much you made your way out of Mexico City with no one the wiser. You're not the invisible woman, you know, you're an heiress; your father has someone in Mexico City reporting back to him on what you're doing. And he told me he was going to get the FBI—"

"Someone on the tech lab staff is watching me?" she cried. "Oh, how—how horrible! How could he do that? When am I ever going to be able to do something on my own, without him breathing down my neck? I hoped—it's Ramona, isn't it? I wondered when I found her in my room, but she said she was looking for a candle—oh, how can I trust anyone when I don't know whether they're spying on me?"

I couldn't summon even a perfunctory response. I leaned back in the couch. The springs shifted and one poked me in the butt. That might be the only reason I didn't go to sleep on the spot.

"How come you're here?" I said, keeping my eyes open with an effort. "How did you get my name?"

"From my dad," Alison said. "First he called up with all this insane stuff about Martin. He asked was Martin with me, and I said, of course not, I hadn't heard from him since the end of the summer. I said we'd all gotten this e-mail from Jari—all of us who were Breen fellows this summer, I mean—asking if we knew where Martin was, which was how I knew he'd disappeared. My dad didn't believe me; he thought I was shielding Martin, which got us off totally on the wrong foot. And then he said you were looking for Martin, and I was to tell him at once if I heard from you."

"And that made you leap on a plane for a six-hour flight without even knowing if I was in town."

She flushed. "I saw the news about Martin's grandmother. How someone killed her, I mean, and attacked his mom. I thought you would know if he showed up."

Mr. Contreras came back with a glass of water. He'd arranged a plate with mixed nuts and apples cut into quarters. "You eat something, young lady. You're worried and you've been on a plane all day. You'll feel better with something inside you."

Alison flashed a smile and a few exclamations of how kind he was, how beautiful the food looked. She'd spent her life with avuncular friends of her parents fussing over her; she knew how to respond.

"I'd better have a cup of coffee if you don't mind rustling one up," I said to my neighbor. "We probably have a long night in front of us."

"Sure, doll, sure." He bustled back to the kitchen.

"He's very sweet," Alison said.

"Solid gold, so don't patronize him," I said. "If you're so worried about people reporting back to your dad, what makes you think I'm not working for him myself?"

"The way he talked about you," she stammered. "This sounds rude, but he said you weren't much of a detective, and that you'd be like a bull in a china shop because you didn't know how to be subtle."

"How clichéd," I said, "although, really, he should have called me a cow in a china shop."

Alison blinked at me, puzzled.

"Just because I don't know how to be subtle doesn't make me masculine," I explained. "Moving on, why did the fact that your father thinks I'm useless make you believe you could trust me?"

Her lips quivered. "Please don't make fun of me. I told you I knew it was rude, but I did look you up, I saw you'd solved some big cases. I saw you were willing to go head to head with the police or FBI or people like my dad if you needed to protect a client, and I didn't know what else to do or who I could turn to."

I sat up again, my back sore from the broken springs. "You're right, Ms. Breen: I shouldn't poke fun. I've had a long day and a hideous week trying to find out what Martin is up to, so I'm not at my empathic best. Tell me what happened after your dad called to accuse you of shielding Martin."

Mr. Contreras arrived with coffee and milk, for me, a glass of grappa for himself. Through some mysterious dog mathematics, Mitch and Peppy distributed themselves so that both were equidistant from all three of us. I gave the old man a quick précis of what Alison had told me so far.

"Someone from the FBI came to my computer lab looking for

Martin," Alison said. "Dad hadn't warned me that he'd called them in, and when an agent of the U.S. government showed up, he got everyone at the lab totally terrified. Mexico kind of looks the other way if the FBI or DEA want to interrogate someone. But when I called my dad, to tell him he'd destroyed the trust the program people had in me, he started yelling at me about national security. He said Martin stole our software, Metargon's software, I mean, and that the FBI is going to find him and I'd better stop being a bleeding heart if I'm ever going to be able to run the company."

She picked at her cuticles, looking very young and vulnerable. "I couldn't talk him out of it. I couldn't make him see that Martin isn't like that."

"What is Martin like?" I asked. "I've never met him, and I can't seem to talk to anyone who understands him as a person, except his high school physics instructor."

"He's a cactus," Alison said. "Hard and prickly on the outside, sweet as honey on the inside."

"Were you dating?" I asked. "Is that why you invited him to the barbecue at your folks' place, even though he wasn't in the summer program?"

She made an impatient gesture. "We slept together twice, but Martin backed away because I wouldn't tell my parents. Martin said it was because I was ashamed of him, but it wasn't that, it's because my dad would have fired him on the spot. Martin belongs at Metargon in a way I never will. I'm a good computer engineer, but Martin, he's special, he sees things in three-D that the rest of us only see linearly."

"Kind of a hard secret to keep," I said. "You sleeping together."

"I see that now," she said bitterly. "Someone who wanted to suck up to Dad gave him a hint. I hope it wasn't Jari, he's a good guy, but everyone at Metargon is so competitive, they're always pushing each other out of the way even if they're all on a project together! It could have been one of the other kids in the summer program. This one girl from MIT, she had a thing for Martin.

"Anyway, someone told Dad, and he said he didn't want some over-ambitious school dropout taking advantage of me. Which was also unfair. Martin wasn't a dropout, he just didn't go to college. He's tak-ing courses part-time at Illinois-Circle, but really, he's so brainy—do you know he got a perfect score on his math SAT and the top score on the physics C exam?"

"People keep telling me that," I said. "His high school physics teacher tried to get him to apply to Caltech or MIT when she saw his scores, but his family were set against college for him."

"Well, there you have it. He has a chip on his shoulder about my family being so rich, and me being at Harvard, but once you knocked off the chip, he was such a sweetheart. Do you know what he did for my birthday? He remembered I told him when I was little I used to beg my dog to talk to me: I was lonely, my dog was my best friend. For my birthday he found this toy dog that looked just like Lulu, and he pro-grammed a chip that he put into her where she sings happy birthday, and says, 'Alison, you're my best friend, no one comes closer to my heart than you.' He even got her tail to wag. He's pretty amazing."

Fatigue and unshed tears turned her honey-colored eyes red. Mr. Contreras nodded approvingly. He thinks *Romeo and Juliet* is a great story except that Shakespeare got it wrong at the end; if he, Mr. Con-treras, had been there, he would have stayed in the tomb with Juliet so that Romeo knew she was just sleeping. That monk was a fool, in his opinion. "You don't leave a girl in a drugged sleep and expect some high-strung boy like Romeo won't overreact," is his verdict on the Bard.

"You tell Vic here what you need her to do and she'll take care of it for you," he told Alison. "You did the right thing, flying all this way."

I grinned wryly at the tribute. "Sure thing. I can handle the FBI with one hand behind my back, which is good, because Homeland Security is already tying it there."

"Oh. I wasn't really paying attention when you said they could be bugging your apartment. Why are they—is it because of my dad? Is it because of Martin?"

"It's because of some papers I found in the house downstate where Martin's mother had been living. I only found a few documents—I think there were others which Martin took. The ones I found were stolen from me before I could get them to a lab for analysis. Homeland Security doesn't believe me. They think Martin and his mother had a file of nuclear secrets that I'm hiding. Do you know anything about this?"

"Be reasonable, cookie," Mr. Contreras said. "How could she, when she don't even know what you found."

"It's possible Martin confided in Ms. Breen," I said. "He was a lonely guy; he had to talk to someone."

Alison shook her head. "He never claimed he knew anything about weapons. And he didn't talk to me about his mom, not like that, anyway."

"But when he went to that party at your folks' house, Martin saw something that rattled him. What?"

Alison's face scrunched up in misery. "I don't know. He was always pretty quiet, and even quieter when the rest of the group was around. All I can tell you is it's something he saw when I took the group up to my granddad's workshop."

"What, your grandfather designed his computers in your house?"

"Granddad always had a workshop at home, even when he got to be famous. All the kids wanted to see it. They probably thought if they saw where Granddad came up with his brilliant ideas, some of his brains and his luck would rub off on them if they looked at the workshop. It's on the third floor of our Lake Forest house. Even though he designed the core for Metargon-I in his first workshop, behind the garage in his Hyde Park house, all his scale models and papers and stuff are in Lake Forest."

I nodded. "So everyone went up there. Who suggested it first?"

"I honestly don't think it was Martin," she said defensively. "Not because I'm shielding him, like Dad says, but because, oh, the chip on his shoulder. He wasn't going to admit he cared about something a rich and powerful man did. Anyway, everyone was playing with the scale-models, and admiring the letters—Granddad had framed letters from all these incredible people, Nobel laureates, President Eisenhower, you knew he'd done something special, just seeing who wrote him."

"And one of those letters or papers or something upset Martin. Think! What was he looking at?" I demanded.

"I told you, I don't know!" she cried. "Tad, that's one of the guys in the summer group, he didn't like Martin because Martin rewrote some of his code without consulting him. Anyway, he was standing next to me. Actually, he had an arm around me."

Tears spilled over the edges of her eyes. "Martin came over to me. He said, 'Something doesn't add up. How much do you know about your grandfather's work?' I asked him what he meant, but Tad made this snide comment about how the human calculator was always right, and that if Martin said the Metargon-I didn't add up it must have been an illusion that it worked so well all those years."

She fished in her backpack for a tissue, but Mr. Contreras was ready with a napkin, dabbing her cheeks for her.

Alison thanked him with a watery smile. "So then Martin took off. I ran after him, but he said, 'I need to think this through. I hope you haven't been making a fool out of me.'

"I said, 'What, you mean with Tad?' and he said, 'With Tad or any other way.'

"That was the last I heard from him. I tried calling him later and he didn't answer, he wouldn't answer my texts or my e-mails, so I wrote a pretty nasty message."

"Oh?" I prompted.

"'To hell with you, mister, my dad was right, you are just a blue-collar boy with a chip on your shoulder.'" She mumbled the words so quickly I barely made them out.

"Of course I didn't mean it," she added, "but why wouldn't he write back? Why didn't he tell me he was going dark? All these weeks in Mexico, I thought he was avoiding me, until I got the message from Jari. Jari said he'd gone into Martin's ISP servers, he'd tracked Martin's e-mails and his cell phone. Martin hadn't sent any messages since the day he disappeared, and he hasn't been in his in box, either on his cell phone or his e-mails—Jari found five addresses for him. They're all untouched."

I drummed my fingers on the couch arm. "I'd like to see your grandfather's workshop: I want to know what Martin saw."

"I can't take you up there! I don't want Dad to know I'm here. Besides, if it was the Metargon-I design he was looking at, like Tad said, anyone can see it: it's in every beginning computer engineering textbook, where they step you through the history. What von Neumann and Bigelow did at Princeton, what Rajchman did at RCA, and what Edward Breen did in his old coach house." Despite her distress, she couldn't help ending on a note of pride.

"If we looked at the drawings, would I be able to follow them?" I asked.

"I could step you through them, but I don't know what the model or the drawings would tell you," she said. "I don't know what they told Martin, or even if that is what he was looking at."

Maybe Cordell Breen was right and I wasn't enough of a detective for a case this intellectual. "What's next to the drawings? Could it be something else that he saw?"

She made a helpless gesture. "I studied everything near where Martin had been standing. There's the original drawing Granddad made for the Metargon-I core, just a sketch of the idea, when he was sitting on some battlefield during the war. That's what's on the wall. There's a letter from Stan Ulam, the mathematician, saying that Granddad's proposal for memory registers was bold and revolutionary, but they were too far down the road at IAS to change designs, especially when it wasn't clear that the Fermi surfaces could be calculated accurately."

I definitely would not gain anything from Alison stepping me through the computer's design: a Fermi surface already was more complicated than anything I could follow.

"A few weeks after your party, Martin went downstate to where his mother was living," I said. "That was when they argued over these papers that have disappeared. Did he ever talk to you about her?"

"You mean, her being a drug addict? Yes, it weighed on him. It was why he didn't think he should have children, in case they turned into crackheads. I couldn't convince him that addiction wasn't genetically determined."

"He didn't say anything about wanting to talk to his mother that night at your party?"

She shook her head. "He did say me not telling my parents about him and me was like him not telling his gran that he sometimes visits his mother. He didn't tell his grandmother about us, either, although he said that was because she had gotten so strange, he just didn't want to introduce me unless, well, you know, if we got really serious."

I rubbed my gritty eyes. The coffee hadn't helped; I was unbearably tired. "Yes, well, speaking of that, it's going to be impossible to keep your parents from knowing you're in town right now. Someone—this Ramona you mentioned—will have seen you leave your place in Mexico. Even if she doesn't report that to your dad, they'll put out an APB on you in Mexico City when they can't find you. If you used a credit card to buy your ticket, you already left a trail. If Homeland Security is, in fact, watching this building, they'll ID you from surveillance photos."

Alison's shoulders sagged in misery. Mr. Contreras went to put an arm around her but frowned at me. "Why get her all upset, cookie? She's here, we got to figure out what to do with her."

"She can't stay here," I fretted. "We're too exposed, too vulnerable. Ditto for taking her down to my office."

Mr. Contreras started to protest reflexively that he could look after Alison, but stopped himself mid-sentence. "I could if it was just ordinary punks, but not when it's the government and her dad and all. Come on, doll, put on your thinking cap. You gotta have some kind of hideout."

I gave him a tired smile. "Like Br'er Rabbit's briar patch? Whatever you do, don't throw me in there?"

The words conjured up an unexpected chain of associations. "I may know a place at that. Come on, Ms. Breen. Let's put on some disguises."

30

PLAYING DRESS-UP

YOU BOYS KNOW how to get to Union Station? You sure I don't need to ride downtown with you?" Mr. Contreras said loudly.

"Come on, Grandpa, we've made this trip a million times." That was Alison, who made a compact boy in jeans and a T-shirt. A backward baseball cap covered her glossy hair.

"I don't know," the old man fretted. "It's late, there are perverts on the train. I should ride down with you."

"You've got the dogs, Grandpa. No one's gonna mess with us." My cousin Boom-Boom's old hockey jersey was a little heavy on a warm night, but it hid my breasts; away from the streetlights, with my own baseball cap, I could pass for the older grandson, who was nineteen now and a freshman at Northern Illinois.

Mr. Contreras clapped my shoulder in a hearty squeeze, hugged Alison, who squirmed away from him just as his own younger grandson might. He blundered around the station entrance with the dogs. This gave me a chance to see if any of the late-night riders who cursed him for not controlling his animals were keeping up with us. It was hard to be absolutely certain, but I was ninety-five percent sure we were clear.

I'd only sketched out the scene, but Alison and my neighbor had risen nobly to their roles. I fed my CTA pass through the machine and lolled at the bottom of the stairs, reading the notices. When I heard an outbound train approaching, I grabbed Alison's arm and we sprinted up the stairs. The doors were closing as we jumped on board.

We were both tense. We didn't talk during the milk-run up to Howard. Alison, who felt at ease navigating the labyrinth of Mexico City, had never been on the L; she kept looking around with a nervous frown anytime a late-night beggar started a sales pitch in our car. We were lucky at Dempster—we just made the Skokie Swift's last run of the day.

At the end of the line we had a mile walk to Kitty Binder's. Boom-Boom's jersey hid not only my breasts but my picklocks, a flashlight and my gun. By the time we got to the bungalow on Kedvale, the flashlight was hitting my rib cage in an unpleasant way.

It was well past midnight and the little houses were shut down for the night, or so I hoped. The last thing we needed was for an insomniac dog-walker to spot us.

Alison's nervousness increased when she saw the police tapes and a Cook County State's Attorney seal on the doors. "If we get caught, won't they put us in prison?" she whispered.

"If we get caught, you hop off like a bunny; if anyone stops you, say that I kidnapped you," I muttered: a prison-yard guttural doesn't carry the way whispers do.

The authorities hadn't bothered to seal the garage, which had a back door with a simple lock. While Alison held the flashlight in an unsteady hand, I quickly undid the tumblers. We were inside within thirty seconds. I put a hand over her mouth as she started to speak, counted eight slow breaths in my head. No one shouted out or tried the doorknob behind us.

I used the flashlight sparingly, since the garage had a couple of skylights in the roof. We could see a workbench where Len had kept his tools. They were dusty now, but chisels and wrenches were laid out on a cloth in careful size order. He'd hung pictures of himself with his grandson across the wall behind the bench. I'd seen the one with Martin and the rockets, but others showed the two of them playing ball, or working on a car together. Alison gave a crow of delight when she saw them and insisted on taking them down from the wall to carry into the house with her.

On the far side of the bench, a door led into the kitchen. It, too, was easy to open. Strange that Kitty, with her fears, and all the dead bolts on her front and back doors, had left this easy route into her home. Odd, too, that the intruders, who'd torn up the house with a ruthless hand, had left the garage alone. Maybe they'd found what they were looking for inside, or maybe they hadn't been looking for anything. If these were drug dealers going after Judy Binder they might have trashed the place on principle—or lack thereof.

Inside the house, the crime scene hadn't been touched. Books and papers were still strewn across the floor. What I hadn't noticed when I ran through here on Friday was that the intruders had also emptied flour and sugar canisters and dumped the contents of the freezer. The food was beginning to rot. A trail of ants led from under the back door, which had been boarded over, to the spilled sugar.

Alison wrinkled her nose in disgust. "This smells as bad as the barrios I pass on my way to one of our schools. We can't stay here."

"Unless you want to call a cab and go home, we don't have a lot of choice right now. Let's do some cleaning, my sister," I said. "It'll make it all seem bearable."

I didn't want to run appliances or turn on lights that might alert someone to our presence. I stopped Alison as she switched on the exhaust fan. Inside the basement door was a rack that held brooms and mops, garbage bags and Clorox. I set to work with a grim will. After a moment of staring at me like a tragedy queen, Alison gave her head a shake, dislodging the baseball cap and her shiny chestnut hair, and joined me.

"Martin's room is downstairs," I said softly. "I think he has blackout curtains, so we ought to be able to clean in there more easily."

Alison volunteered to take care of that while I finished the kitchen and Kitty's bedroom. I helped her down the stairs with the flash, warning her there would be dried blood on the floor. The disarray in Martin's suite wasn't as horrible as the kitchen because he'd left so few belongings behind. Alison looked less miserable as she started to explore the space her sometime lover had grown up in.

I left Alison fingering Martin's rockets and went up to the second floor. I put Kitty's mattress back on her bed, hung clothes in the closet, folded her stretched-out bras and torn underpants into a drawer. What rule says you have to give up beautiful underwear after you collect Social Security?

I couldn't bear to sleep in the bed, even though Kitty hadn't been killed there. It was an atavistic revulsion to death, or perhaps to Kitty's tormented life.

I found a second bedroom across the hall, painted white, with white and pink curtains. It must have been Judy Binder's childhood room, but it looked as though Len had moved in here for the last years of his life. The bookshelf held World War II histories, especially the rocket and A-bomb projects. He'd also tucked away some Loren Estleman westerns.

Len had displayed more photos in here. Their frames had been ripped apart, but the pictures were more or less intact. One was of Judy at five or so, sitting on a trike, grinning up at the camera with her front teeth missing. In another, an eight- or nine-year-old Judy was posed on an armchair, stroking a cat.

It was hard to reconcile the angry scarecrow of a woman in restraints at the hospital with this active little girl. What happened to that child on the tricycle? Living with someone as unbalanced as Kitty would create uncertainty in a child, but why had Judy fled into narcotics? Or was it one of those things that happened without her realizing what she was doing? Looking for love, for warmth through sex, getting high, getting higher, leaving the atmosphere and not being able to reenter planet earth.

I swept the glass and broken frames into another garbage bag, straightened the rug, looked in the dresser drawers. These were empty, which explained why the chaos in the other rooms hadn't been replicated here. I made up Len's bed with sheets I found in a hall closet. They were so worn they were transparent down the middle, but they were clean.

I wanted to fall on my head into the bed, but I went down to the basement to check on Alison. She was sleeping soundly, despite having all the lights on. Her day had started in Mexico City almost twenty-four hours ago: she was entitled. She had scrubbed the floor around Martin's bed and replaced Feynman's *Lectures on Physics* to pride of place on his desk.

She didn't waken as I moved around the room turning off the lights. When I got to the desk lamp, I saw an envelope sticking out of Volume II of the *Lectures*. It was from the Department of Commerce, and dated the week before Martin's disappearance.

Dear Mr. Binder:

Your request under the Freedom of Information Act for documents pertaining to Martina Saginor returned no results. Your request for documents pertaining to Gertrud Memler produced one letter, which is attached.

The attachment was a photocopy of a letter from the Inspector-General's office in the Department of Commerce to the Office of Immigration and Naturalization.

We are applying for an expedited visa for Austrian national (Dr.) Gertrud Memler. Dr. Memler worked at the weapons installation in the Austrian Alps, near the city of Innsbruck, helping design Reactor I-IX. She was trained as a chemical engineer and was sent to the Innsbruck facility to conduct underground tests of early prototypes of weapons.

Major Edward Breen of the Office of the Joint Intelligence Objectives Agency has affirmed that Dr. Memler's role at Innsbruck was in the area of pure research. He has made certain that she was a member of the Nazi Party only because it was necessary if she was to work in any kind of university or research facility.

The Innsbruck facility included a major bomb production facility. Memler shared working and living conditions with the women who were brought to the facility as conscripts, working as forced labor in weapons production. Memler says that while perhaps in some places, such workers were malnourished, that was never the case in Innsbruck. Nor did Memler ever witness or hear about beatings or other severe punishments meted out against anyone brought there as forced labor. In any event, she was never in charge of any work details; her assignment was strictly in the field of pure research.

Dr. Memler's work will be of vital importance in advancing America's rocket and nuclear weapons program. Your cooperation in issuing an immediate visa is greatly appreciated.

I stared at the letter for several minutes, as if the text held some secret that would appear if I looked long enough. Alison turned in her sleep and muttered something in Spanish. I stuck the letter into the back pocket of my jeans and switched off the desk lamp.

31

MUSCLE CAR

I T WAS THE MIDDLE of Tuesday afternoon before I woke again. I showered in Kitty's bathroom, which made me uncomfortable, as if she were sitting on the bed watching me. In the kitchen, I found Alison eating peanut butter out of a jar with a spoon.

"We threw out all the bread last night," she said. "I found a package of bagels in the back of the freezer, but I didn't know if it was okay to turn on the toaster."

"I don't think anyone's monitoring the power use, so go—" I broke off mid-sentence: I'd just realized Alison was texting one-handed while she continued to lick peanut butter from the spoon. "What are you doing?"

"Letting my roommate know I'm okay, why?"

"You told me last night that you left Mexico City without telling anyone, but here you are, broadcasting your location to anyone who knows your phone number!"

"It's my Harvard roommate, not the one in Mexico City," Alison assured me. "She's working with an NGO in Botswana, and we text each other, like, twenty times a day, so she was upset when she didn't hear from me."

"Alison. Ms. Breen. You're the Whizzo Wizard of Computerland, not me, but don't you know that anyone who knows your phone number, whether it's your father or Jari Liu or Ramona in Mexico City, can track your location if your GPS signal is transmitting?"

"Oh," she said in a small voice. "I'm so used to texting, it never occurred to me—I looked at my phone when I got up and thought I'd forgotten to take it out of airplane mode, and Caitlin, my roommate, she said if she didn't hear from me by the end of the day in Chicago she'd text my mom. What should I do?"

"How long have you had your phone on?"

"Since I got up, maybe thirty minutes ago. I kind of do it automatically. I had about twenty texts from the people in Mexico, and then my roommate, and my folks had both texted saying they'd heard from my program director, and they called Harvard, so—"

"So you'd better get up to Lake Forest and let them know you're okay," I finished for her.

I hadn't thought this through last night. Too much Echezeaux had made me overlook how many people would start looking for Alison the instant she disappeared.

"But what can I tell them? I don't want to say I came back hoping that Martin might show up."

"No, but can't you tell them a part of the truth? Tell them siccing the FBI on members of your Mexico program is undoing all the good work you've been putting in. Tell them you needed to have this conversation face-to-face, that it's too delicate a matter to handle by texts and phone calls."

I wasn't really paying attention to her problem; I was wondering whether there were unusual noises coming from the side of the house.

"And if they realize from my GPS signal that I was at Martin's house?"

"Ask them why they were tracking your cell phone and tell them you'll get a burn phone that you throw out every month if they don't stop breathing down your neck."

There were unusual noises on the perimeter. I leapt across the room to the kitchen door and stood flat against the wall, gun in hand.

"Get down," I said to Alison, "get under the table. Someone's here. I don't want to hit you if I have to shoot."

Alison stared at me, still holding her peanut buttery spoon.

"Get on the floor," I hissed in fury.

She was too frightened to move: we both had seen a face appear in the window over the kitchen sink. The flaming hair topping it off was unmistakable. I put my gun back in my holster and left the kitchen through the garage door, since the back door was boarded over.

"Voss Susskind," I called, stepping into the Binders' yard. "What are you looking for?"

He spun around, his eyes wide with terror. "Who are—oh. You're the detective who's looking for Martin. Have you found him?"

"I'm not even close. What are you doing here?"

He'd been standing on a cement block under the kitchen window. He hopped down, his face almost as red as his hair.

"Ever since you came to see my folks, I've kind of been keeping a watch on the house. When I got home from school just now I thought I saw something in the kitchen so I came over to investigate before I called the cops."

"Well done," I said with a heartiness I didn't feel. "We were looking for any clues the police had missed. You didn't happen to be watching the night Ms. Binder was murdered, did you?"

He traced a circle in the hard-baked yard with the toe of his sneaker. "If I say, will you promise not to tell my mom?"

"Scout's honor," I agreed solemnly.

"It was two guys. I saw them break down the back door, and I ran to get my mom, but before she could even call 911, we heard these shots, and my dad, he said, better stay out of it."

"Can you describe them?" I said. "If you can, I promise I won't tell the police it was you I heard the details from."

He shook his head unhappily, looking at the circle he'd been drawing. "They wore dark jackets, or sweaters, and their faces were all flattened-out funny. I think they'd put ladies' pantyhose over them, that's what I decided later, you know, I was talking about it to Aaron Lustic at school the next day and we agreed ladies' stockings would squish your face out funny."

"But you're sure they were both men?"

"It was how they walked," he said simply.

I smiled. "You have the makings of a superior investigator, Voss. Now I wonder if I could ask a favor. That's Martin's girlfriend in the kitchen; she's been helping me search the house but she needs to get up to her folks' place in Lake Forest. Can she borrow your bike? She'd get it back to you tomorrow."

"I, gosh, sure, yeah, I guess, but she should take Toby's if she can handle it. He left it here when he went to Rochester."

We went back into the kitchen through the garage. I introduced Voss, whose eyes widened when he saw Alison: he hadn't expected Martin to have such a cool-looking girlfriend. He became both shy and aggressive. He'd show her how to handle Toby's bike, he'd ride over as far as the Hubbard Woods bike path to make sure she didn't get lost.

Alison was as used to youthful adoration as she was to avuncular elderly men. She thanked Voss with suitable flattery, telling him she'd love the escort since she didn't know Skokie. I shooed them both out of the garage. When Alison turned to thank me I told her it could wait until we were all home free, just to get going.

As soon as she and Voss disappeared across the alley, I started to look for the Subaru's keys. For once, I was lucky on the first pass: Martin had left the car keys in the garage, on a hook by the garage bay door. I didn't see much point in leaving surreptitiously. With Voss's arrival and departure, anyone on the block who was watching would know we'd been in the house. I made sure I had everything I'd arrived with: gun, picklocks, flashlight, toothbrush and Boom-Boom's jersey.

The Subaru had that musty, moldy smell that unused cars get, but the engine turned over immediately. I needed to drive to my office, to see what havoc Homeland Security had wrought there, but I stopped at home first. Mr. Contreras deserved an update; besides, I'd left my laptop and iPad with him last night.

I parked the Subaru six blocks from my apartment and walked home by a zigzag route that let me check for tails. After telling Mr. Contreras about our night, and Alison's decision to go home—with his predictable criticism of my letting her bicycle off with a neighbor kid—couldn't I have driven her to Lake Forest? What was wrong with taking extra time to give the girl the support she needed?—and getting the dogs a much-needed workout, I headed down to my office in the Subaru.

My leasemate, who wrestles gigantic sculptures out of steel and railway ties and any other really big piece of material, was in Cape Cod with her parents this week. Usually when I come in, there's some kind of blowtorch or bandsaw going, along with her music mix. The quiet in the warehouse we share was unnerving, as if monsters were lurking in the shadows.

I flipped on all the lights, got Natalie Maines to sing "Not Ready to Make Nice" for me at top volume, and set to work. Homeland Security hadn't been as destructive in my office as they'd been in my home. I guess because they'd taken the drives from my Mac Pro, they didn't think they had to dump all my documents onto the floor. They'd left my cabinet drawers open, with enough disarray in the files to let me know they'd been in them, but they hadn't strewn paper about, for which I was grateful: my tax dollars at work.

I shut the drawers without trying to reorganize them. I've always thought of housework as a spectator sport, not a participatory one, and

I'd done more cleaning in the last week than I usually do in a year: scoured out a meth pit, cleaned up a major crime scene at Kitty Binder's, and started putting my own apartment back in order. Enough.

Without my big computer I was somewhat hamstrung, but I still had all my reports backed up in the Cloud, assuming some zealous federal official hadn't erased them. I managed to return client calls and get a respectable amount of work done. I saved all my work to thumb drives to keep it out of the Cloud.

As I returned calls and filled in the blanks on some of my reports, I kept wondering if I should tell my clients that their confidential files had been broached. Yes, they had a right to know. No, they'd never trust me with their work again.

My mother's voice rang in my head the summer I was ten. I'd gone to Wrigley Field with my cousin Boom-Boom, traveling our usual route: scrambling up on the platform of the commuter train so we could board without paying the fare downtown; climbing the girders to the L at Roosevelt Road, hoisting ourselves over the back wall into the bleachers. And we'd been caught. Boom-Boom shrugged it off, but I was grounded for two weeks. When I tried to lay the blame on my cousin my mother was angry and contemptuous: *"Don't add* viltà— *cowardice—to your other problems."*

Right, Gabriella. I sent an e-mail to each client, explaining that an investigation had roused Homeland Security wrath, that they had impounded my hard drives, and that while I would take extra precautions in the future (what, I didn't say because I didn't know) I couldn't guarantee the safety of their confidential data in the present.

Sometimes not only is honesty the best policy, but it actually helps. One of the law firms I work for wrote back to say that they were talking to the federal attorney for the Northern District to demand guarantees of privacy for all my data. Another client, also a law firm, was going to the federal magistrate to demand the return of my drives. A couple of customers weren't so happy. They asked for refunds on their retainers, but on the whole, I felt it was V.I., the Solo Op, 1, Homeland Security 0.

I was writing out the last of the refund checks when I got a call that the ID identified only as coming from Palfry. I was tempted to let it go—I didn't think I could take Sheriff Kossel's hearty laughter—but picked it up right before it rolled over to my answering service.

"I'm looking for the detective? V. I. Warshawski?" a woman said.

I knew the voice but couldn't place it. "Yes, speaking. And you are—?"

"This is Susie Foyle from Lazy Susan's?"

"Of course, home of the world-famous BLT. What's up?"

"This—I'm not sure I should be telling you this, but Bobbie Wenger and I talked it over this morning with Jenny Orlick, because she's Glenn's partner, and we finally decided you ought to know."

I made reassuring noises.

"This is a bit awkward, you know, because what if we're making something out of nothing?"

"If it's something out of nothing I will not do anything with the information," I promised.

"It's Glenn, Glenn Davilats, the deputy, you know."

We established that I knew who she was talking about: the deputy who'd waited with me while his pals went into the cornfield after Ricky Schlafly's body. Jenny Orlick was his partner.

"He's driving a new Charger. I know for a fact he's got two babies and a mortgage that he's behind on, so where he got money for a brand-new muscle car, it's worrying Jenny, so she talked to Bobbie. Bobbie's her aunt, you know."

I didn't know, but in a small town everyone is connected.

"Anyway, well, like I say, maybe he won the lottery, and if he did, I'm embarrassed to be bothering you with this."

"No," I said. "It's not a bother, and don't be embarrassed."

As Susie continued to talk herself into a happier frame of mind, two

Palfry images came to me: standing in the motel parking lot at four in the morning, watching a Dodge Charger roar away from me with the two punks who'd busted my trunk lock to steal the dresser drawers.

Even more vivid was the memory of standing by the cornfield in the hot sun. I'd asked Deputy Davilats to help me put Delilah, the emaciated Rottweiler, into my car. She'd been gentle with me, she was sweet with everyone at the clinic, but she'd bared her teeth and shown hackle at Glenn Davilats.

32

CHOP SHOP

MY FIRST IMPULSE was to call Sheriff Kossel, but for all I knew, the whole Palfry County sheriff's department was working with local drug dealers. Roberta and Frank Wenger had said there were at least two other meth houses in the county.

It could be that one of the dealers had bribed Davilats to work with him, but no one else in the county knew about it. My experience of police corruption said otherwise. You didn't usually get a solo bad apple: people don't feel immoral when they're doing what the group is doing. The two deputies who'd answered the 911 at the motel had been unenthusiastic about tracking the Charger: maybe they only suspected it belonged to their buddy. On the other hand, they could be getting a cut.

I wandered up Milwaukee Avenue toward the Subaru, so involved in my tortuous thinking that I almost got hit crossing the three-way intersection at North Avenue. That would be a gallows-humor ending—surviving a shoot-out in a drug den only to die under a semi.

Davilats's being on the take explained the two sets of people paying attention to me. Homeland Security was watching for action on the King Derrick auction of nuclear secrets, but Davilats wanted any valuables I'd found at the meth house. Davilats knew I'd found the desk drawer, because he'd heard about it during the Palfry football game.

Homeland Security had read my e-mail to Cheviot Labs, saying I'd found the drawer with papers stuck to it, but they didn't know about the theft. That was why they hadn't believed me.

So far so good, or so bad. Davilats had been in the Lincoln Navigator that Judy Binder tore off in. He or his accomplice had shot Ricky and Bowser.

I paused in front of a sushi restaurant. Judy gave Freddie Walker the Navigator in exchange for a little oxy, but Freddie did drugs, not cars. License plates, though. There'd been a stack of plates next to the drug cabinet. I wondered if Ferret Downey or his evidence techs had thought those worth bagging and tagging.

A woman with a stroller, talking animatedly into a headset, ran into me from behind. "You don't own this sidewalk," she snapped when I turned around, rubbing my leg.

"And a good day to you, too, ma'am. Be careful in the intersections: you wouldn't want your phone hurt in a crash."

I jogged up the street, her angry insults following me. At Wabansia, I collected Martin's car for the slow slog to Freddie's place, wondering for the ten thousandth time why they call it "rush hour" when you can't move faster than a crawl.

Freddie didn't live in a part of town where cleanup happened in a hurry. Tape still covered the surveillance camera, the car battery I'd stood on was still by the door, which still had police seals on it. Shaq and Ladonna were camped out on a curb up the street.

When they saw me ringing the doorbell, and then once again setting to work with my picklocks, they slowly moved my way. I could hear Ladonna's labored breathing as I got the complicated dead bolt to click back.

"Freddie made bail," Shaq volunteered.

I paused with the door partly open. "He home now?"

"Don't think so. Think he's at his place up by Lake Geneva. Got himself a big house there, boat, everything."

Freddie Walker, floating on a tide of coke, nursing his wounds in Wisconsin. "How about the guy Bullet, who hit his head on the stairs?" I asked.

"He still in intensive care," Ladonna said. "Freddie, he ain't paying a nickel, and Bullet's ma, she so far gone, she don't even understand he's hurt bad, so it's up to the county."

"Makes me proud to be a taxpayer," I said.

"Police know you're breaking those seals?" Shaq said.

"Do the police care if I'm breaking these seals?" I said. "Freddie has something that I want, unless the police took it."

"Ladonna and me, we can keep watch, if you like," Shaq suggested casually.

I thanked him gravely and held the door for them, but didn't wait for their slow progress up the stairs. I stopped on the second floor to look at the two apartments there. These seemed to make up Freddie's home, when he wasn't living it up in Wisconsin. His outsized bed, with a ceiling mirror, was covered in animal skins, in imitation of Wilt Chamberlain, and the rest of the rooms were furnished in equally expensive if unappetizing taste: glossy varnished liquor cabinet, baby blue piano, giant stereo speakers. A kitchen with Viking appliances that didn't seem ever to have been used. The refrigerator was full of Charles Krug champagne. Two hundred dollars a bottle and Freddie had a couple of cases stashed in here.

By the time I'd finished my tour, Ladonna and Shaq had huffed their way to the third-floor landing. The police had sealed the drug shop, but I opened that without compunction, too. I couldn't believe Ferret Downey or his team would ever revisit this site.

When the door was open, Ladonna and Shaq made a beeline for the drug cabinet. The police had taken away the contents, but the two hunted diligently and found enough loose pills on the shelves to keep them happy for a few days. I was even happier: Lieutenant Downey had left the license plates behind.

"That what you wanted?" Shaq said, astonished: he'd obviously thought he'd have to fight me for any loose drugs.

"Yep. You any idea what chop shop Freddie uses?"

Shaq and Ladonna exchanged glances, shook their heads, keeping a nervous eye on me. They were as frightened of car thieves as they were of Freddie, and they lived in this neighborhood. I didn't.

It didn't really matter. I wasn't going after car parts, I only wanted to know who owned the Lincoln Navigator Judy had fled in. With any luck, the license plates would lead me there. I went back down the stairs, but Shaq and Ladonna stayed behind, digging through Freddie's desk drawers, looking for cash or powder or anything else they had the strength to carry.

I didn't head straight home, but drove to the Naked Eye, a store that specializes in equipment for the fearful. Surveillance is not fun, especially not for the solo op, so I don't often do it. I have a few pieces of basic equipment, night-vision glasses and so on, but I wanted something that would tell me if there were any tracking devices on my car. If the Mustang was clean, then I'd know I was overreacting to the threat of being followed. I also picked up four burn phones, each with two hundred minutes, just in case.

What I needed wasn't cheap, but, as the Naked Eye's slogan proclaimed, "Peace of Mind Is Worth the Price." I paid cash, which meant that I also had to stop at a bank to get more money.

I put the Subaru into a covered garage on Broadway, about half a mile from my apartment, where I tested the sweeper on it. Martin's car seemed clean.

My Mustang was a different story. After I lugged all my equipment down to where I'd left my car, I found one bug inside the trunk, a second under the exhaust manifold.

I studied them thoughtfully. They were tiny, only about an inch square, but they were attached by powerful magnets, very difficult to pry loose. They didn't have any manufacturing or patent information on them, so whoever used them was working hard to stay anonymous. And whoever used them had access to top-shelf electronics.

That could mean my pals in Homeland Security, but I wondered as well about Metargon, "where the future lies behind." Metargon could and likely did make this kind of tracking gadget. Cordell Breen had a tight connection to the FBI, that was clear from how easily he got an agent to question the staff at Alison's computer lab in Mexico City. If Homeland Security had seen Alison arrive at my place last night, Cordell could have persuaded them to bug my car so he could keep track of his daughter.

I put the bugs back where I'd found them and drove home. I used the sweeper on my place, on Jake's and on Mr. Contreras's. There weren't any devices in our rooms that I could detect, but phone lines are tapped remotely these days, and there wasn't any way I could tell if there were outside ears trained on the building. Life as a paranoid person is not fun.

Despite realizing that I genuinely was under surveillance, I fired up my laptop and went into a database that gets me DMV records. Besides being hideously expensive, it is illegal, so if Homeland Security wanted to rat me out to the state's attorney, I was in trouble. I was betting on their incurable penchant for secrecy to protect me.

Of the seven license plates I'd taken from Freddie's, two had belonged to Lincoln Navigators. One was a two-year-old model reported stolen nine months ago. The second belonged to Phoebus Fleet, a leasing company whose headquarters were in Dallas.

It was long after the end of business hours, but a leasing company must have round-the-clock staff to respond to customer emergencies. I spent half an hour in fruitless conversation with a representative who could neither confirm nor deny that one of their vehicles had been stolen and who certainly was not going to give me the name of the lessee. Neither would her supervisor, nor the supervisor's manager. Unless I had a subpoena, the information was totally confidential.

I hung up in a snarly mood. Why couldn't the Nav have belonged to Sheriff Kossel, or someone else in Palfry?

I took a bottle of Torgiano out to my back porch to call Jake. He was rehearsing the double-bass solo in Rautavaara's *Angel of Dusk* for a performance with the San Francisco Symphony. He stopped work to talk to me, but when he said he had to get back to the rehearsal, I asked him to leave his phone on. Hearing him play was all I needed from him right now. He attached his phone to his bowing arm and I sat watching the clouds gather in the eastern sky, listening to the music.

Even after he hung up, the calm of the night and of his music remained. I sat on the porch, drinking a second glass of wine with a plate of cheese and salad, thinking of nothing in particular. I didn't hear my front doorbell ring. The first I knew I had company was Mr. Contreras, slowly climbing the back stairs.

33

LAP OF ELECTRONICS

S ORRY, DOLL, but he wouldn't take 'no' for an answer." Mr. Contreras was holding the top railing, puffing for air, after his climb.

Peppy and Mitch, who'd run up ahead of him, were now standing on the top step, facing down. They were growling softly, that deep-throated sound that says a dog is serious. In the dim light from the alley streetlamp, I could just make out a tall, wide shape below them.

"Who is 'he'?" I put my wineglass under my chair, out of reach in case things became physical. The Smith & Wesson was in my tuck holster but I wasn't going to draw it on a crowded porch.

"You Ms. Warshawski?" the shape called.

"Yes." I leaned forward in my chair, thigh muscles tensed so I could leap or duck in an instant. "And you are?"

"My name's Durdon; I'm Mr. Breen's driver. He wants to see you."

"I thought he was married," I said. "Anyway, I'm in a committed relationship." The language of Facebook sounds stupid when you say it out loud.

"Huh?" Durdon took another step up and Mitch gave a warning bark. "Can you hold your dogs? It's hard to talk with them sitting there."

"You came around without an invitation," Mr. Contreras said. "The dogs live here and you don't, so say what you want to say from where you're standing."

I love Mr. Contreras. I went over to the dogs and put hands around both their collars.

"Tell Mr. Breen I'm very flattered, but I'm not interested."

"What do you mean, you're not interested?"

"It's the age-old story, Mr. Durdon. Person X wants to see Person Y, but Y doesn't reciprocate. X persists; Y gets an Order of Protection. Good night."

Durdon stuck a hand in his pocket. I let go of Peppy to reach for my gun, but it turned out just to be his cell phone. He hit a speed dial number and communed with someone. After a moment, he held the phone out to me; I stretched a hand over the dogs for it.

"Ms. Warshawski?" The familiar warm baritone came on the line. "This is Cordell Breen. I've asked Durdon to drive you up to my home tonight. We need to talk."

"Mr. Breen, I pay rent on an office so I can have my evenings at home the same way you do. I went out of my way to visit you at Metargon last week. It's your turn to show some flexibility."

"I'm going to use the same argument I did last week. Your place isn't secure and mine is. I don't want Homeland Security or my corporate rivals to listen in on me. Alison told me the hoops you jumped her through last night to get some privacy. I'm not going to a dead woman's basement to talk. You can bring your neighbor; Durdon tells me he's involved in your business."

I gave in, only because I wanted to see the Lake Forest home anyway. I handed the phone back to Durdon.

"Want to come with me?" I asked Mr. Contreras. "See how the billionaires live?"

He was delighted and bustled back down the stairs to put the dogs inside his place. I told Durdon we'd meet him out front. I took my mother's wineglass inside and ran water over my face, hoping it would jolt my brain awake: a long day and two glasses of wine are not the best preparation for a high-wire conversation. I changed Boom-Boom's jersey for a red knit top, but kept on my worn jeans.

Durdon had arrived in a Maybach sedan. I'd never actually seen one, just heard about them in the way one hears about unicorns. They're made by Mercedes for people who think a Mercedes is a downmarket car. It's only the pit dog in me that made me wish I'd kept on Boom-Boom's sweaty jersey.

Durdon was a good driver, the car was well sprung and upholstered. I dozed against the leather headrest, mumbling assent to Mr. Contreras's running commentary: he'd had a phone call from my cousin Petra. He moved from Petra's Peace Corps saga to the annoying nature of people like Cordell Breen, who expects people like us to drop everything at his whim.

"You need a union, doll: the bosses never pushed us around when I was a machinist, because they knew there'd be heck to pay with the union if they carried on the way this Breen fella does."

"Yep," I agreed. "The detectives union, I like it. We need a strike fund. Any of your horses win today?"

Mr. Contreras sniffed. He bets at an offtrack place over on Belmont, but no matter how carefully he studies the form, he rarely brings home more than twenty dollars on his winning days—which are not as numerous as his losing ones.

We rolled off the Edens Expressway and turned up Green Bay Road. After about ten miles, Durdon swung the Maybach onto a side road. There were no streetlights, but in the headlights I saw we were on the edge of one of the steep ravines that lace this part of the lakefront. The road dead-ended at a set of gates, but Durdon barely slowed— Metargon's electronics included some type of transmitter for the car that opened the gates while we were still fifteen yards from them.

We cruised up a long drive lined with faux gas lamps. The drive ended at a white-painted brick house. It was three stories high with double wings extending toward the lake. When Durdon stopped next to a porticoed entrance and opened my door, I could hear the lake breaking beyond us in the dark.

Durdon strode to the front door without bothering to see if we were following, so Mr. Contreras and I decided to check out the terrain. I knew I was being juvenile: I'll show you who's boss, when I'd already agreed to be here, but Durdon still should have treated us like guests, not servants.

We'd reached a paved terrace on the house's north side before Durdon realized he'd lost us. When Mr. Contreras and I moved to the center of the terrace, security lights came on; it was easy enough for the driver to sprint over to us.

The lights were bright enough that I saw him for the first time. He was a squarely built man, somewhere in the forties. He might have been nice-looking, but a purple-yellow welt covering his left cheek made it hard to tell.

"Mr. Breen is waiting for you," he said. "You can't wander off wherever you want."

Before I could fire off an appropriate reply, Alison opened one of the doors that led onto the terrace. "Vic! I just learned that Dad summoned you. It's okay, Durdon, I'll bring them in through the music room. We'll let you know when Dad is ready for you to drive them back to the city."

On her home turf, Alison sounded older and more confident than she had at Kitty's this morning. It was only when we got inside, and she stopped under the chandelier in the middle of the room, that I saw the lines of strain around her eyes and mouth.

"I'm glad I spotted you out there," she said. "Dad wants to chew you out for corrupting me or misleading me or something totally stupid."

The music room had been built back when Chicago's robber barons were truly baronial. The high ceiling was covered with paintings of the muses playing music for the deities of Mount Olympus. A grand piano still stood in one corner, but the couches and chairs arranged in little islands made it look as though the Breen family used it for more ordinary entertainment.

A door opened at the far end of the room; a woman in a silvery sweater and black trousers appeared. "Alison, your father is looking for his visitors."

Her tone held an undercurrent of warning, or perhaps pleading. Alison grimaced, but introduced us to her mother. Constance Breen was a slender woman about my own age who had the same amber eyes as Alison, and the same stress lines around them.

"We're at sixes and sevens here tonight," she apologized. "We weren't expecting Alison to come home in such a dramatic way and Cordell is—Cordell and I are off-balance. Mr. Contreras, why don't you and I have a glass of something in my studio while Ms. Warshawski talks to my husband."

Her voice was slurred: she'd already had a few glasses of something. Mr. Contreras let himself be led off through one set of doors while Alison escorted me out another.

"Mom is a painter," she explained. "She hasn't had a public exhibition for a lot of years, so it will be fun for her to show her work to Mr. Contreras." It was a gallant effort, but her tone was doubtful.

She took me to the door of her father's office. It was the room of a modern technocrat, with a flat-screen TV on one wall tuned to world market reports and a battery of equally flat computer monitors on the glass-topped desk in front of him. The room faced the lake, but the windows were so thoroughly soundproofed that we couldn't hear the water.

Breen didn't bother to get to his feet or even to look up from his monitor. I guess being kept waiting was supposed to make me feel nervous.

"Good to see you too, Mr. Breen," I said. "If that's all, let's get Durdon to drive me back to Chicago."

As I turned to leave, I saw Alison's eyes widen—admiration or alarm, hard to know. I gave her a reassuring smile.

Breen said, "You came up here to see me. You'll wait until I'm ready."

I paused in the doorway. "It's true, I would like to see Edward Breen's workshop. Alison, why don't you take me up there while your dad plays games with his computer."

"Neither Alison nor anyone else will take you to the workshop. The last time I let her take strangers up there, a valuable picture disappeared."

"Dad, don't start that again tonight, please," Alison cried. "Martin did not steal the drawing. It was there at the end of the evening."

"What's gone?" I asked. "Your pet Picasso?"

"More valuable than that," Breen snapped, "at least to us. Edward's rough sketch of what became the BREENIAC, the Metargon-I, has vanished. Apparently angels or vampires made off with it, since Alison claims it was still here at the end of her irresponsible party with one of our employees. Who definitely should not have been in this house."

"Dad, please!" Alison said. "We've gone round on this all day. Jari Liu has told you himself that Martin could dance rings around all the summer fellows, so why do you need to keep insulting him? Besides, he did *not* steal Granddad's BREENIAC sketch."

"Oh," I said slowly. "Is that what Martin was looking at when he said something didn't add up?"

Alison held up her hands, a gesture of helplessness. "I don't know. It's true that it's vanished, but I'm sure it was here when the party was over. Besides, Martin was wearing a T-shirt and cutoffs to the barbecue; you can't stick a framed drawing inside a T-shirt without it showing. One of the other fellows would have said something. Especially Tad: he goes to MIT. He couldn't stand that a guy taking night classes at an urban campus could out-program him."

"It's why I don't trust young Binder." Breen smacked his desktop with his palm. It must have stung, heavy glass against skin, but he didn't flinch. "He has a chip on his shoulder, he was taking over chunks of Fitora from other programmers. Maybe, as Jari says, he was only trying to improve the program, but maybe he was getting a handle on more of its components."

"What does the sketch show?" I interrupted. "I thought it was just the outline for a computer that is completely obsolete these days. Is there something else on it that makes it worth taking?"

For some reason, the question took Breen off-guard. He didn't answer immediately. "It's valuable to collectors," he said, but he sounded like a kid in a classroom making a wild guess at the answer.

Alison said, "Even if I could believe Martin stole it, it wouldn't mean anything to him, I mean it doesn't contain unusual electronics. It's a very rough sketch of the central grid, with arrows pointing to input and output paths. Granddad did include equations for a hysteresis curve."

"Hysteresis?" I repeated. "I can see how computers make you hysterical, but is that how they're built?"

Alison smiled involuntarily. "That's what everyone says in their first computer engineering class. Hysteresis is hard to explain, but it has to do with the way you can lag output behind input and use the same site both to read and write memory. One of the biggest problems with early vacuum tube memory was the way tubes amplified distortion in the electronic signal. Granddad's big breakthrough was understanding that if you used a magnetic core instead of a tube, you could rely on hysteresis to control the distortion. The sketch had equations in the top corner for electronic Fermi surfaces and for hysteresis. They seem to be how Granddad's thinking led him to a ferromagnetic core."

"That's what makes it valuable to a collector," Breen cut in. "It's drawn on fragile paper, an old piece of newsprint that Edward had—he probably tore it out of *Stars and Stripes* when he was in the last big push of the war. He always said he created it under battlefield conditions.

"This Binder jerk wouldn't know to protect it, which proves the point I've been making all day to Alison—she wants to trot around the globe on her own, hobnobbing with the poor and undereducated, but she doesn't have horse sense. If I'd had somebody keeping an eye on you here at the house while your mother and I were in Bar Harbor, Binder could never have walked away with the sketch."

"Dad, he *didn't*!" Tears were spilling out of the corners of Alison's amber eyes.

"Oh, Sunny!" Breen got up from his desk and went to put an arm around her. "I'm sorry to make you cry. I'm going nuts, worrying about you and Binder and the Fitora software, and to find Edward's drawing missing has tipped me over the edge."

"That's very touching," I said, "but it doesn't help me understand why I needed to be out here."

Breen looked at me over his daughter's head. "I wanted to talk to you in person, not over the phone, because I wanted to see your face and how you react. Have you found Binder?"

I shook my head. "Not a whiff of him. How about you?"

He made an impatient gesture. "I told you when I met you last week that I didn't think you had the skills for this search, and your failure confirms it."

I smiled. "Unless you've shoveled him into a hole in the ground someplace that no one knows about, you're clueless yourself right now. I gather Homeland Security and the FBI are as well, or they wouldn't be messing with my home and Alison's Mexico City program."

Again, something I'd said unsettled him. It was impossible to know what, but he paused almost imperceptibly, as if power had been switched off in him briefly.

He recovered quickly and added, "Beyond the question of Martin

Binder, you need to understand that you must not interfere with my daughter. You crossed a line last night when you took her to that dead woman's home. You are fortunate that she survived unharmed, but it was irresponsible at best, criminally negligent at worst."

"Dad!" Alison shook his shoulder. "*I* went to Vic. *I* sought *her* out, she did not try to find me. She was protecting my privacy because I was being a chicken. I should have been brave enough to come out here right away to talk to you, instead of involving her in my problems."

One of the computers on Breen's desk pinged. Breen kissed his daughter's forehead and trotted back to his desk. "Okay, Sunny, okay, we're all rattled right now. At least you're showing the spine you're going to need to run a company."

His last remarks were offhand; his real attention was on the computer. It was as if that "ping" was what he'd been waiting for all throughout our conversation.

I moved around the desk to see what was so absorbing. At first, I couldn't make it out, but after a bit I thought I was watching traffic on Chicago's expressways. There were thousands of streaks of light on the monitor. The Ryan was dense-packed, especially through the Loop, but I-55 was moving fast, as were the outlying toll roads. When the computer dinged, one of the streaks would pulse red.

"Just another of our programs that I'm testing here at home," Breen said. "No wonder Alison wanders off on her own: I'm not attentive enough, even when I'm angry about her recklessness."

He closed the tab and switched his attention to another monitor, one that was scrolling lines of code that meant nothing to me.

34

GADGET MUSEUM

BREEN'S SUDDENLY MELLOWER MOOD led him to tell Alison she could show me her grandfather's workshop, after all. We collected Mr. Contreras from Constance Breen's studio, a large, glass-enclosed room at the end of the north wing. Constance said she'd pass; she'd already seen the workshop more times than she wanted.

One of the large windows facing the water was open; Ms. Breen was standing there, her back to us, a wineglass in hand. Alison started to say something to her mother about how much she'd had to drink, but her mother simply walked through the open window toward the lake. Alison looked after her irresolutely, but finally squared her shoulders and told Mr. Contreras and me to follow her up the stairs. When we reached the third floor, Alison clapped her hands and lights in old-fashioned sconces came on.

Mr. Contreras and I both stopped in amazement. We were at the entrance to a small museum, one where all the objects were out in the open for anyone to play with. There were models of magnetic memory, which looked like iron Tinkertoys, cylinders that had deep grooves cut into them. A scale model of the BREENIAC, or Metargon-I, was set in the middle of the room; you could take off the panels and see the famous ferromagnetic core. Along the wall closest to the stairs were the actual Metargon computers, from the BREENIAC to 1970s mainframes.

Mr. Contreras was fascinated by the display of Edward Breen's old machines, the bandsaws, drill presses and so on for creating his prototypes. He played with the flywheels, told Alison one of them was out of balance and that he could fix it for her, but she said that her father really would kill her if she let someone tamper with Edward's machines.

The framed letters Alison had mentioned, from Hans Bethe and other physicists, from a raft of presidents starting with Truman, were on the walls in between the computers and the machines.

An old-fashioned pigeonhole desk had open notebooks on it—another museum touch; these were Edward Breen's notebooks, showing his drawings and the steps he went through to engineer and test his early machines.

"Where was the BREENIAC sketch?" I asked Alison.

She waved at an empty place on the wall above the desk. "It was the star attraction, so Granddad had it over his head when he sat. As I said, I don't remember him, but from everything I hear about him, he had an ego the size of Mount McKinley, so I imagine he liked to think of it as the halo above his head."

"How sure are you, really, now that your dad is out of earshot, that Martin didn't take the drawing?"

Alison gave a wry smile. "Physically, I suppose he could have tucked it into the back of his cutoffs, but he was so upset, I don't think stealing was on his mind. I was over there"—she pointed at a table holding a model of a data cylinder—"and Martin came over. I told you that part last night, how he got so agitated and took off. Anyway, I really think I would have noticed if the drawing was gone when I got the rest of the kids out of here."

"Any hunches on who else might have taken it?" I asked.

"It can't be anyone who works here," she said. "We've known all of them for years. A lot of businesspeople come here; Dad thinks it's a better atmosphere for getting people to agree to work on projects with him than the corporate offices. He's getting into solar, which means wooing investors, and they like seeing Granddad's shop. It's all I can think of, that someone couldn't resist taking the sketch."

She pulled out her iPhone and typed in a URL. "Look—this is the photograph of it they use in electronics texts."

I bent over the tiny screen. The web page showed the Metargon-I's interior, which didn't appear much different from what we could see in the scale model.

"Looks like a deep-fat fryer," Mr. Contreras said. "Like what my pa used to make French fries—he was a fry cook at the Woolworth's in McKinley Park."

I thought it looked more like the potholders we used to make for our mothers in grade school art. "Where were the equations you mentioned?"

Alison slid the image to the right and pointed to the top left corner. "He wrote them in this tiny hand, not like his usual writing—I guess in a battlefield he had to conserve paper. And then there was a name next to the grid, someone called Speicher. He was probably one of Granddad's buddies, Dad says. I always picture him talking over the design with his buddy, and then his buddy dying, so Granddad included his name when he drew up the schematic."

She tapped the screen again and moved to the lower right side of the image. "In this corner there was a circle with a design in it. Interlocking triangles and maybe a sunburst; it was kind of hard to make out. Dad couldn't tell me what it meant, so I thought it was part of his tribute to his dead friend. I mean, 'Speicher' could be a Jewish name, and the design could be a deconstructed Star of David."

"A little circle with triangles inside?"

My voice came out queerly, even to my own ears. Alison and Mr. Contreras stared at me.

I took the iPhone from her and went to the Virtual-Bidder site, to King Derrick's effort to sell the details of the Innsbruck reactor.

"Was it like that?" I pointed to the small circle at the bottom of the FOI document that I'd noticed yesterday.

"It might be." Alison peered at the screen. "This is so grainy I can't be sure."

She went to her grandfather's desk and fished a magnifying glass from one of the cubbyholes. When she held it over her phone, we could see jagged lines like a child's drawing of the corona of the sun.

We heard Cordell Breen on the stairs just then. Alison went to the door of the workshop to meet him. "Look, Dad." She held out the phone. "Isn't this queer? This is the same logo that is on the BREE-NIAC sketch."

Breen snatched the phone from her and stared at it. "What the—what is this? Where did you find it?"

I told him about "King Derrick's" auction, now shut down. "Just part of my ineffectual search for Martin Binder. Until he was murdered two weeks ago, Derrick Schlafly was his mother's landlord."

Breen used his thumbs on the screen with the speed of a teenager. "I don't get it. This is an FOI document about the Nazi nuclear weapons program. This makes no sense at all for the same image to be on it and on the Metargon-I sketch."

He used his thumbs some more. "I'm e-mailing the URL to our research department, see if they can get a handle on it. I owe you an apology, Ms. Warshawski—you were ahead of my whole team on this one. Thanks for sharing. If we turn up anything, I'll let you know."

A buzzer sounded. Mr. Contreras and I both were startled, which made Alison and her father laugh.

"We have computer monitors for the house up here," Alison explained. "Dad and I both like to work up here when we've got a tough problem to solve, but we're so remote that we don't hear anything in the house. Mother insisted that we install them."

I hadn't noticed the monitors, but I saw now that there was a modern worktable against the far wall, behind the row of Metargon machines. I walked over and saw the gates we had come through. A car was on the far side. We couldn't see the face behind the steering wheel, but the license plate was being photographed.

Someone inside the house was speaking through an intercom, which garbled her voice. We heard the driver say that he would wait for Breen, either outside the gates or inside the house, but that he wasn't going to leave without seeing him.

"You listening in on one of your fancy gadgets, Cordell?" The electronics flattened the voice into a quack. "I'm tired of you hiding behind the wall of secretaries and pit bulls you built out of Edward's little machine."

"Dad, who is it?" Alison cried.

Breen made a shushing motion and spoke into an invisible mike. "We don't have anything to talk about. You turned a trivial event into the crime of the century and you want to drag me down into a pit with you, but I'm not going there, my friend."

"I'm not your friend, Breen, not for one second. Someone using my name was digging around in the university archives. If that was you—"

Breen pressed another button, cutting off the man in the car, and switching to a room in the house where a woman in jeans and a sweatshirt was standing. "Imelda, let him in. Tell Durdon to take him around the back; I'll meet him there in a minute."

He turned to his daughter. "Sunny, you up to driving Ms. Warshawski and her friend home? I need Durdon here. This is a crackpot who's been threatening me over patent infringements. It's outrageous that he's stalked me here at home and I need Durdon's big shoulders to make it clear this is the last time he does that."

Alison demanded that he call the family's lawyer. Breen laughed easily. "Sweetheart, the legal beagles know all about this guy. I want to make it clear to him personally that he can't charge into our home as if we're a public meeting. In a business like ours, there are always going to be people who think you took their ideas and this jerk is one of them. You get our guests back to the city, okay?"

Alison agreed, reluctantly. She sent Mr. Contreras and me down a third staircase that led to an underground garage; she wanted to stop to tell her mother where she was going.

My neighbor and I went through a room the size of an auditorium that held a golf practice range, a full-sized pool table, and a small basketball court. On the other side was the garage, which was as immaculate as the rest of the house. The cars ranged from the Maybach sedan to two convertibles, a Miata and a Lotus, which I figured as Breen's testosterone car. A Land Rover and a 1939 Hudson completed the collection.

When Alison rejoined us, her face was still troubled. "Mother doesn't know anything about this man, although Dad isn't very good at letting her in on company business. Now that I've been away from home for a few years, I'm beginning to see how hard it is on her."

She pointed to the Land Rover. "Mother told me to take this. The Miata's mine, and I adore it, but one of you would have to curl up in the trunk. Probably you, V.I.; you're more flexible."

She was trying to lighten her mood; Mr. Contreras and I both laughed obligingly. We climbed into the Land Rover, me in the backseat. Alison hit a button on the SUV's steering wheel and the garage door opened onto a steep drive at the back of the house. I looked around for the car that had shown up on the monitor, but didn't see it.

Another tap on the steering wheel opened the gates at the end of the drive, letting us back onto the narrow road that skirted the ravine. The lighting was bad, but Alison drove so fast that Mr. Contreras demanded she slow down.

"There's a cop car at the light up ahead, case you hadn't noticed," he added.

At the red light on Sheridan Road, I looked at the squad car, but the officer inside was focused on his tablet, not on reckless drivers. As Alison turned south onto Green Bay Road, the squad car turned right, toward the Breen house. I could see the markings, dark brown on tan, but couldn't read the jurisdiction. Had Breen felt threatened enough by his visitor that he'd called the local cops?

35

PHISHING

I T WASN'T UNTIL we were back on the Edens Expressway heading south that I brought up the logo we'd seen on the Innsbruck reactor report.

"You realize, don't you, that it's that little design that must have upset Martin when he was here for your picnic," I said.

"I know," Alison agreed, her voice small. "But that doesn't mean he stole Granddad's sketch."

"He might have borrowed it," I suggested. "Here's the thing: his mother stole a set of papers from his grandmother about seven years ago. Martin saw them at the time, but he was only thirteen or so; they didn't mean anything to him. Those little triangles on the BREE-NIAC sketch made him remember the same design on those old documents. He could have taken the sketch down to where his mother was living, to compare it with the papers she'd stolen. After seeing his mother, he knew he had to go into hiding. Whether it's because he's afraid of Derrick Schlafly's killers or some other reason, we won't know until we find him."

Alison swerved around a line of cars, accelerating to eighty.

"Slow down, gal," Mr. Contreras said. "Vic don't mean you no harm, and driving like that could get us all killed. It don't matter so much at my age, but you got your life in front of you."

"Mine, too," I murmured.

"I thought Vic was my friend," Alison protested.

"I am your friend," I said sharply. "But we can't get anywhere if I have to play 'Let's pretend.' You know Martin, I don't. I believe you when you say he wouldn't be interested in selling it or the Fitora code. He's not a guy who cares about money, he cares about his work: I get that. I'm just saying he might have taken the sketch, fully planning to return it. Is that so awful?"

"I guess not," she agreed in a subdued voice. "But where could he be, after all this time?"

Her father's odd reaction when I'd said he, too, was clueless about Martin's whereabouts, unless he'd shoveled him into a hole in the ground, came back to me. It wasn't so much that he'd shown alarm as that he'd been taken off-guard. Surely Cordell Breen hadn't murdered Martin. But what about Durdon, the muscle who could make it clear to late-night callers that they needed to stay strictly away? Would he murder on Breen's orders?

"Tell me about Durdon," I said. "Is that a full-time job, driving for your dad?"

Alison seemed happy to change the subject. "Driving wouldn't keep him busy full-time, not when all three of us like to get around on our own. He's a good mechanic, so he looks after all the cars and keeps on top of the plumbing and stuff in the house."

"It looks as though one of your machines fought back," I said. "That was quite a bruise on his cheek."

"That was the first thing I saw when I came home this afternoon," Alison said. "Durdon told me he'd been clumsy with one of the lifts in the garage."

"Must've been lying there funny to take it on the side of his face like that," Mr. Contreras said. "He could have got his whole face crushed."

"Don't!" Alison said. "It sounds terrible when you put it like that."

"You're close to him?" I asked.

"No," Alison said slowly. "He's been with us since I was little, but—well, some of the staff, like Imelda, went out of their way when I was a kid, but Durdon, he always seems a bit—oh, like he's polite because it's his job, but he doesn't really like me."

"He lives in the house?" I asked.

"He and Imelda, she's the housekeeper, they both have suites in the south wing. An outside contractor keeps up the grounds and Imelda has someone come in three days a week to do the heavy cleaning. Do you think someone from the cleaning service could have taken the sketch?"

"Something to keep in mind," I said.

When she pulled up in front of our building, I asked if she thought she'd feel better spending the night with us, but she wanted to get back to Lake Forest; she was worrying about her mother.

"I ought to be getting ready to go back to Mexico," she said. "But I kind of don't feel like going until I see what's—well, you know—Martin, the sketch—and there's my mother—" She broke off unhappily.

Mr. Contreras gave her a rough embrace. "You just keep your chin up, Alison, leave the rest to Vic and me. We got your back, okay?"

She produced another gallant smile and hoisted herself back into the Land Rover. I went outside with Mr. Contreras and the dogs. It had been a long day and I was tired, but I tried to listen to my neighbor's rambling: he'd had a long day, too.

Constance Breen had shown him her paintings while she worked her way through a bottle of chardonnay. "You'd think she might paint that gal of hers. Alison's got the kind of face I'd like to hang on my wall, I told her. She laughed at that, said she'd do a portrait for me."

He chewed it over in his mind, then added, "These pictures, they're like they're the inside of her head out there on a piece of canvas. Lots of gray paint with one spot of red, like it was a red dot of anger in the middle of her body."

It was an impressive summary, which dovetailed with what Alison had said, her mother feeling shut off in the Lake Forest mansion, away from other artists, her husband lost in the world of machines and money. Her daughter, too, at least the machine part. I wondered about Constance Breen's relationship with Durdon, the driver-mechanic-muscle-man. Did she like him, trust him, sleep with him, keep him at arm's length?

I finally went up to my own place, where I'd started the evening three hours ago. I went back to the DMV site to check the license plate of the car that had been outside the Breen gates when Cordell hustled us out of his mansion.

It belonged to a seventeen-year-old Honda. Which was registered to Julius Dzornen. My jaw dropped. Julius demanding an audience with Cordell Breen? I rubbed my aching eyes.

Cordell had been dismissive of Julius tonight for crying over what he called sarcastically "the crime of the century." However, Julius's reason for driving up to Lake Forest took Breen by surprise: he didn't know someone had used Julius's name to get into the library. That in itself was an odd thing—why had it made Julius angry enough to drive so far late at night? Perhaps he was drunk. Or it was the last straw, the final insult in a half-century of them?

More interesting were the little triangles on the BREENIAC and King Derrick documents. Breen had looked surprised when Alison showed him the design, but I wondered if what surprised him was my connecting those two dots. I was supposed to be the imbecile that he could run rings around while he chewed gum, texted and played the tuba.

I didn't believe anyone on the cleaning crew had stolen it—someone looking for quick cash wouldn't think a page of equations had any street value. I needed to talk to Judy Binder again, to find out what she could remember about those documents she'd lifted from her mother. I wanted to see Julius, as well. I needed to find a way to get him to tell me what crime detectives should have dealt with all those years ago, when he and Cordell were both teenagers. It had to be connected to the drawing.

I groaned. It was late, I was exhausted. Unless I was going to drive down to Palfry and actually dig up the ground around the Schlafly house, I couldn't do anything more tonight.

36

A CHILDHOOD OUTING

WHAT WILL YOU GIVE ME if I talk to you?" Judy Binder smiled at me slyly. "Your son," I said. "You are the only person who may know how to find him."

"Doesn't anyone care about me?" Binder said, her voice a high-pitched whine. "You come in here all worried about Martin, but what about me?"

Last night, despite my exhaustion, I'd lain awake a long time. I kept turning pieces of information like a kaleidoscope, trying to make a comprehensible shape out of them. Julius, Cordell, Martin. Kitty, Martina, Judy. Benjamin Dzornen and Edward Breen. The meth house.

I went to my computer to see what unsolved crimes in Chicago dated back fifty years, with a few years on either side. I didn't turn up anything that sounded as though it connected to Julius and Cordell.

Judy Binder had just been born fifty years ago, but Julius's old crime was tied to Kitty and to the Breens. Her whole life in Chicago, Kitty had thought someone was spying on her. Lotty said it was a constant obsession with her; she wouldn't have kept it a secret from her daughter.

Kitty had witnessed a horrible crime, or been the victim of a horrible crime, involving the Breens and the Dzornens when she first came to Chicago. They had bought her silence with the bank account that Herta Dzornen robbed, but Kitty was always afraid the Dzornens or the Breens would do something else to her. Judy might not know all the details, but she'd known enough to try blackmailing Herta.

I finally went to sleep, but in my troubled dreams, Martin's skeleton was grinning up at me from a hole in the bottom of the meth pit. Alison Breen was weeping over his bones while Kitty Binder wrung her hands, crying, "I told you over and over, if you don't know they're after you, you're not paying attention."

I slept late, despite my unquiet dreams. When I finally got out of bed, the weather had turned, as it does in Chicago: heat-crusted drought one day, cold and rainy the next. I couldn't bear to run in it, much as I needed the exercise.

I threw balls to the dogs from Mr. Contreras's back porch, sipping a double espresso, trying not to resent Jake for sounding so happy when he called me from San Francisco: the Rautavaara had been a huge success. I was truly glad, but I wanted some successes of my own. They seemed hard to come by these days.

It was after ten when I finally got to the hospital, where Judy Binder greeted me with all her usual sunniness. She had just finished taking her first walk since the shooting, as far as the nurses' station and back. I walked into her room in time to hear her snap at the nurse and therapist who'd applauded her progress: she wasn't two years old, she wasn't fooled by pretty words, so they could shut the fuck up.

The nurse helped her into a wheelchair, carefully arranging the IV stands so that the lines didn't cross each other. Judy had four, which disappeared into the folds of her hospital gown. Her thin arms were scaly, with so many collapsed veins the nurses had had to go into her back for sites to insert the needles.

"If Martin wants to disappear, let him disappear," Binder said when I tried to talk about her son. "He treated me totally disrespectfully the last time I saw him."

"You don't go out of your way to make people want to respect you, Ms. Binder."

We both thought she was going to start screaming abuse at me, but she shut her mouth halfway through. "Goddamn bitch, mind your own—" Her face took on a puzzled look, as if she'd heard herself for the first time and wondered what she was saying. After a brief silence, she said sullenly that she had no idea where Martin was.

"I believe you," I said, "but I need you to tell me every detail about the papers you and he argued over. He came to you because he'd seen an odd logo on an old drawing, a pair of linked triangles with something like a sunburst in the middle. He thought he'd seen the same design on a paper he'd once found in your possession. What did he say about it?"

"He came barging in, not even bringing me a flower or anything, the way you think a boy would do for his mother. He just demanded to see those damned papers."

"These were papers that you found at your mother's house when you went there for Martin's bar mitzvah, right?"

"Are you saying I stole—"

"I'm not here to make any accusations. I need information, and I need it fast. Your son's life may depend on it."

She scowled. "Yeah, Martin's life, what about mine?"

"You're alive because your mother called me in time to save you. Now I'm asking you to do the same for your own child," I said.

She tossed her wiry hair petulantly. "I think you're letting Martin dramatize himself, but, okay, I found this envelope in Kitty's under-wear drawer. I started feeling unwell at the bar mitzvah party; I went to lie down and was looking for a—a clean handkerchief."

She stopped, eyeing me to see if I was going to comment on her snooping, but I didn't say anything. "So Kitty screamed the house down when she realized the papers were missing. But I was just preserv-ing them!"

"Yes, so you said." I tried to keep the impatience out of my voice. "What did you do with them?"

"Nothing. I mean, nothing back then. I was looking for an aspirin, only then I saw there was a savings book in the packet, and it had my name in it! That was definitely mine. Kitty was coming up the stairs, and first I thought of asking her why she was stealing from me, but I decided to take the packet home with me to see if there were any other financial documents she was keeping for herself."

I didn't point out that she'd first been looking for a handkerchief. "And were there any other financial instruments?"

"No, just papers with numbers. I showed them to Martin one day when he came to see me, back when he was in eighth grade, I mean. He's always been good with numbers, I thought they'd be, like bank accounts or something, but he said they didn't mean anything to him. Then he wanted to know where I got them. He was only thirteen, but he had the nerve to accuse his own mother of stealing papers when they belonged to me in the first place. Kitty must have been whining about the papers disappearing."

Along with Kitty's pearl earrings and a certain amount of cash, I remembered, but I didn't want to toss a grenade on the conversation.

"So I stuffed them into a drawer and forgot about them, but then, like I told you, a few weeks ago Martin came barreling down to Palfry, wanting to see them again. He tore the place apart looking for them. I kept telling him I didn't even know if I still had them, but he found them with my birth certificate in this old shoe box in the front room. He got all excited and said, 'These were supposed to come to me! Why didn't you show them to me before?'

"I told him I'd shown them to him when he was thirteen and he hadn't been interested. Was I supposed to wait on him hand and foot, checking every morning to see if he cared about some stupid old papers?"

Judy pounded the arm of her wheelchair with a feeble fist. "It was always like that with him, me, me, me. Why couldn't he ever see *I* had needs, too! Even as a baby he was always selfish. It's why I had to give him to my parents, I couldn't cope with someone that selfish."

"Yeah, babies tend to be thoughtless that way," I said, my throat so tight I had trouble getting the words out. "Why did he think the papers should come to him?"

"Because he could understand some stupid equations in them. Then he started squawking at me; he said didn't it mean anything to me when I read the cover letter and saw who asked them to be sent to Kitty?"

"Who?" I felt my pulse quicken.

"Some woman named Byron. Ada Byron. How special does that sound?"

I felt let down: I'd been sure they were from Martina, or Benjamin Dzornen. "Was Byron a family name? I mean in your family, your dad's mother, or the family your mom lived with in England?"

"Oh, those people! No, their name was Painter." Judy giggled unexpectedly, an unpleasant sound. "He was a builder whose name was Painter, pretty funny, huh? Painter the Builder. They adopted Kitty and she *adored* them." The word was a honeycomb of sarcasm.

"They were the man and woman with the girls in the snapshot your mother kept in the living room? What happened to them?"

"Oh, she could never stop crying about it, even though it happened years before I was born. When the war ended, Painter the Builder wanted to put up a house on a bombed-out street in Birmingham. England, not Alabama. Kitty was at school when the mom and dad and sisters were inspecting the site. A few minutes before Kitty got there an unexploded bomb went off. So that was horrible, looking for her *real* family, as she always called them, and finding an ambulance and body parts instead."

She gave her repellent laugh again: her mother had described the scene many times and Judy had grown tired of hearing it. I jammed my hands into my pockets to make sure I didn't leap up and shake her, but I had to wait a moment before I could trust myself to ask another question.

"I know your mother was difficult to live with, but can you remember that her life was punctuated by horrifying losses?" I said at last. "Losing her birth mother and the grandmother who raised her. Losing the family that adopted her. And losing you to drugs."

"Don't you guilt-trip me!" Judy's eyes flashed. "I heard that morning, noon and night for the last thirty-five years."

She repeated my words with savage mockery. "'*I'm sure she was difficult to live with.*' Yes, she was fucking difficult to live with. I never could have girlfriends over to play, she was so suspicious of strangers coming into the house. No one ever invited me to their birthday parties or anything because she was creepy. The other moms felt uncomfortable around her. She always thought people were following her. In high school I finally started finding my own friends."

She was panting, the anger exhausting her frail body. She leaned back in the wheelchair, her face pasty, like buttermilk, with red flecks floating on it. I let her rest, but when she opened her eyes, just a bit, little slits studying my reaction, I started again.

"Who was following her?"

"Don't ask me. She'd say the FBI was monitoring her mail, or sometimes it was the CIA. Like one blue-collar refugee from Austria was important enough for J. Edgar Hoover to snoop on."

"She never talked about an old crime, something that happened before you were born?"

Judy seemed to realize this was an important question. She took time to think about it but finally shook her head. "Not unless you mean the Dzornens robbing her of her inheritance, she talked about that plenty. It always upset my dad, he worked hard, he supported us, we lived as comfortably as anyone else around us: What did she want that guy's money for, anyway? he used to say."

Poor Leonard Binder. He sounded like a decent guy whose only crime had been marrying a woman badly scarred by life and war. At least he'd had those joyous moments with Martin, when they filled the garage with dry ice and set off the rockets.

"Your mother talked to you about the Painters. She also told you about the Dzornens, didn't she? How they mistreated her? Did she think they were the people following her?"

"I told you I don't know!" Judy tried to shout but she didn't have enough strength in her abdomen; the words came out in a grating rasp.

"You knew a lot about her." I kept my voice neutral, neither praise nor blame, merely a chance to open a curtain and see a new landscape. It actually got Judy to think: once again she cut herself off mid-curse.

"She wasn't always angry. When I was little, sometimes we had fun, my dad and mom and I. My dad loved going to the park or the zoo, and he was good with tools, he could build things, mechanical things—Kitty always did the woodwork. They even made me a wagon with a motor. Kitty could sew anything. Once she made a wardrobe for my kitten. The girls at school were jealous when I brought Ginger with me to show-and-tell."

"Do you remember what happened to change your mother?"

Judy looked at her knotted fingers, the fingers of a much older woman. "She wasn't always happy, either, don't go getting that idea! The first words I ever heard from her were how her birth mother didn't like her, how she only cared about equations and atoms. Her mom liked Lotty better, Mom thought Lotty was a show-off." She smiled slyly. "Of course that's why I went to Lotty when I got pregnant; I knew it would piss off Kitty no end."

I nodded. I didn't like it, but I could understand it.

"And like you said, she lost everybody. I heard it so many times it stopped being about real people, it was like a bedtime story, the nasty kind that gives you nightmares."

I nodded again: Judy's drugs made a certain sense to me. If your life had been filled with horror stories from the day you were born, you would want something to blunt the images. That made me think of "duck and cover." I asked Judy how that came into her history.

She gave an involuntary glance at the door. "If I tell, you have to promise not to say."

"That's okay: I promise."

"And shut the door. I don't want those nurses listening in."

I shut the door and pulled the visitor's chair over next to her.

She looked from me to the door several times, deciding whether she was really ready to jump off the high dive, but she finally made the leap.

"It was when I was seven, right after my birthday, when Mom had made these clothes for Ginger. I was playing with him. My mom came in shouting, 'Put down the damned cat. You're coming with me.' She sounded so mad I was scared. I hugged Ginger tight to me and she grabbed him out of my arms and threw him onto the bed. I was screaming, I thought she'd killed him, it was terrifying."

Tears began welling at the corners of her eyes. For the first time I felt real pity for her.

"We went in the car. I don't know where, but it was a long way, out into the country. We went into this gas station, it was in the middle of nowhere, and this old lady was there. She and my mom, they spoke in German. My mom used to talk to me in German, and I could understand some, but I didn't like it. The old lady asked about somebody and my mom said she was dead.

"Next the old lady wanted to know who followed us, and Mom said, no one, I was careful, and then the old lady knelt down next to me. She looked me in the face and asked was I a girl who liked nature and stars or a girl who liked dolls and sewing.

"I didn't know what to say, I didn't know what the right answer was, so I said, I loved my kitten and Mom had sewn beautiful clothes for him. Mom was teaching me to knit.

"The old lady and Mom started having an argument, in German, it was about—" Judy stopped and eyed me suspiciously. "This is going to sound stupid, so you'd better not laugh at me."

"No, I won't laugh," I said gently. "There's nothing ridiculous in a hard story and yours is quite painful. What were they arguing about?"

"About knitting, I think of that sometimes and I think I can't be remembering right. The German word is *stricken*, and sometimes I think they were speaking English and the old lady was stricken by something. But then another car drove up and this man got out and the three of them started having a terrible fight. The old lady was speaking German, but the old man spoke English.

"He said something like, 'I'm not doing anything else, so whatever it is you want, forget about it.' And the lady said, 'You are a weasel.' I remembered that because of 'Pop! Goes the Weasel.' I had a windup clown that sang the song. They were so angry, I thought it was because of me, I was the child, did they think I shouldn't have toys? I was afraid they were going to send me away, the way my mom got sent away, she was a little girl like me when she got sent away from her *Oma*. I thought they were mad because I was knitting and playing with toys. I was so scared, I said, 'Pop! goes the weasel,' out loud.

"They all stared at me, which made me even scareder. I started to cry, which got my mother mad, and the man said the lady was doing something to me, a word I didn't know even though it was in English, something about doctors, I think. I wondered if I had to go to a doctor because of talking out loud. The lady said, 'I would if I could. If I could keep her from turning into a weasel like you, believe me I would risk everything, jail, everything.'

"And he said, 'That's—' I don't know. Maybe he said, 'an outrage.' I was seven, they used a lot of words I didn't know. The lady started saying, 'Tell her, you and tell her, you signed on to duck and cover. That was a cruel lie that you and tell her made up.'

"Mom was shouting, everyone was mad. The man from the gas station came out, so they all shut up, everyone got back in their cars. When we were in our car, Mom said, 'You must never tell anyone. They will put us all in prison if you tell anyone. Don't talk about duck and cover, don't talk about tell her, they'll know who you're talking about.'"

Judy started to cry again. I put an arm around her, awkwardly because of the IV lines and the wheelchair. Her sobbing on top of the stress of the interview was too much for her fragile body; she slumped over in my embrace, her heart monitor sending out a frantic warning. I wheeled her chair to the bed, moving the IV lines with her.

I found the nurse's call button and pressed it, but Judy was so thin, so light, that I could lift her without help. A nurse arrived as I was laying a pillow under Judy's feet.

The nurse took over. "What happened?" she demanded.

I shook my head. "She was talking to me about her childhood and I guess she was more worn-out than I realized—she suddenly collapsed."

The nurse felt Judy's pulse, her eye on the monitor. "I'm paging the doctor, but you'd better leave: we need to get her heart stable again."

Doctors arrived, worried questions were asked, orders barked. I was pushed out of the room. I hoped Ginger the cat had survived Kitty throwing him across the room when Judy was seven. I hoped Judy survived my prying into her tormented past.

37

NUCLEAR UMBRELLA

WHEN I LEFT JUDY, I felt almost as exhausted as she was. I climbed into Martin's car, trying to imagine what to do next, but I couldn't organize my mind. I tried to write up the substance of the conversation on a legal pad, but my arms felt heavy, unable to hold a pen.

I tilted the seat as far back as it would go and shut my eyes. Focused on the breath going in and out, the way my mother always started music lessons.

The morning that Kitty had driven Judy out to the country was the crux of the story. The old lady who'd asked whether Judy preferred stars or sewing—could that have been Martina, not dead after all? If so, why had she not been part of Kitty's and Judy's lives all along?

Not much of a mother, that was how Lotty and Kitty had both characterized Martina Saginor. But if she'd survived the war, even a woman who cared more for protons than people would want to see her only child. At least, I hoped that was true. Besides, Martina hadn't sounded like a melodramatic person, and the meeting in a remote gas station sounded melodramatic in the extreme.

Perhaps it had been Martina's student Gertrud Memler, the Nazi turned anti-nuclear activist. She apparently experienced a deep revulsion against her young Nazi self. Maybe she was seeking Kitty's forgiveness for causing her mother's death.

Memler certainly regretted her weapons work, both in Nazi Austria and in post-war America. Her letters attacking America's nuclear program meant the FBI was hunting her: she lived the last part of her life underground. If she wanted to meet Kitty, she had to do it secretly.

"'Tell her, that was a cruel lie that you and tell her made up.'" I repeated the words out loud and they suddenly changed meaning.

Not "tell her," but "Teller." Edward Teller, the father of the hydrogen bomb.

I pulled the seat back up. Memler attacked Teller for Star Wars, she'd attacked him for the hydrogen bomb itself. She might well have attacked him for signing on to that chirpy civil defense lie, that we could survive a nuclear war if we ducked under our desks and covered our heads with our hands.

Where I grew up, in South Chicago, we might vote Democrat, but we were a hundred percent behind our government and its nuclear weapons. The nuclear umbrella: I could remember the drawing Ms. Jostma put on the bulletin board in my sixth-grade social studies class. It showed a stern-looking Statue of Liberty holding a big black umbrella whose points were all hydrogen bombs. It was a terrifying picture, but all of us knew that the might of the American military kept us safe. Those ugly bombs were an umbrella that was as scary to the Communists as it was to my friends and me. Better dead than Red: my aunt Marie, Boom-Boom's mother, often snapped those words at Gabriella.

"You've never lived through a war, Marie," my mother would say wearily. "When your mother and grandmother are murdered by people of one ideology, you don't long for another ideology to save you."

Judy had heard the "old lady" and the man arguing. She knew part of the quarrel was about her, so when she heard "Tell her," she thought they wanted to tell her something. And then her mother warned her that if she repeated what they'd told her, she'd be punished in a terrible way. For over forty years she had buttoned that fear deep inside her chest: you will go to prison if you talk about duck and cover, or the two people who quarreled over it.

In the early part of the encounter, the older woman and Kitty had talked in German about someone being dead. Maybe it was Kitty telling Memler that Martina was dead. Or the other way round.

What I had trouble with was the picture of someone moving from running a Nazi weapons slave camp to anti-nuclear activist. Some catastrophe must have hit her personally, although what could have been more devastating than war and its aftermath?

I sent your mother off to the Sobibor death camp when we had no more use for her. Can you forgive me? Even someone less damaged than Kitty would be furious in such a moment. *You took everything from me and now you also want my forgiveness?*

Just contemplating such a conversation made me clench my muscles. I got out of the car to get some air and stretch my aching arms. In the middle of Kitty and Memler's argument, a man arrived. The older woman had called him a weasel for signing on with Teller.

Dzornen. It had to have been Dzornen. Breen had signed on with Teller to help design the computers needed to create hydrogen bombs, but it was Dzornen whom Memler and Martina knew back in Vienna.

The man had said, "I'm not doing anything else for you, so whatever it is you want, forget about it." He'd brought her into America, that was one thing he'd done.

That couldn't be right. Would an Austrian Jew like Benjamin Dzornen have supported Martina's Nazi student but left Martina to languish?

On the other hand, that might be the crime that so burdened Julius Dzornen. When the Dzornens left Vienna, his wife, Ilse, probably thought she'd left Kitty and Martina behind forever. I imagined the hot fire of anger and jealousy burning in her, making her persuade herself that Kitty and Martina's fate wouldn't be so bad. She could have kept Benjamin from putting real muscle into finding a lab in America that would accept Martina. They might experience some privation, but Martina deserved that for having sex with Ilse's husband. Ilse's main feeling, as I imagined her, was relief: the fact that her husband was Kitty's father was something she would never have to think about again.

Then Kitty showed up at the Dzornens' Chicago house. Kitty's frenzied journey around the neighborhood, looking for Dzornen, demanding a response from him, would have brought that old wound right back to the surface.

According to his sister Herta, Julius adulated Benjamin and was showing the potential for his father's scientific gifts. Then bam! Kitty arrived and blew his vision of his father apart. Julius would have been about sixteen then, a vulnerable age. He went through the motions for a few years, but by the time he was twenty, he couldn't even keep up the motions. He dropped out of school, dropped out of life.

A security guard came over to me, wanting to know if I was lost or in trouble. I realized I'd been walking in circles around the parking lot in my agitation. "I'm just upset about the person I've been visiting."

The guard watched until I got back in the car and shut the door.

The trouble with the scenario that I'd been imagining was it didn't include the Breens. Julius had gone to Cordell Breen last night. Cordell had mocked him for letting this ancient crime consume him. That wasn't why Julius had gone to Lake Forest, though: he'd arrived at the Breens' furious because someone used his identity at the university library.

My thinking was like a suitcase with bra straps and sweater sleeves sticking out the sides. Every idea I had left me with unpackable loose ends.

I picked up my pen again and managed to scribble down Judy's saga. I included her childhood memories, but also wrote down her more recent past, namely Martin's arrival at the meth house. When he found the papers Judy had filched from her mother's bureau drawer, he was beside himself. The papers should have come to him, and Judy should have known they were important because they came from Ada Byron. The name meant nothing to Judy, and it meant nothing to me.

I drove down to Lotty's clinic. As usual on her office days, the place was packed, mostly with women and children. The handful of men looked awkward; what are we doing in this women's space? their bodies seemed to ask.

Ms. Coltrain, the clinic manager, greeted me with her usual calm. I gave her a note to hand in to Lotty. In a couple of minutes, Jewel Kim came out to get me, much to the annoyance of everyone else who was waiting. I smiled apologetically but followed Jewel into Lotty's office. Lotty herself came in almost immediately, brusque, she didn't like to be interrupted in the middle of seeing patients.

"I never heard of an Ada Byron that I remember. Could she have been the person Kitty lived with in England?" Lotty asked.

"Judy says their name was Painter. But she described a very strange event when she was seven."

Lotty looked at her watch. "Can't this wait?"

"Probably," I said, "but I'm here now."

I told her about the drive to the country and the adults who'd caught her in their angry net. "Judy couldn't describe the woman, just that she was old. Could it have been Martina?"

"I don't see how," Lotty said, frowning. "She was sent from Terezín to Sobibor. That was a death march and there was no record of her in any of the refugee reports; Max checked his networks when Kitty first showed up here in 1956. Last week, he got the Holocaust Museum in Washington to search their records, too. There's nothing about Martina Saginor among the Terezín or Sobibor survivors."

I told her my alternate idea, about Gertrud Memler. Lotty looked disgusted. "A Nazi slobbering with guilt twenty years too late and thinking everyone should bow down and accept her conversion? If Benjamin Dzornen worked with her, then he was truly despicable. The only one I pity is the son, Julius, carrying his father's burden all this time."

Lotty picked up a chart from her desk. "If that's all you wanted, this definitely could have waited until tonight."

38

NEIGHBORHOOD GOSSIP

I FELT SORRY for Julius Dzornen, too, but I wished he would talk to me. I didn't imagine he'd gotten much satisfaction last night from Cordell Breen, when he accused Breen of using his name to dig into the university's archives. If I could learn who'd been impersonating Julius, and what documents they'd been reading, maybe I'd figure out something, like why the BREENIAC sketch mattered so much, or what the little design in its right corner meant. If I presented Julius with a platter of information, I'd have a better lever to pry his old crime out of him.

Before driving to the South Side, I swung by my office. I wanted to see if any of the librarians could recognize who'd impersonated Julius, so I dug up online shots of Cordell Breen and Jari Liu. I wondered about Durdon, Breen's driver-cum-attack-dog, although I didn't picture him as an archival research kind of guy. Anyway, I couldn't find a photo of him, just his first name, Rory, and his age, forty-three. I couldn't even find out where he'd grown up.

The only shot I found of Julius was about a decade old: he and his sister Herta had gone to an event at the Fermi Institute to celebrate the centennial of their father's birth. Herta gleamed like an aircraft carrier ready for night landings: her silver hair was polished, the diamonds in her ears and around her throat sparkled. Julius, slouching next to her, looked morose in an ill-fitting sports jacket. I printed that picture, as well as more copies of Martin Binder's head shot.

I parked at the top of the street where Julius lived. It was a quiet time of day, late morning when everyone was at work or at school. The only person I saw was an elderly woman pulling microscopic weeds from an immaculate rose bed.

I stayed in the car to call the Palfry County sheriff on one of my burn phones. "Sheriff," I said when he'd gotten over the hearty guffaws of greeting. "Glenn Davilats gets around the countryside, always making friends and influencing people."

"What the hell are you talking about, PI?"

"I just learned his prints are all over the pieces of a spandy new Lincoln Nav that got sawed up for parts near the drug shop I broke up last week. I hear your boy's been driving a new Charger: Was that his replacement for the Nav?"

For once, Kossel didn't guffaw, but he was still loud, demanding to know what the expletive I was talking about: just because I couldn't find one pimple-faced teenager was no need to cover his men with Chicago-style shit.

I held the phone in my hand, away from my ear. When it stopped vibrating, I said, "The big question, Sheriff, is who was in the Nav with him? I hope it wasn't Deputy Orlick; I've taken a liking to her."

"None of my crew has been anywhere near your cesspool of a city lately, PI," Kossel snarled.

"Didn't say they were, Sheriff. Sorry I wasn't clear. Deputy Davilats and a confederate drove out to the Schlafly place in the Navigator. They shot Schlafly's dog and they chased Schlafly into a cornfield, where they killed him. While they were doing that, Schlafly's girlfriend jumped into the car—they'd left the keys in the ignition, rookie mistake—and drove it to Chicago. But it's your boy's prints that we've ID'd so far. Any hints on the second party?"

"Says you!" Kossel growled.

"Sheriff, I don't have any power or leverage, I can't issue an arrest warrant or bring anyone in for interrogation. I'm only calling to offer you information ahead of the CPD. And to see if you know who else was in the Navigator. If your deputy is working for one of the other meth dealers in the county, don't you want to know that?"

Kossel didn't say anything else, not even good-bye, just hung up with unusual quietness. Actually, he was right. I was lying. What if I was wrong about Davilats? Just because he drove a new muscle car and a Rottweiler growled at him didn't make him guilty of murder. I was hoping Kossel would take it from here—interrogate his deputy, find out what meth dealer he worked with—unless, of course, Kossel himself was the other person in the Navigator. Had I plugged a hole or dropped a nuke into one?

I left the phone in the car, where it could take messages from cops or robbers, and walked down to the big house in front of Julius Dzornen's coach house. I wondered what kind of arrangement he had with the owners, why they let him live there. This hadn't been Benjamin Dzornen's residence when he was at the university—I'd checked that after my first visit: Dzornen had lived three blocks away, in one of the grand mansions on Greenwood.

I followed the paving stones past the big house to the little one. When I pounded strenuously on the front door, the birds flew off from the feeders with an excited twittering, but Julius didn't respond. I put my head through the ivy and tried to squint through the dirty window. I didn't see any lights, or hear any signs of life. I was tempted to do some on-site research, to see if he'd kept a journal, but as I fingered my picklocks, I thought of the violation I'd felt when Homeland Security invaded my home. Better to go to the archives and see what I could find out by straightforward questioning.

When I crossed the yard again to University Avenue, the elderly woman was still working on her roses a few doors down. I stood on the walk near her and waited until she looked up at me. Her eyes were as cold as the chilly air.

"Excuse me, ma'am," I said. "I'm a detective. I need to ask Julius Dzornen a few questions and wondered if you'd seen him lately."

"Do you have some kind of identification?" Her voice, although thin with age, was as cold as her eyes.

I produced my PI license. She studied it, her nose curling in contempt. Because I was private? Because she was a grande dame and I worked for a living?

"I don't pay attention to his comings and goings, but he hasn't been out while I've been here today."

"It seems odd that he would rent here, so close to where he grew up," I said. "Almost as if he couldn't bear to leave home, but he's seventy-something now."

"People rent out their coach houses for income these days all the time," the woman said dryly. "If you have a question about Julius Dzornen, ask it, otherwise, please leave. It's cold and you're keeping me waiting."

"How long has he lived in the coach house?" I asked.

She gave a wintry smile, as if I'd finally figured out a clue in a complicated game. "Since his mother died." She returned to her roses, but as I walked away she relented and said to my back, "That used to be Edward Breen's home. He had his workshop in the coach house."

I felt as though I'd been hit between the shoulders. Of course. Alison had told me Edward's first workshop had been behind his old house in Hyde Park.

I walked back to the gardener. "Julius Dzornen is obsessed with a crime he thinks he committed around fifty years ago. Do you have any idea what that might be?"

She sat back on her heels and looked at me with the first real emotion she'd shown, but she shook her head. "I didn't know him then, and I've never heard any talk about it—and this is a neighborhood where people are passionate about gossip. I only know that when Ilse Dzornen died, the daughters sold her house on Greenwood Avenue and Julius moved into Edward Breen's workshop. We were all surprised that the Breens still owned the coach house."

Her lips twitched in a contemptuous smile. "I suppose Edward wanted his workshop treated like a shrine."

Breens and Dzornens, united even past the point where death might them part. It was an unsettling relationship, people unable to undo the toxic ties that bound them.

I continued down the street toward the campus. I collected another day pass. Special Collections, which housed the archives, lay along a corridor that connected the main library to its futuristic new reading room. I pushed open the door and found myself in an exhibition space.

The room was quiet in the way that makes you feel quiet yourself; for a moment I forgot Judy Binder's anguish, Kitty Binder's murder, Julius Dzornen's bitterness. I stopped in front of an eighth-century Bible. I pictured monks tranquilly singing psalms in Latin while they copied lines onto vellum in handwriting so careful it could still be read today. Icons of the dead make us think they lived peaceful lives, but murder and chicanery existed long before Cain biffed Abel or Jacob cheated Esau.

A second set of doors led to the administrative area and the climate-controlled reading room beyond, where fifteen or twenty people were bent over boxes of documents.

Three women were sitting at a counter, hard at work over computer monitors. Carts holding blue document boxes stood near them. Several people came up to the counter as I did, one returning a giant box half as tall as he was, the others asking for material. I waited until they'd left before producing my driver's license, along with my PI license.

"What can we do for you?" one of the women asked.

I looked at the ID she wore around her neck: Rachel Turley. "Ms. Turley, I'm a private investigator who's looking into the death of a woman named Kitty Binder. I don't know if you follow that kind of news, but she was killed in the middle of a home invasion about a week ago."

Ms. Turley said she vaguely remembered seeing the story, but added, "We deal here in rare books and documents, not contemporary news, so I'm not sure what we can do to help you."

"Ms. Binder had hired me to look for her grandson," I explained. "He's been missing for several weeks. I've been digging into the Binder family history, looking for people whom he might have contacted, and as I dug, I discovered that Ms. Binder's father was Benjamin Dzornen.

"Someone came into Special Collections recently to look at Dzornen's papers. He had an ID, claiming he was Dzornen's son, Julius. Only he wasn't. I'm trying to find out who it really was, and what part of the collection he was looking at."

Ms. Turley and a woman at the other end of the counter exchanged startled looks, but Ms. Turley said, "We never reveal what anyone using our collection was researching. It's an inviolable library law. Not just here. All libraries."

"Even if your telling me could help find Kitty Binder's killer?"

Turley shook her head. "Even if you could prove to me that it would help you or the police find her killer, I can't tell you."

"Ms. Turley, I appreciate ethical principles as much as the next person, but—"

"There's no but. If you had a subpoena, I'd get the library's lawyer to talk to you, but you're private, not public, right? So you can't get a subpoena. Scholars are a competitive and unscrupulous bunch; if they're both on the track of some new data or theory, they've been known to steal each other's research. They try to break into our files, or even bribe the staff to see whether Professor X is looking at the same material they are. So we protect everyone by scrubbing our servers to make sure there's no trail of who's been requesting what papers."

"What if one of them steals something from the collection? How do you find out who it was if you've been scrubbing the servers?" I demanded.

"We have security precautions in place," Turley said. "I'm not going to share them with you because for all I know, you're pretending to investigate a murder when really you've been hired by one of our more contentious scholars to check up on his competitors."

Her bland smile seemed to say that she knew she was winding me up. I gave her a sour grimace, but pulled my collection of photographs from my bag and laid them on the counter.

Several more researchers came up to the counter; they gave me and my photo collection sidelong looks while they handed in their request slips to the other librarian.

"Do any of these men look familiar to you? One of them is the real Julius Dzornen; the other three are possible candidates for the imposter."

"Ms.—" She picked up the card I'd also placed on the counter. "Ms. Warshawski, the privacy of patrons is more fundamental than the law of gravity. I would not tolerate anyone who worked for me giving you a name or telling you if they'd seen one of these people, and I would expect to be fired myself if I did so."

By this time, everyone in the administrative area was frankly listening—the other staff members, the patrons, even someone from the janitorial staff, who was on a ladder in the corner replacing a lightbulb.

"You're not concerned about imposters in the library?"

"If someone wanted to be in the library so badly that he created a phony ID, I'd like to shake his hand and ask him to make a public service announcement for the American Library Association," Turley said. Her coworker nodded emphatically.

When you've been beaten on all counts, don't keep fighting. "In that case, I guess I need to look at the Dzornen papers myself, to see if

I can figure out what my unscrupulous competitor is up to. How do I do that?"

"You fill out a research request, with a brief description of what your project is." Turley typed a few lines. "The Dzornen papers run to sixty-seven boxes; each one has about fifteen files in it. We limit our scholars to two boxes at a time, so why don't you study the catalog record and see where you'd like to start. We've never had anyone list a murder investigation as a project, but we'll certainly accept that."

39

BYRONIC ODES

RETURNED MY ROGUES' GALLERY to my briefcase and retreated to a counter with a computer terminal, where I grimly studied the record of Benjamin Dzornen's papers: sixty-seven boxes (thirty-six linear feet, the catalog added helpfully). There was a personal biographical section that ran to five boxes. His honors, his lectures, his research and his students took up the remaining sixty-two. Many of the headers were in German.

I scrolled through the lists of students and correspondents, looking for names I knew. Martina Saginor was there for the early thirties, as was Gertrud Memler, but neither name cropped up in the later boxes.

When I checked for Ada Byron, I found a letter from her to Dzornen dated May 1969. This was the only mention of her name, but there were many folders that simply listed "Miscellaneous correspondence from Vienna," or "Family letters from Bratislava," or "Miscellaneous correspondence with students." I'd have to go through those. Which meant many, many folders. I tried not to groan out loud.

I needed an intern. I needed Martin Binder—I didn't think Kitty had ever hired a nanny for him, but maybe Ada Byron was an old lover of Benjamin Dzornen who'd kept an eye on Martin for him. I looked her up online.

According to six million hits on Metar-Quest, she was the long-dead daughter of the poet Byron. Ada played such an important role in the history of computers and programming, they'd even named a computer language for her. Since she'd been dead now for about a hundred sixty years, it was hard to see how she'd written to Benjamin Dzornen in 1969, or to Kitty a mere seven years ago.

Martin knew who she was; he'd disappeared to go look for her. Or he'd been killed, a nasty voice whispered in my inner ear. I rubbed my forehead. The more I learned the stupider I felt.

"Martin, why couldn't you have laid down a trail of bread crumbs for me?" I snarled.

I went back to the catalog record for Dzornen's papers, but I'd had an exhausting morning and was having trouble keeping my eyes open. Philip Marlowe depended on his trusty pint of rye to get him going after he'd been sandbagged. My detecting was fueled by espresso. The coffee bar I'd gone to a week ago was only a ten-minute walk away.

On my way from the reading desk, I saw a young woman who'd been near me when I'd been showing the head shots to the librarians. She was giving me the same sideways glance she'd given the pictures. I walked into the exhibition space, stopping in front of a newer Bible, a mere six hundred years old, written in Hebrew and Latin. I pretended to study it, long enough for a hesitating person to make up her mind.

When I saw her walking toward the reading room exit, I moved slowly out into the hall. In the long corridor, I stood in rapt attention in front of a description of the exhibit. Finally, I heard the door open behind me. I waited another second, then turned to look.

The woman appeared to be about Alison Breen's age. She was wearing the frayed jeans and motorcycle boots that are the uniform du jour among Millennials. She moved from foot to foot but couldn't figure out what to say.

"I went to school here, but I never knew they had a Bible that was thirteen hundred years old," I said. "I also never knew about Fermi surfaces. I sometimes think I wasted my scholarship by focusing on languages and politics."

She gave a nervous smile. "I heard part of your conversation with the librarian, about the Dzornen papers, you know."

"I don't know how much you heard, but I'm a detective." I showed her my ID and gave her a thumbnail sketch of Kitty Binder's death and my search for Martin.

"And you really think knowing who was pretending to be Julius Dzornen will help you find this lady's murderer?" She was twisting a strand of hair, looking around to make sure no one was listening.

"I don't know," I said frankly. "But I've been putting a lot of muscle into searching for Martin Binder and I'm not getting very far. If you know something, I can promise I will not reveal that I learned it from you."

"This is going to sound stupid," she warned me.

"I've been a detective for over twenty years and I've learned that the smallest, silliest things can be the most important. Would you like to get coffee so you don't have to worry about who's listening to you?"

She nodded gratefully and led me along the corridor to the main part of the library. I followed her down a flight of stairs to a coffee shop. It was a Spartan space, part of the old stacks with tables and chairs and bright fluorescent lights. She let me buy her a cola, but I forwent coffee when I saw what it looked like. We sat in a corner where we could make sure no one was eavesdropping.

"Were you really a student here," she asked, "or did you say that to get me to talk to you?"

"I really was a student here," I assured her. "Undergrad and law. My senior thesis was on connections among the Mob, Chicago politicians and waste haulers and how they made sure the city's garbage ended up in South Chicago."

Her lips rounded in the kind of respect people accord a topic that sounds truly boring to them, but she responded with her name, Olivia, and her own senior paper, on witchcraft narratives in seventeenth-century France.

"That's why I'm using Special Collections. Maybe this sounds trivial compared to studying the Mob, but I've been learning Medieval French and Latin and reading some of the old French narratives. Anyway, last week, I think it was Thursday, I was having cramps so I was in the bathroom a long time, and the two librarians who were on duty today came in.

"Ms. Turley, the one you were talking to, asked Ms. Kolberg, did she remember the kid who came in looking at the Dzornen papers a while back. She said he'd called himself Julius Dzornen, and she'd assumed he was like a grandson or great-grandson of Benjamin Dzornen, you know, he worked on the Manhattan Project and was a huge name in physics; they cover his work in the physics core."

Olivia paused, waiting for a response; yes, I remembered the physics core.

"So Ms. Turley said someone else had come in last week, looking for something in the papers, and the box he requested held a genealogy chart. There aren't any young Dzornens, Ms. Turley said. The only Julius is like seventy or something.

"Well, I was really eavesdropping by then, because my dad knows Julius Dzornen. I don't know if you know him, Julius, I mean, but he's kind of a weird guy, a real loner, but he's a bird-watcher, and so is my dad, so they see each other out in the Wooded Isle on Sunday mornings. When I saw my folks that night, I mentioned it to my dad, about a young Julius Dzornen being in Special Collections."

She looked at me unhappily. "I guess my dad told Julius when they were out birding on Sunday, because Monday morning, Julius Dzornen came into the reading room. He was furious, wanting to know who had been using his name. And of course it's against library policy to say, like they told you today. So Julius started to go behind the counter, yelling out threats, and someone had to call campus security."

Olivia looked up at me, her face crinkled in guilt. "I feel so terrible about it. He's this pathetic guy whose dad won the Nobel Prize and he doesn't have any life at all, and it was because of me that he got in trouble. I mean, the librarians thought they were alone in the bathroom; they never would have said anything if they'd known I was in there. Do you think I should tell them?"

I shook my head. "I wouldn't. It's water over the dam. They didn't mean harm, you didn't mean harm, let it lie. And I can tell you this much: as of last night, the real Julius was certainly out and about, not under arrest, so I wouldn't worry about it too much."

I kept my tone casual as I added, "Were you in the reading room back at the end of August?"

Olivia blushed. "My boyfriend broke up with me in August. He was doing research in Avignon and I was in Roussillon, so we were going to meet in Arles and walk the pilgrim road, but the night before we were supposed to meet, he texted me that he'd met someone else. Can you believe that? Breaking up by text without even coming to see me in person? Anyway, I didn't feel like hiking by myself, so I came home and started doing more work here."

I pulled my photos from my bag again. "Any of these guys look familiar?"

"I'm sure it was him." Olivia pointed to Martin. "I noticed him mostly because he and I were the only people in the reading room who weren't like a hundred years old."

"You didn't happen to notice what he was looking at?"

She grinned, suddenly mischievous. "Like, box seven, folder nine? No. I wouldn't have known even at the time. You can't tell across the reading room what anyone is looking at."

She looked again at the mug shots I'd laid on the small tabletop.

"This guy was in this morning, though I don't know what he was doing."

She tapped Jari Liu's face with the eraser end of her pencil.

I half rose in my chair. "Is he still there?"

"I don't think so. He only stayed an hour or so." She blushed again. "I should be translating old French legal documents, not studying the other patrons. Speaking of which, I've wasted too much time today. Thanks for the Coke."

She got up. "You really won't mention this, right, about me and the librarians?"

"What's that about you and the librarians?" I quizzed her. "I don't remember you saying anything about them."

She left quickly, tossing her can in the recycle bin on her way out. I waited until she was partway up the stairs so she wouldn't worry that someone saw her giving me information.

It was after two. I was hungry and I still wanted caffeine, but the Special Collections reading room would close in a few hours. I ate a banana from the snack bar in the coffee shop and hoped that would carry me through the afternoon.

40

THE RADETZKY MARCH

W**HEN I RETURNED** to Special Collections, Olivia was at a table in the middle of the reading room. I pretended not to see her as I scanned the room for Jari Liu. He wasn't there. Why were the Chicago librarians so scrupulous? I would have given my 401k, all thirty-seven thousand dollars of it, to know what files Liu had been looking at.

I spent half an hour compiling a list of the boxes and folders I wanted to see, besides the Ada Byron letter. A note in the file said that most of the correspondence around the Manhattan Project and Dzornen's involvement in the hydrogen bomb still had a top-secret clearance and was unavailable.

I saw that Dzornen had held a number of patents, some for improvements to reactor components for the hydrogen bomb, some in X-ray crystallography. Some were for inventions whose application meant nothing to me, cloud chambers, gas spectrometers, one for an improvement to ferromagnetic drum memory.

Maybe my cynical thought that Breen had hidden the BREENIAC sketch himself was wrong. He'd sent Jari Liu down here to look at Dzornen's patents, because as soon as Julius said someone was using his name in the library, Breen knew it must have been Martin. Breen wanted to see what patent history Martin was looking at. Or perhaps not.

Since I could only get a few folders at a time, I first requested the one that held the Ada Byron letter. I also asked for family papers and correspondence from Vienna between 1936, when the Dzornens left for America, and December 1941, when American entry into the war made it impossible to get mail from Europe.

It was almost three when I got my first set of materials, and the librarians warned me that the reading room closed at four forty-five. The Ada Byron letter wasn't among them; the clerk explained that they were still locating that box.

"It's not missing, is it?" I asked.

The clerk assured me it was merely in transit. That was helpful: it persuaded me that Jari Liu had come to see the Ada Byron letter. Or left after he'd read it.

I looked at the genealogy chart, but it only listed the Dzornens I already knew about, Benjamin, Ilse, the three children they'd had together, along with ancestors in what today is the Czech Republic. A handful had made it through the war, but most had died in 1942 or '43. The chart didn't mention Kitty Binder or her family. I went quickly through the folders in the family history box, but they all related to Dzornen's life before Martina became part of it.

A staff member took those papers from me and handed me the folder that contained Ada Byron's letter, which was in a sleeve about halfway through the folder. The typed name "Ada Byron" appeared in the upper left corner without a return address and there was no address beyond "Benjamin Dzornen, The Enrico Fermi Institute," in the middle of the envelope.

I carefully removed the envelope from the plastic sleeve and took out the letter that was folded inside. It was written on the onionskin paper that I remembered from my childhood when my mother wrote to Italian friends. The text was typed on an old manual by someone not very expert with the keys—a lot of letters had double strikes through them as the writer went back to correct herself. It began without a salutation.

I was sorry to read about your illness. I think of it as part of the long disease of our century, filled as it has been with suffering and death. There is much I would write you, but I do not know if you will ever see this page; I don't know who is guarding you from your correspondents. And anyway, what point is there to rehashing those old quarrels, the ones in public or in private? I'm sorry you felt I did not keep my word, but you were the finest scientist of my time and I couldn't bear to see you abase yourself to those so far beneath you.

Now, though, all I wish for you is peace, so please know that when you are gone, I will keep your name alive in a green and kind way, remembering you from the days of my youth, when ideas poured so quickly and thickly it was as if I could reach out a hand to touch them. Yours were always the most exhilarating, forcing all of us to see the world in a new and different way. That is how I shall remember you.

I know that you have always shared my lack of interest in

The letter ended abruptly there. I looked in the envelope, wondering if there was a second sheet, but didn't see one. Lack of interest in what? Religion? Politics? Children?

I put the letter back in its folder and placed it to one side for photocopying. As I closed the folder, I saw that the header on it noted a two-page letter. I took the envelope out again and inspected it. There was nothing else inside.

I looked through the other documents on the table, to see if it had slipped into another folder, but didn't see it. I took the folder to the front desk and showed the letter to Rachel Turley. She shook her head, frowning in worry. "You're sure it didn't get slipped into other papers on your desk? It's flimsy paper, after all."

"I don't think so, but you can send someone to look through them in case I missed it."

She got up herself and went through the folders on my table one page at a time. I even let her look in my briefcase. I turned out my pockets, but the only paper in them was the FOIA letter about Gertrud Memler that I'd taken from Martin's room the other night.

"This is not good," Turley said. "If we've misplaced it, we're unbearably negligent, but if someone stole it—I guess that makes me negligent as well."

She hurried out the door to the reference area, where I saw her in agitated conference with the other librarian. The two disappeared into a back room.

In a movie, the detective would rub a pencil over the back of the first page and the second would appear, with Ada Byron's address. In real life, the detective felt like chewing the folder in frustration.

I stared into the near distance. Someone writing as Ada Byron had known Dzornen a long time, known him as the preeminent scientist of her youth. She hadn't written under her own name, because she didn't want Dzornen's wife or his secretary to throw the letter out unread.

The conciliatory first paragraph suggested that Ada was really Gertrud Memler. She had attacked Dzornen in public for his support of the H-bomb and his opposition to the 1963 Limited Test Ban Treaty. Who knew what had happened between them in private?

Dzornen had slept with Martina Saginor; that probably hadn't been his only affair with a student. Memler had also been a student at the Radium Institute in Vienna, after all. She became a Nazi, running a nuclear research installation, which meant she was an ambitious and politically savvy Nazi. And on some road to Damascus, the scales had fallen from her eyes and she'd become a pacifist.

I looked at the clock. I needed to get through a lot more material in a short time; I turned to Dzornen's mail from 1930 through 1941. He'd had a large correspondence. I felt a vicarious thrill at seeing Einstein's name on several long letters. Lise Meitner had written Dzornen, as had Fermi, Segrè, Rabi, the whole pantheon of twentieth-century physics. I looked at the letters long enough to see that they were filled with equations or questions about weapons policy. Einstein never wrote, "Sorry about your troubles with Ada, or Gertrud, or Martina, old chap."

I took a quick look at the box of patents. Nothing Dzornen invented seemed connected to the BREENIAC machine, at least as far as I could guess from the single-paragraph description at the top.

Much of the mail to Dzornen from Europe, especially after 1938, was handwritten in German. It was a hard script to decipher when I didn't know the language to begin with. In the end, I thought I identified three letters that might have been from M. Saginor, although the signature, M. Saginor, might have been "W. Oaginow."

Because I wasn't traveling with my smartphone, I couldn't photograph them. I put them to one side for photocopying and slowly continued through the thick folders. I looked at the clock: four-fifteen. I was panicking at the slippage of time and my own inability to figure anything out when I picked up a cellophane folder that held the title page of a book. *Radetzkymarsch*, von Joseph Roth. I thought at first it was in the collection by mistake, but when I turned it over, I saw a letter had been written in pencil on the reverse.

The text was so faded and difficult that I almost passed it over, but the date caught me up. 17 November 1941, three weeks before Pearl Harbor. The text was beyond me and the signature was maddeningly illegible. The writer had printed the address, though: Novaragasse 38A.

Novaragasse, Novara Street, was where Lotty and her grandparents had to move when Nazis evicted them from their flat. I squinted at the signature again. It might be "Herschel." A chill ran down my arms: I was holding a precious piece of Lotty's history.

I carried it and the letters from Martina Saginor to the copy machine. My hands were trembling from excitement; I was afraid I might damage the fragile paper.

Ms. Turley, who'd come into the reading room to remind us we had to wrap things up for the day, saw I was having trouble getting the documents out of their sleeves and came over to help. She took over the letter written on the book title and worked to get the contrast in the faded pencil script as clear as possible. She also helped me copy the three letters from M. Saginor.

She asked me to wait while she went through the reading room to remind the other researchers that they were about to close. I pulled my papers together and went to the reference stand to wait.

"Ms. Warshawski, I'm going to talk to the library director about this missing page. We take this kind of disappearance very seriously, and we'll start an investigation. I just want you to know that."

"If you told me who else had been in these archives, I could probably help you track down the paper—unless Jari Liu or the person posing as Julius Dzornen has destroyed it," I said.

She flinched. "I can't tell you, not even under these circumstances. But if you happen on the second page, please let me know at once: we will want to start a criminal prosecution."

41

BIRD MAN OF HYDE PARK

WHEN I GOT OUTSIDE, the rain had stopped, but the wind was blowing cold through my windbreaker. I jogged over to the coffee bar. While they pulled some shots for me, I took out one of my burn phones to call Lotty. She was still at the clinic, Ms. Coltrain told me, but was going up to Max's afterward. I left a message that I would meet her there.

I took a hummus sandwich to eat as I walked back to Martin's Subaru. I passed the old Breen house on my way up University Avenue. Julius's Honda was still nowhere in sight. On impulse, I cut through to the alley. Lights were still out in the coach house; there was still no answer to the doorbell. The only life came from the birds, pecking each other away from the feeders.

Perhaps Julius had tripped and fallen and was lying in a coma. No one seemed to be watching from the big house, so I got out my picklocks. When I inserted the first wand, the door creaked open. I had my gun in my hand without thinking. I slid in, back to the wall.

Inside the front room, where I'd talked to Julius before, nothing looked different, except that the pile of cigarette butts was thicker. I passed on through to the kitchen, the only other downstairs room. It also looked ordinary, untouched. In fact, it looked as though it hadn't been touched since 1950, with its old Formica countertops and Cold War–era refrigerator.

An outsized black trunk blocked the kitchen door. I opened it, but all it contained were massive sacks of birdseed. It was a safety hazard, blocking the house's second exit; all the windows had the small mullioned panes that would make escape impossible in a fire. I guess Julius was so depressed that he didn't care, but it did send a warning shiver down my spine.

I went up a steep flight of stairs to the bedrooms, two small rooms that overlooked the big house across the lawn. As I watched, two children came out the back door with a set of badminton rackets. Despite the chill wind, they began an energetic if inexpert game.

How strange it must be for Julius to sit in Edward Breen's old workshop, looking at a house that had been part of his childhood. He must have come here often when his father and Edward Breen were working together.

I did a quick search through the two rooms, hoping for a diary, but found nothing except some bird-watchers' magazines, along with back copies of the *Physical Review*. Julius might have dropped out of school, but he still kept abreast of the work in his father's field. That probably would tell an analyst more than it told me.

When I went back to the ground floor, I saw an old photo album on the card table in the corner, half covering the cigarette butts that overflowed the big tin ashtray. I flipped through the pictures. Julius as a toddler with his two sisters, each holding a chubby hand. Julius with his father, standing in front of Chicago Pile Number One, which Fermi had built for the first nuclear chain reaction in 1942. Benjamin Dzornen in white tie next to President Eisenhower. Ilse Dzornen with Julius and his sisters.

In the middle of the book, just after the last of the photos, was a roughly torn square of paper, so fragile with age that it would crumble if I touched it. The left side was filled with equations. Most of the page was covered by a drawing that looked like a deep-fat— No. It was a pencil sketch of a ferromagnetic core for a computer, showing the direction of electric currents through the wires that extended from it. "Speicher" was printed next to it in tiny faded letters, and on the left side, some fifteen rows of equations appeared. In the bottom right was a small design so faded that I could only guess it showed a pair of linked triangles.

I stared at it in utter bewilderment. How had Julius come by the BREENIAC sketch? It had already disappeared before he got to the Breen mansion last night.

I couldn't think straight about this. I'd been assuming that Cordell Breen had hidden the sketch himself, putting the blame on Martin for its disappearance. Maybe Julius was a regular visitor to the Lake Forest estate. He lived here in Edward Breen's old coach house, the two men had grown up together. I suppose Breen's wife or housekeeper could have let Julius in if he showed up unexpectedly one day; they'd assume he was an acceptable, if not a welcome, visitor of Cordell's.

Was this the crime that Julius felt weighed down by, this BREENIAC drawing? Or the computer itself?

I undid the binder rings in the album and lifted out the page that the sketch lay on. I carefully slipped it into the folder with the letters I'd copied at the library. When I caught up with Julius, telling him I had the drawing might finally persuade him to talk to me.

On my way out, I used my picks to do up the double lock on the front door. The children, a girl and a boy about eight and ten, stopped their game to stare at me.

"Your mom home?" I asked.

The girl yelled "Mom" several times, without bothering to go up to the house. After the third shout, a young woman appeared, still in work clothes, wiping her hands on a kitchen towel, a phone tucked between her shoulder and her ear.

I walked over and introduced myself; the woman told her phone she'd get back to it and gave her name in turn, Melanie Basier.

"I'm looking for Julius Dzornen, Ms. Basier, and I'm worried because he hasn't surfaced today. His front door was unlocked; do you know if that's normal for him?"

Ms. Basier made a face. "I think he usually locks it, but to tell you the truth, I try not to pay too much attention to him."

"I don't know him well," I said. "Is he disruptive?"

"Nothing like that, just—he's so strange. He's never worked, he lives on disability or something. My husband doesn't mind him; he says I'm being unreasonable. The two of them talk about birds—Julius has all those feeders up—but—" She gave a nervous laugh. "I always think he's one of those guys who looks quiet on the outside but turns out to be an ax murderer."

"Disturbing," I agreed. "Why do you let him live here?"

"It wasn't our idea: he was already here when we moved in. Our house was cheap because of the bizarre legal arrangement about the coach house. We could never have afforded it otherwise, but I sometimes wish we'd moved to South Shore or even Forest Park, where we wouldn't have such a creepy man on our property."

My brows went up. "It sounds extraordinary. How on earth did this deal get set up?"

"It was in old Edward Breen's will. He didn't sell the coach house when he moved out in 1961, just the big house. When Julius's mother died, the Breens said he could move into the coach house and live the rest of his life there. If he dies or moves out, we have the first right to buy it from the Breen family, thank God! Anyway, we bought here three years ago when my husband took a job in the anthropology department, and I guess that's why he's okay with Julius—my husband looks at him as if he were a science project."

Her phone rang and she started talking into it.

"Ms. Basier—I'll get out of your hair in a minute, but when did you last see Julius?"

She told her phone she'd be right with it and put a hand over the face. "I can't remember. Sunday, maybe, when he got back from bird-watching. He started making a huge racket out in the alley. When my husband went to look, he was breaking china into a garbage can. I didn't see him myself. Okay? I've got to go."

She started talking to her phone again.

"Was someone else in the coach house today? Someone besides me?"

"Cece, someone keeps interrupting me; I'll have to call you back." Basier turned to me. "I'm at work all day. Does it matter?"

"It does, rather. Julius Dzornen's half sister was murdered last week and I'm investigating her death."

Basier looked at her children, her expression changing from annoyance to alarm. "You think he killed her?"

"No. But there's something in his and her past that has been weighing him down, making him the disturbed and disturbing man he is. I think someone was in his house while he was out today, but it's hard to tell. You could call the police, of course, but with no sign of a break-in they won't do much about making it a crime scene."

Basier bit her lip, looked at the children again, and asked me to wait where I could keep an eye on them. She went into the house and returned with a young woman, about college age.

"Mindy is one of my husband's graduate students; she does a little housework for us and looks after the kids between the end of school and dinner," Basier explained.

I went through my spiel again. Yes, Mindy had been in the kitchen around one o'clock and seen someone at Julius's door.

"I think it was the police, though, checking up on him, because the man turned around as he was opening the door, and I saw he was wearing a shoulder holster. I was kind of freaked out, seeing a gun, but then

I looked out front and saw the police car double-parked outside. So I went back to work."

When I'd thanked the two women, Ms. Basier was still worried enough to ask Mindy to stay outside with the children. She wasn't worried enough to stop talking to her phone: as I rounded the corner of the house I heard her having an animated conversation with it.

42

CRASH LANDING

"THE MAN WHO LOST CONTROL of his car on Sheridan Road early this morning when it flipped over into a ravine has been identified as Julius Dzornen, only son of Nobel Prize–winning physicist Benjamin Dzornen. He is in critical condition at Evanston Hospital."

I was half listening to the news as I sat in heavy traffic on Lake Shore Drive, but that jolted me so much that I almost lost control of my own car. The announcer moved on to a story about a lost dog returning home after thirteen months. I tried other stations but couldn't get any more news on Julius's accident.

An SUV riding my tail honked loudly. I realized I'd committed the sin of allowing a car length to develop in front of me. Instead of closing the gap, I inched over to the right-hand lane and exited at Navy Pier.

I drove out to the end of the pier and sat looking at the water. Julius had been angry when he arrived at the Breen estate last night. In any meeting between Cordell and Julius, Cordell would always have the upper hand because he was the cool, successful guy; Julius was the angry dropout living on Breen family charity.

He'd driven up furious about someone using his name at the library, but maybe that old Metargon sketch played a role in the quarrel as well. However the conversation went, by the time he left, Julius must have been in a blind rage, so angry he drove off the road.

A gull swept down to the water in front of me, screeching over a piece of garbage. Four other gulls arrived, all of them screaming, peck-ing each other out of the way until one rose triumphant with a french fry.

Breen was the tough gull. Nice gulls finish last. Julius wasn't a nice guy, merely one who found life overwhelming.

I left the pier and rejoined the slow crawl northward. The hospital where they'd taken Julius was only half a mile from Max's home. I stopped there on my way.

Julius was in critical condition, they told me at the front desk.

"I'm a niece," I said. "He doesn't have any children or family of his own. Is it possible for me to see him?"

They sent me to the sixth floor, where I repeated my tale of being a niece. The ward head told me my uncle had suffered fractures to both arms, his pelvis, and he had a crushed cervical vertebra. He'd been unconscious when he was removed from his car, but scans didn't show damage to the brain.

"He's heavily sedated so he may not wake up, but he will hear you talking to him, so talk about things that are positive, that will soothe him and reassure him—happy family memories, or a favorite pet of his."

I nodded guiltily, since my real hope was that Julius would be in a frame of mind to unburden himself of his own guilty secret. However, talking about it might soothe him more than chatter about a dead cat. I followed the ward head's directions through a set of pneumatic doors.

Julius Dzornen looked like a knight in white armor, so completely was he casted. His breath came in short, heavy rasps. IV lines were inserted through the plaster. The only visible flesh was his face, which looked waxen and unreal. In repose, free of the bitterness that con-sumed him when awake, he looked younger.

I pulled up a chair next to his head and leaned over. "Julius, it's V. I. Warshawski. Vic. I'm sorry you were injured. The ward head said to talk to you about your pets. Your birds are all eating well, Julius;

I was just at the coach house and they looked pretty darned happy. I'll get the Basier kids to keep the bird feeders full while you're on the disabled list, Julius."

I kept repeating his name, hoping it would rouse him. He seemed to stir a little, but maybe it was my imagination.

"Cordell is an angry and arrogant guy, isn't he, Julius?" I said. "You must have really pissed him off, taking that BREENIAC sketch away."

He mumbled something, but I couldn't make out any words.

"Julius, it was Martin Binder, not Cordell, who went into the library using your name. He found Ada Byron's letter to your father. Julius, did you know Ada Byron? Was she another of your father's lovers?"

His eyelids started fluttering and his pulse increased.

I was sweating, scared about whether I was doing him harm. I'd make one more effort and then leave him alone.

"Gertrud Memler. Is that who she really was, Julius?"

"Mem," he mumbled. "Mem-ler."

A trace of spittle fell out of his mouth. I took a tissue and wiped it.

"Memler, Julius? Where is Memler?"

"Root." His lips were cracked and the word came out in a guttural; I wasn't sure I was hearing it correctly. "Root. Sell."

"What are you doing here?"

I jumped at the unexpected voice. Herta Dzornen Colonna had come into the room and was furious at seeing me bent over her brother. "They told me one of Julius's nieces was here. I thought it was my daughter Abigail, but it's you. Get out of here at once."

I got meekly to my feet, but didn't apologize. "I saw your brother arriving at Cordell Breen's house late last night, Ms. Colonna. He was very angry."

"Julius?" She was so surprised she briefly forgot her own rage. "He hates Cordell." Her face tightened again. "How do you know? Were you following him?"

"No, ma'am. Cordell had summoned me to Lake Forest to chew me out. Julius arrived as I was leaving. He accused Cordell of impersonating him to gain access to your father's papers at the University of Chicago Library."

"That's unbelievable."

"Which part?" I asked.

Julius moved restlessly within his carapace and said again, "Root . . . Sell."

Herta moved to the bed and put her fingers against her brother's neck. "Don't worry about it, Jules. Just rest and feel better."

She looked at me. "I don't know why Cordell would want to see Father's papers, unless he thought there was an expired patent he could exploit. He and Julius never got on, but after the launch of the BREE-NIAC, they couldn't be in the same room. Our families stopped having Thanksgivings together. It wasn't long after that Edward Breen moved up to Lake Forest. But if Jules was really angry, I suppose he might have gotten drunk for courage and driven up to confront Cordell."

She sighed and patted the part of her brother's head that lay exposed. "I suppose that's how he lost control of his car."

"If he hated Cordell so much, how come he's living in the Breen's old coach house?"

Herta's nostrils flared with annoyance. "He moved there when Mother died. Bettina and I were beside ourselves! Julius was forty and until Mother's death, he still lived in his old bedroom. He wanted to stay right where he was, but Bettina and I insisted on selling. Julius didn't work, he couldn't even have paid the taxes, let alone upkeep.

"Then Cordell invited Julius to live in the Breen family's old coach house down in Hyde Park. Bettina and I both told him it was a terrible mistake, but all Julius would say is that Cordell wasn't charging him any rent to look after the place. Cordell, and Edward before him, treated the coach house like it was a sacred place—because it's where Edward perfected his first computer. After Edward died, Cordell hung on to the coach house, too! Bettina and I kept telling Julius he'd never get out of his depression if he didn't find an apartment of his own and learn to work for a living, but you might as well talk to a block of wood."

Julius stirred again next to her and she absently patted his head again.

"He keeps saying, 'Root, Sell,'" I said. "Do you know what he's talking about?"

Herta seemed to regret talking to me so frankly. "Whatever it is, it's his business, not yours. I'm not calling the nurse to tell her *you* were impersonating my daughter, but that's only because you could make some sense out of why Julius was on North Sheridan Road. You've still been invasive and even dangerous and I want you to leave."

I mustered what dignity I could and left.

43

TEDDY BEAR, TEDDY BEAR, TOUCH THE GROUND

IT HAD STARTED TO DRIZZLE again while I was with Herta. As I trudged along the dark streets back to the Subaru, a squad car rushed toward me, its lights flashing. I leapt out of the way but my legs still got soaked. The car was tan, not one of the Evanston force's white-and-purple. Perhaps the hospital's security service, trying to look important.

When I got to the Subaru, I was wet all the way through. I turned on the heater and got a blast of cold moldy air. Better to shiver.

Lotty had arrived at Max's almost an hour before I got there. She was curled up in a large armchair in front of Max's fireplace, looking more like a street urchin than a surgeon with an international reputation. I squatted in front of the fire, warming my hands.

"You're wet," Lotty said. "Take off your shoes and socks; Max can find you some slippers."

My teeth were starting to chatter. Max hurried into a back room and returned with a blanket and a pair of wool socks. Lotty went into the kitchen and brought me back a cup of hot lemon water.

"What happened, Victoria?"

"Julius Dzornen." I explained how I'd happened to know he was in Lake Forest last night.

"Julius drove up there last night, loaded for bear, but as always happens in a confrontation between him and Cordell Breen, Breen won."

"That makes it sound as though you think Breen caused Dzornen's accident," Max said. "I find that impossible to accept."

I looked at Max and smiled ruefully. "Nothing would surprise me about any of these people, but Breen is so clever that if he wanted to get rid of Dzornen, he'd use a method that was dead-certain to work, not rely on tampering with Julius's car, or putting Ambien in his brandy. And as it turns out, Julius did survive. He's in rotten shape, but he's alive."

Max nodded. "When you called, you said you wanted me—us—to look at some documents?"

"Oh." I'd been so upset by Julius's accident that I'd forgotten why I'd been on my way to Evanston in the first place. "I went down to Hyde Park this morning to look at Benjamin Dzornen's papers. I found three letters that may be from Martina Saginor, and one from the address I remember Lotty saying she shared with them. Even if I could make out the script, I can't understand German."

I took the folded copies from the folder and handed them to Lotty. She looked at them and looked away, her face contorted in pain.

"Lotty!" I dropped to my knees next to her.

"Victoria! I—that letter—where did it come from!"

She broke off and Max forced her to drink a little wine.

"I'm so sorry," I said helplessly. "If I'd known they would distress you this much, I would never have brought them to you."

"It's not that." Lotty blinked back tears. "It's—this—my *Opa*—"

She swallowed another mouthful of wine. "It's from my *Opa*, my grandfather, Felix Herschel. It's as if the ghosts in my head suddenly came to life."

She tried reading the letter, but finally handed it to Max, who was standing at her other side. He translated it out loud, stumbling over some words where the photocopy was too faded to read easily.

My dear Professor Dzornen,

I hope you and Frau Dzornen are well. As winter approaches, the damp in Vienna becomes raw and bitter, especially here near the canal. Food is hard to find as well.

We miss your beloved student, Fräulein Martina, who has been forced to do work far from Vienna. Her mother and aunts have also left us, as have our own daughter and her husband. A letter came for Fräulein Martina that probably is of no importance, but in these unsettled times, I thought I would let you know so that you can notify her when you next speak to her. We placed it in a familiar family setting, the spot where her own little daughter, Käthe, put our Charlotte's teddy bear.

With all good wishes for your health, my esteemed Professor, yours truly,

(Dr.) Felix Herschel

Lotty's hands shook as she took the letter from Max. "My *Opa*, his own handwriting." She traced his signature with her forefinger. "After the invasion of Poland I never heard from him again, not even Red Cross letters. I kept writing to him from London, to my mother, my grandmother, and never hearing back."

Her voice turned bitter. "Now at least I know the order of their dying: first my parents, then my grandparents."

She added after another silent moment, "My *Opa* loved his books, but he had to start burning them to keep us warm. He held back his favorite titles, but he must have run out of writing paper and used this. I was too little to understand literature, but he often showed me *Radetzkymarsch*, telling me it was one of the greatest novels ever written. That he tore out the title page—I must go to the library, I must see the original."

We all sat quietly for a time. Finally I said, "Can you tell me about your teddy bear? Where did Käthe—Kitty—put it?"

Lotty tried to put her personal distress out of her mind. Her fore-head furrowed as she tried to summon memories she had left buried for most of her life.

"I certainly remember my Teddy. When we were thrown out of my grandmother's beautiful flat on the Renngasse, we had only a short time to pack. They let us take one small suitcase each. They ransacked the rooms, they stole my *Oma*'s silver, her jewelry, even my *Opa*'s World War One military medals. *Opa* took some of his books; the Nazis didn't care about books.

"My *Opa* told me to choose quickly among my toys, that I could take one, and I chose Teddy. He was a beautiful golden brown, and he was my comfort for many years. He traveled to London with me, and cheered me in my cousin Minna's soulless house. In the end, when I learned I'd earned an obstetrics fellowship at Northwestern here in Chicago I had him cleaned and repaired for the children's ward at the Royal Free."

"But where did Kitty put him?" I asked. "Why would your grand-father think that so important to mention?"

"The letter that came to Fräulein Martina must have been impor-tant, or your grandfather wouldn't have written Dzornen about it, right?" Max added. "They didn't really know each other, did they?"

"Not as far as I know," Lotty said. "Of course, my grandfather was a rather important lawyer before the war. Vienna is a small city; profes-sional people crossed paths. My grandparents probably knew the gos-sip, that Dzornen was Käthe's father, but the main thing must have been that the letter held something of value, at least to Martina. My *Opa* knew—must have known by then that they were going to be— that he and my *Oma* would—would not survive. He was sounding casual, hoping the letter would make it past the censors."

"Did Kitty take the bear from you?" I persisted, wishing I didn't have to push so hard on Lotty. "You said she used to come to the

Renngasse flat sometimes, and that you lived across the hall from her when you were forced to move to the other place."

The other place, the crowded rooms in the ghetto. I couldn't say it out loud.

Lotty's eyes squeezed shut. "After we moved to the Novaragasse, there was one horrible afternoon when Käthe and I had seen a man pushed from a roof to his death. There were so many shocking sights back then, and I've tried not to let them fill my head, but that murder—for some reason that death is connected to my bear, but how?"

She hugged her arms around her shoulders, shivering. "Oh, Victoria, if I'd known how much pain these memories would bring, I would never have let you within a mile of Kitty Binder or her daughter. Death is hard enough, but all these deaths, all this violence—everything I saw as a child in Vienna, and now Kitty herself—!"

I took her hands, massaging them between my own. After a moment, Lotty said, "I can't tell you why the man's death made Kitty so angry. I don't remember why we were talking about it, but I was scared that everyone around me would die. We were Jews, we could be thrown from a roof just as that man had been. I think Teddy became my avatar: if I could protect him, I could save my family and myself."

She spoke slowly, bringing the memory into focus. "We were in my apartment. I don't know where my brother and all my cousins were; maybe they were there and I've forgotten. I was wrapping my bear in pieces of a torn sheet, pretending they were bandages, as if Teddy was the man who'd been thrown from the building, as if I thought I could pretend he wasn't dead, just injured."

She stopped again, her eyes still shut. "The other adults came into the room, which ones? Why can't I remember? My *Opa* was there, but who else? Kitty became so angry with me over the bear that she grabbed him from me. She threw him down the stairs? No, it was out the window. We got him back, of course, or he wouldn't have come to London with me."

"Into the street?" I asked.

"Possibly into a courtyard," Max suggested. "That's how all these European apartment blocks are constructed, even in a ghetto like the Leopoldstadt became. The building sits flush with the street, you walk down a hallway that opens into a courtyard. At least in theory, every apartment would have a view of the courtyard. In a big wealthy building it might include a large garden."

Lotty grimaced. "Our courtyard was nothing like that. Any grass was long gone. It was just cobblestones, and racks where people left their bikes, only then the bikes were all stolen from us. People might even dump garbage out their windows. My grandfather tripped on one of the cobblestones when he helped me get my bear back."

I think we all held our breath at the same moment, realizing where Felix Herschel had put the document that had come for Martina. The grandfather clock along the far wall sounded ominously loud. One tick, one second, two ticks, four, sixteen, and then decades had passed.

Would the papers Felix Herschel had hidden still be under the cobblestones where he'd left them? And how could I get permission to look?

Lotty roused herself to ask about the other letters, the ones from Martina to Dzornen. "Although now I'm not sure I can bear to know. Max, you read them and tell us the substance."

Max held them under a lamp, but he still had to squint to read the old script. "The first is about her research, summarizing some articles she'd written that the German science journals wouldn't accept because of her being a Jew. She wants Dzornen to publish them in American physics journals. The papers show that she is creatively attacking the problem of the unstable nucleus of the U_{235} atom; if he can publish for her, that may persuade one of the American universities to offer her a position and a visa. 'Your word carries weight everywhere, Professor. And I will gladly go anywhere, not to such a prestigious university as where you teach. A small laboratory would be sufficient for me.'"

Lotty's mouth twisted. "She's assuring him that she won't be bothering him and Ilse."

Max nodded. "The next letter is after the Anschluss, but before the war began. The laws are strangling Jews—she mentions your family, Lottchen, that they've been forced to move into the Novaragasse apartment complex.

Sofie Herschel manages to be beautiful even while she is starving and wearing the threads of the clothes my mother used to sew her. It's a mystery to us all, but brings everyone pleasure, especially little Käthe, who has every feminine attribute you always say I was born without. I am determined that Käthe will survive this privation. Herr Dr. Herschel is saving money to send his grandchildren to London. If you can send us dollars, I can buy a ticket to send Käthe with Hugo and little Charlotte.

Max looked at the date again. "You went in June of '39, yes, Lottchen? This was written in December of '38, when one could still write a longer letter. The third one is much shorter, in July of '39, to tell Dzornen that Käthe has made it safely to England and has been sent on to Birmingham. A Jewish family there is taking her in."

"And then the war, and then silence." Lotty's voice was harsh.

I wished Jake were here, wished he would play Bach, wished the notes and the strings could reach into the bitter history of the last hundred years and untie the knots that lay at all our centers. Max had the same impulse; he went to his stereo and put in a disc of his own son, Michael, playing Bach's cello suites.

While the music filled the room, Max asked, "What do you think

Herr Herschel hid for Martina? It couldn't be money: that would have been confiscated instantly before the letter was ever delivered. And if it had been a visa—I don't know, but I expect your grandparents would have used it." Max looked at Lotty.

"I hope they would have," she said soberly. "It would be the ultimate twist of a knife in the stomach to know they scrupulously buried a visa in the courtyard where it saved no one's life at all."

Max started to put the photocopies back into the folder, but stopped when he saw the BREENIAC sketch. "What's this? Something that Lotty's grandfather sent to Dzornen?"

"No." I explained the strange story of the drawing. "The current part of Kitty Binder's nightmare began when Martin Binder saw this in the Breen family workshop. He recognized that little design from seeing it on some papers his mother had stolen from Kitty." I pointed to the blurry triangles in the lower right corner.

Max didn't say anything, but went into his study for a magnifying glass. As he inspected the paper, Lotty and I drew near, wondering what he was looking at.

"I'm not an expert," Max finally said. "But you know that for a number of years after the war, I was involved with refugee groups, searching at first for traces of my own family and then helping others. This paper, it looks like the kind of stock we often saw on letters and pictures people created during the war, especially in the camps. It's made out of repulped paper that doesn't have new fiber added, so it disintegrates very quickly. It often came from the cheap newsprint of the papers the guards read and discarded."

"Cordell Breen says his father sketched this during a break in a battle; maybe it's on paper he picked up on the battlefield," I suggested.

Max gave an embarrassed laugh. "This paper doesn't look American to me. 'Speicher' sounds so very German to me."

"Breen says they never knew who Speicher was, but the family assumed he was a battlefield friend who helped his father with the sketch."

Max laid the paper down again. "You say that this is a very rough sketch of a new kind of computer. When I see 'Speicher' next to this center grid, I don't read a person's name: I read the German word for 'memory.' As for the equations, I do not for one minute understand them, but they were written by someone who went to school in the same part of the world where I grew up."

44

HYPERLINK

A T EIGHT, AS I NODDED OFF for the third time over dinner, Max made me
go to bed in a guest room. We had been debating who had written
those equations: Gertrud Memler? Martina Saginor? Perhaps Benjamin Dzornen? Max kept repeating that Martina had not survived
the war.

"But that woman at the gas station." I described the macabre scene
when Kitty Binder had driven out to the country with Judy. "She argued with Kitty over whether Judy should be a girlie-girl, and then she
argued with the man who arrived."

"Victoria, you are so incoherent that you can barely speak, let alone
drive," Max said. "You've had a rough day, but besides that, the letter
you brought has been a deep shock for Lotty. Let's stop trying to un-
tangle this knot and get some rest."

I protested but Max was insistent. He dug up a nightshirt that his
daughter-in-law had left behind on her last visit, found a new toothbrush in his supply cupboard, and pointed me toward a guest room.

In fact, as soon as I lay down, I fell into a well of sleep deep enough
that I didn't even move within the bedclothes.

A bit before five, I dreamed I was in the kitchen of Julius Dzornen's
coach house. I opened the giant black trunk that blocked the back
door and Judy Binder stood up, the skull beneath her skin stretched in
a savage rictus. "Tell her, Warshawski, sell her."

"Of course." My own voice woke me. Root cellar, not root, sell.

Whatever crime Julius Dzornen had committed, or perhaps witnessed, the evidence was under the kitchen in the coach house. That was why Cordell wanted him to live there, rent-free. To keep him facedown in the evidence. To keep new owners from finding the evidence if they decided to renovate or remove the building.

I made up the guest bed and left the nightshirt on it, carefully folded. In the kitchen, I helped myself to a grapefruit and a piece of cheese, and scribbled a note of thanks to Max, which I left on the kitchen island next to the coffeepot. He and Lotty were still asleep, or at least, still quietly in bed. I let myself out through the garage, where the door would lock automatically behind me.

The rain had ended in the night, but the eastern sky was still black when I started south. I drove to my office, not worrying about tails, and left the Subaru in the first space I found near the warehouse.

I wanted to get down to the coach house while Julius was still in the hospital, but I needed to hide the BREENIAC sketch before I did anything else. Gun in hand, I let myself into my building, turning on every light in both Tessa's and my rooms to make sure no one was lurking. Twice before, electronically sophisticated thugs had jumped me in my own place. As my pals in Homeland Security had proven, the most sophisticated security is meaningless for someone with the right equipment.

All was well. Standing at my big worktable, I took the sketch out of its protective wrapper, holding it by its corners with latex gloves. Even so, part of one edge crumbled. I knew flashing light wasn't good for such an old drawing, but the sketch was too important to send off without a copy. After I'd copied it, I cut two pieces of clear plastic from a roll in Tessa's storage closet and laid the drawing between them. I put cardboard backing on both sides and taped a note for the Special Collections librarian to the packet.

Dear Ms. Turley:

I am sending you this fragile document for safekeeping. It was likely created in Germany or Austria in the 1940s and is the initial sketch for what became Edward Breen's first computer. Who drew it and who owns it are two great unresolved questions right now, but several murders have been committed in the last month because of it and I want to make sure it stays in a safe location.

I know this is an imposition, perhaps even a burden, but I am asking you to hold it in the library in some secure place until I can tell you who owns it and whether the library can keep it. I should know within a week.

Sincerely

V. I. Warshawski

I put my packet into an express shipping envelope and went to a twenty-four-hour outlet in the strip mall down the street. I'd handwritten my note to Rachel Turley, just in case there was a Trojan horse monitoring keystrokes on my laptop. At the office store, though, I logged onto a computer so that I could type up a shipping label and handle some of my e-mail.

If I was going to search more thoroughly into Ada Byron's identity, I needed to use my subscription databases. This seemed to be the ideal time to do it, while I was logged on to a machine Cordell or the Feds didn't know about.

While I waited for LifeStory and my other databases to come up with reports on any Ada Byrons between 1940 and 2010, I checked my e-mail. Jake wanted to know where I was and why I hadn't been in touch. By the time I finished a long letter to him, I was getting a signal that results were waiting for me.

There had been thousands of people named Byron in America during the years bracketed by my search. Twenty-three had actually been named Ada, but none of them cross-referenced with either Benjamin or Julius Dzornen, with the Breens, or with Martina Saginor or Gertrud Memler.

After reading the skimpy entries available for the Ada Byrons, only one stood out: a woman who had died in Tinney, a small college town in western Illinois, seven years ago. Right around the time of Martin's bar mitzvah, when Judy Binder had stolen a stack of documents from her mother's dresser.

The Huron County Gazette had written an obituary. Byron hadn't been a computer programmer, just a library clerk at Alexandrine College in Tinney. After retirement, she had volunteered in the town's schools as a tutor. She'd died at 102, leaving no family. In a big city, her meager biography wouldn't have merited an obituary, but her advanced age meant she'd been news in Huron County.

This Ada Byron had been about ten years younger than Benjamin Dzornen. That was all the information my databases could turn up. No sign she'd ever studied physics, no hint that she'd ever left Tinney to work in a lab or a physics department. It was a tenuous link, but she was the only Ada with a date that connected to my story in any way.

I printed the obituary, then checked my e-mail one last time before logging off. Jake, in LA for the last leg of his tour, wouldn't be up for six or seven hours, but Murray had written, complaining that I wasn't answering my phone. I called him on one of my burn phones, surprised that he was awake this early.

"Warshawski, who has always done the right thing by you in Chicago?"

"My dog Peppy," I said.

"Wrong. Me. I have jumped out on more long limbs than are in all of Cook County's forest preserves to help you on stories. So why do you hold out on me?"

"Murray, I'm knee-deep in the old Muddy, and I have to push on, so could you make this less twenty questions and more what your point is?"

"My point, oh girl detective without peer, is that you could have called me about Julius Dzornen."

"What, about his car accident? It was already on the wires. I learned about it on NPR when I was driving home last night."

"And then you went to see him in the hospital."

"How do you know—oh, you talked to Herta, who is not one of my most fervent fans."

"I talked to her after he died," Murray said. "The dead son of a Nobel laureate merits a line—"

"He died?" I interrupted. "When?"

Murray was suspicious. "You really didn't know? It must have been right after you were there. The nurses said he seemed stable, so when a cop came along wanting to interview him, they thought it would be okay. He coded while the cop was questioning him."

Poor old guy, a sad life, a painful death, and all for what? I thought of Kitty Binder's last words as she lay in my arms, the German that Lotty translated as "What was the point of it all?" The misery surrounding all those people from Vienna seemed unbearable.

Murray was still talking; he'd tried calling Cordell Breen for a comment. "He and Julius grew up together, so I thought it would be a good angle. I'm hoping Global will buy my report, but I need to get ahead of the rest of the pack with some unusual angle. Breen wasn't in, but I spoke to his wife, who seemed blitzed. She said it was all very upsetting because Julius had been visiting the house and ran off the road on his way home."

"Yes?"

"And she added that you had been there." Murray suddenly sounded savage. "Why couldn't you tell me?"

"Murray, why don't you join Homeland Security in putting a GPS monitor on me so you know where I am at all hours of the day or night? Why on earth should I have told you?"

"You could have told me what went on when Julius arrived."

I saw that my bill was growing on the computer. I copied all my reports to a data stick and logged off. "I wasn't there. He drove up as I was leaving. I didn't even know until later it was Julius at the gate."

"A crumb, Warshawski. I'm begging."

"It doesn't suit you," I said, but I relented and told him about Julius's arrival, and his accusation to Breen about the library.

"And had Breen?" Murray demanded. "Impersonated Dzornen, I mean?"

"Go talk to the librarians at the University of Chicago," I said. "That's what I did yesterday."

"Save me a trip, Warshawski. You owe me."

"Murray, you know damned well I owe you nada. But I will tell you what they told me: they never, even with burning catalog cards stuck under their fingernails, reveal who has been in the archives. They won't even tell you that I was there."

I hung up.

45

SUBTERRANEAN HOMESICK BLUES

W HEN I GOT to the coach house, the Basier children were fighting over who got to sit in the front seat of the Volvo parked in the drive. They stopped kicking each other to stare at me as I used my picklocks on Julius's front door. The lock turned easily; I waved to them; they quietly climbed into the backseat together. The parents should hire me.

Their father appeared a moment later. I waited until he'd backed the car out before I went to the Subaru to fetch my supplies.

I'd parked in the alley, not for secrecy, of which there was none in this neighborhood, but for expedience: I had gone home for a flashlight and my work boots and gloves, but I'd stopped at a hardware store to buy a crowbar, a pick, a shovel, a flex lamp and an industrial breathing mask. I didn't think I'd find plutonium under the kitchen floor—Julius had lived here unscathed for thirty years—but mold and rats were a distinct possibility. I locked the dead bolt from the inside and went to look for the basement stairs.

I was so sure that there was a root cellar under the kitchen that I was baffled when I couldn't find a door. I probed the cupboards and looked behind the radiators. I pulled all the junk out of the narrow closet that held the coach house's mechanicals but didn't see anything.

Maybe the entrance was outside, next to the barricaded back door. The door was blocked from the inside by the outsized trunk full of birdseed. I tried my crowbar but couldn't budge the trunk with the load it was holding. I climbed over the side and was lifting one of the fifty-pound bags when I heard a banging on the front door.

"Just a minute," I muttered, straining to get the bag over the side.

The door opened; the Basier kids' father came into the kitchen.

"Who are you? Do you have a right to be in here?" he asked.

"Yes," I gulped in air. "Do you have a key, or did you break in?"

"I live in the main house; we were given keys to this place when we moved in. My daughter says she saw you—"

I cut him off. "Come and give me a hand with this birdseed."

He stared at me. The bag tipped over the edge and fell to the floor, bursting and scattering seed all over the kitchen.

Basier backed away. "What are you doing? Are you planning on cleaning this up before Julius gets home?"

"Mr. Basier, I will clean up any mess I make but Julius isn't going to be coming home. He's dead. This is a very labor-intensive job I'm doing, so if you don't want to help, leave. I have too long a day in front of me to waste time arguing with you."

"Julius is dead?" he repeated, stunned.

"You know he was in an accident, right? He died last night." I looked at the space where the bag had been standing and realized I was looking at linoleum. This wasn't a trunk, but a cabinet built onto the floor.

"Hand me the crowbar, will you please?" I said to Basier.

He scowled, not sure whether to demand proof of my right to be in the house or not. After glaring for a moment to make sure I knew he could be tough if he had to, he turned on his heel and left.

I sighed and climbed back out of the trunk to get my tools. Before going back to work, I relocked the front door from the inside.

I plugged the flex lamp into an outlet behind the refrigerator and hooked it onto the edge of the cabinet. I brought two chairs in from the front room and put one on either side of the cabinet wall so I could get in and out more easily.

With the crowbar and the shovel, I moved the bags around until I found the trapdoor. It could be opened with a ring sunk into a groove, but when I lifted the ring and tugged it didn't budge. There wasn't any lock; decades of dirt and warping had glued it into the floor.

I gave it the same glare Basier had turned on me a few minutes before, but that didn't open the trap. I stuck the crowbar into the ring, but still couldn't move the door. Finally I grabbed the pick and started battering the middle of the trapdoor. After five minutes I managed to whack a fat splinter out of it. I could get the crowbar under that; I gave a last mighty heave and the door broke into pieces.

I rubbed my shoulders, but I was too keyed up to waste time resting. I put on the mask and pulled the flex light over to hook on the broken edge of the trapdoor.

Sure enough, steep stairs, little more than a ladder nailed into a rough frame, led to a cellar with a dirt floor. *Oh, V.I., you are a detective without peer. Now detect what is down here.*

I started cautiously down the stairs with my digging tools. My shadow bobbed and weaved against the floor, with the end of the pick looking like Death's scythe. Death had been following in my wake lately; I didn't like being her harbinger. I flung the tools down the stairs; they landed with a dull thud on the dirt floor. I stuck up an arm for the flex light and brought it as far down as the cord would stretch.

The room was small, just the size of the kitchen overhead. A spider as big as the palm of my hand scuttled up the wall and disappeared through a crack in the boards overhead. I wished I'd brought a hard hat.

The walls were lined with shelves, empty for the most part, except for some odds and ends of electrical work, screws, wires, a pair of clippers. Incongruously, in one corner stood a couple of jars of mushy gray stuff. Canned pears, a faded and peeling label said. I couldn't hold back a shudder at the thought of what was in there now.

I took my pencil flash out of my jeans pocket and started a meticulous search of the floor, looking for a place where the soil might have been dislodged to bury something half a century ago. Time hadn't exactly leveled the floor, but it had made the minor hills and valleys uniform across its surface.

I didn't want to dig up the whole floor, and I didn't want to start chopping at it with my pick, in case something fragile lay underneath. I finally went back up the stairs to rummage in Julius's utility closet. He didn't have much equipment, but he did have a few screwdrivers.

I took the two longest down with me to use as probes, delicately twisting them into the soil up to their handles. About five feet from the bottom of the stairs, I struck something hard. I used the curved end of the crowbar as a makeshift trowel and started clearing dirt away from the spot. I shone my pencil flash into the hole I'd created.

Something brownish, matted. I took off my right glove and stuck a tentative hand into the hole. Fabric, heavily layered with dirt. I pulled on it gently, but couldn't bring it up. Bit by bit, I excavated along a line dictated by my probings with the screwdrivers. My neck was sore, my arms and hamstrings quivering, by the time I'd created a trough some three feet by two feet.

I took out my knife and cut away a piece of the fabric, carefully lifting it so that the dirt didn't spill on what lay underneath. I shone my flash again. It wasn't a plutonium bomb, but a suit jacket, a woman's jacket. Mold and damp had turned it a grayish-brown. Only the buttons still gleamed under my flashlight.

I held my breath as I peeled the fabric back. It fell apart under my hand, revealing the bones underneath.

"My God, Julius, you lived with this beneath you all these years? How could you?"

I'd been alone for so many hours I spoke out loud, my voice startling me in the confined space. "Who was she? Martina? Gertrud Memler? Did you kill her? Is that why you thought a detective should come for you?"

But this had been Breen's house, Breen's workshop. Whoever this was, however she'd come to be here, her death and burial were a secret shared by the four men, the Breens and the Dzornens.

I don't know how long I squatted, staring into the hole, unwilling to dig any further, but I heard footsteps overhead, men's voices. I thought it might be Basier, made bold by company, and got to my feet.

I started up the stairs, but my leg muscles had cramped up. As I stood on the bottom step, massaging my hamstrings, I heard a man say, "It's not here. I left it right here."

A second man said, "Look under the sofa, maybe it fell out."

There was a scraping noise and a thud as they tossed Julius's couch to one side. I'd heard the voices before but I couldn't place them. I stuck up a hand and turned off the flex lamp so it wouldn't cast my shadow. Crept up the stairs one at a time.

"The girl over at the house said a detective was here yesterday, a female. That bitch Warshawski more than likely."

The second man grunted.

I slithered through the opening I'd made in the trapdoor. A piece of wood broke loose and clunked down the stairs.

The two men crossed into the kitchen. Rory Durdon. Glenn Davilats, the Palfry County deputy. I was so startled that Davilats pulled his gun before I could react. I dropped behind a bag of birdseed at the last second. He fired but the shots went into the bag. Seed started pouring out around my feet.

"Damn it, man, don't shoot in here, you'll bring in the whole god-damn neighborhood. Use your Taser!"

I picked up the bag and flung it wildly at the men. One swore as the bag got him in the face, but the other was over the side of the cabinet before I could get my gun out of my tuck holster. Durdon.

I kicked his kneecap with my work boot. He grunted and punched at my head. I ducked, grabbed his foot, slipped in the loose birdseed and sprawled across another bag. He lost his balance but I still couldn't get at my gun. I flung my flashlight at his head, grazed his temple, but

Davilats had recovered. He aimed his Taser at me. I tried to vault over the back of the cabinet, but he fired. Every nerve in my body felt as though I'd been seared by a hot iron. I slumped over the cabinet side, unable to move.

The two men picked me up and bundled me into the basement. One of them stuck his hands in my pockets, came away with my papers. I couldn't lift a hand to fight them.

They shone a flashlight on the papers and saw the copy of the BREE-NIAC sketch. "So you did steal the drawing, bitch!" Durdon said.

Underneath the burning pain from the Taser, I felt very cold. The graduate student who minded the Basier kids said there'd been a cop at Julius's door yesterday. Not someone from the CPD, checking on Julius, but Glenn Davilats, planting the sketch. And last night, when Julius died while a cop was questioning him, that had been Davilats, finishing the job for Cordell Breen. Tuesday night, when Alison was driving us home, a squad car had turned onto the street leading to the Breen house. Tan with brown markings. The colors of the Palfry County sheriff's cars. Davilats driving out to Breen's house to get his orders, or get paid.

"What did you do with the drawing?" Davilats demanded.

"What, you planted it here, and Cordell sent you down to get it back before the Chicago cops or the Basiers found it?" My words came out like shapeless gravel; I wasn't sure they could even be understood, but the effort to speak left me short of breath.

Davilats kicked me in the stomach, fingering his Taser. "Where is the fucking drawing?"

"In my office," I said as quickly as my heavy lips would move. "In my big safe in the back. Combination 09-19-06-08-07-27."

"Say it again," Durdon ordered, pulling out a notebook.

I'd used my parents' and my birth dates. I repeated them slowly. Davilats kicked me again, just for emphasis. The two men climbed back upstairs. When they'd scrambled over the side of the cabinet, they pulled the top back on. I lay helpless as they hammered the top back into place.

46

THE PIT AND THE SKELETON

WAS FINALLY ABLE to move my hands. I sat up, slowly, painfully, massaging my fingers, which tingled, as if I'd bathed them in acid. My side ached where Davilats had kicked me. I could feel the darts, one in my left pectoral, the other in my thigh. I pulled the one from my thigh; my jeans had kept it from going in very deeply. The dart in my pec took some doing, first to grab the tiny protruding end in the dark, and then to yank it out. I blacked out briefly, but when I came to, I felt better.

My poor body craved sleep, but I couldn't rest, trapped in a root cellar with a skeleton next to me. I crawled up the stairs and pushed against the cabinet top, hoping I'd been mistaken about the hammering. The top didn't budge.

I'd thrown my flashlight in the struggle, but I couldn't find it when I felt around the floor near the trapdoor opening. I thought I felt furry feet crawling across my hand and let out a stifled shriek. My fingers closed on the cord to the flex lamp. I held my breath, fumbling up the cord to the switch. The light didn't turn on: my assailants had yanked out the plug on their way out.

I felt sick with disappointment. I sat on the edge of the trapdoor, my head in my hands.

When Davilats and Durdon broke into my office safe, they wouldn't find the BREENIAC sketch; they would come back here to finish me off. If I sat here waiting, they'd finish me faster.

I braced my feet on either side of the door hole and pushed with all my might, but the top didn't budge. I put spiders, rats, snakes, skeletons as far from my mind as I could and cautiously stepped my way back down the steep stairway. My throat was parched and my skin still burned. I put those as far away as I could, too.

When I stepped off at the bottom, I stood on one leg and traced a circle with the other foot, feeling for my tools, but I was still dizzy and couldn't keep my balance. I went down on my hands and knees and moved slowly around. My left hand went into the hole I'd dug and connected with matted fabric. I pulled away quickly, but kept feeling the threads, spider feet, clinging to my hand.

At length I came on my burn phone. It didn't get a signal down here, but in the light from the screen, I found my flashlight and my other tools. Flashlight under my armpit, ax and crowbar hugged to my chest, I hoisted myself to the top one painful step at a time. Ten steps. Ten years it seemed to take to reach the top.

I had to sit again. My arms were already weary.

"You have a lot of work in front of you, my friends," I told them sternly. "No whining. Get to work."

I placed the flashlight in a corner where I wouldn't step on it. Pushed the remaining bags of birdseed down the trapdoor opening to make room for myself.

"Sorry," I muttered to the skeleton at the bottom. "Didn't mean to dump it on your head."

I couldn't stand upright in the crate; I had to swing the pick from the top step while bracing myself against the opening. My shoulders shook with involuntary tremors. Dehydration, electrocution, not good for physical labor. How desperate would I get before I opened the jars of gray mush in the basement?

Swing, thud, rest. The outer skin of the cabinet was metal, which was why it looked like a trunk. It bounced back at me every time I hit it.

"I hope you were dead before you were buried," I said to my companion. "If you promise not to tell Davilats and Durdon when they come back, I'm a bit scared. Never show fear, of course: vermin like those two can smell it on you."

I understood what had happened now, but not why. *Swing, thud, rest.* Max had said the equations on the BREENIAC sketch were written by someone who, like him, had been educated in Central Europe. Austria, say, although perhaps Germany or Czechoslovakia. *Swing, thud, rest.*

That meant that it was Martina Saginor, Gertrud Memler or Benjamin Dzornen who'd created the design, not Edward Breen. The little logo, the triangles in the bottom right corner, was the designer's signature. *Swing, thud, rest.*

When Martin saw the triangles, he recognized them from the documents his mother had stolen from his grandmother. *Swing, thud, rest.*

He talked to Cordell, asked him about the triangles. That's what didn't add up for him: the same triangles on the BREENIAC design and on his family documents. That conversation put Breen on the alert, made him look for Martin, pretending to Jari Liu that he was worried Martin would take Metargon's secrets public. Edward Breen had been an engineer, he was clever and saw the potential for the ferromagnetic memory, but he wasn't brilliant: he didn't work out the idea from the hysteresis equations the way the actual inventor had. *Swing, thud, rest.*

When King Derrick posted that nuclear secret document on the Virtual-Bidder website, he signed his death warrant. Cordell Breen couldn't afford for the document to fall into public hands. He got Rory Durdon to sniff around Palfry County to find the deputy-most-likely-to-be-bribed. *Swing, thud, rest.*

Maybe Glenn Davilats was already taking kickbacks from other meth houses, so Durdon knew it would be easy to sell him on digging himself deeper into the pit on the far side of law and order. However the relationship was cemented, the two men arrived before dawn at the

Schlafly house and killed Ricky. Maybe Cordell had sent them to kill Martin—he was the person connecting the dots, after all.

The Navigator that Judy had driven back to Chicago had been leased to Metargon. I'd double-check it if I ever—when I got out of here. *Swing, thud, rest.*

Poor Julius Dzornen. He'd been involved in the death of the woman in the cellar, and the secret so weighed on him that he'd lost the ability to function. It was as if the Breens had Tasered his spirit.

What really did him in was his father's complicity. "Did Benjamin Dzornen kill you?" I asked my companion. "Or was it Edward Breen? Did the two men make Julius kill you, or bury you? You haunted him for many years."

My flashlight battery was giving out and I could only see the side of the trunk dimly.

Swing, thud, rest. The trunk was turning gray. I blinked, sat. Hallucinating, not good. I put a finger on the gray spot: it was a hole, light was seeping in from the kitchen. I was shivering now with a feverish excitement. I took the crowbar and used what was left of my muscles to pry out a chunk from the side. It peeled away like a sardine tin, the metal siding hanging loose like a great lip.

I lay on my back with my boots against the opening. Kicked, kicked again, felt more of the metal give. It wasn't a very big hole, but it was wide enough for me to slither through. I landed in an awkward heap on the old linoleum.

Sunshine on Lake Michigan had never looked as clean and bright as the dim light seeping in through the ivy-shrouded windows. I lay for several minutes, soaking it in, breathing in must and mold on the linoleum as if it were bottled oxygen.

An old industrial clock over the sink told me the time. Three P.M. I'd climbed into the crate six hours ago. Time to get help, time to move on. I turned on the kitchen tap, held my head under the stream of water, gulped down great mouthfuls.

I didn't want to move, but Durdon and Davilats might come back at any second. If they'd broken into my office, the combination I'd given them wouldn't open my safe. They could blow it open, but it was possible they'd come back to torture the actual combination out of me. Or the BREENIAC sketch's actual location.

I took my flashlight and my picklocks to the Subaru with me, but left the digging tools where they were: my shoulder muscles were too watery to lift the pickax again. My back felt as though someone were shooting Tasers up and down the cervical vertebrae.

As I stumbled through the front door, Ms. Basier was getting out of the Volvo with her daughter. The two stared at me without speaking, then scuttled into the house. When I looked at myself in the Subaru's rearview mirror, I didn't blame them. Standing under Julius's kitchen tap, I'd turned the dirt in my hair and skin into mud. My clothes were also caked with dirt. My eyes looked like portals to the Inferno.

I drove slowly, sticking to side streets all the way north. It took over an hour to cover the twelve miles, but by taking the slow route, I could rest my sore back against the seat.

When I got home, Mr. Contreras started haranguing me almost before he had his front door open. He hadn't heard from me since I left the apartment two days ago, he didn't know why I couldn't let him know for a change, and here was young Sunny Breen—he stopped short when I swayed and half fell onto the bottom stair.

Peppy came over and started licking the mud from my face. Mr. Contreras's scolding changed to clucking. Behind him, I heard Alison Breen cry out, "Oh, what happened, oh, please don't tell me that it was my father who did this."

I was too tired to open my eyes. "Rory Durdon," I said. "Rory Durdon and a bent cop he picked up downstate."

I heard her start to sob but I just curled up against the stairwell wall, an arm around the dog.

"What happened, doll, how'd you get like this?" Mr. Contreras asked.

"The guy who drove us up to Lake Forest the other night," I said. My lips were so thick that the words came out slowly, like cold molasses from a bottle. "Rory Durdon. His cop buddy Tasered me. Then they locked me inside a root cellar. I couldn't get a phone signal down there. I had to hack my way out."

"Tasered you? Oh, no!" Alison cried. "I was afraid—after the reporter came, Mother called Dad—she and I, we were both worried—I can't believe—oh, what is happening?"

"She can't talk right now," Mr. Contreras told her, adding to me, "We need to get you cleaned up, doll. Can you make it up the stairs to your own bath or do you want to use mine down here?"

The third floor seemed a great distance away, but I wanted to be in my own place, to get into clean clothes and throw these away. I unlaced my boots; Mr. Contreras got down on the bottom step next to me to pull them off. Without their weight on my feet, I managed to push myself up the stairs.

Alison followed anxiously behind me, asking questions, but I felt as though I were in a swamp in some alien world, unable to think or speak. Mr. Contreras took my keys the third time I dropped them and opened my front door for me. He turned on the taps in the bathtub. When I started to unbutton my shirt, though, he left hastily, shutting the door behind him.

I sat in the tub under the shower, rinsing the mud out of my hair. When I finally felt clean, I filled the tub and lay back, almost comatose, letting the hot water soak into my ripped-up muscles. The place in my pectoral where I'd pulled out the dart was an angry red, but my thigh only showed a small pink circle.

When the water turned cold I finally stepped out and wrapped up in a fluffy dressing gown that Jake had given me for my birthday. In the living room, Mr. Contreras handed me a mug of hot tea that was half milk and filled with sugar. I gulped it down gratefully. Alison took the mug to the kitchen to refill it and came back with a plate of poached eggs on toast.

Mr. Contreras watched me eat, nodding seriously at each mouthful I swallowed. When I'd finished, and was starting to fall asleep, he gave me a shamefaced look but said, "You ain't going to like this, cookie, but I called the doc. She's going to come by to look at you on her way home from the hospital."

"It's okay," I yawned. "We'll have a party."

The eggs and the sugary tea had revived me enough that I was able to give him and Alison a more coherent description of what had happened in the coach house. Alison's sensitive mouth quivered, but she had herself in hand and didn't turn my experience into her own drama.

When I finished, I said to her, "I heard you say a reporter had been to the house. Was that Murray? Murray Ryerson, I mean?"

She flung up her hands. "I don't remember his name. He's big, with reddish hair, and a Mercedes convertible?"

"Yes, that's Murray. He came out to ask why Julius Dzornen had been at the house Tuesday night, didn't he?"

"Mother didn't know what Mr. Dzornen and Dad talked about, but when she called Dad over at Metargon, he came roaring home. He's never done that, not when I fell as a kid and broke my arm, not even when Mother started hemorrhaging after her second miscarriage, so I was pretty tense.

"First he threw the reporter out, then he started shouting at Mother, how could she be so stupid as to have let him inside to begin with. And Mother said, she said—" Alison's eyes got bigger and her voice wavered.

"What?" Mr. Contreras demanded.

"She said Tuesday night she'd heard Durdon banging away in the garage; it's beneath her studio. She'd gone down and seen him under Mr. Dzornen's car! Dad was so furious he almost hit her! Then Dad said he'd better not find out that Warshawski—Vic, I mean—had taken the BREENIAC sketch and I said how could she, because it was already gone when she was up at the house on Tuesday! And he said he was sending Durdon down to Hyde Park to make sure she hadn't taken it from the coach house, and the whole thing was so insane I couldn't bear to be around them. I couldn't go to any of my friends' houses, even if they were home, I can't tell anyone what's going on, so I drove down here."

Her voice petered out. Mr. Contreras patted her hand comfortingly. Lotty rang the bell about then. When the old man went to buzz her in, I asked if he'd bring my iPad back with him: I wasn't up to talking to the police, but I needed to alert them to the skeleton I'd uncovered in the coach house—especially before Alison's father had another brainstorm and sent Durdon down to dig it up and dispose of it.

I wrote an e-mail to Conrad Rawlings in the Fourth District, putting Murray Ryerson in the blind copy line.

> I'm leaving police business to the police, but this morning I stumbled on a body buried in the cellar of a Hyde Park coach house. I would have written you sooner, but two goons, one named Rory Durdon who works for Cordell Breen, the other a Palfry County sheriff's deputy named Glenn Davilats, Tasered me and locked me in the cellar. It's a long story, but you might want to dig up the body before Cordell Breen comes down himself to haul it away.
>
> Ciao, Vic

Lotty came in as I was hitting the send key. She'd spent six hours in the operating room and was tired herself. She forbore from any barbed words, just inspected the wound sites with gentle fingers. I'd gotten the whole dart out of my thigh, but the point of the other one had broken off in my shoulder. Lotty injected me with a topical anesthetic and pulled it out, covered both wounds with an antibiotic salve and gave me a course of antibiotics to take.

"I will say this is a first in our acquaintance, Victoria," she announced when she'd finished. "No drownings, shootings, stabbings or acid, but a poison dart. Worthy of Sherlock Holmes, no?"

"Something like that," I mumbled. "My shoulders—I've torn up those muscles from digging up part of a skeleton, and then whacking the side out of my prison."

"Yes, you'll feel that for some weeks, I'm afraid."

"Can you do something for me? I can't afford to lie in bed for weeks, or even days."

"Even if I could implant new muscles in you, it would take months for them to take hold," Lotty said. "Let Nature take her course for once in your obstinate life."

I shook my head. There was something I needed to do, something urgent, and I couldn't remember what it was.

"I need to be able to act. I need to drive, I need to hold my own if I'm attacked again. I can't do anything right now but sit like a squawking bird! Can't you give me something, whatever modern miracle steroid they inject into football players to get them back into the lineup?"

"What, so your joints can rot like a football player's in another decade?" Lotty's eyes turned darker with anger.

I looked at her gravely. "If Martin is still alive and I can save him, I need to risk my joints. It's not as though I take cortisone every week."

She frowned. "Even if I wanted to let you get this kind of injection, it must be done in a hospital with an X-ray machine guiding the anesthesiologist's hand. Even so, it would take several days before you'd be strong enough to be up and about. I can give you a muscle relaxant, but it will knock you out very quickly. You'll sleep a long time. If you're worried about your safety, you may not wake up easily."

"Will I be better in the morning?"

"Oh, even if you aren't, you will be rested enough to throw yourself in front of a herd of raging elephants, or jump from a plane without a parachute, or some other action that will prove to you that you're outside the usual laws of human mortality," Lotty said crossly.

"I'll stay with her," Alison told Lotty. "After all, it's because of my dad that she went through all this."

She turned her earnest young face to mine. "I hate to bother you when you're so tired, but was the BREENIAC sketch in the coach house?"

The BREENIAC sketch. Was that the urgent action I had to take? No, I'd shipped the drawing to the Special Collections librarian this morning. Durdon and Davilats had taken the copy from my pocket. Along with the obituary of Ada Byron.

The two goons didn't know enough of the story to connect the dots, but if Cordell Breen saw the obituary, he'd be off to Tinney, Illinois, like one of his father's rockets. And if there was any evidence about Martina Saginor or Gertrud Memler, or even why the BREENIAC sketch mattered so much, Breen would destroy it before I could get there.

NEVADA, 1953
The Lost Lover

T HE MOUNTAIN AIR at night bites her skin. She used to love that sharp
high-altitude cold. Back when she climbed the Wildspitze, she slept
on the mountainside so she could start her cosmic ray experiments at
first sun. Stepping out of her sleeping bag, jumping into a glacier lake,
leaping out and running naked around the meadow to dry herself, she
would feel braced, embraced by the air. She thought she could taste the
air; it was tingly, like sekt wine, but lighter, crisper.

In those days, she encountered the physical world like a lover. Pho-
tons and gamma rays, cold air, steep climbs, all exhilarated her. She lies
now on foreign ground, watching the stars. The constellations are the
same that her papa showed her when she was a little girl, but they don't
pulse with the life she once found in them.

She crumbles the soil underneath her fingers. There is no point to
the work she is doing here; it's the same mind-numbing drudgery she
performed at Uranverein 7. There is more food, her shoes fit, the body
is properly housed, but the same high fences, the same guards sur-
round her every morning when she walks from her room to her lab.
Her mind is turning to a desert as arid as the one at the bottom of this
mountain.

Once men discovered they could use the atom to make bombs, they
lost the excitement of the hunt for its secrets. Even her own work has
been degraded by the quest for a bomb. The array she had designed,

why had she put it on paper to begin with? Tempting the gods, who will always laugh in your face.

"I know you, Fräulein Martina," the woman Memler had snarled the morning she was sent from Innsbruck to the east. "You can't stop drawing and scribbling and imagining equations and machines. I want them now. You will have no use for them, after all, when you reach your journey's end."

She had stared unflinching at the younger woman. Why had she not noticed the coarseness of her expression when Memler applied for a place in her lab at the Radium Institute in 1934? Why had she assumed that this young woman shared her passion for unfolding Nature's heart?

Benjamin was right, after all, when he said Martina lacked something essential for human relations. He had meant love, perhaps he'd meant she should adore him, but what she was really lacking was judgment.

She had shaken her head a little in the cave at Innsbruck, sad at her own blindness, but the Memler interpreted that as insolence. Her guards stripped the dress from Martina and easily found her papers, sewn into the hem. The sight of her own coarse stitches made Martina think of her mother. *Even in a slave labor camp you don't have to sew as if you had donkey's hooves instead of human fingers,* she heard Mama saying, and smiled, careful this time to keep her expression to herself. Still, that interior smile allowed her to watch impassively as the Memler put her papers inside a notebook.

The guard flung Martina's dress at her feet. After she put it on, and put on the threadbare joke of a coat, she said, "My last words to you as your professor, Fräulein Memler: you cannot think clearly or do meaningful research if you are consumed by rage or spite."

Memler struck her hard across the cheekbone with her ring-crusted fingers, and Martina felt the blood lace down her face. So her poor body still had some blood in it. Her monthly flow dried up long ago and she wondered sometimes if her whole body had turned to something inanimate, a piece of skin filled with sawdust.

"I should lock you in the pit," Memler growled, but the guard reminded her that the transport to Vienna was waiting: they'd already given the escort the number of prisoners who were in transit. Locking up one prisoner meant redoing all the paperwork.

It was Martina's last sight of Memler, rubbing her rings, as if the blow to her professor's face had also cut her own fingers. Her last sight until six days ago.

The Memler's thick flaxen hair has darkened; she's cut her obscenely fat Hitler-Jugend braid into a fashionable Debbie Reynolds perm, but her posture—the obsequious bob of the head to the senior man in the group, the arrogant gesture to the work crew—Martina would have known her anywhere.

The Memler is even more astounded by the sight of Martina. She stops what she's saying to the men in mid-sentence.

"*Du bist aber tod!*"* she gasps at Martina, her skin turning an unhealthy white.

"You are not the queen of the uranium torture field, now, Fräulein Memler," Martina says, also in German, in a voice of ice. "If you must address me, you will do so politely, or not at all."

Red blotches appear in Memler's face. "*Was machst du—was machen Sie hier?*"†

"The better question is, what are *you* doing here? Do your new masters know what you did in the caves beneath Innsbruck? It will be most instructive for them to find out."

The Memler smiles unpleasantly. "I'm helping defeat Communism. The past is of no interest to them."

She turns to the men, who are looking at her curiously. "A lab

---

*But you are dead!
†What are you doing here?

technician I used to know in Austria. Forgive us for speaking German; we haven't seen each other for many years."

Her English is heavily accented, but grammatically correct. Memler was always a hard worker, that was the good thing one could say.

"Ah, the concussion you suffered in the Nazi weapons plant has affected your memory." Martina smiles at the men around Memler. "You came to the Institut für Radiumforschung as my student. I remember how eager you were then to learn from me. And now you are here, perhaps you may learn again."

Martina asks one of the work crew what it is they're installing. A computing machine, something built in Chicago to help Professor Dzornen's team with their neutron scattering computations. Martina starts to walk past them, then sees the little smirk lingering at the corner of Memler's mouth, the mouth that shouted "Heil, Hitler" not so long ago. She stops to stare at the computing machine, walks around it, inspects the side panels as the men watch her uneasily. The Memler is shifting her feet, unable to hide that Martina's behavior is making her nervous.

"I would gladly see the interior," Martina says to an electrician, one of the crew who has often worked with her. "The design would be most interesting."

The electrician looks cautiously at his own boss. Memler says sharply that it would be a serious error to tamper with the machine, that he is most strenuously forbidden to unscrew the side panels.

Martina smiles tightly at Memler. "You have just shown it to me, Miss Memler. *Ich gratuliere dir.*"*

Martina goes to her own lab, really, to her own two meters on a bench, where she is working out what she's seen in the bubble chambers.

Her first months in Nevada were spent gulping down papers and books, learning Feynman diagrams, the Lamb shift, quantum electro-

---

*I congratulate you.

dynamics, tracing the new particles. At first the physics came back to her slowly, like the return of her flute playing, like the English she studied in Gymnasium, but has forgotten. After seven months, though, she's suddenly confident in all those arenas—although her English has acquired the southwestern twang of the machinists and electricians around her.

She pines to be at Cornell, where Bethe is developing his theories of the meson, or at Columbia, where the most exciting new experiments are unfolding. She is not a shirker, though. Despite the fact that her project could be done by a beginning graduate student, she works through her equations meticulously, passes them to her lab partner to recheck, just as she will, tomorrow, recheck his results.

Today, she stays until everyone except the guards has left the lab. She returns to the computing machine and calmly unscrews the panels herself. This is not the interior of the computer put together at Princeton by von Neumann and his team. Even though the Princeton work is highly classified, she's managed to see photographs and sketches. This Chicago machine is two-thirds the size of von Neumann's and there are no vacuum tubes. Instead, there are a series of plates with wires extending from them; it looks like a loom for making copper tablecloths.

Martina screws the panels back into place. After dark, she goes to the mountain to think. A soldier patrolling the perimeter of the camp reminds her that she can't climb any higher than this. Martina nods at him, acknowledging the order. She doesn't speak; the sight of barbed wire and guards turns her stomach into knots.

In the morning, she watches as the Memler is given a tour of the lab, of the base. Martina chats with the work crew in a way that's alien to her. The men tell her Memler used to be here in Nevada, but she's been assigned to the Chicago project in order to work for the man who sponsored her immigration. Edward Breen is an electrical engineer, they tell Martina; he served with the U.S. Army in Europe; at war's end, he found the Memler in a weapons lab near Innsbruck and brought her back to help with rocket and weapons research for the United States.

The men talk freely with Martina, not because she has an easy camaraderie about her: she doesn't. She talks to them formally, but she respects the work they do. Unlike a number of other scientists, she consults them on equipment design. They respected her at first for her work ethic, but after fifteen months of seeing her close up, they've come to a grudging admiration: she's a woman, she's a foreigner, but she's a born problem solver. *One smart cookie,* they say to each other. It's most unlike her to want to gossip, but the crew are happy to oblige.

"The Memler dame was here for a couple years, but when Breen went back to Chicago to work on computing machines, he took her with him. Good riddance, too. Damned Kraut—pardon my French— always acted like we were too dumb to know which end of a soldering iron to pick up."

"She's not on the University of Chicago faculty, is she?" Martina asks.

"As for that, I couldn't tell you. I just know she's attached to the project that's working on computations for the Super.* You want to see the inside of Breen's machine, we can show you after Memler and her ass-lickers take off—they're heading back to Chicago after lunch."

Martina smiles her thanks, doesn't tell them she already looked. While her department head is seeing Memler and her sycophants onto their waiting C-47, the work crew unscrew the panels and Martina once again sees the magnetic lattice board inside. This time she inspects the wiring more closely. Not perhaps the most efficient design— she would have used a finer wire and coiled it around the armature—but probably a serviceable enough way to organize the counters.

Martina thanks the men, returns to her lab, but at the end of the

---

*The hydrogen bomb.

afternoon, she drops into her department head's office. She tells him that the Memler was her student in Vienna.

"She was a secret Nazi during the thirties while the Party was outlawed in Austria, but after the Anschluss, she became quite public and boastful about her Party connections. During the war, they put her in charge of the part of Uranverein Seven that was working on fission bomb design."

"We know Miss Memler's wartime history, Miss Saginor. Many people felt compelled to become Nazis to protect their jobs, and that was true for Miss Memler, as well."

"Uranverein Seven ran on slave labor and I was one of the slaves," Martina says. "The Memler woman took great pleasure in overseeing our torture and punishments. When the Germans ran out of money and interest in building a nuclear weapon, I was among the expendable: the Memler sent me east to the concentration camps."

Martina makes no effort to smile, to be the good girl asking for a favor. This isn't because of the war, the deprivations and tortures at Uranverein 7, or the march from Terezín to Sobibor. For ten years in Vienna she was a research leader, the acknowledged equal of her male colleagues, her opinions valued by the Institute director.

Martina expects respect, but her American department head isn't used to women scientists. Unlike the machinists and electricians on the base, who may not understand her physics, but see her mind at work, the department head can only see her as a technician sent to Nevada from Chicago.

"Miss Memler's past has been thoroughly investigated," he tells Martina. "She has a high security clearance and is a valuable member of our project. People like you need to overcome your grievances and get over the past."

"Watching people die in nitrogen chambers is not a grievance, but it was a peculiar hobby of the Memler," Martina says.

"She told me that you yourself were a Communist, and that you might come to me to defame her," the head says. "It seems you spent four years in the Soviet Union at the end of the war."

"I was trapped behind Soviet lines at the war's end, like other people in my situation. They put me in a gulag; I escaped with difficulty and walked west. You can't investigate my past, because all my documents were destroyed in the war, but I have never belonged to any ideological party. However, the Memler's Nazi affiliation, and the power she exercised at Uranverein Seven, are easy to find out."

The department head stares at her. "If she is correct about your Communism, your own status here may be in jeopardy. I'd be careful about the mud I threw around."

The warning means not just that the conversation is over. It means she can be deported. Without a hearing of any kind.

Martina returns to the barracks where she's been given two rooms, a bedroom and a living-dining-kitchenette. There's a phone, although of course all calls are placed by operators. She asks the operator to put her through to Chicago, but the woman tells her that her outgoing calls are temporarily restricted.

She goes to the small garden outside her barracks where she watches the sun set behind the mountain. A guard is now patrolling the front of her building. She smiles sourly. The land of the free, the home of the brave.

Back in her rooms she changes into corduroy trousers, laces up her hiking boots, dons a jacket, and fills two canteens with water. Food. She should carry something to eat, although she still—despite years of near starvation—often forgets meals. Raisins, an apple, a slab of something the Americans call cheese, that will do. She has a hat for when the desert sun comes up.

These mountains are rugged, but she crossed the Carpathians on frostbitten feet after she escaped from the Moldova gulag. She waits until full dark, then slips out the window in her bedroom. She crouches on the ground, but the sentry in front hasn't heard her land in the gravel underneath. Nor do the two soldiers patrolling the road notice her when she reaches it.

The Army relies on the terrain, steep, inhospitable, on the barbed wire that rings the base, on the signs warning of nuclear explosions, to keep out trespassers. They rely on the fences, on fear of wild animals or rocks falling from the outcroppings to keep the inhabitants inside. The patrols are just an extra.

In the starlight, Martina finds a gully that she's used before. She climbs to where the wire fence is camouflaged by the brush. She knows where a boulder has raised the fence enough that a thin woman can slide beneath.

She has no compass, but the stars are the same she learned with her father, the same that she saw from the Wildspitze in the Austrian Alps.

She looks up at Pegasus, blinking back tears. She's spent her whole life in love with light and that point in the infinite where beauty is so unbearable that it feels like pain. Is it so much to ask of the Universe to let her return to that point? I don't need a lab, I don't need publications, only the harmonies, she pleads. The stars give her no answer, no mercy, but their light will at least guide her up the mountain, away from the barbed wire and barbed words of a weapons factory.

47

WHERE THERE'S A WILL

WE WERE ON THE ROAD before the sun was up, Alison driving my Mustang. I'd taken the tracking magnets from the exhaust and the trunk—still held shut with a bungee cord. Alison recognized the magnets: they were Metargon products. She tried to suggest someone had stolen them, but stopped herself mid-sentence, flushing with shame. Her education into her father's activities was rocking her world.

At the entrance to the Kennedy Expressway, I told Alison to pull over. I stood on the curb until an eighteen-wheeler showed up at the entrance to the northbound lanes. I quickly stuck the magnets under his rear axle.

"Hope you're going all the way to Seattle, buddy," I muttered, jumping back into the Mustang.

The drug Lotty had given me knocked me out for over ten hours. I'd finally forced myself out of bed, bullied my sore muscles into bending, stretching and lifting. Even with a second espresso, I was still dopey when Alison and I got under way, nowhere near ready to fling myself in front of a herd of raging elephants.

Once we'd off-loaded the trackers, we headed for the westbound interstate. I should do all my driving errands at the crack of dawn. Traffic was starting to build, but we were all going well above the speed limit. Alison covered the fifty miles to the far reaches of the suburbs in under an hour.

As soon as we were clear of Chicago, the traffic thinned and we could check for tails. When I saw we were clean, I leaned back in the passenger seat and slept until Alison slowed for the Tinney exits some three hours later.

"Which exit?" she asked.

"Let's start with the college," I said. "But first, food and more caffeine."

A billboard at the entrance to the town gave us Tinney's population: twelve thousand and counting; told us it was home of the Alexandrine Explorers Division III hockey champs in 2003 and 2010; gave us meeting times for the local Rotary, Kiwanis and Lions clubs; listed a number of houses of worship; and extolled the beauty of nearby state parks. The sign didn't mention Ada Byron.

Tinney lay like a long snake on a high ridge over the Illinois River. Alexandrine College, where Byron had been a library clerk, was a bulge about halfway along the snake's middle. It was built from limestone, with the campus laid out around a square, New England style.

Alison followed signs to "Visitor Parking." One hour for fifty cents. If the company that gouges Chicago over street parking saw this, they'd have massive coronaries when they learned that someone somewhere could park without getting fleeced.

As Alison stretched out the muscles in her neck, I watched the students—couples walking hand in hand along the edge of the bluffs, others playing Ultimate Frisbee in a nearby field. I even saw one who was reading. With the buildings glowing soft gold in the autumn sun, the place looked like a Hollywood set for a college.

I stopped a Frisbee player to get directions to the campus library. We couldn't miss it, he assured us; it and Admin were the two oldest buildings on campus and they faced each other across the main quad. The youth gestured vaguely to the highest spot on the bluff, so we walked along the path above the river to the entrance to the quads.

The drought had turned the river into a sluggish stream. Sandbars stretched long fingers down the middle. Tree branches that had started upriver had halted in the shallows here. The banks on either side were filled with brown grass and dying bushes.

The path divided at the edge of campus, one fork following the river behind the school, the other leading into the quadrangles. Inside the quads, the grass was green. Parents pay a lot of money to send their kids to schools like this; it takes a lot of water to create a good impression.

As the Frisbee player had said, the library was easy to find. That was the first and last easy part of the day. No one in the library had heard of Ada Byron, which I ought to have realized—even if she'd worked until she was ninety she would have retired decades ago.

If I could find her home address, maybe the current owners would know something—we all leave detritus in our passing. New owners might have found diaries or a cache of nuclear secrets. The college didn't keep old phone books, but the reference librarian said the town library might. She also said the college's benefits office might have Byron's address in their pension payment records.

To summarize the fruitless hour we spent being shunted from one clerk to another: as far as Alexandrine College was concerned, Ada Byron had never existed.

I pulled out Martin Binder's photo and showed it to everyone we talked to. Had he been here, asking questions about Ms. Byron? The reaction was instructive: an imperceptible drawing back, a withholding of reaction. Martin had been here. They were protecting him.

On our way to the town library, we finally stopped for food. Alison had been too tense to eat before we left Chicago, but the long drive and the dispiriting search had given her an appetite. We found an indie coffee bar that served sandwiches and continued our quest.

It didn't surprise me to learn that the town library had gotten rid of all their old phone books. When? Oh, the librarian said vaguely, recently, when they were debating their storage needs, what needed to go into remote storage, what needed to be kept.

"After Martin Binder came here asking for them?" I suggested, holding out his photo.

The librarian flushed and looked away, but she wouldn't budge: she'd never seen Martin, all libraries were making difficult decisions these days.

At the *Huron County Gazette* on the far side of town, a staff member agreed that they'd run an obituary for Ada Byron seven years ago, but couldn't dig up anything else in their morgue on her. What about the schools where the obituary said she'd volunteered? The staffer couldn't say—they'd just printed what the funeral parlor had given them.

Back in the car, Alison and I tried to figure out any other way to find Ada Byron's home, or anyone who would admit to having known her. If she'd been born in Tinney, her birth certificate would be on file in the county building. If she had left a will, a copy would be filed with the county probate court.

LaSalle, the Huron County seat, lay about fifteen miles farther south. It was after three; I took over the wheel and drove to LaSalle as fast as I could. We got to the courthouse forty-five minutes before they closed.

This far from Cook County, I'd been imagining spry and helpful court officers, but the Huron County clerks were just as sullen and overweight as those at home. The two women behind the counter in the records room were arguing over the best way to make lasagna. It took them several minutes to acknowledge us.

The woman who finally came over sighed as if we'd asked her to go through the county's landfills personally looking for a document, but she gave me a form to fill out, sighed again loudly with a pointed look at the clock when I handed her the form, and shuffled into a back room, massaging her gunstock for comfort.

She returned with the news that there was no birth certificate on file for Ada Byron, but for ten dollars, we could get a copy of Byron's will. Finding a will at all had seemed like such a long shot that I stared blankly for a moment.

"Do you or do you not want a copy? Because I'd like to get out of here on time."

"Right," I said hastily, pulling a ten out of my wallet.

Our clerk slowly filled out a receipt, slowly stamped the form "paid," and returned again to the interior. She came back just as the clock behind the counter turned to five. She already had her jacket on; she was clutching a Buy-Smart Values catalog, but she handed me a three-page document, The Last Will and Testament of Ada Byron.

"You can look at it *outside*. We're fixing to lock up now."

Alison and I sat on one of the benches in front of the county building to read Ada Byron's will. The benches faced a public square; county employees were streaming across it to the parking lot. Deputies were changing shifts, getting into their cruisers. A clutch of boys was jumping skateboards up a low wall across the square from us.

Ada Byron's house, at 2714 Tallgrass Road in Tinney, was left for the lifetime use of a Dorothy Ferguson, on the condition that all the contents be kept. *It is not necessary to keep them on the premises but they must be housed in safe storage.* Byron donated her telescope to the Tinney Public Library for their children's science program.

It was the second page of the will that made my hair stand up. Byron left her papers in trust for any descendant of Martina Saginor who could prove both their descent and an appreciation of Martina's work. The heir didn't have to know physics, but did have to show a love of science.

I handed the will to Alison, but the landscape and skateboarders were swimming around me in a way that made me put my head down on my knees.

"What, she didn't leave you nothing?"

It was the clerk who'd brought us the copy of the will, staring at us with an unpleasant avidity.

I lifted my head and managed a smile. "On the contrary, she made me her sole heir. It's the shock of knowing I won't have to sell the farm to pay for Mama's heart surgery that knocked me off balance."

The clerk scowled but shuffled on to the parking lot. Alison gave a spurt of laughter. "Vic, you're so amazing; you knew just the right thing to say to her. I don't understand this will at all. How could Ada Byron know about Martin's great-grandmother?"

All along, I'd been wondering if Martina had survived the death march to Sobibor Concentration Camp. Ada was Martina, or someone so close to Martina that she cherished her interests.

If Martina survived, why had she never gone to see Kitty or Kitty's offspring?

She did: she summoned Kitty and Judy to a meeting somewhere in rural Illinois. She stayed close to Chicago to keep an eye on her family, so she knew about Judy's addiction. She died before Martin was old enough for her to evaluate his character.

Why was she in hiding?

That I couldn't guess at.

48

ALI BABA'S CAVE

O N THE OUTSKIRTS of Tinney, we stopped at a gas station for a street map. Tallgrass Road curved away from the river at Tinney's north end. Most of the houses this far out were frame boxes, placed at sparse intervals; a number were attached to small farms. We passed cows and signs for organic eggs or "pick your own tomatoes."

2714 Tallgrass was near the end of the paved road, where it joined the gravel county road. Open fields stood to the north and west. The nearest neighbor was a good quarter mile distant.

The one oddity about Ada's house was a high platform built behind it, as if she'd created a hot tub level with her attic windows. It was filled now with flowering plants.

Whoever lived here had a child—a swing set stood next to the staircase leading to the platform, and as we walked up the shallow steps to the front door, Alison bent to pick up a stuffed lion.

A screen door was set into a frame that was curiously ornate for so small and poor a house. This wasn't Chicago: behind the screen, the front door stood open. Before I could ring the bell, a woman around my age appeared. Without opening the screen, she asked if she could help us. The words were cordial, but her tone was forbidding.

"I don't know," I said. "Are you Dorothy Ferguson?"

"Why do you want to know?" Her tone moved from forbidding to menacing.

"My name is V. I. Warshawski," I said. "This is Alison Breen. If you are Ms. Ferguson, I'll be glad to explain myself. If you're not, I'd appreciate knowing where I can find her."

A second woman appeared in the doorway. "Who is it, Meg?"

"Strangers looking for Dorothy Ferguson."

The second woman moved past Meg and came out onto the small porch. She was in her eighties, with thinning white hair that stuck out in tufts around her head, as if she'd just gotten up from a nap. She was short enough that she had to look up to see me, but despite the wild hair and her age, the eyes under her hooded lids were cold and shrewd.

"Who are you two, and why are you looking for Dorothy Ferguson?"

I looked at her steadily. "It's Ada Byron that I'm really interested in, but I can't explain further until I know who you are, and whether I can trust your discretion."

The woman's wide nostrils flared—amusement or contempt, hard to tell. A girl of perhaps four came running around the side of the house. Her brown pigtails were tied up in pink ribbons and she had on a Hello, Kitty pink sweatshirt.

"Is it Grace, Auntie Dorothy? Can she sleep over?"

"You get inside, Lily, you stay with your mom until I tell you it's safe to come out again. And Meg, you go get the shotgun and keep your phone handy in case you have to call the police."

Auntie Dorothy's voice was so fierce that Lily put a hand over her mouth and ran past us into the front hallway. I don't like guns pointed at me any more than the next person, but I suddenly felt too weary to stand, no matter how many muzzles were aimed at my head.

I collapsed on the top step and leaned my head against a scarred post. Alison squatted easily on her haunches.

"Until an hour ago, I had never heard your name," I said, "but I read it in the will that Ada Byron signed and which you executed."

"Herman Voles let you read Ada's will?" Dorothy exclaimed. "How could he be so untrust—"

"Ma'am, anyone can read the will: it's a public document. I found it in the county courthouse over in LaSalle. I am desperate for information about Ada Byron, and Martina Saginor, and Martina's great-grandson Martin." I heard Meg cock the hammer, but didn't bother to look up.

"Desperate? That's a strong word to use for something so ephemeral as information."

"My name is V. I. Warshawski." I fished in my bag for my wallet and took out my ID.

Dorothy barely glanced at it. "A Chicago detective. Am I supposed to be impressed, or become weak at the knees?"

"You're supposed to reciprocate with confirmation of your own identity," I said.

"Hmmph." She snorted again, this time more obviously in amusement; she called into the house to Lily, telling the little girl to find her big pocketbook and bring it to Meg.

Lily found the heavy purse and dragged it to her mother. Meg slipped the driver's license through the screen door: Dorothy Ferguson, eighty-six years old, living at 2714 Tallgrass.

I accepted the charade, although it would have been easy for me to go into the house, disarm Meg and look around for myself. They were very vulnerable, these two tough-talking women.

"This is a long story, Ms. Ferguson, and I am taking a calculated risk in trusting you," I said.

"Go on," Dorothy said.

"We are looking for a young man named Martin Binder." I pulled his photo from my case and handed it to Dorothy. She glanced at it, but laid it on the porch railing without saying anything.

Alison looked anxiously at Dorothy. "Please: if you've seen Martin, please tell me—tell us!"

"Are you his girlfriend, then?" Dorothy asked.

Alison flushed. "A friend. A coworker, at least, we worked on a project together this past summer. He was at my house right before he disappeared, and I'm terribly worried about him."

"Easy to say, young lady, hard to prove."

"Everyone in this town is anxious to protect Martin," I said. "I couldn't understand it—the librarians, the newspaper—he'd clearly been in Tinney. He's a stranger, but he has the town behind him. You have the forceful character it would take to line up the rest of Tinney. Were you their mayor?"

Dorothy narrowed her eyes at me. "You can say you're terribly worried, but who's to say what you're worried about?"

"Martin's grandmother was murdered last week," I said. "The killers shot Martin's mother, but she survived. Martin's great-uncle, Julius Dzornen, died two nights ago in a car crash because someone tampered with his brakes. I'm worried that the men who killed all these people have Martin in their sights."

Meg gasped. Dorothy's mouth worked as she tried to decide what to say.

When she didn't speak after a long moment, I tried not to sigh audibly, but recited the history of Kitty, Judy, the papers Martin and Judy had fought over, and the BREENIAC sketch.

"When Martin was arguing with his mother about these old papers, what excited him most was seeing a letter from Ada Byron."

I looked at Alison, who accepted her cue to explain why Ada Byron's name would be a red flag to anyone who knew the history of computers.

When she'd finished, I picked up the story again. "Martin knew who the original Ada Byron was, so he guessed, as we did, that it was a fake identity. I'd bet just about anything that Martin found Byron's obituary and that he came here, to Ms. Byron's house, to ask you the same thing we did: Did she leave any other papers behind?"

Dorothy pursed her lips. "Maybe he did, maybe he didn't. Why should I trust you with any information?"

I looked up at her. "A number of people care about what became of Martin and the documents. Homeland Security wants any nuclear secrets Martin may have. They're tracking an old Nazi rocket scientist who used to thumb her nose at the FBI, and they think Martin has secret documents she made off with. The head of Metargon thinks Martin is selling his top-secret code to the Chinese or the Iranians."

Next to me, Alison gave an involuntary cry. This wasn't news to her, just hard to hear in public.

"Ms. Breen and I slipped out of Chicago undetected, at least, I think we did, but I don't know how much time we have before they find the same trail we followed. Goons working for the head of Metargon knocked me out yesterday; they stole a printout of Byron's obituary from my jeans pocket. We may have company before the afternoon is over."

Dorothy looked at the house, as if wondering how little Lily could be protected. My own eyes widened as I followed her gaze—not to the inside of the house, but the frame around the screen door. Inside the carved decorations, I saw tiny camera eyes, identical to those Martin had mounted in the doorway guarding his basement hideaway in Skokie. In the middle of a bunch of grapes was the same minute speaker.

I got to my feet. "Ms. Ferguson, if Martin isn't here now, he's been here, and spent a considerable amount of time here."

"Martin's here?" Alison cried.

She came up the stairs behind me as I opened the screen door. Meg tried to stop her. I moved fast, ducked my head, used my shoulder to hit Meg in the diaphragm. She cried out and her hold on the shotgun slackened. I took it from her.

Alison ran past us into the front room. "Martin! Martin! It's Alison! Where are you?"

Little Lily had been watching television, but she turned to stare at the live drama in the doorway, a finger in her mouth. Meg rubbed her abdomen, her face pinched more in anger than pain: I'd embarrassed her in front of her family.

Dorothy followed us into the house, weariness in the lines of her face. The three of us stood in the entryway, listening to Alison calling Martin's name from the back of the house.

"I'm sorry," I said. "I really need to find him before Cordell Breen's goons do. Will you take me to him?"

"Who is the girl, really?" Dorothy asked.

"Her father owns Metargon, but she's on Martin's side. At least, I hope she is."

"I guess if you're going to break in, show us up for not being strong enough to defend ourselves, I'll have to let you see the house," Dorothy said bitterly.

Meg scowled at her, but didn't speak, just went into the living room to sit next to her little girl on the floor. Dorothy took me on through, showing me the dining room, the kitchen, the two small bedrooms beyond it, as if she were a realtor and I a prospective tenant. The kitchen held a computer monitor connected to the cameras embedded in the front door. I watched a school bus trundle past the house, heading north toward the open prairie.

At a narrow staircase that landed in the dining room, Dorothy told me to go up on my own: her legs didn't like climbing up and down anymore. I smiled sourly: she knew I would find nothing. The climb was payback for disarming her niece. Today my legs didn't really like stairs, either, but I pretended to be detecting things, examining the risers with a magnifying glass while I was still in Dorothy's sightlines.

The room at the top was Lily's: the bed was covered with stuffed animals, the drawers filled with sunsuits and tiny T-shirts. Since I was up here anyway, I pulled down the hatch to the attic crawl space and hoisted myself up, my abdominal muscles protesting mightily, to look at a layer of dusty insulation.

When I was back on the ground floor, Dorothy said, "There's also the basement. Your young woman is down there."

She opened the door and turned on a light, a naked forty-watt bulb that dangled from an old wire, but stayed in the kitchen.

I took a deep breath and started down the stairs. My legs were unsteady and I began to sweat. Not muscle fatigue, but terror. I did not want to be underground again. Everything connected to Martin Binder lay underground, his Skokie bedroom, the secrets buried deep within his grandmother's family, the body in his uncle Julius's basement.

I tried to sing under my breath, but the only song that came to mind was "O terra, addio," when Aida is walled up in the tomb to die. Not helpful. I called to Alison instead.

She met me at the bottom of the stairs, shoulders drooping, tears streaking the dust on her cheeks. "Vic, what made you think Martin was here? I've looked everywhere!"

"The cameras in the front door," I said. "They're the same as the ones in his bedroom door in Skokie. These two women have computers connected to them: they saw us coming. Meg was at the door before we rang the bell." I spoke loudly enough for Dorothy to hear me up in the kitchen. I was a detective, people should know when I was detecting.

"Then where is he?" Alison said. "Has he disappeared from here, too?"

"He has to be here, or at least, there must be some sign of him besides the cameras."

I walked around, testing the walls. This was a real basement, not a root cellar. It even had a couple of small windows, so if Dorothy nailed the door shut we'd be able to scream for help. Although who would hear us?

The usual mechanicals were there, furnace, water heater, a washer and dryer. The floor was made of rough-poured concrete. Since the only lighting was the naked bulb at the top of the stairs and another over the washer, both Alison and I stumbled on the uneven surface.

Dorothy, or perhaps Ada, had put up cheap white shelves that covered the walls next to the washer and dryer. They held gardening tools and enough screwdrivers and pliers for basic repairs, along with the usual detritus of a home: a Christmas tree stand, remnants of a vacuum cleaner, old gym shoes, a moth-eaten bear's head. Perhaps the most unnerving object was an urn on a low shelf labeled "Mother's Ashes."

I lifted the bear's head, but the urn didn't move. I unhooked the latches to the top.

"Vic!" Alison was shocked. "You can't dig through someone's ashes."

I ignored her, inspecting a vase with fine ashes in it. Human remains don't burn down to the kind of neat pile newspapers make. I lifted the vase out. Underneath was a number pad.

"Your turn," I said to Alison. "What numbers would someone like Martin use to control a door?"

"Vic! What—is there a secret door?"

"There's a secret something," I said. "If Martin programmed it, what numbers did he choose?"

"I don't know. He told me that Feynman broke into all the safes in Los Alamos because he knew that physicists love the fine-structure constant, so I don't think—unless—and we don't even know how many digits."

"Try something," I said impatiently. "The fine whatever it is, or pi or anything."

"You usually only get three tries for something like this." She typed slowly, nervous about making a mistake. Nothing happened. She tried again, even more slowly, but still nothing happened.

"Think back to what Martin said when he talked about Feynman breaking into people's safes," I said. "Take your time. Think if he joked about what constant he—"

"Of course!" Alison's face lit up. "Only, I don't know it off the top of my head. Can I turn on my iPhone?"

Another calculated risk. I nodded, and she powered up her device. "Six-six-two, six-oh-seven," she breathed. I typed in the numbers.

We stared at each other in chagrin, feeling we'd run out of chances, when we heard a grinding, scraping noise. I couldn't help imagining the ceiling falling on us, but it was the wall behind the white shelves: it was slowly sliding open while the shelves remained oddly in place.

The room behind the shelves was bigger than the basement we were standing in. The walls were paneled, the floor covered in tile with Navajo rugs scattered around. A bed was set up in an alcove to one side.

Bright lights shone over a long worktable that was covered in metal and wires. A young man with dark wiry hair stood next to the table, holding a screwdriver, gazing nervously at the open door.

When he saw us, his face relaxed.

"Alison. You remembered Planck's constant."

CHICAGO, 1953
In the Workshop

B ENJAMIN, WE MUST SPEAK."
   He's getting out of his car when she appears in the shadows. She can hear the sudden gulp, the intake of air. She may have startled him, but her arrival can't be a surprise. The Memler will have been to him long ahead of her, and someone will have told him of her own disappearance from the proving grounds.

She knows she's not public news: she's read newspapers along her travel route, sometimes heard news on the radio in various bus stations across the Southwest. But she's vanished from a secure weapons facility; the Memler has told the Americans that she's a Russian spy. Unless they imagine she was eaten by a bear, they will be looking for her.

It's taken her a week to get here. The first day, when she climbed down the mountain, she hitchhiked. She figured she had until noon before they realized she was missing and sent out an alarm. She found a ride to Las Vegas, and then went by Greyhound to Albuquerque.

She's been the hare in front of the hounds for most of the last thirteen years, so she's adept at hitching along back roads, or hoisting herself into an open boxcar on a slow-moving freight. Away from the proving grounds she even relaxes at times. No soldiers stopping buses, poking through hay, looking for a Jew on the run. Americans are friendly, by and large, even trusting.

A woman in a small Texas town tells Martina she's known hard times herself, goes into her kitchen for an apple and a sandwich of bread and drippings. The fat on the bread: Sofie Herschel's nursery, the prism on the floor, flashes through Martina's head, makes her momentarily weak: Sofie, the nursery, her mother, her daughter, the light itself have all been stolen from her. The Texas woman gives her sugary iced tea to revive her, takes her into the house to lie down on an old sofa that smells of cats and buttered popcorn.

In St. Louis, she mingles with the crowds at the bus depot, buying a boxed lunch, lingering at the women's toilet, stopping on the benches in the waiting room to pore over an abandoned paper. No one is paying attention. She buys a ticket and finds a seat near the rear exit, wide awake at every stop on the route. The bus rolls into downtown Chicago at nine in the morning.

A nickel in a phone booth gets her the information that Professor Dzornen is in Chicago but is spending the day at the Argonne lab. No, she won't leave a message, she'll call again tomorrow.

She rides a bus from the center of the city to the neighborhood around the University of Chicago where Benjamin Dzornen has bought a house, a mansion, she thinks when she walks over to look at it.

She imagines ringing the bell in the middle of the morning, of seeing Ilse Dzornen's shock giving way to fury: *You were supposed to be dead.*

There's no record of a Martina Saginor's arrival in America: she had found passage to the States on a passport plucked from a purse in a crowded Vienna train station. Martina spent a week in Vienna on her long route from Moldova to America. She hoped her daughter might have returned looking for her. None of the refugee aid societies had any trace of Käthe Saginor, in England or in Austria. Vienna was in ruins, bleak, hunger-filled, mother, aunts, cousins, all dead, nothing to keep Martina, and so she continued west, found a way to get passage on a ship in Lisbon bound for Montreal, slipped across the border to America, to Chicago, to Nevada. How adept she's become at crossing borders.

She's sure Benjamin never told Ilse about her arrival fifteen months ago, how stunned he was. His shocked face, his stammer: you survived, anyway, that's good.

Yes, I survived, by luck first: our train to Sobibor Concentration Camp broke down, we were herded off in the snow, many shot, but the snow was falling thick. I fled to the woods and survived somehow, with partisans, with farmers, until the war's end found me in Moldova and then detention in paranoid Stalin's camps and finally the long foot journey across the mountains back to Austria.

What did she want? he asked. *My life, my physics, a job, a real job,* but he bundled her off to Nevada. So quickly that she was on a train with a security pass before she had spent a night in Chicago. His hollow promise that this was temporary while he found a real place for her.

She'd gone to the university that first time, not to his house. What had she been hoping for? News of Käthe, for sure, but some sign, perhaps a ghostly remnant of his affection for Martina herself that might cause him to sponsor her. None of that remained.

He'd shown no interest in whether Käthe survived the war or not. Perhaps it was guilt for doing so little to help the child. Käthe had been a sullen little girl, using no arts to attract him on the days Martina took her to the Institute. He didn't want to bring Käthe when he left for America, although Martina pleaded for her child. He apparently hadn't wanted Martina, either, his brightest student, his ablest colleague as he'd once called her. Had it been Ilse who slammed the door on them, or his own fears or indifference?

Tonight her business is just that: business. She speaks to Benjamin in German; it's easier, she doesn't have to organize and reorganize sentences in her head.

"The Memler surely told you she saw me. You must have been expecting me."

"You can't speak to me here," he hisses at her in English.

"I will speak to you anywhere," she says coldly, still in German.

"Do you wish to take me inside? Do you want a moment to call the FBI? Do you know what the Memler did at Innsbruck? Does it matter to you that people were dangled in cages above smelting ovens, that she watched, smiling, while prisoners roasted to death? Or that she had prisoners put in chambers filled with nitrogen to see how they would burst apart? I saw her more than once laughing at the spectacle of a naked prisoner in shackles being raped and then beaten to death. Men as well as women."

He tries to stop the flow of words but she won't be quiet.

"And now I find her here, with unfettered access to planes and money, working on a computer whose designs she stole, and I am told that I must not grieve for the past but commend her for being a warrior against Communism. Listen to me, *du*, I have been in Nazi camps and in Communist camps, and one is not different from the other, except that in the Soviet Union no one tried on purpose to murder me."

Ilse comes to the front door. "Benjamin! Is that you? Is someone with you? Julius and I ate dinner two hours ago. Everything is cold now."

"Yes, I know, I'm sorry. We ran late at Argonne," he shouts back. "I'm just finishing a conversation. I'll be in right away."

He turns back to Martina. "What is it you want?"

"I want the rights to my computing machine. I want the Memler denounced as a war criminal and sent to prison or even executed. I want a place in a top lab. I want my daughter. I want American citizenship. My wants are enormous, Benjamin, and I will find a way to satisfy them. I only start with you, I don't end with you."

Ilse is still in the doorway, her body a square silhouette, Brünnhilde, ready to slaughter those who wound her, even her own husband. She calls again to Benjamin, who fumbles in his wallet.

"Do you have money?" he whispers to Martina. "Go to the Shore Drive Motel; it's only a few blocks away. I'll call you there."

"I no longer sit in apartments or hotel rooms waiting for policemen to arrive so that I can be led to the next deportation station. We talk now, you and I, or not at all. Believe me, my next conversations will be with Edward Murrow and Walter Cronkite. Even if you and my department head in Nevada have no interest in the Memler's war crimes, I believe Mr. Murrow will pay the story some attention."

Ilse starts down the front steps. "Who is it who's talking to you, Benjamin? Is it a beggar? Shall I call the police?"

A youth appears behind her in the doorway. "Who is it, Mama?"

Dzornen thrusts Martina into the backseat of the car, calling to his wife and son, "It's someone from Nevada with an urgent message. I'm driving her over to Breen's house. I'll be back in half an hour."

He climbs into the car, slamming the door shut to signal his fury. "You cannot blackmail me over your child. You never came to me during your pregnancy; for all I know, any man in Göttingen could be your child's father."

"Oh, that is beside any point," Martina says. "I am not here tonight because of my daughter, but because of this Memler monster stealing my machine and giving it to your friend Edward Breen. He has built it and claimed it for his own, and you, you are using it to build a heinous weapon that can kill every mother's child on this planet. I can control nothing in this world, or very little, so I cannot stop you prostituting yourself for money or power or whatever it is you get from prancing around with men like Edward Teller. But I can stop the Memler from making one more schilling's profit off my back. That I will do."

Breen lives only four blocks away; the rest of the short ride is spent in silence. When Benjamin pulls the car over to the curb, he asks Martina what she proposes to say to Breen.

"I will introduce myself. I will see what sort of a man he is."

The lights are on in the big house on University Avenue. Benjamin rings the front doorbell. A brief wait, then Breen's son Cordell, named for the Secretary of State for whom Breen once worked, opens the door for them. Cordell knows Professor Dzornen, and tells him his father is in the coach house, which contains his private workshop. Cordell looks curiously at Martina, whose corduroy trousers and hiking boots are stained with travel, but he sends her and Benjamin up the flagstone path to the coach house.

In the workshop, any idea of a polite introduction, a conversation about who Breen is and does he know he created a machine from a stolen design, dies before it is born: Gertrud Memler is in the room.

"The Nazi swine is digging up other people's acorns?" Martina says to her in German.

Color floods Memler's face. "You were dreck in Germany and now you are dreck in America. The FBI will be glad to know you have shown your ugly Jewish face."

"The FBI will be glad to hear how you tortured ugly Jewish faces," Martina says. "They will also like to hear how you stole my equations and my designs in the middle of your bestiality." She fingers her face; a scar from Memler's last assault on her runs across her left cheekbone.

"Oh, *your* equations, *your* designs, as if Fermi wrote equations for you alone that no one else in the world was clever enough to understand."

Martina gives a tight smile and says to Breen in English, "Tell me how you realized the electronic Fermi surfaces were the key to using hysteresis in constructing a ferromagnetic core."

Breen shakes his head. "My designs and my formulas are patented; I don't share them with strangers."

"Forgive me." Martina bows slightly. "I am Martina Saginor, doctor of philosophy from Göttingen, 1931, working on ferromagnetic properties in crystalline lattices. Professor Dzornen supervised my research. The Memler woman became my own student three years later. She then became my warden when I was a slave labor physicist near Innsbruck. The designs she stole while I was her prisoner are perhaps what you used to build your Metargon-I. I will know as soon as I see your blueprints."

"So you can claim them for your own?" Breen says, contemptuous.

"I wasn't born yesterday. Anyone can pretend to have made a design once an engineer produces a working model. That's why we have patent laws in this country."

He turns to Memler. "Is this the woman you said would come here to blackmail me?"

"The patent laws in your country, yes, I know about them," Martina says. "That is why I applied for American patents to my initial lattice designs in 1939. When the patent office produces my application, we can compare my drawing to the sketch the Memler stole from me, and to the sketches you made of your own work. We can watch the thief try to wriggle out of this little spiderweb she wove for herself."

"Dr. Memler has been most helpful in supplying suggestions for my design," Breen says, "but all the initial ideas and work were my own."

"Edward!" Memler's eyes flash. "That is not—that isn't—you know I only gave them to you because I couldn't get funding myself."

"You have American citizenship," Breen says calmly. "You were well rewarded. The patents are in my name."

There is a moment's silence in the coach house. Memler suddenly picks up a chisel and lunges at Martina.

"I should have had the guards kill you in 1942," she screams. "I wanted to see you hang over a furnace, watch you roast, but they put you on the train instead."

Benjamin, who's been standing silent, grabs at Memler but can't stop her. Martina darts behind a bench and Memler follows her, knocking over vacuum tubes, retorts, burners. Benjamin tries to wrestle with Memler, Breen tries to protect his equipment. Wires and chisels and arms and legs all tangle together.

Breen's old sidearm, the Colt he carried as an officer in Europe, is on a shelf. They all see it at the same time.

49

ISAAC NEWTON'S *OPTICKS*

Y OU SAW THE BREENIAC SKETCH at Alison's barbecue," I said. "We know that, but we don't know what you did between that and going to your mother's house three weeks ago."

We were sitting at the worktable, trying to put the different pieces of the story together. Dorothy was with us: she'd come down the stairs when she realized we'd unlocked the secret entrance.

She nodded sourly when she saw Martin standing a few feet from Alison. The two had run to meet each other, and then stopped, as if both realized the size of the obstacles between them.

Dorothy shouted upstairs to Meg that Martin was okay, and would Meg bring down tea. Meg carried down a pot of hot water, mugs and a bowl with teabags in it, but stomped back up the stairs. She was not going to fraternize with a person who disarmed her, no matter what her aunt chose to do.

"I was doing research," Martin answered me. "I knew I'd seen the design, you know, the triangles at the bottom of the drawing, before. They're Newton's prisms, of course, but besides that."

"Of course," I said dryly. "What fool doesn't recognize Newton's prisms?"

"Me," Alison said. "I saw those my whole life and never thought of Newton. Why did you, Martin?"

"His experiment with prisms is the first thing you look at when you start thinking about light." He spoke matter-of-factly, as if the whole world thought about light the way he did. "I knew I'd seen them drawn like that someplace else. As the party went on and this one guy, Tad, got drunker and more annoying, it came back to me, that they were on some of the papers my mother had, uh, well, stolen from my grandmother. It didn't add up for me. I knew there had to be a connection between the BREENIAC and my family, but I couldn't figure out what."

"Is that when you went to see Benjamin Dzornen's children?" I asked.

"Yes, but they wouldn't talk to me." His mouth bunched in remembered annoyance. "See, I was wondering if it was Benjamin Dzornen who had drawn the prisms on the BREENIAC document. I knew he'd worked with Edward Breen on the hydrogen bomb, and it was possible that he'd given the sketch to Edward.

"My gramma always claimed she was Benjamin Dzornen's daughter, so I wondered if Dzornen had left her some of his papers in his will, you know, as a kind of proof that he was her father. But when I tried to explain this to Julius Dzornen and his sister, they both slammed the door on me."

His tone of bewildered indignation made him seem younger and more accessible than he'd appeared at first.

"They thought you wanted money," I said.

"Money?" He was indignant.

"Sorry, but your mom had put the bite on them more than once."

He closed his eyes, an involuntary reflex to pain. "Of course," he said, his voice bitter. "Of course, she would have. She always claimed that Herta Dzornen had stolen money from her. I should have put those twos together."

I cocked my head, thinking I heard footsteps. It was only Lily, the little girl, looking for her aunt Dorothy. She climbed up in the older woman's lap, clutching the stuffed lion Alison had picked up from the front steps.

I looked at a monitor on the workbench, which was also connected to Martin's door cams. I worried about lingering here: I worried that someone from Metargon or Homeland Security had seen our location when Alison turned on her iPhone. I wondered, too, whether Breen's goons had shown him Ada Byron's obituary.

"Did you talk to my dad before you disappeared?" Alison asked in a small voice.

"I talked to Jari Liu, and he told your dad, I guess, because your dad called me from Stockholm. I was trying to get more information on the history of the Metargon-I. You probably know this, but after the war, your granddad was part of this thing called Operation Paperclip. They brought Nazi rocket and bomb experts over to the U.S., even some who'd committed terrible torture. One of the people Edward kind of whitewashed was this Nazi named Gertrud Memler, who'd been a student of Martina's.

"I was trying to find what the connection was between, well, your family and mine, through Memler's history. I got her file through the Freedom of Information Act, but there wasn't much in it, and she'd completely dropped out of sight after 1953, except for these letters to different magazines she'd sometimes fire off. Memler worked with your grandfather on setting up Metargon-I at the Nevada Proving Grounds when they were just starting to test hydrogen bombs."

"My grandfather was not a Nazi collaborator!" Alison cried.

"I'm not saying he was," Martin said quickly. "It was the Cold War; everyone was cutting corners. Anyway, I did a patent search to see what patents had been issued to Dzornen, and none of them connected to the BREENIAC, at least not to that first model they used in Nevada. I looked for Memler and Saginor, and here's where it got weird. The index said that a patent had been issued to Martina Saginor in 1941, but the database didn't show it. I wrote the patent office, but when they digitized all the pre-1970 patents, they threw out all the paper files, so they didn't have any way of locating a file. If it's not online, it's like it didn't exist."

"So you don't know what the patent was for?"

He shook his head. "But I keep thinking it must be something like that drawing that's on Alison's dad's wall."

"If that's Martina's work, how did Edward Breen get hold of it?" I asked.

Martin shook his head. "I don't know."

"My grandfather didn't steal the design," Alison said, her voice quivering on the brink of tears. "He was a brilliant engineer! The BREENIAC was a masterpiece; every history of computers describes it as more elegant than von Neumann's machine, and ahead of its time. Don't talk about my family as if we were a group of crooks!"

Martin glanced at her stormy face and turned his attention to his tea, turning the cup round and round in his hands.

"I'm sorry, Alison," he mumbled. "It's not a crime to collaborate with someone on a project as big as a new computer design. Steve Jobs didn't think up the Macintosh all by himself, either."

"Why did you go dark?" I asked, when Alison didn't say anything.

"That was after I talked to Mr. Breen. I guess Jari talked to Mr. Breen and Mr. Breen called me. He was in Stockholm, at Metargon's Swedish plant, and he made me kind of, well, nervous."

"Did he threaten you?" I asked.

"Not in so many words." His glance flickered at Alison, sitting very still; he turned back to the tea as if it held the secret of dark matter. "He told me I didn't know how big a mistake I could be making if I didn't leave these matters strictly alone. 'That patent expired in 1970,' he said, 'so don't go imagining there's money to be made from it.' Then he went on about national security, nuclear secrets and staying the hell away from Alison, from his daughter.

"I couldn't tell if he thought I was hoping to get Alison to support me, or if he thought I was going to uncover something shameful from the U.S. bomb program, but he said if I meddled in things that were none of my business he'd know and he'd take appropriate action. He reminded me how easy it was for Metargon to track people. I worked on some of those programs, so I knew he could find me anywhere I left an electronic—not even footprint—toenail fragment."

"I can't listen to you talk like this," Alison burst out, getting up from her chair.

"I'm not saying this to hurt you," Martin cried.

Alison made a gesture of frustration and ran up the stairs.

"You're talking about her father," I tried to explain. "Girls hold their daddies sacred. She doesn't want to believe you, even though she knows it's true."

Martin looked toward the stairs again, but said, "When Mr. Breen hung up, I knew I had to figure out some way of proving that all I cared about was where the first idea for the BREENIAC came from. I mean, nobody could build a computer from that sketch on his workshop wall—it was the central concept, but miles away from workable memory. I knew, though, if I was going to do research, I couldn't do it online. Even if I created a separate online identity, Metargon could tell if I was mining data that was relevant to the BREENIAC or Edward Breen or any of the people involved in the hydrogen bomb.

"I went down to my mom's place. I was hoping she still had these papers she'd taken from my gramma's dresser, and I found them. One of them was this letter from Ada Byron, saying that Martina Saginor had applied for a U.S. patent for ferromagnetic memory back before America entered the war, and the person who found the patent could prove that Martina had created the design for the Metargon-I.

"As soon as I saw Ada Byron's name, I knew I had this huge clue, because of who she was, in computer history, I mean. So I figured it was a cover name. I went back to Chicago and looked her up in the public library. One of the reference librarians did some work for me; she found Byron's name listed in the catalog of Dzornen papers."

"So you went to the University of Chicago and stole the second page of the letter she wrote Benjamin Dzornen when he was dying?" I said.

He flushed. "I'll give it back. I thought if someone, I don't know, like Jari Liu, followed the same trail I did, he'd get to the letter—the second page had this address here in Tinney on it. So I came here and passed the tests that Martina left. Then, when Dorothy let me into the workshop, well, then I realized that Ada was really Martina. At first I couldn't believe it, but the more time I spent down here, the more real it became."

"How did you figure it out?" I asked.

He grinned suddenly. "It wasn't hard: she wrote her name in all her workbooks. I thought—I don't know what I thought, that it was really Gertrud Memler pretending to be Martina, or—I didn't know. But Martina made a list of all the publications she'd produced back in the 1930s, when she was in Vienna. She wrote out the steps she went through in solving some of the problems, and she said—"

He broke off to pick up an old notebook and flipped through the pages. "See, she wrote it in German and in English: 'I am putting down all these steps so that anyone can see that it is I, Martina Saginor, who made these discoveries.' And then, she had the prisms at the beginning and end of all her workbooks. Plus, she had copies of the letters she'd written under Gertrud Memler's name."

"So those letters really came from Martina," I said. "Not a Nazi getting a conscience after seeing the horrors of nuclear weapons. But why did she keep quiet all those years? Why not be in touch with Kitty—with your grandmother—and your mother? Did she come over before the war? Were all the records of her having been in Terezín and Sobibor false?"

Martin shook his head, his thin face troubled. "I don't know any of that. If she left a personal journal, it's one of these German notebooks."

He picked up another old school exercise book and showed us the faded German script. "Her notebooks in English were only about physics. Even at the end of her life, she stayed current with physics; she was thinking about problems in dark matter and supersymmetry. She had a telescope, she kept a star journal; she tried to work on gamma ray bursts."

Dorothy nodded and spoke for the first time since we'd found the hidden workshop. "She used to invite me out here to look through her telescope—she kept it on that platform outside. She never told me she was really an Austrian scientist, although I could tell she had a bit of an accent.

"Learning who she really was explained something to me. Ada— Martina, I should say, but I knew her as Ada for fifty years—Ada knew more science than I did, with my master's in chemistry, but she claimed she never went to college. She'd give talks on physics and astronomy over at the high school; she'd let the kids come out and look through her scope, tell them about black holes, make it all come alive for them. She used to tutor the college kids in physics, help them with their problem sets, that kind of thing.

"In my early days here, I pushed her to get a degree and try for a job at a big school, but she said she liked small-town life, she liked the slow pace, not having to be competitive or look over her shoulder. I finally let it rest."

"I wanna see the telescope," Lily said.

Dorothy laughed. "You can, sugarplum, it's over at the library for you and any little girl in Tinney to look through."

I wondered about the skeleton I'd found yesterday. If Martina hid from the FBI under a double identity, as Ada Byron, or sometimes as Gertrud Memler, was that the real Memler, buried in Edward Breen's old basement? Who had killed her? Who had buried her?

"How did you know to let Martin into the workshop?" I asked Dorothy.

Dorothy gave a bark of a laugh. "Ada said if someone claimed to be from Martina's family and claimed to know physics, see if they could solve a problem set. Like a prince in an old fairy tale, pulling the sword out of the rock, Martin worked the problems in the first few days after he got here.

"When I saw those problems, after the lawyer gave me all the documents Ada left behind for me, they took me a month and I still couldn't solve them very elegantly. Ada included a couple of different answer guides and Martin worked out two problems according to what Ada called the best solution; his other three solutions were clumsier but still—he got them in three days! And he knew the Saginor family history; he knew that his grandmother was Martina's daughter."

"What are you doing here in the workshop?" I asked Martin. "Hoping to find information on the patent?"

"I'm trying to rebuild the BREENIAC from Martina's notes, sticking to what she dated from before 1953. I thought if I could prove that Martina designed the first magnetic memory, Mr. Breen would have to stop threatening me. Martina used a special gauge of wire that I don't think Edward Breen had thought of, so Martina created a more reliable current than he designed, but I can't quite get it to work."

It seemed ludicrous to me, completely practical yet utterly impractical, like filling a garage with dry ice to freeze a model rocket. "You need to abandon it for now," I said. "It's only a matter of time before Cordell Breen or Homeland Security gallop up to Dorothy's door; we don't want to be sitting ducks for them. Why don't you gather up the most important of her papers and your notes; we'll get them into safekeeping in Chicago."

"We'll go over to my bank in Tinney right now," Dorothy said. "We can rent a safe-deposit box there. Better than putting them at risk by driving all over Illinois with them."

Martin tried to protest. "I'm so close, and really, I'm safe down here. It was only Alison remembering my saying I'd use Planck's constant instead of the fine structure that opened the secret door for you."

I shook my head. "Metargon and Homeland Security, whoever gets here first, have such sophisticated electronic spyware, they'll break the code in a second. Or Metargon's goons will simply take an ax to the wall. You'd be trapped in here."

Martin's jaw jutted in obstinacy, when Alison appeared on the stairs. "Martin! Vic! You need to come up! There's a story on TV about Julius Dzornen and a dead woman!"

50

MALWARE

WHEN WE GOT to the front room, the station had gone to commercials. We watched a woman extol the virtues of a new drinkable yogurt, followed by a man driving an SUV through the La Brea tar pits.

Beth Blacksin, one of Global Entertainment's news anchors, finally appeared. "Today's top story is the dramatic discovery of a skeleton that's been buried underneath the kitchen of a Hyde Park home for at least fifty years, and perhaps longer."

She was standing in the cellar where I'd been entombed yesterday, gesturing to the hole in the floor where police had dug up the skeleton. I wanted to be outside, breathing real air, but I forced myself to stand next to Alison and watch the screen.

"What makes this story both more tragic and more important is that this coach house was the site of Edward Breen's original workshop," Blacksin was saying. "Breen, whose revolutionary computer design led to the creation of the world-famous Metargon company, allowed Julius Dzornen to live here after the Breen family moved to Lake Forest.

"In a statement today, Edward Breen's son, current Metargon CEO Cordell Breen, said he was shocked that Julius Dzornen had taken advantage of the family's generosity by murdering a woman and burying her underneath the kitchen."

Meg took Lily to the kitchen. "She's only four; she doesn't need murder and what-all in her life yet."

The scene switched to Metargon's headquarters. Breen spoke from his office, the Rothko painting in the background.

"This discovery is a shock to all of us in the Metargon family." Breen's mellow baritone was appropriately solemn. "Julius Dzornen's father, Benjamin, collaborated closely with my own father to design America's nuclear arsenal. When Julius and I were boys together, everyone thought he would become a scientific giant like his father. Instead, he became depressed and reclusive and dropped out of school.

"Julius often spoke of having committed a terrible crime, but I always assumed he was referring to squandering his scientific gifts. I can't begin to fathom what made him commit such a heinous murder, but he came to see me on Tuesday night, speaking as if he wanted to confess. In the end, he didn't reveal his horrible secret, but it was after leaving my house that he drove his car into a ravine on Sheridan Road."

That was all Breen had to say. After Breen's speech, Murray Ryerson appeared outside Metargon's headquarters.

"Police currently have no clues as to the woman's identity," Murray said, "but a button found with the body was given to Chicago Fashion Institute historian Eva Kuhn. Kuhn says it's from a Dior suit cut in 1952, so the dead woman was possibly murdered in '52 or 1953. Police are anxious to talk to Chicago investigator V. I. Warshawski, who discovered the skeleton yesterday, but has since disappeared. This is Murray Ryerson, live in Northbrook."

Murray was replaced by a couple of men waist-high in cranberries. Dorothy muted the sound.

My skin turned cold. Cordell Breen had pulled off a very neat stunt. He'd landed Julius with sole responsibility for the dead woman. There was no way to refute him, since Julius was dead. My assumption, that the Breens installed Julius in the coach house to avoid anyone finding the body, was only an assumption, after all.

Alison was jubilant. "See! My father didn't have anything to do with Julius Dzornen's death. Durdon wasn't tampering with his brakes. I shouldn't have listened to you, Vic, you've been making me scared of my own father."

"Alison, Rory Durdon tried to murder me yesterday." I was close to screaming in frustration.

Alison's eyes were bright, as if the effort to live in denial was making her feverish. "Dad sent him down to the coach house to see if Julius Dzornen had taken our sketch. Maybe he overreacted to seeing you there, but that doesn't mean my father—"

"Dorothy!" It was Meg, calling from the kitchen. "An SUV just pulled up out front. I'm taking Lily over to Gracie's, see if her mama will let us watch *Clifford* with her."

Dorothy said to us, "Go back to the workshop and shut yourselves in. If these men mean trouble, stay in there until I give you an all-clear."

Martin and I moved quickly back to the basement, but Alison lingered, peering at the street through a crack in the living room curtains. The switch to close the secret entrance was under the worktable. Martin had his finger on it, but waited in a sweaty silence, hoping Alison would come. At the last minute, as the men began hammering on the front door, she ran down the basement steps to join us.

Martin pressed the switch. We watched the sides of the wall slowly move. The edges came together with a series of bumps, and then a click locked them into place.

I turned to the monitor on the worktable and saw that the men on the porch were Moe and Curly. "Homeland Security," I muttered.

"See?" Alison hissed. "My father is not tracking you!"

I was trying not to panic, but I didn't think I could take being sealed in a basement two days in a row. "Martin, is there another way out?"

"At that far wall, under Martina's telescope platform."

Through the mike Martin had embedded in the front door, we heard Dorothy's gruff voice, demanding to know the men's business.

We watched Moe and Curly whip out their federal credentials. Dorothy said they could talk to her from the front porch, she didn't let strange men into her house no matter how many badges they flashed at her.

"That Mustang parked out front belongs to a woman who is wanted by the Chicago police, and we have reason to believe you're harboring another fugitive," Moe said.

"We can open this door without any trouble," Curly put in. "We're giving you a chance to cooperate in an investigation that involves our national security."

"You watch too many cop shows, young man, if you think that kind of talk impresses me."

While they were talking, I saw another car pull up behind the SUV. We couldn't see the driver as he got out of the car, but we watched him bend over to pull a large, oddly shaped bundle out of the backseat. As he came up the walk, I thought at first he was carrying a mannequin, but when he got closer to the house I could see he was holding a woman, a skinny scarecrow of a woman with wild graying curls, her bare legs little more than flesh-covered sticks.

"That's my mother!" Martin was shocked. "What—how—?"

"With Durdon?" Alison whispered.

Their arrival was also a surprise to Moe and Curly, who stopped haranguing Dorothy to look at them.

"Who the hell—oh. It's the guy from Metargon," Curly said. "What are you doing here?"

Durdon set Judy down on the stairs, where she fell against the stair rail. "We've come for the kid and the documents."

"This is a federal investigation into a matter that may involve international terrorism," Moe said.

"Yeah, we know. It was Mr. Breen who told you we might have a rogue programmer selling defense secrets overseas," Durdon said. "We've kept an eye on your investigation. I followed you out here to bring back the proprietary secrets the Binder punk stole from Metargon."

"Who's the skeleton?" Moe pointed a toe in Judy's direction.

Durdon flashed an ugly smile. "Our boy genius's mother. We'll let her go if he turns himself in." He elbowed past the federal agents to face Dorothy through the screen door. "You want to go give young Binder that message? We know you've got him here."

"You don't know much, then, do you? You got what looks like a real sick lady with you. She needs to be with a doctor; we'll call an ambulance for her."

Durdon pulled on the screen door so hard he yanked it from its hinges. We heard a loud cry from Dorothy, and a thud, as if she'd fallen, but we lost sight of the men once they moved through the door and out of the camera's eye. Moe ordered Curly to keep Dorothy from calling for help, but then moved out of mike range. We could hear feet pounding overhead, Durdon and a Homeland guy ripping their way through the small house.

Martin started to push the button to release the workshop entrance but I pulled his arm away. "I'll take care of your mother. You have one chance to get yourself and Alison away; go, now, before they find this room!"

I ran to the back wall where I saw a staircase tucked into the ceiling. I tugged on a handle. The stairs came down with a great screeching. A pot filled with geraniums also came down, almost hitting my head: the stairs acted as a trapdoor up to the platform.

I thrust the Mustang keys into Martin's hand and dragged him to the stairs. "Get out of here now! Alison Breen, show some steel. Get to your feet, get going. Martin needs your help to find his way out of Tinney. I'll get Judy to a hospital."

Someone began pounding on the workshop's outer wall. A gunshot sounded and then another. The wall shook, but didn't open.

"Just go!" I screamed.

"My machine, Martina's designs!" Martin cried. He darted around me and scooped up an armful of journals. With his other hand, he grabbed Alison and dragged her to the ladder.

I watched them disappear through the opening, heard their feet on the wood planks. A moment later I heard shouts but couldn't make out voices or words. I had my gun out of my holster and was on my way up after Alison and Martin when Moe's face appeared in the trapdoor.

"We're coming down. You stay where you are."

"Let him down." It was Dorothy, her voice barely recognizable. "They found Lily, they've got Lily."

51

POWER DOWN

I **BACKED AWAY** from the stairs, tucking my gun into my waistband, hoping Moe hadn't seen it. He lowered himself into the room, grunting slightly.

"Open that door!" he barked, gesturing at the far wall with his gun.

"Why?" I said. "You're already in here."

"You don't have your dog, you don't have your lawyer or your interfering neighbor to protect you, and we have the little girl and the junkie mom. I think you'll do what we want."

"Whose side are you on, anyway?" I demanded. "Are you freelancing for Metargon, or is terrorizing the citizenry part of your—"

He hit me across the mouth with the flat of his gun. My mouth filled with blood. When I spat it at him, one of my front teeth felt loose. I caught his arm and wrenched it down. His gun came out and skidded across the floor. I beat him to the gun, but Durdon had reached the bottom of the stairs. He was carrying Lily. The little girl was screaming. The pink ribbons had come out of her pigtails and her face was streaked with dirt.

"Drop the gun, Warshawski," Durdon ordered.

I dropped the gun.

"And that one stuck into the back of your pants."

I dropped the Smith & Wesson.

"You were lucky yesterday, weren't you," Durdon added, his tone contemptuous, "but Mr. Breen wasn't impressed. If you thought you were smart enough to outwit him, it proves how stupid you really are."

I was stupid, no question about it. I shouldn't have left the Mustang out on the road, for one thing. And I should have gotten Martin and Alison away from Tallgrass Drive at once, instead of lingering to talk.

"Where's your pal Deputy Davilats?" I asked.

"I don't need him, not when I've got federal agents to back me up."

Alison and Martin were climbing down the stair ladder, Dorothy and Meg slowly following. Curly brought up the rear, covering the group with an ugly snub-nosed twenty-two.

Durdon planted Lily on the floor, hard. She was still crying, no longer the shrieks of terror, but the heartbreaking moans of desolation.

"We were heading for your car, but they threatened to shoot my mom," Martin said, his voice dead. His hands were empty. At first I thought he'd dropped the papers, but then I saw Curly was holding them.

"You!" Durdon turned to Dorothy. "Get the brat to shut up."

He pushed Lily toward Dorothy, who carried the little girl to the daybed that stood against a side wall. She sat the child down, cuddling her, smoothing her hair with thick arthritic fingers.

Meg was so distraught that she hadn't registered what had happened to her child. She called Lily's name, looking around in distress until she saw her daughter with Dorothy. She stumbled over to the daybed and sat next to them, taking the child into her own lap and folding her into her chest.

"Why did you let these men come here?" Meg demanded of me.

I had no answer, only remorse, which was useless right now.

"Durdon, why are you doing this?" Alison asked. "Doesn't Dad pay you enough?"

He looked at her in astonishment. "I'm doing this *for* your father. I'm helping him protect Metargon. That's why we involved Homeland Security in the first place, to make sure our assets aren't compromised."

"But not like this," she protested. "I know Dad wouldn't order you to do this, scare little children, beat up people. He'll be terribly upset when I tell him."

"Your father knows he can count on me to do whatever is necessary for Metargon's long-term security," Durdon said. "What I don't know is whether he can count on *you* to do the same."

"I don't believe Dad wants anyone to hurt people to keep Metargon safe," Alison said. "Martin's grandmother—that wasn't you, was it? Why would an old lady need to die?"

"Metargon's secrets are proprietary. Some are vital for America's nuclear safety. The old lady was keeping us from getting back documents that were essential for our survival," Durdon said.

Alison's hand went up to her mouth, an involuntary gesture of revulsion.

"I guess that's the logical outcome of the Supremes deciding that corporations are people," I said. "You start to feel the same fealty to the corp that medieval people attached to their kings. Does Cordell Breen share your devotion?"

"Huh?" Durdon glared at me.

"You know," I said. "Does Metargon come first with him? Would he be delighted to know you were holding his daughter at gunpoint?"

"If Alison paid attention to Metargon the way her father wants her to, this never would have happened. She brought all this on herself."

I kept up a meaningless patter, hoping to distract the three men while I looked for escape routes. I glanced at the monitor on the worktable. The camera feed was still on, but I couldn't see Judy Binder.

"What did you do with Martin's mother?" I asked.

"The junkie?" Durdon said. "She's a lost cause. Mr. Breen told me to grab her from the hospital; he figured even though she's a meth head, the Binder kid wouldn't want to see her hurt, but the bitch can hardly walk. We dumped her in the kitchen once we had Binder and Alison under control."

"Is she still alive?" I was eyeing the ferromagnetic device Martin had been building. Could the loose wires dangling from the grid be used as a weapon?

"What difference does it make? Where did you put that drawing you stole from us? We busted open your safe and looked through all your papers. We searched your apartment this morning. What did you do with it?"

"It's like Mick Jagger keeps on saying, Durdon: You can't always get what you want." I kept my voice light, but I was frightened, worried about Mr. Contreras. I didn't ask if he'd tried to stop them. If I showed my fear, Durdon would add him to their list of potential hostages.

"The drawing?" Alison repeated numbly. "Are you saying—Vic—did you steal the BREENIAC sketch? I thought Tuesday was the first time you were in the workshop."

"It was. But Deputy Davilats planted it in Julius Dzornen's house on Wednesday morning after he murdered Julius. I found it in the coach house Wednesday afternoon. Your father blamed the theft on Julius so it would seem as though Julius had harbored a grudge against your grandfather all these years."

"That isn't true—it can't be true!" Alison cried. "The sketch has been on the wall ever since I can remember. Anyone who visited us could see it. Mr. Dzornen must have stolen it himself."

I shook my head. "No, sweetie, it didn't happen like that. Edward liked to hang it over his desk, to gloat about how he'd pulled a fast one by stealing the design and claiming it for his own. Cordell inherited the sketch and the gloat. It was when Martin recognized Newton's prisms and knew he'd seen them before that your dad became alarmed. He knew he had to get any other papers Martina left behind before Martin made them public. Cordell used his contacts in the Department of Defense to get Homeland Security involved."

"We have a mission to safeguard our country's nuclear secrets," Curly growled. "Whatever crap you're spouting is beside the point."

"Yeah, I know," I said wearily. "National security, blah blah. Do you know, do you care, that Cordell Breen made you an accessory to murder? He sent Durdon down to Palfry to work with a bent cop to steal the papers from Ricky Schlafly. Schlafly was not one of nature's princes, but he didn't deserve to have his eyes eaten out by crows."

"He didn't cooperate!" Durdon said. "And you won't, either. You should have kept your Polish nose out of our business."

"I should have had a keener Polish nose," I said. "I should have recognized you right away when you picked up Mr. Contreras and me Tuesday night. That bruise on your face—that was when I whacked you with my gun in the parking lot down in Palfry. When you were breaking into my car to steal the documents Deputy Davilats told you I'd found."

Alison's legs gave way. She grabbed at the edge of the worktable but ended up on the floor. When Martin went to her side, Moe pointed a gun at him, but decided Martin wasn't going to do anything rash.

"Yeah, it's a nice story," Durdon said. "It doesn't matter what you say or think since you won't have anyone to say it to before too long."

I continued as if he hadn't spoken. "The patent for the Metargon-I expired decades ago, so it's not as though Metargon would lose their rights to the design, but the company could lose a lot of face. Knowing Edward stole the BREENIAC design would make people question products coming to market today. They'd look at things like the Metar-Genie and think it was flawed because Metargon didn't really know how to design computers. The share price could sink, the Defense Department would start to look for someone else to design Princess Fitora."

"You talk too much," Durdon said. "Tell me where you put the BREENIAC drawing, or I'll shoot the little girl."

Meg screamed and lay on top of Lily, who started howling again at her mother's terror.

"It's in the University of Chicago Library," I said quickly. "I put it in an envelope inside a book I returned there yesterday."

Durdon looked at me suspiciously. How could he be certain I was telling the truth?

"What book?" he demanded.

"*Secret Diary of a Cold War Conscientious Objector.*" It was the first title that came into my head.

"She can't open her mouth without lying," Curly said. "Maybe it's in these papers here. Go through 'em before we burn them."

"Don't burn them!" Martin begged. "They're irreplaceable, they're Martina Saginor's work."

"You'll be in a federal prison for stealing national defense secrets, so I don't think you'll have to worry about them," Curly said, not really paying attention to him. He was sifting the papers he'd taken from Martin, dropping them on the floor as he finished with them.

"Mr. Breen needs to look at these," Durdon announced. "He wants to see any other patents that might have been filed around the same time as the one for our first Metargon computer."

"We need a box to carry all this crap," Moe said to Dorothy. "Where do you keep them?"

"They're in the basement," Dorothy said in a dull voice. "On the other side of the wall."

"Show us how to open the door," Moe ordered her.

"You shot out the electric release," Dorothy said in the same heavy voice. "I tried to tell you when you started to shoot it that it has a dead man's switch. The panels lock into place if someone tries to break in."

"You can go around via the stair ladder." I nodded my head toward the exit up to Martina's observatory.

"Someone should have taught you to shut up when you were still young enough to learn," Durdon said. He swung a fist at me again, but I ducked under it and rolled out of the way. "You, old lady, you live here, you have to know another way to get the panel open."

Dorothy looked from his gun to Lily. "There's a button under the table. I don't know if it will still work, though."

"You." Durdon pointed the gun at me. "Do something useful for a change. Push the switch."

I crouched down under the table to look for the button Martin had been going to push. If there hadn't been so many people to look out for, if one of them hadn't been a terrified four-year-old, this would have been my chance.

As it was—as it was, next to the button was a master switch. I pushed the button and the switch at the same time.

The room went dark. Durdon swore and fired, but over the noise from the gun I heard a groaning from the wall panels. Keeping low, I moved toward the sound.

"Meg! Dorothy! Get Lily up the back stairs. Move!" I bellowed. "Alison, Martin, follow me."

Someone crashed into the worktable, knocking a spool of wire onto my head. A hand lunged at my shoulder. I rolled away from it, kicking wildly, but only connected with air.

The opening in the panels let in a pale light from the basement windows. I could see the big shape of Moe looming over me. There was fighting behind me; a fist connected with skin, followed by a deep groan. Moe grabbed me by the hair. I kicked again, hit a kneecap. Moe jerked my head back.

"I've got the boy," Durdon said. "I'll shoot him right now if you don't get the light back on in five seconds."

The Homeland agent released me with a kick to the back of my knees. I limped to the table and fumbled for the master switch. When the lights came back up, Durdon was holding a half-conscious Martin upright with an arm across his chest. Curly had grabbed Alison at the bottom of the stair-ladder. Tears left white tracks in her dirty face.

Dorothy was still sitting on the daybed, but Lily and Meg had disappeared. When Durdon realized he'd lost two of his hostages, he swore.

"Let's get what we need and get going," he said to the Homeland agents. "We can prove we have a right to be here if a local LEO shows, but it would leave us with a lot of loose ends."

Namely Dorothy, Alison and Martin. And me.

"And cuff the detective bitch to the table. She can die in the fire."

"Can't do that," Curly objected. "If they find her after the fire, they'll be able to tell the cuffs came from Homeland Security."

Durdon made an ugly gesture. "Cuff her to Alison. We'll figure it out later. Get the papers and the gadget the kid's been building."

Curly yanked me over to Alison and cuffed us together. Moe went through the open panels into the basement. We heard him flinging things to the floor; in a minute he returned with a couple of empty cartons. He dumped Martin's ferromagnetic grid into one of the cartons and swept all the papers into another.

Martin had recovered from his half-swoon, but he was bleeding around the left eye. He watched in misery as Moe and Curly jammed a chisel into the device he'd been building so painstakingly, but he didn't say anything.

"You go first with the Binder kid," Curly said to his partner. "Durdon and I will follow with the other three."

Moe frog-marched Martin from the workshop, a gun against his ribs. Durdon stuck his gun under Dorothy's armpit and said, "On your feet, Granny."

She stood slowly. "I suppose even a sociopath like you had a grandmother once. And unless she was as horrifying as you are, she would be disgusted to hear you talk to me like that."

He hit her. "What is this, a TV talk show? First the detective bitch and now you? Shut up and move."

"That's the Metargon spirit, Durdon," I said heartily. "It's where old Edward Breen started all those years ago, bringing Nazi collaborators into the country, then murdering them and burying them in his basement. No wonder Cordell likes you so much."

"You can say what you want; it doesn't matter." Durdon refused to be provoked. "Mr. Breen already covered that issue with the police. They know it was that loser Dzornen who buried the woman."

"Cordell *told* them that, but that doesn't make it true. We'll find what happened to Gertrud Memler when we get Martina's German journals translated."

"Get Warshawski out of here," Curly said to Durdon. "She's stalling until the other woman gets back here with a cop. Don't argue with her."

"You take them," Durdon said. "I'll bring up the rear with Granny. Gun's at the base of her neck, girls, so move along double-quick if you don't want her dead at your feet."

Curly took Alison's free arm. He pulled her forward so hard that she stumbled. My feet got tangled in hers and I almost fell. He kept us moving fast, his gun in Alison's neck.

Martin and Moe were at the top of the stairs.

"Martin?" Judy's scratchy voice came down to us. "What have they done to you? Did this man hit you? Why did you do that to my baby?"

"Oh, get out of the way, you dried-up drug-fucked cunt," Moe said.

She was outlined in the doorway above them, swaying. "You don't talk to me like that and you don't hurt my baby," she rasped.

She suddenly grabbed a mop from the brackets at the top of the stairs and shoved it at Moe's head. He jumped out of the way, but he lost his hold on Martin, and stumbled backward on the stairs.

I felt Curly move his gun away from Alison. I grabbed her hand below our cuffs and dragged her up the stairs. "Move!" I yelled, as she hesitated.

Moe recovered his footing. He lunged for me just as Curly shot up the stairs at us. Moe bellowed in pain and fell heavily in front of us.

I yanked on Alison, got her over Moe and out the door at the top of the stairs. Judy had collapsed, clutching the mop. Martin was bending over her, not sure what to do.

"Martin, pick her up, carry her outside," I ordered.

"But Dorothy?" Alison quavered.

"Meg's gone for help," I said. "If we split up, they won't shoot her: they'll have to explain it to the sheriff. Go, go, go!"

I wrenched Alison out of the doorway and slammed the basement door on the agents. Martin collected his mother and followed us out the back door.

52

VIRTUAL REALITY

W E'D BEEN with Tinney's police force for an hour, stuck in separate interrogation rooms, telling our many different stories, when Cordell Breen arrived. He'd flown in on Metargon's Gulfstream with enough lawyers to start a good-sized firm right on the spot. He also had with him the Chicago-area Director of Homeland Security, a brisk woman named Zeta Molanu.

When Molanu and Breen arrived, the Tinney police chief, Duke Barrow, brought us all into his office to sort out who was going where with whom. Barrow had grown up with Meg Ferguson. He cut off one of Breen's lawyers mid-sentence to order a patrol officer to take Meg home with Lily and Dorothy.

"I'm going to have an officer spend the night at your place, so don't worry, just get some sleep," Barrow assured Meg.

"These women are making accusations against two federal agents," Zeta Molanu objected. "You can't release them."

"This isn't a courtroom, Ms. Molanu," the chief said. "You can complain about it for weeks in front of a judge, if you want. I'm just a cop trying to decide who gets arrested and who gets to sleep in her own bed after being beat up this afternoon."

It was thanks to Meg knowing Chief Barrow that we'd made our ultimate escape. While Martin was struggling across the yard with

Judy in his arms, Curly and Durdon had roared out of the kitchen, firing at us. Before they managed to hit us, the patrol cars Meg had summoned pulled up.

One squad car took Judy Binder to the Tinney hospital, with Martin sitting in the backseat with her. When a unit went inside to collect Moe and Dorothy, they saw that Moe was bleeding from the shoulder. They called an ambulance for Moe, but sent Alison, Dorothy and me into the police station along with Curly and Durdon.

Molanu told Barrow that he didn't have any authority to arrest Homeland Security agents. "If my agents have gone beyond the scope of their orders, we'll deal with that as a matter of internal discipline."

Curly's face turned crimson. "But ma'am, Director, you told us to cooperate with anyone Metargon assigned—"

"You are always to use good judgment and discretion in the field, Bonner. Neither you nor Gleason showed good judgment when you held a small child hostage."

"We were doing what Breen's man told us, Director," Curly tried to argue, but Molanu said that could all wait until they were back in Chicago.

The local chief protested on different grounds. He wanted the FBI to look into a charge of kidnapping; he'd already called an agent in the Peoria office to come interrogate Durdon and the two Feds for seizing Lily and Meg; someone was supposed to arrive at any second.

"We're in the middle of a giant misunderstanding here," Breen began in his warm baritone. "I don't think the FBI—"

"Don't worry about that," Zeta Molanu told Breen. "I'll sort it out with the head of the Northern District. I know you were concerned that defense secrets were heading into Iranian hands, which may have made your staff overzealous. We'll take young Binder in for questioning so we know exactly what he was doing with the Fitora code."

"No," Alison said.

"Sunny—" Cordell began.

"No 'Sunny,' Dad. I am not a sunshine person. You cannot accuse Martin Binder of stealing the Fitora code. You know he did nothing with the code—Jari Liu told you and me and Vic that there's not a whiff of interest in the code anywhere on the Net or among our competitors. You know that all Martin's been doing is looking for what work his great-grandmother did before Granddad stole her design for the ferromagnetic memory core."

"Sunny, you've had a lot of shocks this afternoon," her father said urgently. "The Warshawski woman got you into something deeper than you could handle. We'll be filing separate charges against her before we get back to Chicago. Chief—Barrow, is it?—do you have a room where I can be private with my girl?"

"We're not going to be private, Dad." Alison's face was stony, her voice like flint. "If you take any action against Vic or against Martin, I am going to the Board to explain how you've been abusing your power. I will vote my shares against you and I'll get Mom to vote hers, too."

Breen's ego was built on the grand scale. He said, "Alison, you're in shock; we'll talk when you're feeling more yourself. We're going back to Chicago in the Gulf; you can get something to eat in the plane, get a nap and you'll get over this."

"No, Dad. I'm not getting over you acting like a rhinoceros on a rampage. It would be such a big help if you listened to anyone. No wonder Mom drinks the way she does; she's tired of you acting like she isn't there."

"Your mother does not have a drinking problem," Breen said. "It's very wrong of you to discuss our private home life in public. Haven't I told you that a thousand times?"

"I tried to warn you about her," Durdon said. "I told you I didn't think you could trust her loyalty."

"We'll get you to see a therapist, Sunny. You're suffering from Stockholm syndrome," Breen said. "Chief Barrow, I think my lawyers have dotted the *i*'s you need. I'm taking Durdon back to Chicago with me. And you don't need Alison anymore, either."

"Dad, I'm staying with Vic and Martin. If you want Durdon to blow them and me up, I guess you'll give the necessary orders. Or you can talk this Director Molanu into doing it for you; she seems eager to please."

Under Molanu's makeup, her face turned a blotchy red. I wondered if she was sleeping with Breen.

"That is enough, young lady!" Breen blazed, grabbing her arm. "You'll come home with us, you'll get some therapy and we won't have any more of this nonsense."

"Dad, no!" She pulled away and ran to Martin's side.

Breen seemed finally to realize that he had lost her, at least for the time being. Or he was just worried about how much fuel he was wasting, with the Gulfstream's engines still running. He let Durdon and the lawyers take him away.

After that, Chief Barrow wrapped things up with us in short order. He was angry at having his authority usurped by Homeland Security; he saw Martin, Alison and me as ranged on his side of the table and gave us his cell phone number—"In case anyone tries to bother you while you're in town."

One of his officers drove us back to Dorothy's house so I could collect the Mustang. Martin wanted to retrieve his great-grandmother's papers, as well. Dorothy and Meg were less than ecstatic at seeing us again, although they thawed a bit after Alison gave them an earnest apology on behalf of her father and Metargon.

"I'll see that someone rebuilds Martin's great-grandmother's workshop, if you want," she promised. "It feels like, oh, sacred space, this lady who survived the Nazis, working here all these years, staying involved with physics and looking at the stars. Wouldn't you like to see it restored to how it was before they tore it up today?"

Dorothy said gruffly that they'd think about it. "But I still don't understand what they were after, why they had to attack Lily and do all that damage."

"Breen was protecting Metargon's reputation," I said.

"But he's destroying it!" Alison cried. "When people learn what he's been doing, they'll lose confidence in him as CEO."

"I'm not defending him," I said. "He's indefensible. I'm just trying to understand what's been driving him. I think it's his idea of Metargon's reputation as the great innovator in computing and technology. Metargon, 'beyond energy.' 'Where the future lies behind.' Those are your company's mottos.

"When Wall Street learns that your grandfather didn't create the BREENIAC, that he stole the design from a Holocaust survivor, it's what I said earlier—people will lose confidence in you. The public isn't going to be very forgiving, either."

"But why were they chasing me?" Martin asked. "I knew Mr. Breen was upset about the prisms, but he didn't know they were Martina's signature."

"But he did know. He wanted all of Martina's surviving papers so he could destroy any evidence connecting her to the BREENIAC sketch. Besides, he wanted the copy of the patent that was mailed to Martina. You said the Patent Office's copy of it had disappeared, that there's a record of her getting the patent for the design in 1941, but no trace of the actual document in their files. This long after the fact, we'll never know what happened to it, but I'm betting that Edward Breen, who had a lot of contacts in Washington, got someone to remove the file for him back when he realized he could make a fortune from the stolen BREENIAC sketch."

"Why did they think I would have something?" Martin persisted.

"If the documents that were mailed to Martina in 1941 survived the war, Cordell thought you'd lead him to them."

Martin shook his head. "I never saw those, either here or in the papers from Martina that my mom stole."

"I know where they are," I said. "At least, I know where they were in November 1941."

VIENNA, NOVEMBER 1941
Letter from America

E VER SINCE THE CHILDREN LEFT for England, the overcrowded flat on the Novaragasse has felt empty, hollow. But now, two years into the war, it is truly empty. His beloved daughter, Sofie, his Butterfly, weak from her difficult pregnancy, was taken from him yesterday, along with her husband and his parents and all the aunts and nephews and cousins.

A father should be able to protect his daughter. A father should not sit uselessly by as men point weapons at his daughter and force her to her feet. A father should not have to see his daughter so thin and weak from malnourishment that her breastbone and ribs protrude like a plucked pigeon, but so he has done. He wants to sit on Sofie's mattress and tear his hair out, wailing. He eyes the bedding, neatly folded by his wife after their beloved's departure, her hands trembling, folding the thin blanket and stroking it over and over as if it still held her child. If he sits and howls he will never get to his feet again and his poor Charlotte will be left to cope on her own.

Felix Herschel blinks back tears, puts on his one remaining suit and shirt—the others long since bartered for food—and follows a lifetime of habit. He shaves in cold water, brushes his teeth, boils water to make a cup of ersatz coffee for Charlotte.

At least little Lotte is safe in England, with her brother and Käthe Saginor. Before the war began, before Europe was sealed, they received two letters from their Lottchen. He worries constantly about how his wife's cousin Minna is treating their darling. Minna is an angry woman, always jealous of his wife, spiteful toward Sofie. He worries that she will abuse their little Charlotte, but what choice did they have? Only the children were allowed visas into England.

He goes down the four flights of stairs and stands in the street to do the breathing exercises that have been part of his morning routine since he was a university student at the turn of the century. He tries as much as possible to follow his decades-old schedule: shaving, dressing for the day, bringing his wife her morning coffee.

It's been two years since he last was in the office on the Park Ring, where he was once a highly regarded attorney. Until the war, a number of his clients continued to consult him surreptitiously: Felix Herschel's advice was always carefully and intelligently crafted. He knew what could and couldn't be done even after the Anschluss.

In exchange, he received the gold coins that his wife sewed beneath the buttons in Lottchen's waistband. When she reached cousin Minna, little Lottchen wrote carefully, *Hugo and Käthe and I are safe. I still have all my buttons. I love you and miss you, Opa.* Minna would have been as likely as the Nazis to steal the small hoard that Felix intended for his granddaughter's survival; the message told him that she has managed to hold on to her legacy.

Before the war began, Felix tried to persuade his wealthy clients to pay him with visas, to anywhere, Argentina, Cuba, even Iran, but they did not feel so loving toward him that they would use up their own stock of government favors on a Jew's behalf.

As Herr Herschel stands in the doorway, rotating his arms, the postman arrives. So little mail goes in or out of the Leopoldstadt these days that the arrival of mail is always an occasion. His heart beats faster: perhaps something from his granddaughter. Since the war, they have received two letters from her, twenty-five words, mediated by the Red Cross and still censored. They don't know if their own letters to her made it through or not.

There is nothing for his family, but the postman has a letter from America addressed to Miss Martina Saginor, 38A Novara Street, Vienna 2, Austria. Herr Herschel carries it upstairs. A letter from America carries with it so many possibilities that he can hardly breathe.

Felix shows the letter to Charlotte, who has finally risen, has combed out her long waterfall of hair and pinned it around her head and is shaking their bedding out over the courtyard. She nods, and he helps her replace the thin blanket. She takes a hairpin from her coiled braid and slits open the envelope.

It's an official government document, but not the visa they'd been praying for. U.S. Patent D124603, for a ferromagnetic device that can store data. The sketch that Fräulein Martina submitted with her application two years ago is attached to the grant, which will expire seventeen years from the date of issue.

Felix cannot bring himself to look at his wife, but she squeezes his hand. "After all," she says, "if it were a visa, how could we leave Vienna with our darling Sofie somewhere in Europe and in trouble?"

53

KILLER APP

LOTTY WAS VERY PALE. When we reached the corner of Novaragasse, she stopped, eyes shut tight. She had last seen this street early one morning when she was nine years old, when her father walked her and her brother and the wailing Käthe Saginor to the train station. The police, who treated her deferentially on this visit, had poked bayonets into her teddy bear to make sure her family wasn't hiding jewels in it.

"Okay," she said at last, opening her eyes, taking a deep breath.

Herr Lautmann met us at the entrance to Novaragasse 38A. He was from the public works department, the man who provided the permits and the workmen to excavate the cobblestones in the courtyard.

Max had found Lautmann after I announced my intention of flying to Vienna to look for Martina's patent. Max had been amused: "Vienna is not Chicago, Victoria. You can't suddenly show up at a building and start dismantling the cobblestones. You need a permit, you need an official, probably two or three officials. Don't show your gun to the concierge and imagine he or she will want to help you."

"I'm capable of subtlety, Max," I answered, full of dignity.

"I'm sure you are," he said. "I hope one day you'll show it to me. For this errand, you need someone like me, who speaks German and knows how to steer a boat through a set of bureaucratic locks."

Max had set about sending e-mails and making phone calls until he was put in touch with Herr Lautmann. A process that might have taken months or years was compressed into a few weeks thanks to Max's connections in refugee and Holocaust survivor circles.

With Max making all the arrangements, both for the trip and for the excavation, I turned my attention to shoring up relations with the clients I'd been neglecting.

I was also answering a lot of questions from the Cook County state's attorney. When I suggested to the SA that the dead body in the coach house probably belonged to Gertrud Memler, they contacted the FBI. The Feds were excited: they'd been hunting Memler for fifty years. The trouble was, no one had any DNA samples for comparison.

The infuriating part of the post-Tinney weeks was my inability to get the state's attorney to pay any attention to Breen's role in Julius Dzornen's death, or in my own incarceration by his minions in the root cellar below the coach house kitchen.

The SA said it was ridiculous to think that the head of a company like Metargon, which paid eight million in state income taxes last year, would be involved in the kind of crime I was describing. As for the man Durdon, Mr. Breen had made it clear that he was led astray by some overzealous Homeland Security agents when Durdon was hunting for missing computer code.

"Eight million in taxes, but two hundred thousand in campaign contributions, which is more to your point," I snapped. "Will Breen continue to try to murder Martin Binder, or can young Binder go peacefully about his business?"

The assistant state's attorney advised me to tone down my language. Mr. Breen had issued a formal apology for suspecting Martin Binder of trying to sell proprietary code. If Metargon was prepared to let matters rest, I should leave things alone, too.

At least Sheriff Kossel down in Palfry was taking matters seriously. He was trying to get the Palfry County state's attorney to file murder charges against Deputy Davilats and Durdon. I promised Kossel that I would testify if he was able to bring either or both men to trial.

In the days after Tinney, I was spending my small squares of free time with Jake, who'd returned from the West Coast. Lying on his couch, listening to him practice, or lying with him in bed after a late night of music and dancing, was restoring my spirit.

Alison decided to take a leave of absence from Harvard. She thought first of returning to Mexico City, to the program she was setting up, but the more she talked about it with me, the more tainted it felt to her.

"It's so corporate: I was providing them with Metargon products—it's like using a charity as a front for turning Mexican schoolkids into Metargon customers. We give the kids Metar-Genies and then they have to buy the apps and the games from us. I need time away from all that corporate stuff. And then, too, with my dad bringing in the FBI when he thought Martin might be in Mexico City with me—they don't trust me now."

She rented an apartment in the Ravenswood neighborhood, about a mile from where I live, and entertained herself by finding furniture at estate sales. When she learned about the Vienna expedition, she wanted to join us.

"You don't think my dad will come after you in Austria, do you, Vic?" she asked.

"I don't know," I admitted. "It depends on how much that patent matters to him."

I'd gone back to using my own phone and my own computer identity—conducting business in secret is almost impossible and sucks up way too much time and energy.

If Breen was still obsessed with forestalling any publication of Martina's patent, he was almost certainly tracking Max's and my e-mails. Which meant he was also tracking Max's exchanges with Herr Lautmann in Vienna.

I didn't see Alison often after we left Tinney, but she dropped into my office from time to time to use me as a sounding board. When she persuaded Max that she had a legitimate need to be present at the No-varagasse excavation, she stopped by to talk to me about Martin.

"I know he has a right to be there, too: it's his great-grandmother, after all. But he won't let me buy him a ticket."

"That's good," I said.

"How can it be good? He has so many expenses, and no job right now. My dad fired him, he's put a lot of negative words out with other software companies, which means Martin is having trouble getting work. His mom is in serious rehab, you know, and even though she's got Medicaid, Martin's paying all the extra expenses."

When Judy Binder was judged strong enough to leave the Tinney hospital, she moved into a halfway house in Chicago with the dog Delilah. It was her idea: rescuing Martin had been a turning point for her, or the last point in a turn that started when her mother died in an effort to protect her.

"Delilah and I, we've been through a lot together. She'll look after me," she told Martin when he heroically offered to let her join him in the Skokie house. She was still volatile, hot-tempered, often mean-spirited; her recovery went in fits and starts. You don't change a thirty-five-year habit in a week, after all, but Martin reported that she seemed seriously committed to the process.

Mr. Contreras was disappointed when he realized we couldn't keep Delilah, but Judy's halfway house was only a half-dozen L stops north of us. He took to riding up to see the dog, impervious to Judy's mood swings. Just the fact that she had a regular visitor was also a help in her recovery.

When Max agreed that Martin could be part of the trip, Alison gave up her first-class ticket to ride coach with him. And with me. And with Jake.

"I've been too laissez-faire about letting you go off into oubliettes and dungeons," Jake said. "My attitude was that as long as you knew what you were doing I wouldn't interfere. Especially since interfering carries a high probability of losing my bowing arm, or even my fingering."

We were lying in bed, his long fingers on my breasts. Bowing and fingering gave him a magician's touch on my body and I rolled over to lie on top of him.

"Nothing's changed. I still know what I'm doing and I would be distraught if anything happened to your fingers. I'd love it if you came, but I don't need you to do so."

"Victoria Iphigenia, you jump off cliffs not knowing if you packed a parachute. I'm coming to Vienna so I can play a dirge if someone drops your body into the Danube."

And so there were four of us in coach, five if you counted Jake's bass, which required its own seat. We arrived in Vienna late in the afternoon. While Max pampered Lotty in the Imperial Hotel, the rest of us stayed more modestly in a pension Jake knew from his professional trips here.

We were only a few miles from the Novaragasse, and could have gone by tram, or even on foot. However, Max—concerned about how well Lotty would weather her return to the old ghetto—hired a car, which picked us up after breakfast the morning after our arrival.

We drove around the Ring, so-called because it circled the city where the fortifications used to stand. We passed streets where the gray buildings stood wedged so tightly together that we couldn't make out the sun. It was depressing to see the same gang graffiti that cover Chicago bridges and walls on apartments and bridges here.

Once we crossed the Danube Canal, which was a sullen gray, not the oompah-pah blue of the tired old waltz, we were in the Leopoldstadt, the section of Vienna that Hitler had turned into a ghetto. The car dropped us on a side street, near a memorial to the deportees from the Leopoldstadt. Lotty wanted to see if her family's names were included among the victims.

"They called it the 'Mazzesinsel,'" Max said, "the 'Matzo Island,' because so many Jews lived here. Freud grew up here and so did Billy Wilder, the physicist Lise Meitner, oh, many famous people."

When Lotty found her family—Herr Doktor Felix Herschel (1884–1942) und Frau Doktor Charlotte Herschel (1887–1942); Mordecai Radbuka (1908–1942); Sofie Herschel Radbuka (1907–1941); Ariadne Radbuka (1940–1940)—she called to Martin, who'd been standing apart from the rest of us, as if he didn't feel he belonged.

"Here is your grandmother's grandmother—the woman who raised Kitty, just as she raised you."

We all crowded respectfully closer to look at the inscription: *Liesl Saginor (1885–1942).*

"Her husband had died of tuberculosis, I think it was, soon after Kitty and I were born; that's why they're not on this wall. They were so young," Lotty said. "Even my grandparents, and Kitty's grand-mother, were younger than I am now."

She took a map from her handbag. "I don't remember these streets, though I walked them every day for more than a year. Of course, then the shops were empty. All this food, these stores filled with electronics— our shops were our grandparents, bartering a book or a coat for a loaf of bread."

Martin hesitantly held out a hand. She let him take her arm and the two of them studied the map. Novaragasse was only a few short streets away. When we got to 38A, Herr Lautmann was there with a couple of workmen carrying picks and shovels.

"It looks familiar but not the same," Lotty said.

"Bomb damage," Herr Lautmann said. "This street was bombed badly; these apartment buildings, some could be—what is the word— *gerettet?*"

"Salvaged," Max supplied.

"Yes, some could be salvaged, but some were new-built."

We went up four flights of stairs, Lotty shutting her eyes, letting memory guide her feet to the right door. A Turkish family lived in her family's old apartment now. The woman who answered the door, a toddler in her arms, was at first alarmed at the sight of so many Europeans, but after Lotty spoke to her in German for a few minutes, she nodded, said something to Lotty, who turned to us.

"The women can come in, but the men must stay in the hall; there is no man home right now, and the neighbors will talk. Max, you and Martin and Herr Lautmann can go below and I will throw something, see where it lands."

The Turkish woman stepped aside and spoke again to Lotty; I made out the word "coffee," but Lotty declined.

Alison and I followed her inside. The apartment was filled with furniture and bright hangings. A large TV stood in one corner, with a map of Turkey framed above it. Two children were watching German cartoons.

"Very different from when I was here," Lotty said. "My six Radbuka cousins, Hugo, my parents, my grandparents, we were crowded onto four mattresses. We had a few chairs, no drapes, nothing to hang on the walls."

She spoke again to the woman in German, and we were allowed to go to a back room that overlooked the courtyard. The yard was a small irregular circle, with bicycles, baby buggies and a few outdoor grills covering the cobblestones. Lotty emptied her handbag, handing the contents to me. She opened the window and tossed the bag down.

Martin had reached the courtyard ahead of the other men. He picked up the bag and kept his foot on the cobblestone where it landed.

Lotty thanked the woman, talking to her at length. Judging by the way she was using her arms, she was describing herself as a small child living here, explaining why she had thrown her bag. The woman nodded, put a hand on Lotty's arm, eyes bright with tears. She gestured at Alison and me with her free hand—*"Ihre Töchter?"*

Lotty smiled, but shook her head. Down in the courtyard, Herr

Lautmann set his work crew to digging up the cobblestones. We quickly drew a crowd, the usual assortment of drunks, out-of-work men offering to help, women with children too young to be in school.

The crew worked quickly, prying up about a dozen stones in a circle around where Lotty's purse had landed. They dug up the ground underneath and sifted it through a large kind of grater. There was an amazing assortment of detritus, old pens, hairclips, the head to a porcelain doll. As they finished shaking dirt from their findings, they stacked them neatly on a small tarp.

The packet lay under the stone nearest the building. They handed it to Herr Lautmann, who gave it to Lotty.

A square of oilcloth was wrapped around a piece of black silk that had turned a rusty green. "I think this was from an umbrella," Lotty said, fingering the silk. "The oilcloth—where did they get that, I wonder? Cut from an old mackintosh, perhaps."

We all bent to stare at the envelope inside, with the three-cent U.S. stamps on it, and the address, typed on a manual machine: Miss Martina Saginor, 38A Novara Street, Vienna 2, Austria.

Dear Miss Saginor:

I am pleased to inform you that the United States Office of Patents has issued you U.S. Patent Nr D124603, for a ferromagnetic device that can store data. This patent will be in effect for seventeen years from the date of issue, which is May 13, 1941.

Please let me know if I may be of further service to you in the future.

Yours sincerely,
Lester Tulking
Patent Attorney

Attached to the letter was the official notice from the Patent Office, and a copy of Martina's drawing, a grid that looked like it might hold potatoes in a deep-fat fryer with wires dangling from it, the word "Speicher," in neat printing, a series of equations, and the twin prisms in the bottom right-hand corner.

Alison stared at it. "It's the BREENIAC sketch. It's true: we did steal it from her."

Lotty rewrapped the patent and gave it to Martin, who didn't quite know what to do with it. At Max's suggestion, we went back to the Imperial Hotel's business office, where Martin scanned the patent documents. We sent a copy to Murray, with photographs Martin had taken of the courtyard on Novaragasse and the excavation process. I wrote out a history of the patent, and what we were able to guess, or piece together, of how Edward Breen had acquired it, and told Murray he had a twenty-four-hour exclusive before we put the story out on YouTube.

After that, we spent another three days in Vienna. Max took Lotty to see her grandparents' old flat on the Renngasse, the place where she'd lived until the Nazis forced her family into the ghetto. They also visited her grandfather's office on the Park Ring, where the earnest young lawyer using it today took them to lunch and let them linger behind her grandfather's rolltop desk.

Jake and I wandered through the city's parks, where we met his musician friends for drinks that lasted until dinner and then became informal recitals at one apartment or another.

Martin dragged Alison to the Institut für Radiumforschung. The director of the Institute patiently let Martin tour the place. Apparently Martin's enthusiasm for quarks and leptons was such that he was allowed to sit in on an Institute seminar, which seemed to thrill him even more than recovering Martina's patent.

By the time we returned to Chicago, Metargon's stock had halved in value. One of Metargon's outside directors was my own most important client, Darraugh Graham. The afternoon after our return, Darraugh summoned me for a private meeting to find out how much I could verify of the stories that were now circulating in the financial pages.

We talked so late into the afternoon that we ended up at the second-floor bar in the Trefoil Hotel on Delaware, drinking their legendary Armagnac. By the time we finished, Darraugh said that it was all deeply troubling.

"That history, that patent, it's water over the dam by now," Darraugh said. "Don't know why Breen would be so obsessed with it."

"It's got something to do with the skeleton in his father's workshop," I answered. "The literal skeleton that I found last month. We'll never know what happened there, we'll never know who shot her, but the two sets of fathers and sons, the Breens and the Dzornens, all were part of the burial. It weighed Julius Dzornen down, but it made Cordell Breen think he was so far above the law that he could get away with anything, including murder.

"Breen knew his father had stolen the patent from Martina Saginor, or at least from Gertrud Memler. When Martin challenged him about the BREENIAC sketch, Breen thought Martin was just one more fly to swat. When I got involved and the situation began to spiral out of control, Breen wasn't thinking anymore; he was just carrying on as if he were, I don't know, Napoleon or Hitler on their way to Moscow, maybe."

Darraugh gave his dry bark of a laugh. "Good lesson in there for the rest of us CEOs, Victoria. I'll talk to the other directors. The girl, what's her name? Alison? She's a bright young lady, as well as a major shareholder, but she's much too inexperienced for the executive floor."

CHICAGO, 1953
Sacrificial Lamb

DAD? DAD, WHAT'S GOING ON?" It's Cordell, who's heard the shouting and
fighting in his bedroom across the yard in the main house.

Martina is startled by his appearance. She looks at Cordell, she
squeezes the trigger. The noise, impossibly loud, fills the room. Breen
grabs the gun from her. It goes off again. The Memler clutches her side,
the rage in her face turning to surprise. Blood flowers on the white shirt
underneath her Dior suit; she sways for an instant, then collapses onto
the workbench.

In the doorway behind Cordell another youth is standing; he's been
sent by his mother to see what Benjamin is doing. He cries in horror,
"Papa!"

*Edward Breen decided I was to be the sacrifice: he would call the police
and report me as a murderer, the end of a fight that started years ago in
Vienna. That last statement might be true, but not the first. I am no one's
sacrifice any more times in this life. When Benjamin put up the feeblest of
protests to Breen, I walked out of the workshop, and disappeared. Once I
was safely away, I wrote Benjamin a promise that I would bother him no
longer. Only keep an eye on Käthe for me, poor Käthe who lives with so
much trouble in this world, I begged, but he did not. Only once more did
I see him, when our granddaughter was seven: I sought a fugitive meeting
near the Argonne Laboratory, to see if our daughter's child might carry
some spark within her.*

54

LATE MAIL

ALISON WENT TO SEE her mother and came back with a disturbing picture of her father, one, though, that bore out the reading of his character I'd given Darraugh.

"He seems to be insane, Vic. I mean, literally. He's marching up and down the halls at home quoting from *King Lear*, about me, the ungrateful daughter, and threatening revenge on me or any shareholders who challenge him. Jari Liu told me my dad is giving orders that no one can follow. He wants Jari to find a hitman to kill Martin, and then he says he'll do it himself if no one else has the balls."

That was so frightening that she agreed to go with me to the state's attorney. The SA was still reluctant to act, but when the Skokie police found Breen and Durdon creeping up on the Binder house with a full arsenal, the two men were finally arrested on attempted murder charges and weapons violations.

The legal process seemed likely to make my ex-husband, whose firm represented Breen, even richer than he already was. The only positive out of it was that Breen's wife decided she'd had enough; Constance wasn't going to stand by her man. She rented studio space not far from Alison's apartment and began painting seriously again. How well that would work was anyone's guess, since she still seemed to find answers to many of life's questions in a Sancerre bottle.

The other plus, one that delighted Max and Lotty as much as it did me, was Martin's acceptance at Caltech. When he decided to apply, Max and Darraugh both worked their networks to get the college to consider him.

Like Alison, Martin dropped by my apartment and office a number of times in the weeks after we returned from Vienna. We had a lot of conversations about his life, his family history, his legacy from Martina. Should he go to Caltech, or find a job with a computer start-up company?

"If you want to become an Internet billionaire, you have the skills and the smarts to turn computer apps into money," I said to him. "But if you want to follow Martina, then you should work with the people who can help you understand her work. That patent, that was a throwaway idea for her, don't you think? Her real passion was for those things you say she wrote down, supersymmetry, how to understand dark matter, all those places where light bends and mortals like me drop our jaws in amazement."

The January day was cold and bright when Martin stopped by my office to tell me Caltech was letting him start in the middle of the year. He was driving the Subaru out to Pasadena, but he traveled light: his modest wardrobe, his computers, his poster of Feynman and his set of Feynman's *Lectures on Physics*.

"You've been great, Vic, really great. I know my grandmother hired you—I found your contract when I was packing up her things to put the house on the market. I can't pay your bill right now, and even if I could it wouldn't come close to what I owe you for finding Martina's patent and coming to Tinney to save me and all those things. But if the book makes any money—"

"Stop," I said. "If the book makes any money you'll do something in Martina's memory. Anyway, Dr. Herschel is taking care of my professional fee."

We'd hired Arthur Harriman, the young German-speaking librarian at the University of Chicago, to translate Martina's journals. They seemed interesting enough that the Gaudy Press had given Harriman and Martin a contract to write a memoir, threading her story together with the history of nuclear weapons.

One afternoon, I went with Martin to the Special Collections room at the University of Chicago Library. We returned the second page of Ada Byron's letter to Benjamin Dzornen, which Martin had lifted back in August. We talked to the librarian, Rachel Turley, about the BREE-NIAC sketch, which I'd sent her. Alison came with us: we had a kind of formal ceremony, in which Alison relinquished any claim to the sketch on Metargon's part and Ms. Turley thanked us for the bequest, and said she would overlook Martin's removing a library document.

"Anyway, thank you, Vic," Martin said the afternoon he stopped at my office. "I'm going to head west now. I'm spending the night in Tinney. Dorothy's forgiven me for all that mess back in September. She knows it wasn't my fault or yours, so I'm stopping there on my way to California. Will you visit my mother sometimes? I mean, not take her on, she's not easy to be with, but just so she's not completely on her own?"

I promised.

"And Alison. She's kind of in a difficult place right now. Hard to believe a billionaire could be in a difficult place, but, you know, her father's been arrested, her mother is still drinking, and she's kind of on her own. Can you let her know you haven't forgotten her?"

I promised him that as well. He and Alison had decided that their lives were on such separate tracks these days that a romantic relationship wasn't possible, but they were remaining friends, as their generation was able to do.

I sympathized with Kitty, angry with a mother whose mind searched the outer reaches of time and space but had little room to spare for a human daughter. Perhaps Martin, inheriting his great-grandmother's powerful gifts, would forge a life that held more balance.

I waved good-bye to Martin. At the end of the evening, I drove over to Lotty's apartment. Angel, the doorman, warned me that she had an early surgery call in the morning.

"I have a package for her," I said, "Something I know she'll want to see."

While the librarian, Rachel Turley, had been meeting with Alison and Martin, I had requested a file from the Dzornen papers. I'd performed a little sleight of hand at the photocopy machine. I was preserving, I was confiscating, I was restoring.

When I got off the elevator at her floor, Lotty was waiting for me in her red dragon dressing gown, her face anxious, wondering what new crisis I was bringing to her.

I handed her the packet. When she opened it and saw the letter from her grandfather to Dzornen, written in pencil on the title page of the *Radetzkymarsch,* she stared at it for a long moment. "Oh, Vic, oh, daughter of my heart. For this—oh, thank you."

TINNEY, ILLINOIS
Finding the Harmonies

SHE KNOWS THE JANUARY AIR is cold, but her bulky coat gets in her way when she's making adjustments to the lenses. She doesn't shiver as she unwraps her telescope. It's as if she were eighteen again on the Wildspitze, embracing the glacier water.

The heavens lie open above her and her heart, that aged frail muscle, stirs as it always has at the purity of light.

Benjamin said to her on their last night in Göttingen, "You are not human, Martina. One does not lie with a lover to talk about spectral lines, one seeks the comfort afforded by our human bodies. It's as if you have no feelings in you."

"I was never a cold person, Benjamin," she says tonight: like many old people who live alone, she doesn't realize that she's thinking out loud. "But my passions were too intense for you. I thought you shared my longing for the harmonies. I thought with you I might find the place where the music is so pure that the sound itself could ravage you, if it didn't first shatter your mind. These bodies, yes, we live inside these bodies and must tend to them, but I wanted to be inside the numbers, inside the function where it approaches the limit. I long for the stars. I know their red shift and their spectral lines, but I don't want to describe them: I want to be inside the light."

She's weeping now, her tears turning to ice crystals on her lashes. And then, because it seems the most natural thing in the world, she unbuttons her jacket and her shirt and lies on the deck, opening her arms to the heavens.

HISTORICAL NOTE

Some years ago, while thumbing through my husband's copies of *Physics Today*, I came on an article I actually could understand: a tribute to the Austrian physicist Marietta Blau. I had never heard of her, but she did groundbreaking research in cosmic ray physics in the 1930s. She was a member of the Institut für Radiumforschung (IRF) in Vienna.

The IRF, which still exists in the original building under the name Stefan-Meyer-Institut, was unique in the era between the world wars for its aggressive hiring and support of women scientists. It was the first research facility in the world to hire a janitorial staff, instead of demanding that women researchers also clean the labs. They were also the first, and perhaps remain the only institute to require the same number of toilets for women as for men. Before the Anschluss, thirty-eight percent of the research staff were women. With Nazis in power, the Jewish staff and the women were fired within relatively short order, and the IRF lost its cutting edge in research. Blau's work was so highly regarded by Erwin Schrödinger (Nobel Prize, 1933) that he kept nominating her for the prize, which she never won. As war closed in on Europe, Einstein tried to get an American university to find a place for Blau. He was unsuccessful, but at the last possible second, he found her a position in a high school in Mexico City. Her enforced exile from the heart of physics meant that at war's end, Blau had lost her edge as a researcher. She worked briefly at the Brookings Institution in Long Island, and died in obscurity in Austria.

Blau's story haunted me for years. *Critical Mass* has its origins in Blau's life, but the physicist I created, Martina Saginor, is a work of fiction. None of Martina's biography is based on Blau, except for her position as a researcher at the Institut für Radiumforschung. It's also true that one of Blau's students, Hertha Wambacher, was a secret member of the Nazi Party when the party was outlawed in Austria. However, Wambacher was not involved in weapons work or in torturing prisoners.

The Technische Hochschule für Mädchen, which Martina attends as a student and where she later works as a teacher, is my own invention. Despite the IRF's welcoming policy toward women, the University of Vienna did not pay them a stipend. The IRF director, Dr. Stefan Meyer, paid women out of his own pocket, but many had to augment that stipend with other paying jobs.

The German effort to release enough energy from the atom to create a weapon of mass destruction took place through an institution called the Uranverein, or Uranium Club. There were a number of sites in Germany where scientists and technicians tried to create reactors that could produce a self-sustaining nuclear reaction. I created a fictitious site near Innsbruck, Austria, Uranverein 7, but to the best of my knowledge, there were no actual reactor installations in Austria.

At the end of World War II, when U.S. policy concerns shifted from Fascism to Communism, the American government brought in many Nazi weapons and rocket researchers. Under the name "Operation Paperclip," the United States did a perfunctory investigation, or none at all, into the background of Nazis it brought into U.S. weapons labs. Some of the people had engaged personally in horrific acts of torture.

For the background and history of the IRF, I used Maria Rentetzi's *Trafficking Materials and Gendered Experimental Practices*, New York:

Columbia University Press, 2008, as well as Brigitte Strohmaier and Robert Rosner, *Marietta Blau, Stars of Disintegration*, Riverside, California: Ariadne Press, 2006.

Dr. Johann Marton, deputy director of the Stefan-Meyer-Institut, took a day from a busy schedule to show me through the Institute building on Boltzmannstrasse, and to give me a personal history of the Institute, and the way in which it was affected by the Nazi era.

For details about Operation Paperclip, I read Linda Hunt, *Secret Agenda: The United States Government, Nazi Scientists, and Project Paperclip, 1945–1990*, New York: St. Martin's Press, 1991.

For background on physics and on the race for the atomic bomb, I read Richard Rhodes, *The Making of the Atomic Bomb*, New York: Simon & Schuster, 1986; Steven Weinberg, *The Discovery of Subatomic Particles*, New York: Scientific American Press, 1983; and Richard P. Feynman, *QED: The Strange Theory of Light and Matter*, Princeton: Princeton University Press, 1985.

For the history of computers and the development of the hydrogen bomb, I used George Dyson, *Turing's Cathedral*, New York: Pantheon Books, 2012; and Stanislaw Ulam, *Adventures of a Mathematician*, New York: Scribner's, 1976.

Although the physics in Frank Wilczek and Betsy Devine's *Longing for the Harmonies* was beyond me, they express so perfectly my own longing for the harmonies that the book helped guide me as I created the character of Martina Saginor.

In the best books, the ending often comes as a shock.
Not just because of that one last twist in the tale,
but because you have been so absorbed in their world,
that coming back to the harsh light of reality is a jolt.

If that describes you now, then perhaps you should track down
some new leads, and find new suspense in other worlds.

Join us at www.hodder.co.uk, or follow us on
Twitter @hodderbooks, and you can tap in to a
community of fellow thrill-seekers.

Whether you want to find out more about this book,
or a particular author, watch trailers and interviews, have
the chance to win early limited editions, or simply browse
our expert readers' selection of the very best books,
we think you'll find what you're looking for.

And if you don't, that's the place to tell us what's missing.

We love what we do, and we'd love you to be part of it.

www.hodder.co.uk

 @hodderbooks

HodderBooks

HodderBooks